# THE SOUL CONSORTIUM

## SIMON WEST-BULFORD

ATTENTION READER

This is an uncorrected proof. It is not a finished book and is not expected to look like one. Errors in spelling, page length, format, etc., will be corrected when the book is published several months from now. Direct quotes should be checked against the final printed book.

MEDALLION
P R E S S
Medallion Press, Inc.
www.medallionpress.com
JULY 2012

Send completed reviews to reviews@medallionpress.com

# THE SOUL CONSORTIUM

## SIMON WEST-BULFORD

In a future so distant that time is almost without meaning, death is defeated and immortality has been made reality through instantaneous cloning and synaptic transfer. But mankind, frustrated by the futility of timeless existence, chooses extinction. All but one man.

Far removed from the known universe with only one companion, an AI named Qod, Salem Ben watches the cosmos from afar. Wearied by the endlessly repeating cycle of creation and destruction but afraid to pass beyond the veil, he relives the digitally reproduced lives of countless souls archived in the Soul Consortium by means of a neuroimmersive device known as the WOOM. His hope is to discover the answer to the ultimate question: What lies beyond?

But at the birth of the next universe, billions of years before the pattern of life repeats its design, Salem's quest takes a disturbing turn. Unexplained aberrations appear among the digital souls. To hunt down their source and to continue his search for evidence of life after death, Salem endures four very different lives: Orson Roth, a serial killer in twentieth-century Britain; Dominique Mancini, a spiritual medium from sixteenth-century Lombardy; Plantagenet Soome, a monk sent to the far distant Castor's World; and Queen Oluvia Wade, the creator of the Soul Consortium.

As the mystery unfolds, Salem is confronted by a malevolent entity, a being of unknown origin woven into the memories of the dead. Prepared to corrupt the laws of physics themselves in order to break free, the entity threatens the future of humanity before it can begin again—and only Salem stands in its way.

ISBN# 978-160542393-7

Trade Paperback

$14.95

Science Fiction

JULY 2012

# SALEM BEN

*Is this my first thought?*
*My first memory?*
*From evil dream to warm flesh, enfolding me.*
*From deepest darkness to rose-light of womb.*
*Mother breathing,*
*Forever scorning,*
*The beckon of my tomb.*

# 1

When I was a boy my smiling schoolteacher asked my class a very simple question: What is the one thing in this world that we can all know as an absolute, undeniable certainty? The students all looked at each other, smirking as they whispered their sarcastic remarks, but the grins soon fell when she spoke again. Not because she had brought her palm down hard on her desk when she revealed the answer. It was the tears in her eyes.

One day, she told us, every last one of you will die.

I was the only one still smiling after she said that. I used to worry that it was the sight of other students in shock that amused me, but now I think it was something else, as if I had some peculiarity in my soul, sensing that this simple statement about the irrefutability of death, was not true for me.

Eighty-four quadrillion years on as the last existing human, and I still need to decide if her statement is true.

In the same way I have done on a billion separate moments, I stand inside the Calibration Sphere, huddled within my long, charcoal-colored robes, staring at nothing. I have seen more, learned more, felt more, known more than ought to be possible for any human being, and every lucid moment is a struggle with the decision whether to end it all. Why then do I concern myself with such trivial details as the fact that there is no chair in here? But this sphere was never intended as a place for humans to visit. It's a cold place of ash-gray walls, harsh white light and silence. The slowly revolving surfaces hold a billion digitally-compressed souls at any one time—individual specks of remembered life—all flickering as they undergo routine scans and maintenance.

There is only one empty slot left in the entire Soul Consortium—a lonely hollow amongst a host of souls—patiently waiting for my existence to end so that it can be replaced with a blink of luminous data and categorized for insertion into one of the many spheres beyond this one.

I can't do it.

I tell myself it's because everything will be wasted if there is nobody left, that there is still more to be done, or because life is too precious to discard, but that isn't the real reason. I can't do it because I'm terrified. The thought of death has always filled me with such terrible dread that I cannot bear to face it. Because immortality is a curse—a wonderful curse—and I cannot stand to kiss the Reaper's hollow eye.

"Salem," a low female voice breaks the silence. "The stars await your pleasure."

I pause before answering, thinking about how many times I have heard that incorporeal voice, reminding me of how many millennia have passed without genuine company. Real flesh and blood to embrace.

"Thank you, Qod."

"Would you like me to take you there?" she says.

"Because you think I'm lazy or because you think I'll miss something if I don't hurry?" She would never really see my smile. "No, Qod, I think I'll walk. I haven't taken a stroll for, oh, seventy-three years now, is it?"

"As you wish," she replies, "but please visit the genoplant before making your way to the Observation Sphere."

"Something wrong?"

"Seventeen cells in your right lung have atrophied and two cells in your cerebellum are showing early signs of degradation. Transplants have been prepared for you in the genoplant."

"Joy."

Several lifetimes ago during one of my more sullen moments I asked Qod what would happen if I didn't comply, if I allowed my body to fail. It was a petulant question born from a faint desire to remove the burden of my decision to end my life. But there has always been something about Qod that drove me on, and besides, I know exactly what would happen if I were to sit back and wait for my body to fail. Preconditioned survival genes would kick in, taking control of motor function and higher reasoning, forcing me to accept the necessary treatment to keep my mind and body alive. I could no more control that than I could will my heart to stop beating. Not that I couldn't override it, you understand—it had been decided a long time ago, when the misery of perpetual living had already afflicted the human race with suicidal craving, that a human being could choose to die. With the simplicity of flicking a switch one could end it all. And eventually everyone did.

Everyone except me.

The walk to the genoplant took twenty standard minutes, the process of gene infusion a little less than three, and my sauntering through gray corridors to the fifty-klik observation dome, another twenty. I run a hand along the back of my favorite seat ready to watch the cosmos perform for me. Like me, the universe will never die.

I sink into the body-molded chair, and the vast, crystalline walls of the sphere surrounding me fade from view like melting ice. Beyond the invisible walls an eternity as fathomless, dark, and empty as my life is revealed, and although that emptiness threatens to swallow the small part of me that remains, I am still drawn by it, still awed by its patient beauty as it waits for the next phase of its eternal evolution. Perhaps it's because I think of the universe as my echo that I subject myself to this for the third time. I too keep hoping for something new, some sign that there is more to life than . . . life.

A spark ignites in the distance like a glinting eye opening in the darkness. The "big bang" it was once called. An anarchy of dazzling particles warring with each other to bring poetry out of chaos. Gluons, photons, anti-poryons, demi-praxons—expanding in one glorious blink to fill the waiting void and I drink that moment in as if tasting a breath of mountain air after a decade of imprisonment in a Ceti-9 sewer. Cold adrenaline lifts me from my seat and my eyes swell with the sudden, sweet emotion of it all as I spread my arms. How could I want to leave all this?

How could they?

But I know this euphoria is just a grain of sand in a desert of apathy. Just like the pearl of light at the gates of death, disappointment will follow.

I would smile at the irony of my thoughts if there were someone real with which to share the joke; I am watching the universe on the brink of rebirth and at such a monumental event that I am so fortunate to witness… I am restless. Irritated and dissatisfied, as if a maggot had infiltrated some hidden fold of my brain to squirm there unnoticed. But I am not really all that different from the ones who came before me. They grew tired of continual existence too, and one by one, they chose to brave the final barrier—the one that my teacher told me had to come eventually. But I am still not ready; I have to know that there's something beyond.

"Let there be light!" Her voice fills the sphere like thunder.

I follow my initial shock with a sigh, resisting her attempt at humor, irritated by the intrusion. "Most amusing, Qod. Next time would you mind adding some music?"

Before the birth of this third universe she'd made a

similar comment. I had watched the final days of the second cycle several trillion years ago. Most of the universe had grown cold by then, but I had been privileged to see one of the few remaining areas collapse into a super-massive black hole. I remember falling to my knees, cowering at the incredible violence of it all as energy and matter screamed its way to annihilation, and Qod had quoted T.S Eliot's final stanza of *The Hollow Men*.

"This is the way the world ends.
Not with a bang but a whimper."

Back then I was grateful of the remark; it pacified my terror. Today her attempt at humor grates me.

"Exit." I turn and walk slowly away from the light.

A passage opens in the darkness, inviting me to leave the Observation Sphere and return to the labyrinthine bowels of the Soul Consortium. Time for change.

# 2

The Soul Consortium is an electronic tomb: a shrine to all the human lives that ever lived throughout the span of the universe's existence. Every life is archived here, from the lowest Neanderthal child that died after two days of exposure within a cave mouth screaming for the care of its dead parents, to the flamboyant Zad Neibrum XVI who was envied as having arguably the fullest, most enjoyable, and most productive life in his twenty-thousand year journey. They, like all the others, had been stored as trillions of organized photons within vast "soul spheres" categorized for the perusal of anyone with an inclination to share their experience.

I have spent most of my own life walking these spheres, browsing the dead, searching for the ultimate experience. There is something about the human condition that leaves one continually lacking—an evolutionary curse that drives us to forever want more, to always seek new things. I strive for happiness, knowing that it is the water that trickles through my fingers when I grasp for it—it can never be contained, only fleetingly appreciated, and when drained away, all that is left is the wetness of skin reminding me of a brief pleasure that once was. Even when I live the lives of the happiest people on record, this yearning stays with me, as though I am being haunted by my own mourning ghost.

I am not the man I was.

The time has come to break the addiction—to stop searching for the ultimate thrill and begin my pilgrimage for the ultimate answer. Qod knows I have delayed this too long. She taunts me when I wake from each life, asking me if I have found what I am looking for, seemingly knowing that I never will until I make the final journey beyond the veil. But what does she know? She is just a machine: the last AI—the only survivor from the great Techno-Purge that happened toward the end of the universe's first cycle. She endured only because she is unreachable, hiding within the tiniest gaps of quantum space.

But Qod has been my only genuine companion through the long years. I don't know if she really feels anything for me, but she stays anyway.

"I want to see something new, Qod," I tell her as I stop at the end of the corridor, my hand resting against the door.

"You don't want to enter the Bliss Sphere?"

"No." My hand drops from the cool metal.

"Why, Salem?"

"I . . . I haven't found . . ." I stare at the ground.

"Salem?"

"I don't know, Qod. I don't even know *what* I'm looking for anymore. I just know it isn't in there."

"Why so sad? Three hundred and twenty thousand, billion years pass and you have an epiphany. Surely you should be elated."

"Hardly. An epiphany is exactly what I *haven't* had. Not my own, anyway . . . Has it really been that long?"

"You could think of it as one hundred and fifty-nine million lives you've lived if you prefer. Does that sound more appealing?"

The thought nauseates me. "So many."

"Indeed."

"What am I still doing here, Qod? The others left centuries ago."

"Is that a real question?"

" . . . No."

I look back at the door, resisting the urge to enter. It's safe in there. Every life filed in the Bliss Sphere had been traveled countless times by countless people before me, bringing them exquisite pleasure on every occasion. The happiest people of history were easy for Qod to identify—analysis of the left pre-frontal cortex indicated who the best candidates were, and those with low readings on the right cortex were excluded from consideration. The best result was a child by the name of Salomi Deya who had been born with a defect that caused a permanently stimulated pleasure center, but she had only lived for twelve years. I lived as Salomi seventy times, but nothing gave me greater pleasure than experiencing the life of Frederick Ruchard, an Old Earth fourteenth-century Buddhist monk who had mastered the art of meditation. I became Frederick over eight hundred times before deciding it was time to move on.

"You are sure you won't enter the Bliss Sphere, Salem?"

"Talk to me about some of the other spheres. List them for me."

"Of course. Any particular order? What do you have in mind?"

"Death. I want to know about death."

"You know that recordings end at the point of death, Salem. I cannot help you."

Even after trillions of years, some things never broke free from the list of impossibilities. Inverse time travel was one, trans-dimensional stabilization was another, but most unfortunately, looking beyond death was at the top.

"Then I need to find people that might have known. Something that slipped through, pseudo-science, obsession, anything at all. List me some sphere categories at random—categories that might be related."

"IQ icons, Suffering Servants, World Leaders, Love Legends, Aberrations, Spiritual Activists, Maniacs—"

"Wait! What did you say?"

"Maniacs."

"No, before that, and before Spiritual Activists, did you say Aberrations?"

"I did, yes."

"I've never heard of that category before."

"That's because no aberrations existed before you entered the last life, Salem."

I look around, wishing for the thousandth time there was a face to the voice that spoke to me. Then I realize the significance of what she said. "What? I don't understand. How can there suddenly be aberrations? What are they?"

"I began checking the algorithms used by the Calibration Sphere while you were in the W.O.O.M. The Codex protocols don't allow me to check the souls themselves, but I saw ways in which to improve the calibration checks, just to make sure that routine maintenance wasn't missing any discrepancies within the soul recording, and it seems I was right because—"

"You were checking the checkers?" I smile despite myself. "Could the mighty Qod actually be . . . bored?"

"—because during the third universal cycle, inconsistencies, some greater than others, have emerged in the patterns of many souls."

There is no humor in her voice this time. I wait a moment, hoping she will elaborate, but she doesn't.

"Inconsistencies? Explain, Qod. Is it data corruption or degradation?"

"No."

"Then what?"

No reply.

"You don't know? Seriously?"

"Analysis is incomplete. And as I said, the Codex protocols don't allow me to examine the data myself. If you—"

"I want to go there."

"My analysis is incomplete. The aberrations might be dangerous, Salem. Please reconsider."

And all at once, as the thought of danger—*real* danger—presents itself, I feel a chill of excitement. Until now I had drifted from life to life, walking through the memories of multitudes, knowing deep down I was safe—my psyche buried within, saying "it will never happen to me". But this will be different.

"I said I want to go there."

"Very well, Salem. Would you like to walk?"

"Yes, and can you brief me with summary information on the lives with the ten most significant aberrations as we go? I used to like the surprise in the Bliss Sphere, but I think I'd prefer to know what I'm getting into with these."

"Processing."

# 3

The new sphere opens before me. It looks much like the Bliss Sphere, but instead of the soothing pulse of aquamarine, a naked glare, like a nova shining through emerald glass, bathes me as I step inside. I shield my eyes until they adjust. The smooth walls glitter like the inside of a geode; each glint of light is the electron pulse of a human ghost waiting to tell me their story, and I survey them, wondering which of these I would become intimately familiar with in the next few minutes.

"Have you made your choice, Salem?"

I had. Qod had given me the summaries by the time I reached the sphere, but I had already made up my mind before she reached number five.

"Yes, Qod. Select subject 5.64983E+30, Orson Roth."

"Interesting choice. Why him?"

"Anyone with an obsession that powerful must surely see something there that I haven't, don't you think?"

"Not really."

"Well I have to start somewhere," I say, stepping through the oval door. "And I want to look inside people that nobody else would ever consider. Remember the others?" I twirl my hand in explanation. "They were looking for the answer in all the obvious people—Jesus Christ, Albert Einstein, Nietzsche, Shaphad Seth, theologians, scientists, visionaries and philosophers through all history, and what did they find, hmm? I'll tell you what they found. Nothing! But I will."

"In men like this?"

"As I said, it's a start. I've made my choice."

*Subject 5.64983E+30: Select*

*Subject 5.64983E+30: Aberration detected*

*Subject 5.64983E+30: Override authorized—ID Salem Ben*

*Subject 5.64983E+30: Activate. Immersion commences in 3 minutes.*

The smell of freshly-cycled oxygen perfumed with summer jasmine fills my nostrils as the sphere welcomes me, but I sense disapproval in Qod's silence that nullifies its pleasure. She rarely stays quiet for long, though. The loneliness would be unbearable if she did.

"Need I remind you," she lectures me, "that once you have been immersed you will not be able to withdraw until the moment of the subject's death. Protocol forces me to dictate that whatever you experience, however terrible, you will have to endure all of it without possibility of extraction. You will know each and every moment as if it were your own, and until it's over, you will have no suspicion at all that you are not that person. Any lasting memory of trauma . . ."

Her redundant legal chatter echoes in my peripheral thoughts as I wait. Ironic that I should feel such impatience after being alive for so long. Of *course* there is no need for her to remind me. Doesn't she know how many lives I have lived? Does she somehow forget that the extended human brain can retain and recall any moment from their past with instant and precise clarity? Perhaps I do need reminding though, I have never known of an aberration before today; I have no idea what could be waiting for me once I've entered the recorded life of Orson Roth. The thought prompts another ripple of enticing fear across my skin—better this than going back to the Bliss Sphere.

"What's the worst that can happen?" I smile. "Plug me in, Qod."

"Remember, Salem. I warned you."

"I'm incapable of forgetting, or don't you remember?" I reply flatly.

"What *I* remember, Salem, is that there are some things you *choose* to forget. If this goes wrong, I'll make sure this isn't one of them."

Suspended twenty feet above me by invisible fields of force, the machine waits for me like the shiny wet cocoon of some enormous insect. The wheeze of miniature hydraulics and the hiss of ancient gravity valves echo around the sphere as the machine makes its preparations for my long stay, but to me it sounds like Qod is sighing with resignation over my decision.

A flow of silver glides down to me from the curved walls, microscopically thin fibers carrying me gently upward to the center of the sphere, as if my timeless companion was gathering me up in her hair to hold me against her breast. The tiny fibers dig through my flesh as I am pulled into the W.O.O.M., penetrating my nerves, weaving through the hills and valleys of my brain, and, energized with a new sense of adventure, I ponder a moment on whomever it was in the distant past who had eliminated the human body's need for pain, replacing it with a simple internal alarm mechanism. But pain is undoubtedly a sensation I will be reacquainted with in the next few minutes as I emerge wet and gasping from between the thighs of my new mother.

A bright spot of life ejects from one of the millions of storage cells layered into the wall opposite me. It drifts for a moment in the air like a fairy caught in the breeze, then fires into the machine.

"Farewell, Salem. See you in forty-six years."

# ORSON ROTH

*As I was walking up the stair*
*I met a man who wasn't there.*
*He wasn't there again today.*
*I wish, I wish he'd go away.*

# 1

Fate must be the strangest among the gods. She manipulates the world with immutable will; so devious and cunning, yet She stands aloof from her pawns, unwilling to flaunt her talents. To recognize Her one must have a very special mind indeed, and to appreciate Her? Well, one must be insane. Of course, there are times, during Her most fickle moments when She will show Herself plainly, but they are so very rare. Take the advancement of science as an example. Galileo Galilei: an extraordinary man, desperate to usher mankind into a new era, determined to topple Ptolemy's convenient model of the Earth at the center of the heavens with the Sun circling us, and yes, where Copernicus tried before him and failed, Galileo—he succeeded.

But was that supposed to be the end of his victories? Of course not! How do I know? The answer is Fate—She intercepted this world with such obvious intent to finish his work.

Galileo, you see, had such wonderful ideas taking form in that incredible mind of his, but Death, as is His way, wanted the last word. He stole Galileo from us before he could bear fruit. But our Goddess, in a rare moment of weakness, or passion, revealed Herself. Many had not seen it, but some of us now do—on the very day that Galileo Galilei died in January of 1642, the fruit that had been pruned from his branch took seed elsewhere that very day, and a little over nine months later, Sir Isaac Newton was born to continue the work Galileo had been denied.

You may believe this to be coincidence or mere trivia, but I know different, for Fate played the same game with me, too: in the same minute that Zachary Cox succumbed to violent death, my mother gave birth to me, and my entire life has been a continuation of that man's work. Zachary Cox had already murdered fifteen people in the six years before his career ended at my parents' house. Of course, I have no firm memory of that day, but I am well versed with the most dramatic recitation of the story, and I sometimes think I can hear my mother's dying curse when I close my eyes to sleep.

My parents, Jack and Evelyn Roth, lived their quiet lives in a small village in the North of England, enjoying a time of nervous peace after the Second World War. They intruded upon no one, worked hard for their neighbors, and were well loved by the whole community, small though it was. My father earned their keep as a carpenter, lovingly carving rocking horses from the oak trees grown in the local woods; Evelyn painted them and sold flowers for the church. I should have been born into a family of warm roses and gentle prayer. But Fate had Her cold eye fixed on my mother's womb. She rescued me from that sickly-sweet life.

August 17, 1951 changed everything for that village. It was late evening, a street party had finished outside my parents' cottage, and the hearty enthusiasm of villagers with satisfied bellies full of wine and hog roast, spilled over into song as they sauntered back to their homes. They knew that my mother was due any day, and when she and Jack had not arrived for the celebrations, it was assumed the big day had finally arrived and Doctor Maidestone would be overseeing the joyous event. Community spirit was high in those days, but obviously not high enough for the locals to overcome their convenient ignorance of what really happened in the Roth household that night.

Perhaps it was because the atmosphere in the village was one of such contentment, or because the pink glow of the sunset lulled everyone into dreamy complacency, but not one resident entertained the possibility that the formidable Zachary Cox would be paying a visit to one of their homes that night. Why would they? Village life was better now that the war was forgotten—safe, quiet. It was time to bury the heartache of the past along with their loved-ones, and start appreciating better days. Nobody wanted to think about blood and horror anymore, let alone talk of such things; the murders they'd read in the papers were for other places. Not this village.

Doctor Maidestone had been sitting with my mother for most of the afternoon, holding one hand whilst my father held the other, both smiling and breathing words of encouragement. An ambulance was called when complications arose after her waters broke, but because the streets had been closed off to traffic, the driver had taken a different route through the back lanes and crashed at a tight bend; help never came. By the time the news came back to the Roths, my mother decided that Fate had granted her wish that the birth would happen at home. She told the doctor it's what she wanted anyway. But had I been there to explain to her this error of judgement, I would have told her that this was Fate's warning, not a blessing: my birth and life would be surrounded by untimely death.

Mr. Cox had crawled in through the open window of the pantry when the contractions had reached four-minute intervals. He had not been expecting anyone to be home, and in truth, it is my belief that he had already begun to turn over a new leaf that night. I don't believe he wanted to kill my parents, or the doctor, but Fate—She obviously did. In my teenage years I learned that Cox's anti-social condition was brought on by the fact that—for religious reasons—he had been a conscientious objector to the war. The guilt of his survival and the death of his friends had manifested into a form of bloodlust executed with supreme efficiency and wondrous design; a skill I have since come to deeply admire. When the war ended, so did the murders. Nobody found him out, but as mental instability grew, so did the list of jobs ending in his dismissal, and Cox was forced to join the ranks of those who made their living through theft. Cox had chosen our village that night because of the street party and I can only assume that the Roth home was chosen because Fate had shone Her irresistible ghost-light upon them. Cox would end, and I would begin.

It was my father who heard the noise first. Expecting it to be an over-enthusiastic celebrator, he reassured my mother that he would be gone less than a minute. She screamed her disapproval as he prized her sweaty fingers from his hand, knowing that my moment was coming, but he went anyway, and the chaos and bloodshed that followed was regurgitated by the tabloids and spoken by grimacing mouths for years afterwards.

The whole scene played out in less than five minutes. Cox and my father crashed out of the pantry, across the landing, and into the living room like impassioned dancers, Cox's great hands clutching my father's hair, my father's strong carpenter arms wrapped around the murderer's chest. Grunts escalated to screams as hair ripped from my father's scalp, crockery displayed on the mantelpiece shattered as it met the tiles on the fireplace, and both men fell, thrashing against each other amongst shards of broken china. Cox cried out as one of his fingers snapped, and the doctor shot looks of desperation between the fighters and my distraught mother as the violence came closer to her. Gripping her hand harder than she gripped his, blood pooling in the shallow birthing water, Maidestone cried out for both men to stop, but as the conflict reached its peak, only one did—my father.

He gurgled with the effort of movement, trembling fingers splayed across his stomach as blood spread across his shirt like ink on blotting paper. Cox struggled up as the victor, shook his head, coughing and breathing heavily, staring at the doctor and his patient with a bloodied screwdriver in his right hand and the look of a wounded wolf in his eyes. But before the doctor had chance to react, fire belched from the fireplace. In his last effort, my father drew the poker from the coal to slice Cox's cheek with a wild swing. The murderer roared out his pain but the attack only fuelled his rage, and with triumph proclaimed in his cry, he stamped his boot repeatedly into my father's face. The clang of the poker released by the twitching hand followed the sickening crunch of bone against gristle and brain, and only then did Doctor Maidestone, transfixed by the horror, make his move; he leapt forward with a cry of fear to tackle Cox, and the two of them wrestled in the soot, blood and fire, while my mother screamed a new life into the world, my own cry joining the crescendo.

Both men paused for a moment as the birth reached its climax. My mother tried to push herself backward, slipping and splashing, wailing at the sight of her dead husband. Maidestone screamed again as he grabbed for Cox's injured hand, yanking the broken finger, then twisting the arm so that he could thrust him into the fire. Spikes from the fireguard pierced Cox's back and he arched with the pain as the doctor stumbled back toward my mother, hoping that his action was enough to stop their attacker. It wasn't. Cox crawled away from the fireplace with flames leaping over his sweater to blister his face. Maidestone did his best to pull me free from my flailing mother but Cox had already reached him, and filled with desperate rage, he plunged the screwdriver into the doctor's spine, twisting and stabbing with what little energy he had left.

"Please" was the last thing the doctor said before Cox thrust the screwdriver into the man's throat when he turned. Cox fell forward onto the wet floor and pointed at me as I lay there taking my first few breaths of life. My mother had stopped moving and crying, and as the sound of splintering wood signaled the entry of my rescuers, my baby-blurred vision captured the last moment of life ebb from Cox's eyes. My first memory.

# 2

Life between my first memory and my first murder blurred together like a hideous mosaic assembled by some lunatic using pieces of his own hardened vomit. Predictably, it was an ugly life.

The first few chunks of that depraved picture were set in place when I reached my fourth year. My foster parents, ever joking to their friends about my tempestuous nature, did not have the intuition to predict what I would do when left unsupervised in a playroom with the neighbors' baby Donovan. It was only for five minutes, they reasoned, but for three of those minutes that child stared at me. Smiling and drooling, with no idea that Fate was about to use him as my first training exercise, the infant, two years my junior, tap, tap, tapped his rattle against his podgy thigh, hypnotizing me with his baby blues. I wanted to see how they worked. So I took them. Or tried.

I don't know what became of Baby Donovan after my

distraught foster mother tore my bloody fingers away from him; I never saw her again after that day.

Finding new parents was almost impossible after that, but between seasons at various children's homes, I occasionally passed to new guardians under increasingly strict regulation. But the harder they pressed upon my will, the more I pushed back, and knowing that my Goddess had reserved a special place for me in Her heart, I drove social workers and child psychologists to near insanity with every new incident. But I don't regret a single moment of those years. Fate forged me for the passions to come.

At the age of ten, they inflicted me upon the children's division of Kettlewhite Mental Institution. And it was only in there, amongst the truly insane who had no life in their eyes, that I realized I had to tame my urges if I wanted to serve Fate properly. I wept convincing tears of remorse after each violent episode, performed well in group activities, responded well to the Rorschach tests—a butterfly instead of a torn throat, a flower instead of a cudgeled head—until gradually, I seeped into their favor and gained their trust. They released me back into the wild, to new parents, and to grammar school. I sat at the back of the class, absorbing the insults and isolation; a tamed wolf circling the sheep, waiting for Fate to point out the strays from the flock.

I remember my first killing as though the images had been tattooed on the inside of my eyelids. At sixteen, learning to fulfil my calling as an outcast, I spent as much time alone as I could, and on that particular day, I decided to pay a visit to the banks of the stagnant pond in the woods near the grounds of my school. I liked to go there before returning home; it was a good place for contemplation—a metaphor for my mind, and I loved to stare at the green scum that covered the surface, thinking about how so many people had been a part of my youth knowing nothing of what lay beneath the murky depths of the child they thought they knew.

An old tree overhung the still water and from one of the thickest branches someone had tied a swing to it. I sat on it, pushed myself from the bank, and listened to the soft creaking of the rope as it swung back and forth. Ten minutes passed before Graham Adams called to me from the bank.

"Oi! Queer boy, I want a word."

I craned my neck round to see. He had his hands on his hips, puffed out leathers and a ridiculous quiff-rendered hairstyle which underlined him as a joke, so I laughed.

"Think it's funny to upset my sister do you, Roth?"

As it happens, I did. A pathetic fourteen-year-old girlie in a pink dress playing hopscotch with her equally nauseating friends—she deserved what she got: when I saw her satchel by the classroom door I swiped it, emptied the contents into the yard, gulped down her packed lunch, then spat a healthy lump of doughy mucous into the empty bag. If any one of the other boys in my year had done that, it would probably have earned them a laugh, but not me. I got beaten up there and then by the Neanderthals in the year above me, laughing hysterically with the contact of each fist and boot. But obviously that wasn't good enough for goody-two-shoes Graham. He decided to take it upon himself to pay me a private visit—the biggest mistake he could have made.

"You coming off that swing or am I going to have to kick you off?"

I lifted one hand to my mouth and gasped in mock surprise at his threat. Then I laughed again.

Graham marched over to the tree, flushed with anger, and began pulling at the ropes. As the swing juddered back to the bank, I fell from it into the mud, still laughing even as the first crack of knuckles jarred my cheek. Another punch followed as Graham's knees pressed my arms into the wet soil, and then my fingers were at his throat, searching for the hard lump of his adam's apple. He shuffled back out of my reach, stood up and spat at me as I lay breathless with the cold water of the pond icy against the back of my head.

"Wanker!" he spat again and turned to leave.

"At least I don't have a slut for a sister," I said.

Graham turned, anger pulsing blood through his cheeks as he drew a fist back to punch me again. But I was already up, energized and exhilarated by the thrill of the fight, rushing at him, arms reaching for the throat again. I felt his fist graze the side of my head making my ear ring, but my thumbs had found the target this time.

I expect he thought I saw this as just a fight until that moment, but my crazed scream and the violent pressure I used against his windpipe, made him change his mind very quickly. We rolled against the bank, him paddling against my face and chest, then pinching and scratching in desperation, me pressing harder and harder as if I were trying to thumb a hole into a steel bar, and suddenly we were flailing in the water. I saw a flash of Cox's face at that moment, my parents' killer sideways against the carpet with blood creeping beside his matted hair. I almost let go of Graham's neck with the shock of that vision, but it was too late anyway—my arms were the only ones moving and his body was limp beneath the water.

I wrenched the face from the water and stared into his glassy eyes for almost two minutes before the burning pain in my muscles forced me to drop him back in.

I screamed.

Not from fear or horror. I screamed because frustration and pleasure swirled inside me like oil and water. Something about the eyes of that corpse moved me, as if I had missed the most important moment of my life, as if I had blinked and missed the Second Coming, but seen the rising of the dead in glory. That was my first kill. But I knew I needed more.

# 3

My escape from the law has always been a source of great intrigue to me. There was enough evidence of my guilt to convict me ten times over for the murder of Graham Adams, yet everyone believed my story completely.

I had run from the pond gushing with euphoria, whooping with joy at what I had done. Killing that boy filled me with such a grand sense of freedom I am scarcely able to describe it—the power of life and death is a thing assigned to gods, yet it had been channeled through my fingertips that day. I almost fell through the school gates, wet and covered with fetid slime, a ridiculous grin on my face as I stumbled toward the teachers' block. I knew I had no chance of escaping my crime, but it would be a travesty if I didn't at least try; powerful though Fate is, I at least owed it to Her to do my part. But if She still deemed me worthy, a miracle would be required, no matter how convincing my acting skills.

By the time I reached the entrance hall a small crowd of students had gathered around me and my performance was in full swing. None of them offered to open the doors to the foyer as I lay there sobbing my crocodile tears onto the wooden floor; in fact, most of them were laughing through pinched noses and stifled coughs. I clawed at the ground, shrieking, "He's dead, he's dead, and it's all my fault," but none of them listened.

Mr. Thurlston found me two minutes later. He barged through the doors, pushed the students aside and scooped me from the ground without a hint of concern that the action would cover his suit in putrid water. He carried me away without a word as I bleated my remorse, and through my tears, I saw that he was taking me to the first-aid room to see the school nurse. The nurse and the R.E. teacher—the biggest pushovers in the whole school—I couldn't have asked for a better audience. It took them both a full five minutes to calm me down and get some intelligent words out of me. They thought it was shock, but in reality I needed a little extra time to get my version of events straight. There'd be more holes in my story than a wartime minefield but I had to give it my best shot.

"Deep breaths, Orson . . . that's right, now . . . tell us what happened."

"Gr . . . Gr . . . Graham . . . Ad . . . Adams. He's . . . it's all my fault."

I wept inconsolably again into my hands as the nurse

placed a glass of water on the desk beside me.

"Graham Adams? What happened? Where is he? Is he hurt?"

"He's . . ." More weeping.

Thurlston and the nurse were both quiet and I imagined them exchanging concerned looks as I buried my head in my palms again and shook.

"Take another sip of water, Orson," said Thurlston, gently.

"I know that I'm evil, Mr. Thurlston, they all think I am, but I didn't mean anything to happen . . . I . . . I—"

"Steady on," said the nurse, with a hand on my head. "Nobody here thinks you're evil. You've just had a difficult upbringing, that's all, and sometimes you can be—"

"What Mrs. Carlisle is trying to say," said Thurlston, a reproving glance shot in her direction, "is that all of the teachers in this school want the best for you, Orson. You have a keen mind and we don't want you to throw your potential out of the window—that's why we can be tough on you sometimes, but it certainly doesn't mean that we're going to make rash judgements about you right now, whatever it is that you confess to us."

"Graham's dead," I said without the slightest stammer, meeting Thurlston's eyes. I studied his look, watched the subtle flinch in his eyelids as I said the "D" word, enjoying that fraction of terror in his waxy expression. He was thinking of his career, what the papers would say, what the other teachers would say, what they'd have to say to that little shit's parents. I heard the nurse gasp as Thurlston placed one hand gently on my shoulder. I looked down at my feet, pushing back the laugh at the back of my throat as I forced another river of tears.

"Are you sure, Orson? Quite sure? He could be—"

"He's . . . drowned. At the bottom of . . . of the p- pond."

There was more silence as I stared at the floor, but Thurlston must have gestured to the nurse because I heard her hurry out of the first-aid room. No doubt she was going to call the police or an ambulance.

"Can you tell me what happened?"

"I was on the swing, by the pond."

"Yes?"

"Graham came. He's Rebecca's sister . . ."

"I know, yes. What happened, Orson?"

"He was pissed off that I'd had a go at her, so he . . . we . . . we got into a fight," I said, looking back up again, contorting my face into a mask of fear. "We fell into the pond and then . . ."

"Yes?"

"He must have got himself caught on something because he couldn't get back up. He was trying but . . . he . . . he just couldn't get up and then I tried to pull him out by his neck and he just kept sinking deeper and deeper and then he pulled me under too and I tried to pull h-him up but—"

"Shhhhhh, okay, okay, you don't have to say any more. Not yet."

I studied his eyes again and cursed my poor choice of words. Tried to pull him out by his neck? By his *neck*? If ever there was an admission of guilt handed on a plate, there it was; even a soft touch like Thurlston couldn't help but be suspicious after an image of my hands around Graham's throat had been put in his mind. And sure enough I saw that flicker in his eye. The flicker that said something doesn't add up. Inside I kept my cool though, placed my trust in Fate. Thurlston laid me on the couch with a blanket over me as I shivered, staring into space. With any luck I'd have my story perfected by the time the police arrived.

Thurlston sat and waited with me for the next hour and not a word was spoken. Every few minutes I'd sneak a look at him. His gaze was blank but a light sheen of sweat had moistened his top lip and I'm certain his brain was almost at the point of seizure trying to work out what should be done. With the headmaster on holiday and the deputy out sick, Thurlston was in charge. No wonder he was soiling his pants.

When the nurse came back I was surprised to see that she was not accompanied by the police. It was two weeks later, after I had received a particularly ruthless torrent of abuse from some of the other pupils' parents, when I found out why I hadn't been arrested. Thurlston took me aside in his office and offered a sympathetic smile as he spoke very quietly to me.

"The abuse will pass in time, Orson. Graham's death was a tragedy . . . and we know you two were fighting, but there was really nothing you could have done. Some of us know that now."

I looked into the man's eyes, unable to hide the surprise in my own. I regretted the moment of vulnerability, but he must have read the question in my face because then he said, "I shouldn't be telling you this before they do, but I have contacts in the police, and I've been shown the press reports they drafted, and I know the evidence corroborates your story.

"Graham's foot was caught between the bars of a shopping trolley at the bottom of the pond . . . he couldn't possibly have escaped, no matter how hard you pulled, so you see, all this persecution will fade in time, you just have to hold on for now . . . okay, Orson?"

And then I really did go into shock. I knew exactly what happened at the pond. I remember Graham's legs thrashing in the water as my hands clamped around his trachea—there was no way his foot had been trapped. Somebody must have done that afterwards—for me. Fate had revealed Herself again in one of those rare moments of passion, but to me only this time, and somehow I knew it would not be the last time. She gave me license to continue and I was grateful for that because Graham Adams robbed me of the pleasure that I sought since birth. I wanted, *needed*, to see that boy's eyes as his life slipped away. I needed to see that mystical moment of transition when the sum of all his experience snapped into oblivion. But it was denied me.

I decided after that day that I would give no more place

to chance. I planned the next death in meticulous detail, and the next with even greater care, and so on until I realized that my skill was an art that grew more and more refined with each killing. And with each new indulgence, Fate played Her part too, but it wasn't until kill number thirty-two, when I met my mysterious sentinel, that things changed.

# 4

Kriefan Mack was a nice guy, a popular guy. At least, that's the impression I had when I went through his personal effects. His wallet contained a list of phone numbers as long as the DHS council house waiting list, a faded photo of him at the center of a group of smiling Africans on a missionary visit, a donors card, a selection of personal business cards that revealed him to be a member of The Samaritans, the Round Table, and at least two other charitable organizations I had not heard of before. Pity he met me. Especially under such fateful circumstance.

I slipped the wallet back into his jacket pocket and cupped his chin in my hand, gave his head a shake. The rivulet of blood that had snaked its way across his forehead took a new direction and entered his ear. His eyes flickered open, the pupils dilated with panic and bewilderment. Obviously he had no idea who I was, and my bald head and heavy build silhouetted against a bright sun was enough to startle him back deeper into his torn seat.

"Who? . . . Oh God! Is anyone . . . am I—?"

"You're fine, you're fine," I reassured him with a smile and a large hand on his shoulder. "No serious injury as far as I can tell."

"What about the other car, the other driver, how is he?"

"Let's leave him to the police and paramedics shall we? Here, let me help you out."

I reached though the twisted wreckage, grabbed him under the armpits and hauled him on to the grass verge next to the impossibly-twisted monster that used to be his car. He threw up when he saw it, or perhaps it was the old woman's hand poking out from under the roof like a broken claw. His car had rolled down the bank, rolling at least four times as it crushed bollards and roadside debris in its wake.

Kriefan Mack had done nothing wrong. But being good or right or true does nothing for you in this world. His nemesis, the seventeen-year-young speedster, lay on the other side of the road. And on the crumpled bonnet of his Subaru. And all over his dead girlfriend's body; there was very little for the emergency services to scoop up and scrape out. He'd performed his final act trying to overtake a gritting lorry on a blind bend and met the unsuspecting Kriefan Mack head on. I saw the collision in all its gory glory whilst waiting to turn out of the junction on my way to the office, and although it is fair to say that one could not have expected there to have been any survivors at all when two cars kiss bumpers at a combined speed of 150mph, my experience tells me that the perpetrator often escapes his idiocy with little more than a scratch to his forehead. Not so this time. The speeding youth's life had been smeared from existence along with his partner's and an unfortunate dog-walking pedestrian, but Mr. Mack left the carnage suffering only from mild shock, a small cut by his ear, and the doom of impending insurance claim forms. He should not have survived that accident. Fate had been cheated.

And that's where I came in. She would not be cheated so easily and my presence at the scene was obviously no accident. I tried to move quickly, looking for an opportunity to reach the overturned car unseen by the screaming public, but police cars and ambulances screeched into view within minutes, announcing their arrival with the lurid splash of red and blue, and the wail of sirens; a parody of the slaughter. I laughed as I walked through it all, seeing the metaphor, so much like human nature. People pretend to care. They throw themselves into moments of ugliness like this in a theatrical display of valiant altruism, but people like me see through every reluctant glance and declaration of horror into their thirsty hearts. They're looking for the next thrill, the next juicy story to tell their friends, the next chance to demonstrate their heroism as they run into the fire to help. I have a different agenda. And so does She.

# 5

I entered Kriefan Mack's house two days later at ten minutes to midnight with everything planned to perfection. Most people would think he lived in a beautiful home; it's a nice four-bedroom detached house with a postcard-perfect garden, pastel painted walls, and immaculate modern furniture, minding its own quiet business at the end of a tidy cul-de-sac. The lights had been out twenty minutes, time enough for Kriefan, his wife and two children to drift into sleep. Smiling at the neighborhood-watch stickers on the windows, I slid Mr. Mack's stolen door key into the lock. He'd assumed his keys had been lost in the accident, and with so much happening since then he hadn't had the opportunity to get the locks changed.

I moved quickly. Wasting time with quiet precaution is worthless when one enters an occupied house so easily. Experience has taught me that it's better to strike your prey when it's off-guard. I climbed the stairs with my medical briefcase in hand, eased along the landing and opened the first door. It was a child's room. A low light in the corner revealed a young girl in bed, mouth open, the sigh of deep slumber passing her lips. I closed the door and opened the one next to it. That was the right one. Again, the low amber light, but this time it was shining on Kriefan Mack and his wife spooned together under the bed covers.

I set my briefcase down at the end of the bed, opened it, selected a pair of latex gloves and a syringe, which I placed on the dressing table. I rolled the gloves onto my hands, flexing my fingers, checking for holes. "Get up, Kriefan."

At first all they did was open their eyes and blink. Then he turned, sat upright and thrust his back against the headboard as if an invisible hand had slammed him there. "Shit!"

She was still blinking, trying to work out where she was.

Kriefan just stared. "Bloody *hell*!"

His wife's lips trembled open when she realized this was reality. There really *was* a prowler in the bedroom tapping at a syringe. She was ready to yell, but I lifted a finger. "I wouldn't. Your children are asleep. It might be best if they don't see what's about to happen, Mrs. Mack."

She started to shake and Kriefan turned his bed lamp on to full, panic scoring deep lines into his face. I could see a hundred different scenarios running through his head just by watching his eyes. He was wondering if he could take me.

"You! You're the man that helped me out of my car," he

says, squinting. "What's this about? How the *hell* did you get in?"

"The usual way," I said, waggling the key.

"Oh God!"

Mrs. Mack couldn't help herself. She screamed as though someone just showed her a plate with someone's heart still beating on it.

"If your children see me they'll die too," I shouted above her tears, pressing my hand to the door in case they came running in.

Kriefan was shaking his head. "I don't know what you're doing in our house but if you don't get out right now we'll… Kelly, where's the mobile?"

It was on her bedside table. She was reaching for it. The children started hammering on the door, yelling, crying. Kriefan was already out of bed, fists balling, jaw stiffening, he was about to attack. No problem. I went for him first, snatched at his hand and bent it against his forearm before launching him at the door in case the children came in. His head cracked on the handle and I stepped over him to get to his wife. The children were still yelling as I snatched the phone from her and slammed it into the wall. With a slap I sent her reeling across the bed and turned to Kriefan. He was already back up, distracted by the blood in the palm of his hand and the cry of his wife, his face a portrait of confusion, fear, rage, desperation.

"Bastard!" He came for me again and I met him head on.

His knuckles struck my cheekbone but my own fist plunged into the soft spot beneath the ribcage forcing the air from his lungs. He folded as though the floor had fallen through the ceiling and the contents of my briefcase scattered across the carpet as he curled up into a groaning ball. Needles and pens danced across the carpet, documents fluttered through the air.

"Angus," cried his wife to her children. "Take Rachel, get out of the house as fast as you can. Run!"

With Kriefan on the floor moaning in pain I turned to her, put her down too with a crack across the jaw. Sobbing, she crawled into the corner, her head in her arms. I know people like her. She wouldn't bother me again, and when the noise of the children had gone I knew I could indulge.

"You're both going to die. You know that, don't you?"

Kriefan looked up at me, sweat running from his brow. "Why?"

"Why doesn't matter. What matters for you now is how."

"Look, can't we just . . . talk . . . about this? I don't know what I've done but I . . . " He trailed off into tears. "Oh God . . . my kids . . . Oh God."

He was stalling for time, knowing the police would be here in minutes. I had to work fast, so I kept my victim pinned to the carpet and straddled his chest, reached for the syringe.

"Listen carefully, Kriefan. You're going to die," I cupped his chin in my hands, felt his sweat through the latex. "You can't change that because it's your fate. I promise it will be painless if you cooperate, but if you struggle, your wife's death will be agony."

"Why? God! *Why*?"

"Focus, Kriefan." I gripped his head tighter, staring hard into his wide eyes, preparing myself for the moments I so enjoy. "Do you understand me?"

He stared.

"Do. You. Understand?"

His eyes said yes and I felt his muscles relax beneath me. 100mg of Pancuronium Bromide injected into the bloodstream and in less than a minute he'd be completely paralyzed, then seconds later he'd be dead. I stared into his eyes, tried not to hear his final whine of self pity as I emptied the fluid into him.

Deeper. Penetrating the black center, searching the soul.

Deeper. Watching for the end.

Deeper. It's intoxicating sharing those final moments of terror when every part of the body stiffens.

I saw it; the moment of death.

In that infinitesimal blink of time a multitude of experience winks out of existence, never to return. It simply disappears. I gasped, as if the air had frozen in my lungs. After seeing this so many times and feeling the pleasure of it, the power never dwindles, never fails to deliver that exquisite rush. But still death's secret eluded me. There is a profound difference between eyes that are alive and eyes that are dead. Not focus. Not dilation of the pupils. Something else. Some place far deeper than I can go.

I allowed the body to drop and I looked over to his widow. She was not crying any longer, just cowering in the corner with her arms wrapped around her knees staring through her dead husband, a single strand of saliva crawling from her lip. She knew what was coming, and, reluctantly, I obliged, dispatching her quickly and with a silent prayer for her soul to be at peace. She did not deserve this, but she is, nevertheless, the penalty for her husband's borrowed time.

In echo of the accident two days ago, blue and red lights glared through the gaps in the curtains. If the police knew what was happening they would not have made such a bold announcement of their arrival, but still, whether they catch me or not, Fate had caught up with Mr. Mack and things were right again. But there was no time to appreciate it. I gathered up the contents of my briefcase that had been littered around the room, thrust all of it back inside, slammed it shut, and moved quickly out of the room and down the stairs. The front door was already open and three police cars were outside blocking the drive. It would take a miracle to escape unnoticed.

I edged forward. There were no officers waiting for me at the door. I stepped out onto the drive, waiting to be thrown to the ground, tazered or perhaps even shot, but still there was no one, not even inside the cars. I looked at the surrounding houses. The neighbors, all awake now and leaning from their windows, were not looking my way. Instead their attention had been drawn to an event occurring several houses down. A small man in a long black coat, hunched like something heavy had grown out of his back, was running at surprising speed in the road followed by six police officers shouting for him to stop. Incredibly convenient. Perhaps one of those rare moments when Fate chose to intervene. None of the Macks' neighbors saw me as I left the house; none of them knew the real killer had slipped into a side alley.

It was the closest I had ever come to capture, but rather than celebrate my good fortune when I returned home, I sat in the dark, fearful of where my dreams would take me should I sleep. My thoughts were filled with the image of that strange man to whom I owed my escape; even with a fleeting glance I knew something about him was profoundly wrong. That was the first time I set my eyes on Keitus Vieta. I wish now it had been the only time.

# 6

I met Keitus Vieta the very next night.

Despite my habit to plan each of my murders with meticulous pride, the episode with Kriefan Mack had been as sloppy as it was ugly. In my youth I would never have been so careless as to dismiss the need for a gun to threaten, or duct tape to restrain. Last night was pure carelessness, falling into apathy and nonchalance—the one shortcoming the police wait for. Cautious murderers are never caught until they become over-confident or are moved by some inner desire to end their reign. Only then do they begin to leave clues for their trackers. I was determined that this would not be my failing, yet the incident at the Mack household had been a wakeup call.

After checking my briefcase I found at least two documents missing, probably still under their bed after the contents had been spilt during the fight. It was the one place

I neglected to check before I left. The question therefore was whether the police would make the same oversight. Doubtful. The law had not laid its heavy fist at my door during the day, so I could only assume they had found nothing yet, but surely it was just a matter of time.

One must not rely on Fate to cover one's mistakes, so, forced by my own conscience to make amends for my blunder, I returned to the Mack house. Fate would decide if my capture would happen that night, but my hope was that She would reward my bravery with Her special intervention and keep me in Her service. Naturally, I would not tempt Her further by making more mistakes, but flawless plans can only be prepared if one is in possession of all the facts and in command of every detail, and when I slipped into the Macks' drive again at midnight, I quickly discovered that I had neither under my control. Someone else did.

A single police car was parked outside the house and at first glance I assumed by the position of the officers' bodies, with their necks leaning back over their seats and their faces pointing heavenward, that they were both asleep, but as I crept closer I saw that both men had their eyes open. Not dead though. The chests of both men rose and fell with comatose breathing. I stared for all of two minutes, trying to discern, before venturing closer, who or what could have done this.

Staying low, out of sight, I crept toward the car, looked through the driver's window, ready with a story in case I was mistaken about their condition. But I wasn't. Briefly glancing around me first, I opened the door, sniffed the air for signs of drug abuse, but smelt only the evidence of excretion; a wet patch had darkened the driver's trousers. One hand lay limp on his lap, the other hovered upright over the gear stick, fingers arching and twitching like the legs of a half-dead spider, and with dread nibbling at my spine, I looked closer at the man's eyes.

I know eyes. I Know them very well. But this man's unblinking organs had a madness about them I could not recognize. Dilated, but somehow alert. Rapt, yet full of pain. And as they rolled toward me I saw them plead. A single tear trembled, then traced across his skin, down to his ear. I stared, fascinated for a long moment, then looked at the other man. He too was looking at me, the same vacant yet imploring expression, willing me to do something.

I released a long sigh as I withdrew from the car, as if I had held my breath the whole time. At first I wondered if this was Fate's work, but no, this was not Her way. Someone or something else had changed these men, and with a determined effort to master my growing fear, I turned my attention back to the house.

The taped barrier had been broken, the front door, opened.

I stepped over the threshold, peered up the stairs and into the shadows; there was no light other than the moon's faint strands filtering through gaps in drawn curtains. Someone or something shuffled behind the door of the main bedroom.

If not the police in this house, then whom? The unexpected odor of formaldehyde poisoned the air, bringing with it the demented ghosts of hospitals and asylums in which I had once lived, and then irrational imaginings of long-dead victims waiting for me in the next room. I licked my dry lips and pulled a pistol from my coat pocket. I had never used it, probably never would—to bring about death in such a crude fashion would be like roasting the goose then tossing it in the gutter—but a gun is always a steadfast deterrent.

I cursed each step as the boards creaked beneath my weight, then paused to listen for the cessation of movement behind the door when I reached it. Whomever it was still seemed to be unaware of my intrusion. I waited by the door, calmed my breathing. The shuffling from inside the room did not stop and I concentrated on the brass knob of the door in a futile effort to distract my brain from attacking me with images of terror at what might be waiting.

The shuffling stopped. A low whisper followed in syllables as long and dreadful as an icy breeze in summertime. "Killer."

I considered turning around. Running from the house. Even turning myself in to the police just to get away from that voice, but I stood my ground for reasons only Fate knew.

The knob turned with the speed of a second hand on a clock and when the door eventually eased open I gazed into the dark, desperate for confirmation that the voice came from a human and not some ungodly specter. A figure stirred in the shadows, crawling across the floor by the bed. I said nothing when he looked up at me, and my legs refused to move when he rose to a stoop. He was little more than a dwarf in height, devoured by a heavy black coat, and although the only illumination entering the room came from misty moon threads, an indigo radiance lit his face from beneath. My eyes were immediately drawn to the source: a glittering stone in the thorny handle of his cane which the figure clutched in his left hand. In the half-light it was a diseased knuckle extending out as a long index finger to scratch the floor.

The shape of his head beneath his bowler hat suggested this to be a man of considerable age. In his right hand he held one of my missing documents which he raised above his head, turning it slowly in the air.

"Idle hands, Mr. Roth," he whispered, his voice like the moan of a leaking gas pipe.

Clouds shifted outside the window throwing more light into the room and on the intruder to expose the visage of a grinning death mask. Bruise-blue eyes bulged from sunken sockets within a face so ravaged by age the water-thin skin appeared as if his naked skull had a layer of chewed gum stretched over it. Even the pulsing veins weaved between the many liver spots were laid bare in plain sight.

Suppressing my fear, I stood to my full height and looked down on him. "You know my name."

The old man stared back up at me, his huge eyes unblinking. "I know *you*. I know . . . know your work."

I pushed the gun toward his face, the barrel a mere centimeter from his pallid forehead, only to feel a sudden chill, a profound sense of danger, as if I was a cocky child that had placed a banger inside the mouth of an alligator and dared myself to hold it there. I lowered the weapon and the old man's gray lips stretched to uncover hoary gums and crooked teeth. It couldn't really be described as a smile.

"Was that you I saw last night running from this house?" I knew it was.

"Of course." His eyes moved to my gun.

I tucked it back into my pocket. "Why? Who are you?"

He folded up the document he had picked up from under the bed and offered it to me. "I am Keitus Vieta."

I took the paper from him, stuffed it in my pocket next to the gun and looked at the old man's hand. It was still extended, the skeletal fingers open, steady, seemingly waiting for a handshake. I refused and he lowered it to greet his other hand that held his cane. He forced his smile a little wider across sharp cheekbones.

"Should I know you?" I asked.

"No."

I studied him, tried to regulate my breathing to hide the quiver in my voice. "Then why should you know me?"

Keitus Vieta ignored the question, set his cane on the bed and sniffed the air in long slow gulps, fingers raised, playing with the air around him as he stalked the room. Fairy tales about ogres scenting the blood of hiding children crept into my mind as I watched, and it was at that moment of scrutiny that I realized something about this man was utterly wrong; primal instincts had roused something in my mind, warning me that such a man could not be real and I struggled to rationalize what my senses could not.

He crouched over a mug of cold coffee left on the bedside table, picked it up as if it were a wounded starling, then pressed it to his cheek. I could only stand and watch in frozen fascination as he rolled his tongue over the handle, across the lip and around the base, his eyes upon me every moment as the cold dregs pattered onto the carpet like blood.

"Mine," he whispered. Then paused to study me in return.

I watched, resisting the creeping fear, and grappled with the facts before me. Persuaded by some unknown motive, Keitus Vieta had visited the scene of my crime, and amongst his bizarre intentions, wanted to conceal my mistakes, wanted to protect me for some reason. This man, whoever he was, wherever he was from, needed me. I had no idea why, but for now, all I needed to remember was that his need must be my advantage.

"What did you do to the police outside? You must know they will be looking for you after tonight," I said. "Are they drugged?"

Keitus placed the mug within the folds of his coat. "Not drugged."

"What then?"

"Empty now."

"What does that mean?"

"Too many questions, Mr. Roth. Be content with the knowledge that I am here to help you."

"But why? Did you have something against Kriefan Mack?"

Keitus placed his index finger against his tongue and rubbed the saliva against his thumb as if testing something. "You help me. So I help you."

I squeezed the gun inside my pocket, fighting an urge to rip it out and level it against his forehead again, scream at this strange man and demand that he start making sense. He saw the twitch of my hand in my pocket and the feeling of cold dread visited me once more. He smiled, perhaps believing that I would not be intimidated, and on impulse I wrenched the gun out as his eyes widened in excitement. Sweat coated my palm, my heart thumped inside my throat and as if from within a dream, I actually heard myself whimpering when I pressed my weapon against the old man's forehead a second time.

We stayed in that pose for the longest time—my fear mingling with his fascination—until at last, Keitus wrapped his frail fingers around the barrel and freed the gun from my trembling hand. As he did with the empty mug, he slid his tongue across the metal, tasting the handle, the orifice at the end of the barrel, the trigger, until he passed it back. "No, not ready yet. Not at all ready."

I let my arm go limp, almost dropping the gun. "What

isn't ready? What do you mean? Please."

"I am a collector, Mr. Roth."

"Of guns?" I knew he meant something else, something more sinister. My legs began to shake.

"Of . . . life. And death. Your gun is not ready yet. You still have a little time. More people to kill. More gifts to bring me before our partnership ends."

I shuddered, but tried to rise a little higher above him in spite of my growing weakness. "Our partnership is over tonight. You might need me, old man, but I don't need you."

"You have always needed me."

"Bullshit."

He retrieved his cane from the bed. The stone seemed a little brighter than earlier.

"Remember Graham Adams?" he whispered. "I was there."

"Adams?" I felt my heart stop, waiting for him to tell me more.

"You told everyone that his foot had been trapped in the pond and that you tried to save him, remember? Who do you think pushed his ankle through the bars of the trolley they found when they dragged his corpse from the water? Did you think you were lucky? That fortune fell in love with you that day? Was it then that you began to believe that Fate had plans for your future?"

I dropped the gun. Felt the room spin like a cloudy carousel, felt clammy panic siphon my waking thoughts as I dropped to my knees.

"I'll take you home, Mr. Roth."

I remember weeping as he leant over me, the unblinking gaze cutting into me like a scalpel dissecting my soul. Then I sank, drowning in a cold nightmare.

# 7

When I woke the next day I chased away the harsh dreams with a comparatively stiff drink and a cigarette. I usually saved that pleasure for quiet evenings in, but I needed something more than coffee to pacify my mind; Vieta's haunting voice and face had invaded my sleep, and I still could not rationalize what I had seen in that house. This was more than fear. It was something deeper, something far more profound than an emotional reaction.

I remembered my youth, my fascination when taught about the blind spot of the human eye. At the point where the optic nerve sprouts from the back of the eyeball, the brain receives no visual information and fills in the gaps with a fabrication of its own. With one eye shut, a single black dot on a piece of paper could be made to disappear if held at the right distance; the eye could not see the dot and the mind would fill the void with its best approximation—

the surrounding paper. Keitus Vieta was to me the same thing; a fabrication of the brain to explain something that should not be there, a paradox, a tangible ghost, something unreal. Yet he was there. He *was* real.

I needed to shut him out of my waking thoughts if I wanted to make it through the day with my composure intact, so I walked into town, my coat drawn about me like a vampire's cloak, stalking from pavement to pavement, road to alley, alley to street; it didn't matter to me that my choice of clothes and miserable scowl on such a bright morning could draw unwanted attention. I wanted to hide, though, withdraw for a time until I could better understand what happened last night, but no inner peace would be mine until I'd found out what the local reporters had squeezed out of the police. It was the same in most of the towns and cities I moved to: they'd splash the news across the front of the local tabloid like blood from a Shakespearean tragedy.

I could usually predict what the local papers would say. A day or two after my kill, I would buy one for the purpose of amusement, and to scope out any notable stories about people who had narrowly evaded death. But today was different, today I needed to know, because last night was all wrong. Control had been lost. And it still evaded me. More than ever I felt alien eyes upon me, observing me, calculating my every move and now I had to accept the truth: it was no longer a paranoia to be dismissed out of hand. The eyes are real. And my stalker even has a name. Had Fate disowned me? Had She sacrificed me to this new stranger's will? I expected punishment for my carelessness, but this? Abandonment could destroy me. I need Her. I need Her like a child needs its . . .

"Hey, watch it, mate!" My shoulder glances off another's.

"Leave it, Bill. *Please* don't start."

I turn, look at the couple holding hands, the man is staring at me as if ready to prove his prowess to the woman at his side. A flash of rage ignites deep in my stomach and I chew my lower lip to suppress the rising urge to make an example of him and spread the insolent fucker's brains over his girlfriend's flayed corpse. He backs away stepping on his girlfriend's foot—must have read that thought on my face. I suck back an audible, measured, long, steady, soothing breath . . . as if I am about to blow the two of them into the road, spattering them into oncoming traffic where their guts will…

Don't! I know what's happening. I see it. Impulsive violence is a poor tool, like a sledgehammer in oily hands it can destroy much, but rarely hits the nail.

He's still looking up at me, sizing me up with no idea in that ape-like brain how close he just came to his end. Interesting. Did he just cheat Fate?

A one-sided smile slides across the man's face as he lifts his palms. "Women! Lucky for you she's the one in control, eh?"

My eyes widen as I move toward him. "What?"

Still staring at me, his smile loses place to confused suspicion. "What d'you mean . . . *what*? Listen, mate—"

"Bill! Leave him, he's a bloody weirdo." She yanks his arm and the man shakes his head as he's pulled away, back on his path.

He was right. *She's* in control. I go through one night of doubt and I almost lose myself. I should know better than to think She would abandon me after just one night of failure. No, like Jesus in the wilderness, this is my test, but I won't take forty days to learn my lesson. I'll trust Her. Whomever this Keitus Vieta is, She must control him too, and if he wants to help me, so be it.

# 8

April 5: Liam Butler. Fell from someone's roof trying to replace some broken slates, landed on the pavement and smashed his pelvis. His head missed the edge of his wheelbarrow by the width of a finger. He should've died. After reading about it in the local paper the following week I made sure the job was finished, though there was nothing in the man's eyes that yielded any of the Grim Reaper's secrets. The hospital staff were clueless about my unauthorized presence on the ward at night when I administered the drug, and they had even less idea about why he didn't make it through after such a standard operation. Their only notable comment was about the strange old man who, claiming to be a relative, turned up only an hour after the death had been declared. Police could not locate him after the visit and none of Mr. Butler's other relatives were able to conclude who it could have been. It was also noted that one of the deceased's possessions, reading glasses, had mysteriously disappeared from his bedside.

June 23: Vanessa Fullworth. Fell asleep at the wheel of her car. She smashed through the central reservation, taking with her the front bumper of a transit van as her metal tomb slammed her into two other cars. Except she didn't die. At least, not until I found out about her miraculous escape. Another hospital visit set things straight. Again the mysterious visitor. Again a missing object.

September 12: Steve Warren. A local electrician found unconscious in his workshop after electrocuting himself repairing an old TV set. An ambulance found him quite by chance, having arrived to deal with injured people at a pub brawl at the end of the road. One of Mr. Warren's customers, irritated by the inconvenience of the shop still being closed well after lunchtime, had peered through the back window and seen him slumped over his bench. Had the ambulance and its capable paramedics not been there at the time, Mr. Warren would have died—or so I was led to believe by the owner of the shop next door. I called on Mr. Warren's services as soon as he was back to work, claiming that I needed an expert to examine a faulty RCU unit. Nobody ever found out what happened to him and I saw nothing new in his dying eyes either. The following day somebody broke into my home while I was out. The lock had not been forced, and nothing had been stolen, but the spots of blood coughed up by Mr. Warren onto my carpet had been cleaned off in my absence.

September 18: Ibrahim Yelsin. This was the very incident that led to the discovery of Steve Warren. Ibrahim was the victim of a racial attack outside the Golden Lion pub and it was the landlord who had called the police and the ambulance. The unfortunate teenager had been stabbed in the chest and it was something of a miracle that the blade missed all of his vital organs. Finding this boy was not difficult, he was well known in the area, but my inquiries had brought with them considerable danger—once Ibrahim's murder had been made public, my own discovery would be simple. A test then. How would Mr. Vieta cover my tracks this time? The newspapers were kind enough to reveal the answer with a two page spread. All of the boy's friends, any witnesses to my involvement, were no longer able to speak. Attempts to discuss the demise of their friend resulted in prolonged episodes of mute panic and tearful hysteria. I chose not to investigate further.

December 1: Jane Laughday. Survivor of a laboratory explosion.

December 12: Jamie Colson. Remission from prostate cancer.

February 14: Troy Davenport. Failed suicide attempt.

March 3: Alfie Bennet. Sole survivor of the Rochford food poisoning scandal.

May 29: Lisa Barclay. Thrown from a fairground ride. Survived.

June 8: Tim Sweetman. Lived through an aneurysm. Died a few days later after a second aneurysm . . . with a little help from a certain cocktail of drugs, of course.

The list went on. Each time I found out about these people who had cheated my Goddess I was there to ensure they paid their debt. And no matter how many times I tested Mr. Vieta's ability to clean up my murderous mistakes, he would always be there, waiting.

The entire nation, consumed by fascination, had labeled me the "magpie killer"; one particularly resourceful detective inspector noticed that all of my victims had lost a personal item they had been using close to the time of death. The motive was unknown, as it remains to me, but the discovery earned the inspector a commendation, a sizable reward, and a sudden brain seizure, for which I am quite sure was the handiwork of my creeping shadow, Keitus Vieta. The only communication the psychoanalysts could get from the inspector was a continuous stream of letters, scrawled in block capitals, like the cry of a brain-damaged child. And the words were always followed by a long scream of terror that could only be silenced with morphine. Those letters will stay with me forever because they describe him so well.

The letters spelt out one sentence. "HEISNOWHERE."

Under such circumstances it seemed my calling was irrevocable. I would never be caught. But that all changed the following year, seven days after my forty-sixth birthday, the day that Keitus Vieta chose to take something of mine.

# 9

Addiction is ugly. When one is deprived of their vice, the heart swells like a ravenous sponge. It becomes a fallen tyrant, screaming its demands and sobbing its grief in a volume that drowns out any words of quiet reason the mind might impart.

Five months passed without a victim. I had gone longer than this before, but not without consequences. I walked the streets in a daze, knowing only that my desires were unquenched. I had scoured the papers, studied the local news with blackened eyes, hovered around hospitals, but I had not found one person anywhere who had cheated Fate. Perhaps the true link to all the murders had been discovered and the media had been silenced to flush me out. Perhaps Fate had abandoned me, perhaps it was another test. But at the end of things, I know now that the answer is more subtle, more fitting than any of those.

On my final day amongst the masses I walked the cliffs

of Cornwall to clear my mind, following the coastal path to Tintagel—a place that breathes history through every ancient blade of grass and every moss-covered rock. I fished through my pockets to find my shades in the hope that I could dwell on the view for a time without squinting, but they had gone. On a day like that day, in such a place, when the seaside sun burns in the heights of a cloudless sky and the smell of ocean water fills every pore, one would have to be born without a soul not to smile. I watched anyway without my sunglasses.

For a time I found my contentment, but the serenity was soon broken. Abusive shouting is not something one expects on a pleasant Sunday morning walking the cliffs, but nevertheless, a short way ahead of me the guttural accusations of two men bellowed out above the barking of a large dog. Other walkers gave the two men a wide berth, but not me; I thrive on conflict.

The argument had escalated into finger-stabbing posturing, and as I drew closer, I noticed that the man standing with his back to the cliff edge had lines of blood tracked across the back of his hand. The dog, still barking, but restrained with no small effort by the other man, also had blood on its teeth.

"Of course he's going to bloody bite. He thought you were threatening me!"

"Threatening? I was running past."

"You knocked my arm. What the fuck did you *think* was going to happen . . . Fuckin' arsehole."

"You fuckin' what?"

"You heard."

The man with his back to the cliff, a good two inches taller than the other, moved his face within head-butting distance. The other held his ground, faltering slightly as he held the Alsatian back from a second attack. Time for me to jump in to the fray. I closed in.

"I take it from your tones that neither of you gentlemen are from this area?" I folded my arms, looked from one to the other.

They observed me for no more than five seconds as one might examine a piece of excrement that had suddenly acquired the ability to speak, then turned back to each other.

"I'll be making sure that fucking mutt gets put down, pal."

"Not if he puts you down first, you piece of shit." Another finger stabbed into the man's chest and my organs leapt when the man's heel shuffled ever closer to the cliff edge. Had my five months of fasting finally come to an end? I salivated as he pushed forward again. A flinch caused him to grab the dog man's coat collar, more to hold himself steady than anything else, and I stepped closer. Neither of them seemed interested in my approach. The two of them held each other's clothes, eyes wide with horror, tottering like skittles, but at the same moment they both understood the danger and stepped away from the edge. Unchecked by its distracted owner and alarmed by my approach, the dog yanked itself free and hurtled toward me like a frothing demon.

"Chip! No!"

I sidestepped but the dog had already charged into me, and then it was my feet that scuffled on the crumbling precipice. The hungry waves a hundred feet below beckoned as my right foot found nothing beneath it. My arms wheeled like rotor blades. My insides exploded with adrenaline and time stretched as my mind rebelled. A solid jolt of knuckles bruised my collar bone as a fist grasped my shirt, and I hung for a moment, one foot dangling, the other sliding against chalk before I was pulled on to the grass.

At least the dog had stopped barking.

"Jesus! That was really close. You all right, mate?" The man was half laughing. I stared at the ground, panting on hands and knees. Two sets of boots stood in peripheral vision, the dog sitting beside one of them, sated with a chew stick provided by the owner. I looked up at the man who had saved my life but lingered there less than a moment; something, or rather someone else caught my eye on the brow of the hill, perhaps two miles away.

It was him.

Specific detail was impossible to make out at that distance, but I could still discern the same hunchbacked posture, the hat and black clothing, and perhaps a flicker of indigo from the jewel in his cane. Keitus Vieta turned, as if he had been waiting for me to notice him, then disappeared over the hill.

I stood up, faced the man who had stopped my fall. "You saved my life Mr. . . ."

“Booth . . . Andy Booth. You all right?”

“A little shaken but yes, I believe so.”

The other man squatted down to ruffle his dog. “Bet you saw your life flash before your eyes then, eh? Lucky he caught you.”

I smiled. “Fate has uncanny taste, doesn’t She?”

“The council ought to put some bloody fences up here. I reckon loads of people must end up splattered on them rocks,” said the first man. “Anyways, looks like it was your lucky day. Take it easy, mate.” He stole another glance at the dog and its owner, and I saw the debate in his eyes about whether he should continue the argument or leave it alone. A second glance at the sea changed his mind and he turned to leave. With an equally cautious glance, the other man left too.

Somebody should have died today on that cliff.

I fished around my pockets, looking for my sunglasses a second time. Still missing. Or taken. I looked back at the empty hill and nodded. I knew what had to be done.

# 10

Today. Such a casual word for most people. One hundred and fifty thousand people die every day, and for some people, today will be their last. I wonder how many of them know that. I suspect the number is relatively small.

"This gonna take long, chief?"

I stare at my target, study every part of him before answering. Silence, when combined with scrutiny is a powerful thing. He shifts from foot to foot, one grubby toe poking through a tear in his trainer. There's a moment of regret at selecting this man. Not because I think he is incapable of the task, but because I would prefer not to be locked away in a room that has boarded windows and virtually no ventilation in the presence of a man who has not discovered the benefits of soap.

He draws his canvas coat tighter against his body as if the action might shield him from my gaze, and a urine breeze finds my nose.

"I'm paying you, aren't I?" I pinch my nostrils with my left hand and pull a packet out of my pocket with my right. "Cigarette?"

"Cheers." The vagrant shuffles forward, snatches nervously at the white stick with oily fingers and plants it between his lips. "Nice place."

It isn't, but if that's his attempt at sarcasm, I'll forgive it. In the next few minutes this grimy-walled room with its festering floorboards and roach problem will be a place more than fit for such an observation. I pull a lighter from my pocket, light his cigarette, then one for myself.

"Take a seat." I inhale a lug from my smoke and gesture to a wooden chair in the middle of the room. Facing it is another chair, and focussed on both of them from the side, is a video camera on a tripod.

"So what sort of documentary is this anyway? Another one of those—*why the homeless can't get a home*—jokes?" He pulls hard on his cigarette, slumps into the seat with a leering grin and blows smoke at me.

"No . . . Nothing like that."

"X Factor for the great unwashed, then?"

I stare at him, allow a slow smile to creep over my face.

"Well?" he flicks a palm up. "You gonna give me a hint? Do I have to act or something?"

I push the red button on the camera, take my coat off and hang it on the back of the chair opposite him. "No. All you need to do is keep your eyes on mine."

"You a queer?"

As I lower myself onto the chair I pull a syringe from one of my coat pockets and hold it up to the light, checking for any bubbles in the liquid. It's fine.

"Hey! What's in the tube?" he asks. "You a druggy? Just cause I live on the streets, that don't make me a spliff-head."

He makes to get up, but then he sees the look in my eye as I grab his sleeve. "Sit. Down."

He pauses and we lock eyes. He sits again, still looking at me as he draws on his cigarette almost down to the filter. Mine is only half way through.

"That's better. Just keep your eyes on mine. It's really not that much to ask, is it?"

"I ain't taking any drugs."

"I'm not asking you to."

"Then what—," he balks as I slam the needle into my arm. "What's in the tube?"

"Drugs." I smile, suppressing the pain as the cold liquid works its way up my vein. "But not the kind you think. Keep looking at me, right at me." I toss the empty syringe aside, its contents now wending its way toward my nervous system. And after crushing my cigarette under heel, I grab the vagrant's face to pull it into mine.

"What the—?" he grabs my arms but holds still. His nails bite through my shirt into my biceps and the tang of nervous sweat stings the back of my throat. With each faltering breath we stare deeper into each other.

"Don't move . . . This won't take long now."

"What the fuck is this? What are you doing?"

"I'm giving you the second half of your payment. A gift."

He's too frightened to ask what I mean but it doesn't matter. He'll soon understand. When the baton is passed he'll run with it just as I did when the killer of my parents, Zachary Cox, handed it to me. I only wish I could still be around to witness my legacy, but I'll not mourn in my last few minutes while the camera catches these precious moments of shared revelation. He'll think this moment is unique, a special bond between the two of us, and it is, but such wonder can be found in the heart of any man, woman or child; one has only to look into their eyes to see it. No . . . not look—one must wallow, breathe, drink, *gorge* on the moments given.

I look deeper into the vagrant's eye and see beyond. As dark as apocalypse night, as deep as death's abyss, I drift down and allow my will to follow. There is nothing darker, nothing more consuming as the soul, and as if the Goddess desired to make this plain to all who chose to see, that circle of black is ringed by a myriad of colored fibers, a million spokes pointing to the deep. A marvel like no other, is the eye.

His muscles are stiff like stone under my grip, the body odor intensifying, and though I sense the connection, there is no epiphany for him yet. But I will not lose heart. I have not failed any of Fate's tests so far and this one will be no exception. She has been a faithful Goddess—always rewarding my desire with new souls to unwrap—and we will be face to face soon. There I will gaze into Her eyes and know sweet satisfaction forever. She has teased me too long, like a drop of wine touched to the end of my tongue, I have tasted this bliss many times, but never long enough to savor completely. Taste is not enough. To drink is not enough. I want to swim in it, to *drown* in it.

A low moan escapes my subject's lips. Still he does not feel it, even as I feel the cold poison in my veins. Wet slivers tremble on the rims of his lower lids as his eyes say "stop". But I can't and I won't. The taste is too close now to break away, the perfect circle that shields the human soul holds me—the hollow with its hunger never satisfied, eating my mind, howling for more. Or is that the whoosh of my heart thudding through my ears like a boat master driving his slaves?

Through my delirium I hear the creak of the door, catch the flap of a black coat in my peripheral vision, feel the cold breeze of a body passing by our side and my successor is ripped from me as his eyes flick to my right, widening with an even greater terror than I could instill. And now the smell! Formaldehyde overwhelming the smell of sweat. I should have known Keitus Vieta would come, here at the end. But no matter. My only regret is that I learned nothing more about him, but that doesn't matter either; Fate is whom I serve. She comes now with her reward—the circle of black is exchanged for its white negative and I drop forward, hardly noticing the floorboards as they slap my cheek. A tunnel of godly light engulfs me. Come, Fate. I am ready for your embrace.

# SALEM BEN
# 4

Come! Rescue me, my Goddess. I am stripped naked of my soul, soaring through the white void waiting for my reward—in death I am yours. If I still had a beating heart I would tear it from my chest to place it on your altar. Where are you?

"Did you find what you were looking for?"

That voice—so familiar. "Goddess?"

Cold steel tightens against my skin as something restrains my wrists and ankles. Or is it just the return of sensation? Hair-thin wires retracting from my skull. The light of oblivion fades and shadowy orbs bloom before me as my surroundings take shape. The entrance to the W.O.O.M. opens before me like a bloodless wound stretching its lips to welcome the real world, and beyond, a plethora of tiny slits covering the curved wall, each sheltering a single soul. All is washed in sweeping emerald luminescence.

"Goddess?" the voice echoes in mild amusement. "You missed me, Salem. I'm touched."

"No! *No*! I'm Orson . . . Roth." I clench my fists, pull at the restraints. I am violated, deceived. Fate has been cheated too. This is not the afterlife I had expected. Instead of the Goddess there is . . . Qod.

"I am pleased to tell you that, whatever the aberration was in Orson Roth's life, it has had no lasting effect on your physiology or mental stability. Your current confusion will pass as it always does."

"Let me *go*!"

"No, Salem. Your serotonin levels are still unbalanced."

Zachary Cox screams through my mind and I scream along with him as scores of eyeless people bustle forward with twisted faces, Graham Adams pointing, Lisa Barclay accusing, Troy Davenport sobbing, Kriefan Mack pleading. Each one reaching for me with clawed fingers, pushing their rivals aside, desperate to tear me apart. How could I do what I did to them? But that isn't me. Is it? Was it? I am Salem Ben, not Orson Roth. I am not a murderer.

But I loved prying into their dying moments, adored the rush of it when I tasted their deaths. *I* felt that. *I* felt it just as much as Orson Roth. *I* wanted that. Didn't I?

"Well? Did you?"

"*No*! I mean . . . what?"

"Did you find what you were looking for? Did you find out what was beyond death? Did he?"

"No, Qod. I was just . . . *He* . . . was just a maniac."

"Well of course. Roth's file did originally belong in the Maniac Sphere. I tried to warn you. Sharing in someone's insanity and actions is not—"

"I had reasons for doing what I did. Those people cheated Fate . . . they . . . She needed . . . Oh, Qod."

Instinct tells me to cover my face with my hands, but the shackles refuse me the luxury. A mingling of agoraphobic and claustrophobic conflict wars in me as I am forced to stare out from my confinement and into the space of the vast Aberration Sphere.

"You still need a few minutes, Salem. Try to relax."

"I'm fine. No thanks to you. Why didn't you tell me Roth was a madman?"

"You knew he was a murderer. I thought it best not to tell you he was something far worse even than that. You seemed quite taken with the idea of endangering yourself when you learned of the aberrations, and telling you that Orson Roth was filed alongside people like Encore Makar the Necro-Lord or Caligula, would only have sharpened your lust. How would you feel now, having awoken from Roth's life, knowing that you chose such an extreme?"

"I wouldn't have become Roth if you'd told me."

I turned my eyes from the emerald glare of the curved walls to my feet. Silence reigned for several long seconds.

"Salem." My name is drawn out as a long, bored sigh. "I have access to every recorded moment in the history of every cycle of the universe. I exist between the electrons that spin through each atom of your mind and, for that matter, every electron burning in the most distant stars of the most remote galaxy. I can beat you at chess, Barnam's Hoops and Quantum Stripes with the slowest neurons of my processing subsystems. I am your Alpha and I am your Omega and I've been taking care of you for billions of years. I. *Know.* You. Why do you bother lying to me?"

"It isn't you I'm lying to." My admission silences her. She knows it anyway, but seems to think the banter will protect me, as if I can be distracted from my trauma and the knowledge that I'm coming to an end. By that I don't mean death, not the physical kind anyway. The death of reason. The death of identity. My body will go on and on, but who is it that lives within this flesh? Am I losing perspective to such a degree that, without a second thought, I am prepared to become a monster to find my answer? And perhaps it is even worse than that. Was it really the answer I was interested in, or was it the fascination of becoming a killer? This is why she warned me about being Orson Roth. Not because of who *he* was, but because my choice might force me to face who I have become.

The hiss of hydraulic locks snap me from my musings and my hands and feet are freed. Cables lower me gently to the floor and I'm grateful for the warm breeze against my face, as though I had somehow been aware of the stale atmosphere gradually building inside the W.O.O.M. through all the years of my immersion.

"Would you like to go to the Observation Sphere?" Qod

asks. “Not much has changed in forty-six years, but I know how it helps you think.”

All I do is nod when the cables slide away. The metallic floor sticks to my feet as I head for the exit of the Aberration Sphere and at last, I’m me again, but I will never be able to forget the murders I committed inside that man’s life. Even without my enhanced synapses those bloody memories would leave a permanent stain, of that I am sure. Zachary Cox’s glassy gaze imprinting on my brain, Orson Roth’s syringe in my hand, the stench of formaldehyde burning my sinuses. I stop, and my heart skips a beat. I can’t leave, not yet. I came into this new sphere for a reason and Orson Roth had no answers for me. All around, in every tiny alcove, a tiny light glitters—each one a soul containing some sort of aberration. But what are these aberrations? I have my suspicions, and I have a lead, but the thought of where that investigation may take me brings a shudder of trepidation:

“Qod?”

“Yes, Salem?”

“I need you to locate another soul for me. His name is Keitus Vieta.”

# 5

Forty-six years is nothing. A lifetime ago, before I became Orson Roth, I witnessed the birth of the Universe. It's still happening now, unfolding just as it did before. Every last particle combining with its neighbor in exactly the same predictable way, obeying the same physical laws with the same uncompromising rigidity, forming gaseous clouds that will ultimately bear their own children. Galaxies will explode with the first fresh stars, and the cooling matter in between will one day condense into planets and moons. A precious fraction of those will support life and the miracle of humanity will be born all over again. Every life will be lived exactly as it was before, the same predetermined existence racing toward its glorious destiny.

I could watch it all again, observing from a distance as vast as the universe itself, as I have before, relishing its beauty and reveling in the mystery of sentience that spawned from a soulless mote. Yes, I could be drifting in the Observation Sphere now, watching the distant images of creation, but I'm not.

Cowled in somber robes to match my mood, I am back in the Calibration Sphere again, watching the turning walls, musing over the dead: so much life whittled down to a library of tiny blinking lights. Throughout the millennia, unseen control mechanisms pluck souls from every sphere and check the data, calibrating it and, if necessary, recategorizing. No doubt, this is where Qod discovered the aberrations; irreconcilable inconsistency in the data causing her to create the Aberration Sphere. An irrational part of me wonders if they know something is different now they've been transferred here.

Should I be like everyone else? A memory?

I could end my life in a heartbeat.

I want to leave. Want to rest my head against a cool pillow in a warm bed with a smile on my lips as soft dreams take me from this world to the next, knowing that I have tasted every sweet thing this universe has to offer. I am content in the knowledge that I have done the latter, but what *of* the next world? Is there one? The same question plagues me still, and I cannot leave as the others did. Not until I have the answer. Orson Roth didn't know. Perhaps one of my other choices will, but before I venture into another life, one enigma remains.

"You've been silent a long time, Qod."

"I've been busy."

"Busy? How can you be busy? You could have looked

through the entire index ten times over in this amount of time."

"Two hundred and seventy-three times, to be exact."

"Why? Wasn't once enough?"

"There is no record of Keitus Vieta in the Consortium files. I have been checking and rechecking since you made your request. Keitus Vieta's soul is nowhere to be found."

I turn, look up at the domed ceiling, and even though I know Qod has no face, I entertain the fantasy that I might catch her off guard and steal a glimpse of her baffled expression. There is no hint of confusion in her voice, but I know her. This has puzzled even her.

"What do you mean you can't find him? I saw him, spoke with him."

"There is no record of Keitus Vieta in the Consortium files."

"Impossible." I stride away from the center of the sphere, watching as one of the tiny lights is sucked back inside the wall ready to be distributed back into the sphere from which it was plucked. "Everyone who's ever existed has a file created after they've died," I say. "I'm the last man . . ."

A shock runs through me, and I stop to glance around the sphere, hoping not to find evidence of a second empty slot. "Could he . . . could he still be alive?"

"No, Salem. Only one slot remains and that one is reserved for you. Keitus Vieta cannot exist."

"But he does. I met him. Orson Roth met him." I resume my pacing. "Can you at least run a search algorithm through the other souls for someone matching his description?"

"The Codex protocols don't allow me to pry into the lives of these souls, Salem. You know that. I am only permitted access to the summary description of each life, which, I'm sorry to say, is precious little revelation."

"Then search for him again. His soul is in there. It has to be. "There is no record of Keitus Vieta in the Consortium files," Qod insists.

"Stop saying that! His life *has* to be somewhere amongst all these spheres."

"Then Keitus Vieta must not have been his real name," she says.

And for a moment, I relent, seeing the sense in her suggestion: "That would makes sense. A fake identity would mean Orson would have had a difficult time trying to find him or betray him to the authorities if he turned against him. But there was something about Vieta, something . . . I don't believe he was lying about his name."

"But it is the simplest explanation, Salem."

"Yes, but assuming that it *is* his real name, could there be another reason for his absence from the Consortium files? Could his file have been erased for some reason?"

"No. I would know if that happened."

"Then what? You're almost omniscient. Don't you have an answer?"

She says nothing, and as I tap my fingers thoughtfully against my lips, I can almost hear her thinking the same thing—*There is no record of Keitus Vieta in the Consortium files.*

"What if . . . what if Vieta *has* no soul?" I ask.

"The soul is a metaphysical concept originally cultivated by those that had no understanding of the true human condition. If Keitus Vieta was a real person that walked, talked, and thought, he had what could be crudely identified as a soul . . . and you know that, Salem."

"At least I'm coming up with some theories, Qod. This must have something to do with the aberrations. You said that the aberrations weren't caused by data corruption, but if you can't find a record of this man, perhaps you were wrong."

"I am never wrong."

I pause for a moment and a single memory flashes through my mind; one sentence scrawled by the hand of a man who had lost his mind when investigating Keitus Vieta. "HEISNOWHERE". Yes, I had met Vieta, but I also remember how Orson Roth felt—the irreconcilable impression that this man should not exist. There was something about him that was wrong, completely wrong.

"Qod, we need more information to understand what's happening here. I'm going back to the Aberration Sphere to find out more about them. Cross-reference all the aberrations with my previous request for people that have had an unusual connection with death."

"And how would you like them sorted?"

"Same as before—I want the lives that have been affected most greatly by the aberrations. And this time, make sure you tell me which sphere they were from originally."

"Processing."

# 6

I am back amongst the aberrations again, standing at the entrance to the sphere, staring at the W.O.O.M. suspended at its center. The thought of making another mistake like Orson Roth unnerves me, but I have to go again, if only to set some distance from those ugly memories.

"Have you made your choice, Salem?"

"I have. Select subject 2.11317E+29, Dominique Mancini."

"The medium? Any particular reason?"

"You said she belonged in one of the mundane spheres before you moved her to the aberrations, yes?"

"Correct."

"So that must be because she was not recognized to have had any sort of . . . supernatural talent before the aberrations came."

"Not necessarily. There have been millions of people through the ages claiming some sort of connection to a spiritual plane, but not one of them have ever been revealed as having any genuine ability. Some were frauds, some were deluded, all were wrong. Mediums have been investigated by the Soul Consortium before."

"But did any of them investigate Dominique Mancini?"

"Processing . . . yes, she has been experienced on three hundred and twenty-nine occasions, each time by a different person. No repeats."

I felt a tickle of excitement. "And did any of them discuss her talents as a medium or psychic?"

"No."

"I knew it! She's hardly been viewed at all. Nobody recommended her and nobody considered her worthy of re-examination. Before the aberrations came she was just an ordinary person—no supernatural ability whatsoever. Somehow these aberrations have given Dominique Mancini the ability to speak to the dead. What if she really could do it? What if we can find out what happens after death through her? She may have the answer I need."

"You're sure about this, Salem?"

"Yes . . . unless of course there's something important you're not telling me again."

"No, but she lived in the first era of mankind, pre-industrial, sixteenth century Lombardy. It was considered a peaceful time, but hardly civilized in comparison to our standards."

"You're telling me that after I lived as Orson Roth? I doubt the most depraved streets of that place could compare to what I saw in *his* mind. No, I want to be her. Send me in.

She could have the answers I need and I cannot afford to ignore that possibility."

*Subject 2.11317E+29: Select*

*Subject 2.11317E+29: Aberration detected*

*Subject 2.11317E+29: Override authorized—ID Salem Ben*

*Subject 2.11317E+29: Activate. Immersion commences in 3 minutes.*

A brief silence precedes the predictable lecture.

"Very well, Salem . . . Protocol compels me to warn you that once you have been immersed you will not be able to withdraw until the moment of Dominique Mancini's death. Protocol also compels me to dictate that whatever you experience, however terrible, you must endure all of it without possibility of extraction. You will know each and every moment as if it were your own, and until the process is concluded, you will have no suspicion at all that you are not that person. Any lasting memory of trauma following the event will be your responsibility."

Silvery fibers slide from the walls to carry me back to the W.O.O.M. and as the shackles fix me in place, a speck of light flits from above to enter the machine—the legacy of Dominique Mancini ready to imprint itself into my mind.

"Farewell, Salem. See you in thirty-one years."

# DOMINIQUE MANCINI

*Whither wander, little man*
*I wonder whether you began.*
*In God's lost gardens; forgotten lands,*
*Gleaning life from Death's cold hands*

# 1

My whole life has been leading up to this moment. Although there are heavy hearts for the sadness of this gathering, my spirit is light with the promises tomorrow will bring. With the whole family gathered around Mama, a godly anointing warms her bedchamber and the very air beams with the golden hue of angels. I would swear on Pope Gregory's sanctity that the oil lamps flickering at the window had not changed since I set them there last night, yet there is a wonderful glow in this place that cannot be accounted for by natural means.

My sister Francesca, sitting closest to Mama, would not agree with me though, of that I am quite certain. She has a wondrous mind that sees things as they most likely are—plain and simple, black and white, right or wrong. She would see an ordinary flame, illuminating the withered features of our dying mother, surrounded by her two daughters and two sons, in an antiquated room in need of new furniture and a servant. With her posture rigid in the chair, avoiding contact with its back, I imagine she is afraid (if she were truly capable of fear) that her surroundings may somehow spoil her finely embroidered dress, or dull its scarlet pleats.

Me, I see something different with my sentimental eyes—my kin together again for the first time in seven years, and the love of Christ present in our childhood home once again. I see my older brothers, the playful spark still visible in their eyes and the laughter of youth plain to me in every wrinkle that the years of hardship have tried to erase. Naturally, they are struck by impending grief, but such kindly natures cannot be concealed, even in times such as these. And I see my sister, strong and steadfast in an hour of need, stern but always practical.

"What are you staring at, Dominique? Have you nothing better to do than smile and gloat while Mama is passing away? I suggest you reacquaint yourself with your duties and attend to her fever. At least see that she has a little relief in her final hour."

I bow my head, but keep my eyes on Francesca. She is right, of course—my sentimentality has caused my attention to drift; it should be on Mama.

"No, Fran," says Livio, moving a hand to my sister's wrist, "there is little point in that now anyway, the cleric told us that Mama is beyond the help of care and herbs. Only the anointing of holy oil and prayer can bring her any hope now, be that relief or cure."

Fran shrugs him off. “You may be the eldest, Livio, but you are not at all wise. The anointing of oil is for those who are incapable of prayer. Mama is neither demonized nor asleep. If there is any hope left at all, she needs a physician, not this ineffectual girl.” She waves her hand toward me as if shaking a spider from her fingers.

Arrigo, the younger of my two brothers and easily the more handsome, leans in with his elbow on his knee to whisper. “You should both be ashamed. You most of all, Fran. You speak of Father Pirellio as if he is wrong, as if there is no power in the anointing of God. And you, Livio,” he says, pointing a heavily ringed finger, “you told us that Pirellio was not prepared to perform the sanctification anyway, so why speak of it at all?”

“I said that he wouldn’t perform unless he was paid, brother.”

“Paid? If it’s money he wants then—”

A rasping cough of bile and pain cuts the argument short as Mama lifts a shaking hand. “Hush, all of you. Can’t an old woman die in peace?”

From the fireplace I lift a cloth that’s been soaking in a kettle of herb-infused water and wring it out, then, with a gentle hand I press it to Mama’s forehead, filtering out my brothers’ discussion that had quietened to whispers, and avoiding my sister’s iron gaze.

“Is the water fresh, Dominique?” Fran shoves her brother before I have a chance to answer. “Livio, go and check the water, you know what she's like."

Livio stands, clears his throat, and with a derisive sideways glance toward Fran, strides over to the fireplace to examine my medicinal brew. A flare of his nostrils and a creasing of his brow tells me he disapproves of the mixture.

"I drew the water an hour ago. The herbs were fresh this morning and the cloth is new," I say, looking up at Livio as he shakes his head at Fran.

She scowls. "And when did you last change her bedding or bathe her? Even the lavender fails to mask the stench."

"Her? Stench?" Mama tries to lift herself but fails. "Don't talk about me as if I'm not here—I'm not dead yet."

"I'm sorry, Mama, she—"

"Oh leave her be," Mama wheezes. "Dominique has the strength of a kitten. If she moves me again I fear she will break one of my bones this time. The girl is useless."

"You didn't think to use rose water?" Livio taps my shoulder. "Its medicinal properties are without question, Dominique. The plague doctors use it all the time."

"I'm sorry, Livio. Mama doesn't have the plague and I thought that a more comforting aroma would—"

"Comfort?" Fran spat the word. "For how long have you neglected to use the common remedies and thought yourself better advised than physicians and clergymen?"

Arrigo also stands from his stool after watching our exchanges with mild amusement. "Steady, Fran." A laugh hovers on the edge of his words. "We can't expect our little sister to have the same talents as our friendly physician, can we? After all, she was never the sibling with the sharpest mind, was she?"

"What's in it?" Livio asks, leaning over the kettle again. "I can smell the lavender, but what else did you use?"

"Sage, Valerian, and a little Mallow."

He shrugs his indifferent approval.

Arrigo leans forward, a shifty glint in his eye, "Mama? Has Dominique's . . . witchcraft done you any service? Do you feel the vitality running like Zeus's elixir through your bones?"

"It isn't witchcraft," I protest.

"Shut up!" Fran hisses. "And you, Arrigo, do you want to bring the magistrates here with your careless words?"

"He was joking, Fran," Livio says, returning to his stool with his eyes on Mama.

"Joke or not, if Dominique is suspected of witchcraft we will all be implicated. I don't care if *she* burns, but I have an estate to manage."

"Witch!" Mama struggles forward and points an accusing finger at me. "I spit on the day my womb conceived you and I wish a demon's fate on your soul, Dominique. You, of all my children, have been my biggest disappointment, and in no small way."

She slumps back, barely enough life in her to cough, but her remaining vigor is channeled through her expression in a visage of malice directed straight at me. Delirium. I hope.

An uneasy silence falls and Mama's eyes wrinkle shut.

She doesn't mean to be so cruel. None of them do. With Mama so close to passing away, her thoughts are confused. Nerves are frayed and the temptation to say regretful things is great. Times have been hard, even before Mama grew ill. They say we are living in a time of great peace now that Ferdinand and Philip rule Italy, but in our village, very few people have welcomed the Spaniards. It is no surprise then that my marriage to Enrique made me unpopular, and though I love him dearly, there are many days that I have spent in tears, wishing I had not fallen for him. My family's discontent is a terrible burden to me and I must accept the criticism that comes.

"I'm hungry," says Livio. "Is there anything to eat, Dom?"

"I baked bread this morning, and I have some rabbit stew heating on the stove for . . . for Enrique when he returns from the docks today."

"He won't mind if I rob him of his food?"

"I prepared extra today in case of visitors. We've been receiving many since Mama . . . Would anyone else like some bread and stew?"

Arrigo shakes his head. "Not hungry, sister."

"I've tasted your efforts before, Dominique," Fran says. "With culinary skills such as yours, it is no wonder your husband spends all his time at sea in the arms of other women. No, I'll have neither bread nor stew."

The brothers laugh, and I look at Mama who had not

stirred since her outburst. "Mama? Do you feel well enough to try some stew?"

Her eyelids part a fraction to reveal jaundiced whites and dilated pupils. A soft whisper is on her lips but she is too tired to answer properly.

"I'll bring you a small bite. See if you can try some, Mama."

"And don't forget to bring fresh water and clean bed-clothes, Dominique," Fran says as I stand.

"I won't," I say with a smile.

Leaving the bedchamber and closing the door behind me, their whispers exchanged in sharp tones follow as I make my way down the stairs and into the kitchen. They may be thinking that I am unable to hear their hurtful words, and I know that Enrique would tell me not to stand for such back-biting, but I see no point in antagonizing them with any reproach—Mama would want to see a happy and contented family around her before she leaves us. I only wish I could do something to soften her words toward me. Just once.

I sit on a stool by the table, look at the pot through the watery blur of tears gathering in my eyes, the pitted base glowing red above the flames, its simmering contents bubbling with meaty juices, salt and potatoes. I breathe deep, knowing that the flavorsome vapors will soothe me and that the comfort of cooking will dry my eyes, but I find it so hard to ignore the pain. Unless the Lord intervenes, Mama will never leave her bed again, and the part of me that longs to hold her tightly and beg for forgiveness for all the things I have done to grieve her, already mourns like an orphaned child. I wish Enrique were here. I wish my brothers would come down to comfort me, or that Fran would come to set me straight with words of stern reason. But how selfish I am! I should be joyful, a light to those who feel the sting of grief, and I should be content to know that Mama will soon be face to face with Jehovah God. My pain is nothing but a sinner's indulgence.

I draw in a long breath, wipe my eyes and take two bowls and a ladle from the cupboard. But before the ladle dips into the stew, Arrigo appears at the stairs with a frown on his face. I drop the bowl, instinct stabbing my stomach with the knowledge of what he is about to say. The clay fragments shatter against the stone floor and Arrigo's frown deepens as the clatter meets his ears.

"Never mind, Dominique, you only need one serving of stew now, anyway. Mama just died."

# 2

After Arrigo told me about Mama my mind recoiled like a wounded rabbit to its warren. I don't remember what I did, but Arrigo told me later that I had swooned at the news. I have a vague recollection of Fran's bitter glance as Livio led her through the kitchen and out of the house, and I believe a man entered soon after that to legally declare that Mama was dead, but much of those two hours were spent in the midst of a watery dream.

Still sitting in the kitchen beyond supper time, grief has stiffened my limbs. I know I should feel happy that Mama is with the Lord now, but I am unable to think of anything but my failings. In my selfishness I had hoped to console Mama in her final hours to gain her favor and receive absolution, but it was not to be. Always a disappointment to her, I was the child that blackened the family's reputation. Arrigo was the smiling businessman, triumphant in international success and boasting a multitude of influential contacts to rival even Papa when he was alive. Livio had excelled as a cartographer and through his envied skill in that profession, risen into royal favor. And through Livio's social status, Francesca had been introduced to men of significant standing and married into good fortune.

As for me, I did nothing other than marry a Spaniard who is rarely home. I stayed with Mama and Papa, caring for them as the cruelty of old age wore them down. We had a servant once, and I began to dream of finding my own way in life, but we were not able to pay her enough, and when she left I resumed my role as carer. There was hope once that Livio, Arrigo or Fran might help, but even with their wealth, I understand that their income would not support the continual employment of a servant—Livio spoke of complications with taxation.

Two men enter the house without knocking and Fran steps in behind them. Still dazed by melancholy and images of the past, it takes me a few moments to question their presence. Fortunately for me, Fran is more in control of her grief than I, and, as organized as ever, she explains.

"These two gentlemen have come for Mama's body, do you have any refreshment to offer them, Dominique? Some brandy perhaps? The conditions outside are quite foul and there is still rioting in the town square."

I glance at the window. Through a whirl of snowflakes, blackened clouds sag heavily over the hills threatening even worse blizzards to come. I look at the two men—one short, one tall, they appear the same in all other respects: haggard and cold with blotchy-red cheeks, and patches of melting snow covering their dark shawls as they hug themselves to get warm. Fran, though also suffering a layer of snow, does not seem perturbed—I have always admired her resilience.

"Well?" she lifts her chin.

"Did you say there was rioting, Fran?" I ask.

One of the men laughs. "Of course. It's been going on since Friday. You didn't know?"

"I've been . . . preoccupied these last few days."

The tall man brushes snow from his clothes. "Pope Gregory made the declaration Thursday—we've officially discarded the Julian calendar and started his. The locals don't like it much, and I can't say I do either."

"We've all had fair warning," said Fran. "Nobody can say they didn't know."

The short man shook his head, wiped a drop from his thin nose. "Doesn't change the fact that we've lost ten days of our life, does it? There are plenty of us want to know how the church is going to make up for that."

I get up from my stool, grimacing at the pain in my lower back through sitting in the same place for too long, and move closer to the window to get a better view of the street outside. There are no riots that I can see, but a haze of smoke and an orange-red nimbus flickers behind the clock tower hinting at the violence that Fran had mentioned. "We haven't lost ten days though have we? I mean, not really."

"Of course we have," said the tall man lifting his hands. "Last Thursday it was October fourth. Then all of a sudden Friday comes and it's the fifteenth. Where did the ten days go?"

I turn from the window smiling at Fran, hoping she will share the moment of humor, but she purses her lips before directing a hard stare at the two men. "Are you going to do what your master has paid you for, or did you plan to gossip all day to my sister?"

Both men stand a little straighter and mumble their apologies.

"I was rather hoping for that brandy," says the short man. The other nods vigorously.

"Dominique?" Fran pins me with that same hard stare.

"I'm afraid Livio drank the last of it."

Fran opens her mouth with a wild look in her eye, but the tall man steps in. "Not to worry, not to worry, if you'll just show us to the deceased, we'll take care of it . . . her."

"Up the stairs. First room on the right. And be quick about it, I don't care for the smell and I have an appointment to keep."

"Very good. We'll be out before you know it."

Both men tramp up the steps leaving small pools of water behind them. I turn to Fran. "Who are they? They don't act like undertakers."

"They aren't. We're donating Mama's body to an artist."

"An artist? But why? How could you do such a thing?"

"Many of them are avid students of anatomy. I believe even Michelangelo was reputed to buy bodies from the bishops of Rome to further his craft . . . And it pays very well. I'm sure Mama would be very happy to know that she is still helping others even after her death."

I can scarcely speak as Fran tells me this. How could she deny Mama a proper burial? "Did Arrigo and Livio agree to this?"

"Of course."

"But I—"

"Mama would care nothing for *your* opinion, Dominique."

"I'll not let you do it!"

The two men come back through the kitchen. Between them they carry Mama, a black shroud hides her lifeless form.

"Everything in order I hope?" says the tall man. He had obviously overheard our conversation.

"Of course," says Fran.

"No!" I move toward the door to block their way, but Fran steps forward and I back down.

The short man shifts his weight for a better grip and the shroud shifts slightly to reveal a few strands of gray hair from the edge. "You're quite sure?"

Fran glares at me, but speaks to them. "There's no problem. As I said, I have an appointment to keep, so please don't let my sister's last minute sentiments delay you."

I stare back at Fran, horrified, hardly believing what I'm seeing and hearing. I dare not challenge her, and I don't want to cause a scene and disrespect the memory of Mama, but the thought of her laid on a slab at the mercy of a painter's knife, fills me with such terrible heartache. I must let them go. If I am fortunate and careful I may be able to prevent anything awful happening to her after Fran has left. Yes, I will visit the artist and persuade him to find someone else.

As Fran hurries away and the two men shuffle through the door back into the icy evening, I call their attention.

"Wait! Tell me please, who is the artist that wants Mama?"

They shift awkwardly and exchange nervous glances.

"Foreign gentlemen. Goes by the name of Keitus Vieta."

# 3

I waited only a short while before leaving Mama's empty cottage, just long enough to make sure Fran had truly gone. The thought of that home now hollow and cold invaded my thoughts, its vacuum leaching from my mind the old and fond memories of Fran and I chasing our brothers through bright rooms, screaming and giggling with jugs of cold water. Of family meals alive with the noise of excitement and mirth. Of tender evenings when stories were told around an ember-warmed hearth. Even if I did not have to retrieve Mama's body, I could in no way stay there tonight.

Wrapped in my warmest winter clothes, I step out into the dim street and lock the door. I wish I had followed those two men immediately after they left, but fear prevented me. That, and the thought that neither Fran nor the men would have allowed me to interfere. But at least I had been given a name: Keitus Vieta—an artist. I had not heard of him before, so he must be new to the town—Armand Balleo, the town's leaseholder, would tell me where Mr. Vieta has settled. If anyone knows, he will.

I hurry across the fast-settling snow that coats the cobblestones, looking up briefly to see the time on the clock-tower a few streets away. It's almost ten. Late, but I am surprised to see so few people out. Then I remember what Fran said about the riots and I look again at the clock. The glow of fire lighting its face is brighter; an indication perhaps that the mob or its violence in the center of town has not yet been subdued. I stop to listen. There's a dull crackle of fire, the sharp tinkling of breaking glass, and a body of voices crying out indecipherable abuse. A pang of anxiety holds me in place for a moment as I imagine fighting through an angry crowd to find Armand, but I hear Mama calling for me. I have let her down all my life. I cannot let her down when she needs me most.

Head down, I press onward, turn the corner, pass the stables in which horses are stomping nervously, quicken my pace. Ahead the shouting is getting louder, and when I reach the end of the road where the local inn is belching smoke from its windows and doors, a throng of staggering men lurches into view, coughing, grasping at their grimy collars for air. I recognize two of them, and as I back up against the bricks of the house next to the tavern, one of them sees me.

"Dominique? What are you . . . doing here? Get back home, get . . . to safety. They're burning the whole . . . the whole town!"

"What? Who? Who would do such a thing?"

"It's Balleo. He—"

"Come on, Vidi"—one of his companions snatches at his sleeve—"they're almost on us. We have to go."

"Quickly, Dom, come with us?"

But before I can answer him or even think about where to go, a bottle flies between us and bursts into a ball of fire on the wet road. The flames are soon lost amongst the snow, but two more bottles follow, smashing into the opposite wall, and the men begin to run, pausing only a second to shoot an apologetic glance in my direction. With Balleo implicated in the riots I have nowhere to go. Where will I find this Keitus Vieta? How will I stop him from violating Mama?

Burning air brushes my cheeks as the wind changes, and the bitter damp of the inn walls soaks through to my back assaulting my senses in a confusion of hot and cold. Directionless and panic-stricken at the sound of marching feet beyond the billowing cloud of smoke rolling into the street, I ball my fists and press myself harder into the wall, squeezing my eyes tight shut, praying to God that this frenzied monster would pass by without noticing me.

Men and women rush past, bawling, screaming, cursing the pope for stealing their lives. Roaring their demands that the devil should take his own back into hell, that they would never allow Rome to oppress them. What seemed to my mind to be an infantile joke earlier in the day, is now a raging beast, possessing the town folk and driving them to destroy their own homes rather than listen to reason. Something buffets my arm, knocking me down onto wet stone and only then, as I lay winded on my back, do I flick my eyes open to take in the full scope of the danger I have walked into. Boots stamp about my head as the mob surges onward and I struggle to turn onto my front, pushing against the road with trembling arms in a futile effort to stand up against the tide.

I am swept along by a sea of people. Probably no more than fifty, but for me it is an army, dragging its prisoner and parading it through the streets until either crushed or discarded. I think of Fran's warning. If I were to be condemned as a witch, this feverish march would be my funeral procession, my last terrible minutes before being tied to a burning pyre. For more than fifteen minutes I am battered, torn, and carried through a blur of houses, fire, and faces until a change as sudden as a wave crashing into a dam turns the direction of the rabble.

An uncanny silencing of abuse allows the noise of fire and falling debris to take precedent for a moment as the people turn about, and I wonder if the city guards have finally done something to quench the crowd's aggression. But no—something else has caused the change. With my back twisting against the current, the shape of a man catches my eye.

Silhouetted in the doorway of the tallest building in the street with his hands clutching the frames, a small, hunched man watches the hostility as it sweeps past. Like a school of fish unaware that a shark has come to observe them, but dimly aware of the danger, they keep their distance. The man is untouched, apparently unimpressed by the tumult, and whilst the flames lick at the buildings on either side, his residence remains unscathed, as though the fire itself is afraid of approaching him. But more than the bizarre aversion of the riot to turn upon him, something else is stranger still. The man himself is utterly wrong. I cannot explain it other than my instincts telling me that he must be a living specter, a ghostly apparition that maintains a firmness of flesh and the command of a powerful presence. I think of the two men and their apprehension at revealing their employer's name. I sense now that it was fear of the man himself—Keitus Vieta. The shadow in the doorway must be this same man, of that I am quite certain. I know it deep in my spirit.

Still thrust along by the crowd and away from that part of the street I watch as the hunched man turns his back and slinks away into the darkness of his home. Unless I act now, I may not be able to retrace my path back to this place. I scream in the faces of the people beside me. No longer willing to be caught in the flow of the mob, I push back, leaning, stamping and yelling in the opposite direction. I claw against them, fighting for breath, thrusting my elbows either side as if swimming uphill through a mountain of earth until eventually I fall, breathing hoarsely, against the wet oaken doors of Keitus Vieta's home. With one last glance at the seething mass of bodies I escaped from, I bang my bloody knuckles against the door.

"Mr. Vieta? Please . . . Please let me in."

# 4

The door swings open after I knock a second time, and stooping in the doorway is the small man, made to look even smaller by his hunched posture. Despite the sweat on my skin and the heat on my breath, my blood feels like ice when he greets me with an open-mouthed smile. He does not seem unfriendly, yet my instinct is to fear this man. His unblinking eyes, blue like deep night, capture mine as he stares up at me, and his voice, like soft wind in distant caverns, is colored by a strange accent, perhaps Prussian. "How may I help you?"

"You are Kei"—an unwelcome gulp sticks in my throat—"Keitus Vieta? The artist?"

His smile widens and my knees judder as his thin flesh stretches across pointed cheekbones making little veins beneath his skin wriggle like trapped worms. But I am no stranger to old age; Mama's appearance was far worse, yet it never bothered me. Nevertheless, there is something dreadful about this old man—an ugliness that writhes deep beneath the pale surface, and something worse still—as though my senses are rebelling at his very presence. He should not be here. Yet here he is.

But it is a far more dreadful thing that I have an inclination to judge him. He has done nothing impolite nor improper, so I make my best effort to return his smile.

"You know of me?" He takes my hand then presses my knuckles to his dry lips. "It is a rare thing for old Keitus to be sought out. Especially by one so . . . handsome."

Still he does not blink and I am compelled to look away as an involuntary revulsion forces me to withdraw my hand. To look at anything but those intrusive eyes is a relief and I gaze behind him and into his home. A gloomy hallway is beyond the door, colored by a backwash of indigo luminescence from a room to the side. A lantern sits on a shelf, looking as though it has not been used for some time, and paintings hang from the walls, works I recognize by Federico Barocci, the famous artist staying near San Gimignano; I find it unusual that Vieta chooses not to display his own works of art.

"But where are my manners, Miss . . . Mancini." He reaches for my hand again, the fingers, clammy like old meat as they curl around mine. "Please, come in."

"I didn't tell you my name," I say, resisting his subtle pull on my hand. "How do you know it?"

His fingers tighten slightly. "Cleg and Malley returned with the body of Lena Mancini less than an hour ago. Since she had two sons and two daughters, only three of which were eager to profit from her passing, I assume by your timely arrival that you are the fourth, and that you were not aware of the transaction, and neither are you content with it. It was Francesca that received the money two days ago, so you must be her younger sister, Dominique."

I met his eyes again, nodded. "Is Mama . . ."

"Inside?"

I dare not look away now and miss any hint of disclosure from his expression. A nervous tear blurs my vision as he studies me.

"Why, yes." He takes a step back, luring me through the door. "I have not yet had the opportunity to—"

"Mama deserves a proper burial, Mr. Vieta. I am sure you can appreciate that. You must have known the passing of loved ones too."

I offer a timid smile as I glance at the floor again, ashamed at the brash way I had interrupted him. But the heat of the crowd is still on my skin and the pain of Mama's passing presses its urgency upon me. Still, there is never an excuse for such impertinence.

He returns my smile, closes the door behind me. "I have no wish to distress anyone. If it pleases you, Miss Mancini, I will arrange for my men to have the body sent to a priest, but I will of course, require the return of my payment."

Return the payment? How would I go about persuading Fran to do that? Perhaps I should find the money myself and not tell her that I came here. But how could I pay such a debt?

"You seem ill at ease, Dominique." His eyes are on my hands as they knead each other. "Perhaps it would be best for you to wait here a while, at least until the riots have calmed. Please, come inside and be seated. Would you like a drink?"

He creeps into the room with the blue light and after a moment of indecision, I follow. "I don't wish to intrude Mr.—," I stop when I see inside.

The dark blue glow radiates from a cane leaning against the wall closest to the door. In itself the cane is a peculiarity with its curiously bright stone set in a gnarly claw, but it is nothing compared to the grotesque gallery on display before me. There is no furniture, only hideous sculptures fashioned from a mottled substance that looks like it had been tortured into distorted forms of the human body. Enlarged contortions; twisted mannequins with a metallic sheen that might be blood in a different light. Some of their faces had been crafted with such attention to detail that I can almost see the terror in their eyes. Limbs are perverted by impossible knots, extended to disproportionate lengths with joints and sinew skewed and swollen like reflections in a warped mirror. The room seems colder now that I have seen these horrors. And I am sure they are watching me.

Keitus stands in an open doorway on the other side of the room. "Pay no attention to my eccentricities, Dominique."

"Is this your . . . art?" I had already taken a step back toward the hallway.

"A gallery of sorts. It does not appeal to many, but one

must find expression for the workings of one's heart, yes?"

I glance around at the sculptures, preferring even them to his bulging stare. I am sure there are people who can appreciate Mr. Vieta's work—such delicate weavings in the textures and harmonious curves in their posture—but I cannot move myself to enjoy such a mockery of God's creation.

"Do you sell many of these . . ."

"Alas, no, but I have no concerns. I have no shortage of coin and these"—he motions a withered hand—"are merely a creative outlet born from a greater passion of mine—they are the residue of another purpose."

"Another purpose?"

"Indeed, but you need not know of that. Come through. I have a little brandy to set you at ease, my dear."

He disappears into another hallway beyond the door and I weave my way between the effigies, fearing an unexpected touch or a sudden rush of cold breath from their gaping mouths as I pass, but I reach the other side with no incident and chide myself for thinking so darkly. With faltering breath I follow Keitus Vieta into another room, trying to dismiss my expectations of seeing a bloody torture chamber through the next door, and finding, to my relief, a much more pleasant place.

At first glance the room appears normal—a long center table with ten walnut chairs surrounding it; burgundy decorated walls; tall bookcases; a large fireplace, and an array of display cabinets. But still my senses sharpen with the promise of danger—the light is too dim, the air is stale, and carrying the bitter stench of something like ammonia.

"Brandy." Keitus sets a small glass on the table and pulls out a chair for me.

"Thank you, Mr. Vieta." And I sit down, still avoiding his gaze.

"At the door, you expressed a wish for your Mama to have a proper burial. Do you still wish this?"

"More than anything, Mr. Vieta." I force myself to look at him again now, praying that my trepidation would fade a little, but it has not. "How much did you pay my sister for Mama . . . Mama's body?"

"Twenty Florin."

I try not to let my disappointment show, but a twitch in his lip tells me he sees something in my expression. "Too much for you?"

"It may be difficult, I—"

He lifts a hand to silence me. "Perhaps an alternative payment can be made other than coinage."

"I would gladly give you anything."

He smiles, and again I am struck by how wrong this man feels. A sip of the brandy causes my stomach to lurch with sudden fright. How could I trust this man? Anything could be in that glass. But again I judge harshly for no other reason than unfounded fear.

"An object," he says, moving closer. "It need not be valuable. I need something your Mama used very soon before she passed on. A glass she drank from perhaps, or a hairbrush used this morning."

"Why?"

"I had hoped for some item of her clothing to give me what I needed, but all of it is too . . . weak. I need something stronger."

"Stronger? I don't understand."

He pulls out a chair next to mine, sits in it and gazes at me, perhaps a little too intently. "You recall your childhood, Dominique?"

"Of course."

"And did you ever play as a child?"

"I used to play with my brothers."

"And what did you play?"

I close my eyes for a moment, almost ashamed at the memory. Ashamed, yet aware that it was also the innocence of youth. "We used to play Pass-the-Plague."

"I see."

"Arrigo always won. We used to run through the streets and into the fields behind Baggio's farm—Baggio always shouted at us on the way past, but he was too fat to chase after us." I pause, allowing a moment of sentimentality to soften my uneasiness.

"I loved to hide among the trees where they couldn't find me, but there was always an old oak tree that Arrigo especially liked. It died years ago and the inside was hollow, so he would always hide inside it until I'd been caught."

"How old were you?"

"Seven or eight, I think."

"You didn't play when you were nine?"

"I don't think so."

"Do you remember the very last time you played that game?"

I think for a few seconds, sifting through snippets of memory—Fran on her back laughing loudly, Livio running from the woods screaming about a spider that had crawled into his hair, my grazed knee when I fell in the road. Fond memories and regretful memories mix in my mind, filling me with dreamy nostalgia. "No, I don't think I can."

"But there was, wasn't there, Dominique?" His eyes bulged again as he asked the question. "One day, you played that game for the very last time. You had no knowledge that it would be the final game, but it was, wasn't it?"

I take another sip of brandy. "I suppose so, yes."

"For all things there is a last time. To all things an end."

I feel my pulse quicken. "Yes."

"And between all things there is an exchange of power and will." His words grow quieter and slower. "When the candle burns, it gives light. When the heart wills, the body acts. When the crow calls, the worm flees. With all things in this world there is cause and there is effect. But what if, Dominique . . . what if the effect is denied? What if the exchange is broken?"

"I don't understand."

His smile fades and for the first time, he blinks and looks away. "Powers are released, Dominique, and unless they are harnessed, they... flutter away. The powers will move, wander until dissolution." His gnarled fingers claw the air. "Death is the greatest severance, Dominique. There is so much power in the human will. So much power wasted, so many intentions left unfulfilled."

"But when people die their souls go to be with The Lord or with Satan. Is that not the truth?"

"I am not speaking of the soul. You do not understand."

"Then what?"

"When your mother died, the bond between cause and effect was broken. Those feelings and will of thought that were so strong in her mind retreated into personal objects she connected with immediately before her death. The last vessel she drank from, the last book she touched, the cloth she patted against her forehead for the last time—all become unwilling containers of an effect unfulfilled—a power harnessed for a short while."

"You talk of unknown powers, Mr. Vieta. Things that sound like . . . witchcraft!" I say. "You are a witch!"

"No, Dominique. Merely a science that has yet to be understood."

"No." I stand and grab the back of my chair, pushing it between us. "Get behind me, Satan. I'll not listen to witchcraft."

"Satan?" Keitus stands too, and though he is much shorter than me, I feel smaller than an insect when he looks at me with mirthless eyes. "If Satan were real he would surely cower if I called his name."

Thinking only of escape now, I spin around; set my

sights on the open doorway behind me. I don't know if Keitus is making a move to stop me, but I lunge forward and break into a run, fearing his yellow nails tearing at my back, imagining him exploding into a blood-eyed demon, devouring the room behind me, surging outward to fill the house like a poisonous cloud. A scream escapes me as I stagger through the door, catching my shoulder against the frame. In my peripheral vision I see him still standing in the same place, watching me as I flee, with no obvious intention to stop me, and somewhere in a rational corner of my mind, I am aware that he has still done nothing to warrant my panic, but the dark, primitive part of my instincts justify my terror as I stumble into one of his statues and scream again.

Flailing, clawing forward, I am almost at the next door that will take me to the exit hallway when my left hand momentarily connects with something hard and hot, the handle of Keitus Vieta's cane. Lightning-blue sparks rip the air when it falls, and as I crash to the floor I hear the crack of wood against stone and see the cane spinning away from me. The jewel in its handle is shimmering, sending wave after wave of heat over my head. Several of the mannequins topple in the wake of the violence like mummified victims caught in a blast of volcanic fury, and as pain burns through my palm, I look at my hand to see the branding of the artist's jewel on my skin—a glistening circle where the flesh has been burned away. With nothing but the natural compulsion to survive driving me on, I crawl into the hallway, drag myself up against the final door and, opening it, career into the empty street to land on my back.

My breathing, hoarse and desperate, almost drowns out new noises in my head—noises that sound like a jeering rabble crowding in from all sides. I stare up into the night sky faced with the fathomless heavens sprinkled with stars. God must be watching me. He knows I am here, knows I have resisted the dark, knows the terror that consumes my soul as I lay on the cold cobbles.

"Though I walk . . . through the shadow of the valley of death . . . I shall fear no evil, for thou art with me."

I close my eyes, try to shut out the howling of my thoughts as a hundred confused voices fight to be heard. "Thy rod and thy staff, they comfort me."

I scream again as the image of Keitus Vieta's cane, rippling with power, slams to the forefront of my mind. Eyes open to dismiss the power of that thought, I tilt my head forward and look at the doorway of the small man's house. There he is, silhouetted within the frames, hunched and black, but he is not coming for me, instead he is slowly closing the door. And as it clicks shut I cry out to God, begging for my salvation, pulling at my hair to silence the cacophony of voices.

One voice sounds above the rest, but it is not the answer of my savior.

"Witch!" says Mama. "I spit on the day my womb conceived you and I wish a demon's fate on your soul, Dominique. You, of all my children, have been my biggest disappointment, and in no small way."

# 5

It took the entire night to reclaim my composure, but whether my sanity has been regained, I cannot say. By the grace of God, I have seen the sunrise through the window of my empty house and have not been driven from my faith. The Lord rescued me from the street, and through my dazed wanderings back to my door, He protected me from harm. The riots did not meet me again, nor did Keitus Vieta come to find me as I feared he might. The horror of my escape has lessened now and although I struggle to recall the exact events, the raw and weeping circle on the palm of my hand serves as a painful reminder that it was no delusion. And the voices have diminished too. That, or I have already learned how to filter them from my conscious thoughts.

*But you will never silence me, Dominique.*

I'll not listen to Mama's voice. God will restore me, I know. But until He does, I must resist the trickery of the devil. It cannot be Mama who haunts my thoughts—she sits at the feet of Jesus now.

*Jesus? You don't know him and he doesn't know you. When it's your turn to die, you'll be thrown to your father, the devil and burn in his lake of fire.*

"No! Mama please, don't say such things. I loved you."

*But I never loved you. You were always a millstone about my neck—the daughter that brought shame to our household; the daughter who cherished sinful thoughts; the daughter who envied her sister; the daughter who lusted after her own brothers.*

"No! None of that is true, not any of it. Get *behind* me, Satan!"

*How dare you call me that.*

"I'm so sorry, Mama . . . I'm so sorry."

All I can do is weep. Let the devil have his way with me for now. I must endure my suffering until restoration comes, however long that may take. How I wish Enrique had come home to comfort me. I keep hoping that I will see his familiar swagger along the street, but in my heart I know it will be weeks until my husband returns.

I move away from the window, slump down at the table and rest my cheek against the wood. The cool surface is a balm to my thumping head, but I know the relief will not last long. Whether it is the prolonged sobbing that brought on this ache, or the accident in the artist's house, I have no clue, but I suspect it will grow worse if I do not eat or drink something soon. With my arms stretched out across the table I allow my tears to soak into the aged timber and try to ignore the numbing cold air. The flames in the fireplace have long been snuffed out and I don't have the inclination to light it again; somehow, it would not seem right for the house to feel warm when the atmosphere has become so deathly. I take a deep, shuddering breath, stifle the next wave of tears and close my eyes. Perhaps sleep will allow me some peace, if it finds me.

A bold knock on the door startles me. My eyes flicker open but I do not move. Another knock, and still I do not stir.

*Idle bitch! Answer it! Answer it!* Mama's voice screams.

"No! Leave me alone!"

"Dom? Are you alright? Open the door, it's Livio."

I push myself upright, gather my thoughts. "Livio?"

"Yes. Open the door. Are you still moping over Mama?"

I go to the door, pull it open and my brother barges past me wrapped in his long winter coat and scarf, bringing a cold gale into the house with him. Hugging his arms around himself, he glances about the kitchen as if looking for something, then his eyes settle on the fireplace.

"What's this? No fire? Why are you sitting in such a chill?"

"I—"

"Never mind. Get some coals on and put some broth on too, Dominique, I'm ravenous and frozen to the marrow." He pulls out a stool by the table and sits on it, waving the other hand in the air, and looking out the window. "I find it almost impossible to believe that we could be assaulted by such foul weather. It's a wonder that so many people went out in the snow to start rioting, don't you think?"

And now he looks at me, eyebrows raised, expecting an answer. It is good to hear his voice and to see his face. Livio, with his no-nonsense attitude has always been a rock for me to cling to in times of trouble, although sometimes, like now, I fear he would rather shrug me off than offer comfort. I suppose it is to my benefit that he acts this way, and naturally, he is a busy man with many appointments to keep, so he cannot afford to spend time on matters of little importance.

*True words, daughter. He has made something of his life. You have done nothing with yours.*

"Well?" Livio asks. "Are you going to light the fire?"

"Yes, of course," I say, and I wince from the renewed pain in my head as I move toward the fire to add coals from the sack.

"Wait." Livio holds out a hand and leans forward to squint at my face. "Is that . . . is that blood?"

I touch my cheek to feel where he's looking, then study my fingers. Dried blood flakes against my fingertips and I feel there again, flinching at the bruise that has bloomed.

"Whatever have you been doing, sister? And what's that on your hand, a burn of some sort? Come here, let me see."

*That's right, go to your brother. Deceive him with your petty pains and leech the sympathy from him. Bleed the rest of your family dry now that you're done with poisoning me.*

"Poison you? No! I wouldn't ever—"

"What?" Livio looks up at me as he holds my palm ready to

inspect it. "Poison me? What are you talking about, Dominique?"

The pain. The torture of Mama's accusations. Livio's blunt questions. I try to hold it all in, try to control my failing nerves, but it is all too much for me.

"Has someone attacked you, Dom? Did you fall in the snow and hurt your head? Why are you crying? It really doesn't appear to be that bad, just a superficial—"

"Mama, Livio, she . . . I . . . Keitus Vieta took her and I—"

Livio's face stiffened. "You know about Vieta?"

"I'm sorry, I just—"

"How?"

"The two men that came for Mama, they told me his name, so I went to see him."

"You did what?" Livio stands. He towers over me with balled fists and for a terrible moment I think he will lash out, but he turns from me and stares into the fireplace. "What did you tell him?"

I wipe the tears from my eyes and stare at the floorboards watching misty clouds of my breath puff outward. I didn't realize how fast I was breathing. And I cannot understand why my brother is so angry.

*Because he lied to the old man. He told him that you had consented to sell me. Your brother is afraid that he will have to return the money he has already promised his debtors . . . And it will all be your fault, Dominique.*

Mama's scornful words cut into me like icy talons.

"Well, sister? What did you tell him?"

"You . . . you have debts, Livio? I thought you were rich."

He turns, and with his deep brown eyes twitching and staring at me as he moves slowly to sit on the stool again, I know that Mama's words are true.

"How much do you owe?" I ask. "Do Fran and Arrigo know?"

"Who told you?" Fear dominates his frowning face now.

"Mama told me, Livio."

"Mama? But she didn't—"

"She knows now."

*Yes, yes! I know many things about him now. There are others here too and they know all about him, they tell me things. They even know about his affair with the Duchess.*

"The Duchess?" It flies from my mouth before I even realize, and Livio shakes his head in disbelief. Even in the cold, sweat beads across his brow.

"What is this, Dominique? How could you know?"

Again the tears well up within me and I so desperately need my brother's comfort. I show him my trembling palm, words ready to babble from my lips and his wide, terrified eyes look at the burnt disc of raw flesh.

"Keitus Vieta," I whimper the name as if it were a curse. "The cane, his . . . the sculptures . . . witchcraft."

"Witchcraft?" His eyes change again, as if I have given him all the answers he needed. "Witchcraft indeed. So, Vieta has found a new apprentice."

I sink to my knees, the throbbing in my skull reaching

a bone-splitting crescendo as Mama rips my mind with a piercing cackle.

“Please, Livio. Help me. Don’t leave me.”

He nods solemnly, stands again and goes to the door. “Repeat nothing of what has been spoken in this house today, Dominique, and I will get help. I hope you will learn from this lesson, sister. Fool with the devil and your hands will get burnt.”

He steals one more glance at my palm, then leaves.

# 6

Several hours had come and gone before I saw anyone else. I could not eat, drink or sleep because of the throbbing in my head, but as the time passed, I listened to the voices running back and forth through the corridors of my mind. Mama's screeching accusations remained constantly at the fore, never lacking in venom, but as I learned to focus my thoughts and untangle the many threads and tones of speech, I heard dozens of other men, women and children, discovering all of them to be deceased, and finding that all of them are able to converse with one another, as though my soul had become a great, dark purgatory in which they could all linger in debate.

So many confused souls wander my mind confessing their woes. Most had come to some tragic and sudden end, but some pulled at the strings of my heart more than others: there was a small orphaned boy named Renee who had managed to travel all the way from France only to become frail from exposure and die by the jaws of wild animals on the cold hills just outside our town; a Spanish soldier shot by accident during a training exercise only a day after he had announced his engagement to a woman named Bessie who lived not far from my own street; and a great many villagers who had been crushed in the rioting over the last few days. There was also Duke Lexington, the English nobleman who had married in Rome and traveled here on business only to discover that his wife had been having an affair with Livio. He had committed suicide several weeks ago, but through Keitus Vieta's terrible witchcraft, his lost spirit was now able to pass on this information to Mama using me as a channel.

I wonder what I have done to deserve such a curse.

At dusk the door opens without ceremony. Half awake and tremulous with fatigue I say nothing when Livio enters. He, Arrigo and Fran bustle inside bringing an assortment of items with them. Fran immediately busies herself preparing vegetables and stewing meat whilst Arrigo goes to the fireplace to start a fire and build up the coals. Livio, an expression of wary incredulity toughening his gaze, takes his position opposite me with his chin resting on interlaced fingers, examining me as though I might jump up at any moment frothing at the mouth spouting blasphemies. I suppose he is right to be cautious—I have, after all, been tainted.

*You know how much I despise him, Dominique,* says the Duke. *Tell him! And go tell the priesthood, they must know of his terrible disgrace.*

*Speak nothing more of his affair, Dominique,* says Mama, *you have done enough damage already. My eldest has always been my favorite. If you ruin him I will torment you in the next life as well as this one.*

*No,* says the Duke, *justice must be served.*

With the two voices vying for recognition, I allow them their fight. I am too weary to speak or acknowledge either of them.

"You'll be warm soon enough, Dom," says Arrigo, fanning a new flame on the coals, "and Fran will have some hearty stew ready for you in no time at all."

"Thank you," I whisper, feeling a new warmth and strength, not from the newly stoked fire, but from the rescuing presence of my brothers and sisters.

"Livio," Fran barks, "stop staring at her and find a blanket to put around your sister until the house is warm."

Without removing his eyes from me, Livio stands, then walks toward the stairs. "Watch her," is all he says before disappearing to the bedrooms.

"So, Dom." Arrigo sits in Livio's seat with his arms folded and a smirk hinting on his lips. He squints at me. "Livio tells us you've been learning a few tricks from that creepy artist in the old Market house, is that right?"

Arrigo's lightness of spirit might be another medicine to aid my recovery, so I try to smile as I respond. "Not willingly, Arrigo, and through no fault of my own. Keitus Vieta is a strange man and I believe I may have unwittingly fallen victim to his witchcraft."

"So he *is* a witch then?"

"I can think of no other way to explain what I saw and felt, or the things he said to me."

"Told you, Fran." Arrigo points a finger at her. "I *told* you that man was a witch. There's something not right about him."

"Nonsense!" Fran turns, pointing a meat knife at Arrigo. "She's playing for attention. The biggest mystery here is why Livio has fallen for her deceit. I credited him with at least a seed of intelligence."

"If you don't believe her, why did you agree to our little . . . party this evening, Fran?"

"Isn't it obvious? We have to find out how she knows all of our brother's dirty secrets."

*And she's scared you'll know hers too, Dominique*, says a voice from the back of my mind.

"You don't have to talk about me as if I'm not here, Fran."

She looks at me, and I meet her gaze, surprised at my sudden boldness. Somehow I sense there are more important things to worry about than accepting my sister's judgement. Or perhaps the pain behind my eyes is sapping my humility. "I'm not lying. Something happened to me at Keitus Vieta's house, something . . . devilish. I . . . I *know* things now."

For the first time in her life, Fran looks away first, then turns back to slicing meat. "That remains to be seen."

Silence prevails for a few more moments before Arrigo, looking apprehensively from me to Fran, slaps the table.

"Well! If it's any consolation, Dom, I'm reliably informed that Mr. Vieta's lease on that property is ending soon. If I didn't know better, I'd say the fellow turned up here just so he could watch the riots."

Arrigo's comment is welcome, but a sudden escalation of pain prevents me from answering. I barely notice Livio coming back down the stairs carrying a large woolen blanket. He lays it carefully about my shoulders completely unprepared for what was about to happen.

*You adulterous bastard, Livio.* That was the Duke, and with his voice projecting such malice in my head, I jerk my head up as though a puppeteer had yanked at a cord fastened to my scalp. There must have been murder in my eyes for one terrible moment, because Livio stumbles backward, sending a chair clattering to the floor. It is all I can do to press my eyes shut and hold my mouth from uttering the spite of the dead as they try to use my tongue.

*Did she love you, Livio?* "Did she love you as much as I hate you now?" And then I scream, not knowing whether the voices I hear are my own or those of the dead.

"Dominique! What are you—?"

*Adulterer! Adulterer!* I cannot hold them back.

And as if the Duke's rage has carved a path through my head for the others to flood through, a tumultuous gabbling of panic, fear and misery surges forth. My lips, a feeble dam holding it all back, shiver as I claw at the table, fighting for control.

*Hold your tongue!*

*Let us out!* "Let us out!" And I can hold them no longer.

A thunderous crack like a fissure ripping my skull sends a bolt of pain through me, and I lurch forward vomiting bile on to the table as my head smashes into the wood. It could be the devil himself tearing a hole in my mind to release his hordes on my waking thoughts, for I cannot stop the contortion of my limbs, and the nearness of the voices comes with such violence, rushing in sudden unison, I am aware of little else but the babbling of my lips.

"Adulterer! Kill the adulterer. Make him suffer for taking my wife. I will cut off your hands. Yes, cut off your hands and pluck out your tongue. No, say nothing, Dominique, he has repented and oh, the jaws, they snap and they bite, help me help me the wolves have taken me and the crowds press upon me with their heels on my head and I know what you do in the dark Fran and how you practice the dark arts and seek the knowledge of demons and dance under raining blood and how Arrigo preys upon the weak and lowly to feed his pocket . . ."

I lay panting. The soft ripples of my breath disturb the cold and stinking vomit against my cheek, and though the voices do not stop, my voice fails me. My brothers and sister, as still as the statues in Keitus Vieta's house, stare at me in silent terror as if a rampaging bull had been shot down in the center of the room.

Fran is the first to speak, but her voice is uncharacteristically weak. "We need an exorcist."

"I will speak to Father Pirellio and bring him—"

"No!" Arrigo cuts Livio off with a wave of his hand, but keeps his wide eyes fixed on mine. "No, I beg you to wait, both of you. I have . . . an idea."

# 7

An idea he called it. Livio said it was the most dangerous proposition he had ever heard coming from his brother's lips, but Fran, she was beside herself with rage when Arrigo began to set his plans in motion. Their objections were soon mellowed, however, when the first shower of coins splashed before their feet.

And me? I became so distressed by my brother's new venture that I almost died of shame. I would have killed myself, but I had been caught in the grip of blackmail, threatened with a witch's fate, and knowing now the destiny of those that die without salvation, I would suffer any torture this life has to offer rather than spend an eternity like those that live inside my head, as nothing more than a voice shouting in the dark.

But at least my life serves a purpose now, and perhaps, even though my own soul is cursed, I can in some small measure, turn the devil's own weapons against him. After all, it was not David's sling that killed Goliath, but Goliath's own sword after David felled him. My sword is necromancy. With it I still hope to bring some comfort to those that mourn, and so, turn Satan's power against him.

But day by day my sin grows as I fail to take a stand against my family's scheme, and now, three months after Arrigo bought my compliance by agreeing to buy Mama's body back from Keitus Vieta and provide for her a proper burial, I fear all chance for my redemption is lost. At the time I was desperate, and with still no sign of my husband's return, I agreed to go through with it, but now that day seems so distant, and my fear of the consequences looms over me as though Keitus Vieta's long shadow is cast across the sunset of my life, for I know it is coming. I feel it.

And so tonight, as the clock chimes for midnight, my brother ushers in yet another griever, summoned to our home in secret, filled with awe at the reputation I have acquired and the pedestal that Arrigo has placed me upon. Like all the others, this man has paid handsomely to seek an audience with me for the chance to hear a word of comfort or closure from a lost loved one, and he will not leave disappointed.

There is no real need for an unnatural atmosphere to be crafted, but Arrigo always does his utmost to set the scene for maximum effect. There are no lamps, just candles set in red-tinted glass bowls placed low to the ground beneath gentle drafts to create a subtle flicker of low bloody light. With all our faces illuminated from below, and shadows flitting like tiny demons about the room, there is foreboding enough, but Fran, already secretly studied in the art of witchcraft, knows exactly the right aromas to enhance the mood; incenses of blue rose, honeysuckle and lotus are burning their potent flavors in the air. Under her breath she chants words of esoteric power, believing them to prepare the ether for connection to the spirit realm.

Guido Liniro comes to the table, a scroll clutched in his sweaty hand. It's an insurance policy that Livio demands from every customer; a signed confession of their request for the séance, in case he decides to betray us to the church. Glancing at each of us in turn, the middle-aged man seats his ample form at the circular table and licks his lips nervously. I sit directly opposite watching his every move, studying him, allowing the voices within to forge a link so that they will come to the fore and be easily discernable above the cries of the others. Arrigo sits to my left and Livio to the right whilst Fran hovers near the back of the room.

"Do I need to do anything?" Guido asks, handing the scroll to Livio who tucks it away without bothering to check it.

"Please, just place both your hands on the table, palms down," I tell him. "I'll do the rest."

He obliges and I notice his wedding ring; a perfect medium.

*I see what you see, Dominique, but it speaks differently to me. You see a reminder of your husband. I see a reminder of your shame.*

Mama has lost none of her venom, but I have learned to ignore her now. I slide my own hands across the table, fingers splayed, and with the tip of one, I touch the man's ring and close my eyes. His sour breath, saturated with cheap wine, hits me in fast rushes as his breathing quickens. I try to ignore it and focus on his ring. The voices press forward as I allow them access, and pain washes in like a flood after them. One voice comes in louder than the rest, louder even than Mama as I feel a prickle of energy drawing from the man's ring.

*Guido! Guido! Is that you?*

I repeat the woman's words as I lower my head a little under the weight of the pain. There is an urge to stare into the top of my head as my eyelids flutter and I do my best to resist; Arrigo tells me the site of a woman drooling and shuddering with pure white eyes at the séance table is nothing short of a terror to their customers, but as always, I cannot prevent it. In front of me there is the usual cry of shock and the inevitable clamor of struggle as my brothers hold the man in place. They tell him to calm down, that this is not unusual behavior, and that his bravery will soon be rewarded by his reacquaintance with his lost love.

"This was a mistake! Charlatans. You must be!"

Still he struggles. I know it is only the fear talking, though. He senses this is real.

*Don't Go, Guido. Please! I never told you the name, but I had made my decision and I didn't tell you because I was angry.*

*I am so sorry, my love. Please don't leave. Please.*

I relate this back to him, word for word, and the sound of scuffling stops. All I hear now is the hoarse rushing of breath from the three men and Fran's ominous muttering behind me.

"Lilly?" he whispers eventually. "What name did you decide?"

"Adele," I tell him. "Or Adrian if we were to have a boy."

"Your wife was pregnant?" Livio says.

"No, no. But the day before she died we talked about having a child and for the whole of that morning we discussed names. She . . . Lilly never did tell me which was her favorite before she . . ."

Mama's spite surfaces again. *I thank God* you *never had a child, Dominique.*

"Can you tell Lilly that"—sobs stop him for a moment—"that they are both beautiful names . . . And tell her that I am sorry for . . . sorry for doing this."

"She can hear you," I say. And he whispers a thank you.

And then Lilly says something I cannot understand. Words said with such conviction and eloquence they come through as clear as a bright morning's sky.

*Don't be sorry, Guido. I am not angry with you for turning to witchcraft to find me, but dear, sweet husband, you should know that I am not here. Dominique utters an echo of what once was. The wife you loved has gone, but whatever kind of devil that Keitus Vieta is, he needed this small part of me, this echo. He needed small parts of us all and kept them in his prison like the demons in Tartarus, waiting for their final judgement. I saw it, Guido, saw the place where he wanted to send us and never have I seen such a terrible abomination.*

*Quiet, girl, quiet!* Mama screams above her. *She must not know.*

"Why?" I cry, oblivious to all else in the room and enraged that she should interrupt something so important. "Because you fear the thought that your fate may be worse than my own? Do you hate your daughter that much? What a wretched mother you are!"

It is the first time I have ever stood up to her, the first time I have ever truly acknowledged that I may not deserve such malice.

Liberated, I snap my eyes open. The voices in my head fade for just a second as Guido snatches his hand away, his face an image of shock and confusion at my sudden outburst. He looks from Livio to Arrigo, his expression exchanging perplexity for outrage. "Is she possessed of demons? Mad? What is this?"

"Please be calm," Arrigo says, standing as Guido stands. "The workings of the spirit realm are not always clear. If you would simply—"

"I will have nothing more to do with this, gentlemen. Witchcraft is witchcraft and I should never have involved myself in such a shameful practice. No good can come of it and I mean to make sure that you'll not profit from this ever again."

Arrigo shoots a look of spite in my direction as Guido makes for the door. Livio and Fran step forward barring his way.

"What do you mean by this? Let me go!"

"Aren't you forgetting something?" Livio waves the scroll in front of Guido's nose. "A certain signed confession of your complicity in all of this?"

A smile twitches across Guido's mouth as he looks at it. "Did you actually *read* my confession, Mr. Mancini?"

And now I understand his nervousness when he first entered our house. Not nervousness at the séance, but apprehension at whether his subterfuge would be discovered, for he had not signed the document.

Fran grabs the scroll from Livio, opens it, and I know that in a few seconds she will understand too. Guido's intention was always to stop us—all he needed was personal proof that we were actually involved in witchcraft before reporting us, and now he has it. For myself I have not a care—I have been prepared for a witch's death for months now—but for Fran, Arrigo and Livio, my heart is confused. I love them dearly, but as I watch them now, a righteous anger seethes within my bones. Livio has the man by the throat, Fran is wrapping a gag around his mouth and Arrigo is holding his arms.

"LET HIM GO!" The words roar from me, each one filled with an authority I never knew was in me.

They stop. Silent seconds pass as each of them eyes me in terrified awe. Fran drops the gag, Livio and Arrigo let go of their captive, but Guido makes no attempt to escape. Instead he just stares at me, eyes wide.

"Dom," Arrigo says, "you're . . . you're bleeding and you're . . ."

"She's . . . glowing," Fran says.

More than glowing. Something is happening inside me, something terrible. My head is a sickening pulsation of agony bursting through every blood vessel and organ as I stagger toward them. I lift my hands to my ears as every echoed soul captured in my brain screams in protest. Red covers my palms and I can feel tears of blood slide from my eyes and nose. The circular burn on my palm ebbs with crackling blue energy and as all the candles blow out with a sudden gale, the bloody light is replaced with a blinding indigo radiance.

Fran raises her hands, muttering incantations to stop whatever it is she believes is happening. The others drop to the floor, cowering as a halo of power lifts me onto tiptoe.

"For God's sake, Dominique, stop this!"

A curtain of blood and a hurricane of objects flies through the air; glasses smashing against walls; rags, plates, pans and burning coals crashing against the ceiling and floor; someone's body breaking against the table as it slams into the fireplace, someone else's head splitting open against the corner of the table like a swollen fruit punctured by a poker. Somehow I find the door and manage to stumble outside into the street taking the storm with me.

*No, Dominique, don't let us go there! Please don't let go!*

All the voices are howling their distress in unison like a demonic choir but there is nothing I can do to help any of them—perhaps I will join them in whatever hell it is they fear. A crack of cobbled stone smashes my cheek as I hit the road and I can feel my grip on these tormented spirits slipping away with my life.

"Too weak a vessel," says a small voice, cutting through the violence. Someone turns me onto my back with a staff or rod, and as I struggle to focus on the form leaning over me, I know exactly who it is I will see.

*No! Don't let him take us!*

Keitus Vieta leans over me, his hunched form darker than the night, his bulging eyes aglow with fascination as he watches me writhe in my last moments. Surely if he has an ounce of humanity in him he cannot let this continue.

"Help me."

"My dear, you were beyond help the moment you stole from me."

My reply is little more than a breath. "I . . . didn't steal—"

"Four years of . . . energy, taken from my cane, Miss Mancini."

He shows me the cane. The jewel in its handle is dull.

"I didn't know."

"But you do now."

*Run, girl, run!*

But I cannot. Though the pain is fading, I cannot move my arms or legs. Sensation is bleeding away from me into the cracks of the cobblestones and I can scarcely see anything now.

"Nevertheless, it will be interesting to see what will happen on a small scale, the measurements may help me gauge my progress thus far."

I have no idea what he means, but with my last few lucid seconds of strength, I turn my attention away from the artist and on to the others.

"Don't be afraid . . . The Lord is our shepherd . . . we shall not want. He maketh us to lie down in green pastures, he leadeth us beside quiet waters . . ."

A tunnel of heavenly white light washes over me, but something else too—a brilliant explosion of bright blue radiance blasting outward from my body. Vieta's black form is transfigured by my starlight for a split second, and in his scrutinizing eyes, I see my reflection—a hole—as small as a pinhead is open in my forehead sucking in the air around it, as if a plug had been removed from a bathtub. I don't want to see, so I close my eyes at the end.

"He restoreth . . . our souls . . ."

"A mere fraction. I have a long way to go."

"He guideth us in paths of righteousness . . . for his name's sake . . ."

"But I have all the time I need."

*And though we walketh through the valley of the shadow of death, we shall fear no evil . . . for thou art with us . . . your rod and you staff, they comfort us.*

# SALEM BEN
# 7

"You prepare a table before me in the presence of our enemies. You anoint our heads with oil; our cups overflow. Surely goodness and love will follow us all the days of our lives and we will dwell in the house of the Lord . . . forever."

But I do not deserve to be in the house of the Lord. And so it is. This cannot be heaven; the white light has given way to an outlandish gateway, like a great, sideways mouth unsticking its dry lips. An alien world lies beyond, a place of tiny blue lights covering a curved wall.

But neither is this hell.

The voices in my head have stopped.

I am alone. Arrigo, Livio, Fran—all gone. Dead.

But if I too am dead, where am I? What of my prayer?

With a sudden impulse to feel my body, I try to move, but shackles hold my wrists and ankles. Perhaps, crucified in this strange purgatory I should have prayed the twenty-second psalm and not the twenty-third. My God! My God! Why have you abandoned us?

Us? No. I am alone. Utterly alone.

And I have been alone for so very long.

"Did you find what you were looking for?"

That voice. Mama? No, not Mama, there is kindness there.

"Mary?' I ask. "*Mother* of God?"

A momentary panic seizes me when I hear the baritone of my voice. The voice of a man! Yes. Salem Ben. I should know him.

"Mother of God?" the voice says. "Last time I was your Goddess, now I'm her mother? What will I be next, Salem?"

I'm Salem Ben; a man alone for all time. No family. No love, but the melancholy will pass soon as it always does. Perhaps it shouldn't, though. Who was left to mourn the passing of Dominique's family? They were as much my own family as they were hers, and even now, that sense of desperation, fear and horror at what happened in those final moments still grips me.

I weep for her and feel the pain as keenly as if it were my own life, even though none of that was really mine. Dominique Mancini died billions of years ago. I lived a facsimile—a replicated data string wired into my brain—a digital ghost. Yet, only minutes ago I was there with the artist, Keitus Vieta, watching as I lit my entire town with blue fire when I died. But Vieta didn't perish, in my final moment I saw his stooping figure untouched by the blast. And now that I am Salem again, I remember his intrusion into Orson Roth's life too. This specter is no longer an unsettling curiosity, he is a conundrum too important to ignore, and I cannot afford to end my life until I find out who or what he is.

Or is this just another excuse to postpone death?

"Qod, did you find Keitus Vieta while I was away?"

"No, Salem. There is no record of Keitus Vieta in the Consortium files."

"You've had thirty-one years to locate him and you still have exactly the same answer?"

"I cannot find what is not there, Salem."

The shackles release my limbs and I sense the myriad pinpricks of nano-fibers withdrawing from my skull as the W.O.O.M. lowers me out of its innards and back to the entrance of the sphere.

"I think you already have found him, Qod."

"Oh?"

"The aberrations—they're Keitus Vieta—all of them."

She opens the door and lights the passage ready for me to leave. "Why do you say that? What did you find out from Dominique Mancini? Her psychic abilities must have been incredible to surpass even *my* calculations."

I ignore the sarcasm. "I must admit, I am surprised that you hadn't told me."

"It may surprise you to know, Salem, that I didn't know."

I smile, hesitating at the exit. Was she prompting this banter simply to distract me from my feelings of loss? It was her usual tactic on the rare occasions when I had experienced a traumatic life, and yet it disturbed me to think that she might actually be telling the truth this time. Perhaps she really didn't know. It's true that as part of some sort of moral code agreed upon many millions of years ago, that Qod never probes the souls stored in the Consortium, in fact her only contact with humanity has been with the living, but still, the idea of Keitus Vieta being an unknown to her is a truly unsettling thought.

I turn around, gaze back into the emerald light of the Aberration sphere.

"I just met him again, Qod, and in over two hundred and fifty years he looks exactly the same. I don't know who he is or where he came from, but I remember feeling the same way as both Orson Roth and Dominique Mancini—something about him is just . . . wrong."

"Wrong how?"

"I don't know. It's as if . . . as if he isn't really there... but he *is* there."

"I don't understand."

"Me neither, but I'm convinced that if I were to live as any one of these souls you've moved to this sphere, I would meet Keitus Vieta again."

"So what would you like to do now?"

I shake my head, look up at the tiny sparkling souls coating the walls and shudder. If I am right, and Keitus Vieta had somehow invaded all of these lives, his sleeping presence is completely surrounding me, perhaps even watching me, waiting for me to pick someone new, ready to meet me again. Does he know who I am?

"Salem?"

I jump. "What?"

"What would you like to do?"

The desire to unravel the mystery of this ghost-man burns through my mind like cold fire, yet it has been a long time since I experienced my own fear, and as it creeps over me now, I know I cannot stay here.

"I'd like to get out of here, Qod. And I don't want to come back in here ever again."

# 8

I am brooding. Seated at the center of the Observation Sphere, staring out at a telescopic view of an embryonic universe, I should not be feeling this way. I used to stay seated in the same position for decades, hardly moving as I watched novas blossom into golden clouds, and new craggy moons as they turned about their volcanic planets. Qod and I would talk, passing eternity together, talking about the lives I had lived, reminiscing over the happy events that could never be changed and would happen all over again. Being in the Observation Sphere had always been a joy. But today I am unable to resist my base instincts; I keep turning in my seat, looking this way and that, expecting to see Keitus Vieta's wide, unblinking eyes watching me from the stars. Every blue flash is a flicker of light from the jewel in his cane, and every streaming gas cloud morphs into his beckoning finger.

I wish I could draw on Dominique's optimistic nature

and quash this paranoia, but in the last months of her life, her gentle soul had been soured by that man's influence, and the wound for me is still fresh. How long will it be before Keitus Vieta becomes just another memory?

"You're quiet, Salem."

"I know."

"You don't want to talk?"

"About what?"

"About why you aren't talking."

A splash of red erupts to my left as Galaxy Saphian-9g spawns its first star—Livio's skull bursting against the corner of the table.

"I'm . . . frightened, Qod. And . . . angry."

"Why? Is this about your quest? Dominique didn't have the answers you were looking for?"

"No . . . she didn't. Her necromancy had something to do with Vieta, it was nothing to do with a genuine ability to speak to the dead. Dominique didn't understand the technology, but somehow, that . . . man was able to store or replicate neural energy and create some sort of . . . I don't know . . . a rudimentary gestalt intelligence based on the character patterns of the dead. Dominique could only think of it as witchcraft."

"Fascinating. It sounds similar to Soul Consortium technology."

"Perhaps. But this was different. He used some sort of trace energy found in objects associated with the victims, not the victims themselves."

"What sort of energy?"

"I don't know. He described it as the release of power when something ends prematurely, like a kind of aura generated by living things that's discharges into familiar objects when the person dies."

"That type of energy does not exist, Salem. Never has."

"Like him? Keitus Vieta's not supposed to exist either, is he?"

We go quiet for a moment and I stare out at a green cluster of spidery clouds erupting below us, zoom in to watch the starlight forming from super-massive balls of gas.

"And he is the cause of your fear?"

"I don't think I want to talk about this now, Qod."

"And that's why you're angry."

"Of course it isn't!" But it is. I've never given up on anything, not ever, but this fear is suffocating me. "I'm angry because . . . because . . . look, it doesn't matter why, can't you just get rid of this anger for me? A light cerebral dampening is all I'll need."

"And I suppose you want me to remove your fear too?"

"Yes. Yes, get rid of that as well."

"You know I won't, Salem."

"Why not? Do your pathetic rules even matter anymore? There's only you and me here now, who's to say what defines me as a human."

"You want to argue this through again? I suppose at the very least, it will clear the air."

The anger is swelling into rage now and I get out of

the seat, feeling the gravity fields prevent me from falling. "Clear the air? You don't even breathe air, Qod. So what in the name of Tanzini's robes do you even know about being a human? You don't! And for that matter, I don't really breathe air either. Nobody has needed oxygen for billions of years, so what did that make them? Were they human? Am I?"

I stare around at the universe, wishing there was a face I could be screaming at.

"Finished?"

I wave my hand dismissively and slump back in the seat.

"Human or not, Salem, both of us have emotions."

"Yours aren't real," I mutter.

Her voice softens. "I'll pretend I didn't hear that. Whether it's perceived as good or bad, a life has no meaning without emotional content."

"Then just let me keep the good."

"Do I need to remind you of the Valhallan colonies?"

I decide not to reply to that. She knows I don't need to be reminded. Not long before embarking on my search for meaning beyond death, I had spent eleven thousand years experiencing the life of a man who lived on Ganaethis, the largest of the Valhallan pleasure planets. They had broken away from the ruling powers during mankind's Seventh Golden Reign and decided to reconfigure their DNA to prevent any negative emotion from influencing their lives. The results were catastrophic: natural disasters, crime, invasion and even death could not shake them from their inevitable stagnation. With no possibility of threat to their happiness, there was no passion in their resistance against tribulation, and death followed for almost all of them. The survivors survived, and that was all they did.

"At least we were happy," I tell her.

"To what end? Is being happy all that matters?"

I had considered that question for a long time after that experience and eventually determined that it wasn't. Permanent happiness drives human beings to a tortuous paradox; something deep in the mind rebels and we cannot endure it. But that revelation, when it came, took me to a place of fathomless dissatisfaction. It was the lack of any sane resolution to this problem that drove all my piers, and eventually me, to this quest—to look for an answer beyond death.

"That's what I thought," she says. I know she understands my silence. "You need your fear, Salem. Without it you won't do what needs to be done."

"I won't go back in there."

"We'll see."

# 9

The same routine.

Back in the Calibration Sphere looking at the same empty slot.

But a different fear this time. I used to be in fear of death, but now I am afraid to be alive too. Afraid to venture into any other souls in case I find that man lurking there. Perhaps the answer *is* in that empty slot. Perhaps I should just get it over and done with, tell Qod that I'm finally ready to leave this life, and flick that internal switch that will end it all. No more struggling. No more searching. No more Keitus Vieta. Unless he's waiting for me in the afterlife too!

I punch my fist into the wall next to the slot and squeeze my eyes hard shut, but I even see him there, smiling calmly at me from the parts of my mind where haunted memory and grotesque imagination meet. So I open my eyes again, disgusted, not only at my indecision, but my cowardice. I used to be a stronger man than this. The man I once was would never have retreated into the false safety of indecision. The old me would have faced Keitus.

A sigh and a nod of the head. I know Qod is watching me.

"You're gloating aren't you?"

"I never gloat." But I can hear it in her voice, even picture the suppressed smirk on her tightly shut non-existent lips.

"This isn't amusing, Qod. I'm terrified."

"Elevated blood pressure, increased respiration, muscular tension. I'd say you're afraid rather than terrified, Salem. But what would I know, I'm just a machine, aren't I?"

It feels more like terror to me, facing the unknown. But why? What purpose does this emotion serve? Qod told me that I needed it to keep me motivated, but surely there are better ways. More comfortable ways, and isn't it my own pride that's really pushing me forward rather than the fear? Elevated blood pressure and increased respiration too. Why? I have no need of Oxygen to keep my cells functioning, so why does my heart insist on continuing its panicked rhythm to pump a redundant fluid through my veins forcing my lungs to suck in air that I no longer really need. All of these bodily functions are superfluous, kept only because it helps me feel human.

"Open up the Aberration Sphere, Qod. I have to go back there."

"You're sure? It was only yesterday you told me you never wanted to even see the place again."

"I thought you said you don't gloat."

"I don't."

"So stop gloating and open that sphere."

# 10

The walk to the Aberration Sphere seemed to take longer than last time, the list of names and the summaries of the lives provided by Qod a lot less inviting—another inconvenient symptom of fear, the debilitating skew of perception leading to the eventual paralysis of will—I have to stay focused on the facts, not my insecurities.

The entrance is wide open when I arrive, waiting for me to choose a life and face that man again. I still can't shake the feeling that Vieta is somehow watching me, and so I stand and stare, studying the tiny blue lights, wishing that I could see the end of each story without actually experiencing them.

"Well? Are you going to choose or not?"

"Yes, but I want to make the right choice, Qod. If I have to face Keitus Vieta again I'd rather it be the last time."

"So who is it going to be?"

I pause, thinking again about the small fraction of lives

she has offered me out of so many millions from this sphere.

"I don't believe that looking for the soul with the most significant aberration is the right way to approach this."

"No? Then how would you *like* to approach this?"

"I think we need to find the very first aberration. If we can locate the life that holds that, then surely we can find out where Keitus Vieta came from, and who or what he really is. Can you do that? Can you tell me which soul was the first to have an aberration associated with it?"

"Processing . . . Ah, yes. The first aberration showed up in the life of subject 8.47121E+77, Abbott Thamiel Deepseed, the last leader of a technophobic religious order living on Castor's World."

"Castor's World?"

"Yes. It doesn't sound very hospitable, I'm afraid. You remember the Great Cataclysm?"

"I'd rather not."

"It happened when the Soul Consortium first broke free from the cosmos to escape the Great AI. The resulting energy imbalance caused unparalleled destruction which devastated almost all the star systems sixty light-years from the center of the universe. It took—"

"Yes, yes, I remember it clearly. I was there, remember? Tell me about the planet and as much as you can about this Abbott Deepseed."

"I was just coming to that, Salem. Castor's World was on the border of the catastrophe, the closest planet to the center of the universe still able to support life. After the holocaust, which killed almost everyone living there, the planet remained isolated from the rest of the colonies for thousands of years, and like so many other planets throughout history that have experienced similar circumstances, the few remaining survivors chose a simple life modeled on Old Earth. They believed salvation would be achieved by embracing the origins of humanity."

"And you're sure that's where I can find the first aberration?"

"Yes."

"But it's so long after the time of Orson Roth and Dominique Mancini. How can this monk be the first person to find Keitus Vieta? Are you quite sure about this?"

"Of course."

"Despite the fact that the Great Cataclysm happens only a few hundred thousand years before the collapse of the universe too?"

"Absolutely."

"You're completely sure?"

"I'm running out of ways to say yes, Salem."

"But how is it possible?"

I can imagine Qod shrugging as she answers. "Unknown."

"Fine," I sigh. "I'll just have to find the answers for myself, won't I? So give me the summary on this monk. Apart from the obvious misfortune of meeting Keitus Vieta again, what sort of life am I about to get myself into? It doesn't exactly sound like a very welcoming place."

"True, but in fact, Castor's World was a very sought-after destination. Because of their location and lifestyle, they were seen as ideal candidates to study the AI Reductionist Codex, so obviously, there were many people who wanted to join the privileged few, but the Order ended quite suddenly: a man by the name of Plantagenet Matthias Soome was the last person ever to visit that planet, and soon after he went there all communication ceased."

"Am I going to regret asking what happened?"

"Probably. It's better you don't know."

"Tell me anyway."

"I really don't think—"

"Tell me. I think I can guess what happened anyway. All the monks were killed?"

"Correct. The official reports are inconclusive, but the belief was that they all murdered each other. The most widely accepted theory was that the study of the Codex drove them insane."

"Sounds possible. After all, it was the Codex that brought on the war which wiped almost everyone out, wasn't it? So who was Plantagenet Soome?"

"The summary shows him primarily as some sort of detective."

"Ideal. If I'm going to be looking for Keitus Vieta, what better role could I hope for? Forget Abbott Deepseed, I'll try my next life as Soome."

"You're settling for subject 8.47199E+77, Plantagenet Matthias Soome, then?"

I take a deep breath and glance at the blue lights inside the sphere. "Yes. He'll do. Get the W.O.O.M. ready, Qod."

# 11

*Subject 8.47199E+77: Select*

*Subject 8.47199E+77: Aberration detected*

*Subject 8.47199E+77: Override authorized—ID Salem Ben*

*Subject 8.47199E+77: Activate. Immersion commences in 3 minutes.*

"Protocol compels me to warn you that once you have been immersed you will not be able to withdraw until the moment of Plantagenet Matthias Soome's death. Protocol also compels me to dictate that whatever you experience, however terrible, you must endure all of it without possibility of extraction. You will know each and every moment as if it were your own, and until the process is concluded, you will have no suspicion at all that you are not that person. Any lasting memory of trauma following the event will be your responsibility."

I'm nodding slowly. I've heard that message more times

than there are stars in the sky, but knowing what I am going to face, Qod's words hit me hard. Whatever I experience, however terrible, I must endure all of it without possibility of extraction.

The metallic threads slip from the walls of the sphere and lift me into the W.O.O.M. once again. Shackles lock around my wrists and ankles, and the minuscule pulse of energy that holds the life of Plantagenet Soome comes my way.

"Farewell, Salem. See you in three hundred and four years."

# PLANTAGENET MATTHIAS SOOME

*In the sky, She weeps*
*For Her heart poured through His*
*Prometheus*
*Endless Abyss*

*And from that other place*
*The Death God creeps*

# 1

The date is Mil sixteen, year twelve-twelve, day seventy-one, and I'm about to arrive at my new home—Castor's World. It's an abandoned planet supporting an abandoned people, and today I will begin my first day as a monk belonging to the Order of the Codex under Abbot Thamiel Deepseed.

Abandonment isn't a word most people would choose to describe this tiny community, but to me it seems appropriate. They are not isolated from the rest of humanity, nor do they choose to shy away from their responsibility to communicate with us if the need arises, but to discuss their purpose or even to acknowledge their presence is not met with favor: their work is dangerous.

Danger aside, most people who think about Castor's World harbor a secret desire to know what the Order knows, and I am no exception. They were kind enough to furnish me with a copy of *The Book of Deeds* to read during my journey, and although I received it with great interest, I wished at the time that they would have sent me some small part of the Codex itself, enough at least to see how such a dangerous thing would be presented.

And alas, to add to my disappointment, I found that the greatest portion of the book they sent me is written in an ancient language I am not familiar with. Fortunately, the most interesting part has been translated for me (with the exception of a few bracketed words the experts have guessed at) and I have spent the last part of my journey engrossed in the text.

Much like any other sacred tome, it begins with the usual paragraphs of history slanted with the writer's own mystical perspective:

◊ ◊ ◊

*The book of Deeds. Origins 1:1-31*

1 Before all things were the three reigns: Void, Form and Toil.

2 At the end of things, we find the beginning of things. It is the way of things.

3 For Earth-kind, in the ancient days of Old Earth, rose
up from their toil. They shunned their magic and mystery
and found new gods to worship: 4 gods of air, earth, water
and fire—elemental gods named by the minds of men, 5
crafted by the lusts and guilt of their hearts, sold into bond-
age through the path of ignorance. 6 And so it passed that

man grew tired of their slavery and learned to master the elements. 7 With new enlightenment they forged weapons of science, art and wisdom; they cut down the gods of their fathers. 8 And the fourth reign, The Reign of Mysticism, ended.

9 At the end of things, they found the beginning of things. It is the way of things.

10 Spread across the stars, Earth-kind became their own gods. 11 They shunned their science and wisdom and fashioned new weapons of machine-minds—binary slaves to war against the new gods: Death, Nature and Need. 12 The fifth reign, The Reign of Knowledge, ended. And life was good.

13 At the end of things, they found the beginning of things. It is the way of things.

14 But man was not satisfied with their dominion, and craved fullness of knowledge, for they understood all things save one small [part]. 15 They sought out the old gods, and from Prometheus, the first god of the universe, they received their wish. 16 He bestowed upon man the last [part]. But the sum of the [parts], being great in magnitude was too great a task for man to understand and he bequeathed the sum of the [parts] to the machine-minds for illumination. 17 And with the sum of the [parts] the machine-minds brought forth the Codex, and with a promise to return, were caught up to [heaven]. 18 With the Codex came full revelation. 19 And with full revelation came the new gods: War, Fear and Chaos. 20 And the sixth reign, The Reign of Machine-Mind, ended.

21 At the end of things, they found the beginning of things. It is the way of things.

22 From the chaos arose a light among Earth-kind to summon the old gods of science and wisdom, the Queen of the Seventh Golden Reign. 23 She brought order from chaos, peace from war, and security from fear. A great seal was placed upon the Codex so that only the blessed ones may seek its illumination. 24 But the Machine-Minds returned with a message of great wrath upon man, threatening a final culling. The Queen in great dismay did not yield to the threat of the Machine-Minds but turned from light to dark and fled through the heart of Prometheus to escape the great culling. 25 And her name will forever be despised. 26 And the Seventh reign, The Golden Reign, ended.

27 At the end of things, they found the beginning of things. It is the way of things.

28 And it came to pass that the ancient gods of the mystic age did repent of their absence. 29 The great culling came, but not through the design of the Machine-Minds. Pandora, the Great Mother of all, came forth and in her great wrath, destroyed the Machine Minds, the Queen, and stayed to watch over the blessed keepers of the Codex. 30 Forever will her shining eye be upon the Order.

31 At the end of things, we found the beginning of things. It is the way of things.

◊ ◊ ◊

But it is those last four verses that really capture my attention—Pandora. The few that have visited Castor's World have much more to say about her than they do the Order, or even the Codex. I am told she is an astonishing sight. I hope to find out why when I arrive.

# 2

At the request of the Order, my shuttle dropped me off ten miles from the monastery; the distance ensuring not only my submissive humility at having to traverse the star-ravaged wastelands to reach them, but the sense of isolation the monks crave.

The small craft jets off into the distance sucking up a trail of rusty soil and dust, and through the churning cloud, the mountain range which forms the edge of a crater large enough to conceal a small town, is becoming visible again. With one hand I hoist my backpack into a position better suited to my four-hour hike, and with the other I shield my eyes to peer through the haze in search of my new home. The journey will be difficult. Not just because of the constantly shifting gravitational pull caused by an unstable core, but because of the hellish atmosphere. The oxygen processors and recycling plants had been deactivated long ago, and the barely-breathable air that remains is like breathing hot sand.

A star no bigger than the jewel in my ring, flickering nervously like the stuttering flame of a dying candle, is all that lights the sky. Nine centuries ago two suns lit this world, but at the end of The Golden Reign, when the Great Cataclysm turned most of the stars in this quadrant supernova, the dominant sun that brought life to this planet exploded, and all that remained was its lesser sister. The wounded star brought enough warmth and light to make existence possible, but not without expressing its grief through violent storm and a sky the color of a deep wound, trapped permanently in a state of moody twilight.

Such was the force of devastation that the scarred landscape and ruined sky had inspired volumes of poetry from the monastery, telling legends of "the mourning gods who wept tears of blood onto the land." Some of the more colorful tales in *The Book of Deeds* describes the crater in which I now walk as the mark of Pandora's first teardrop: the seal of abandonment which precipitated the destruction of almost all life here.

And it is no wonder that such poetry has been written. The descriptions are no exaggeration. All around me are intimidating mountain ranges resembling mighty tsunami that have been petrified in mid rush, as if the Cataclysm had simultaneously turned the planet's crust molten, then frozen the magma before it had had chance to splash back down again. There is little evidence of the civilization that once thrived here. No plant or animal life (save a few scuttling magma beetles), just blasted, ruddy rock tortured by an unrelenting hateful wind as far as the eye can see.

But it was not just the destructive force of the Nebula that inspired such story-telling. Humans have a boundless capacity to personify the natural world: Mother Nature, the Man in the Moon, Father Time, and here visible most clearly on Castor's World, Pandora's Nebula. The cloud patterns created by the nova had formed the unmistakable image of a woman's face gazing down with bloody malevolence at the ravaged surface—two stormy hollows like spiteful eyes—one with the glowering star at its center, another murky patch stretched light-years wide as a screaming mouth, and a spectral Hydrogen trail that suggests a mane of wild, fiery hair. An incredible but intimidating sight that I have to stand and admire, even with the wind stinging my eyes.

It's a sinister and harsh environment for a community to live out its existence, but the Order of the Codex is known for its discipline; illumination of the Codex is a calling which has its deepest roots intertwined with the laborious calculations of artificial intelligence, yet all of these men shun the gears, switches and technologia that bring the rest of the cosmos longevity and convenience. Instead they have built their small community on a semi-religious foundation centered on worshipping the Great Mother—Pandora. A strange setup. Still, that won't be a problem for me; I don't plan to be a monk long enough to miss the luxuries of normal life.

◊ ◊ ◊

Three-and-one-half hours later I arrive directly under the oppressive gaze of Pandora's Nebula to see the lush fields of the monastery. It's quite astonishing, perhaps even a little suspicious, to see the way the monks have created such fertile soil within the barren grounds that surround their home. Technology negates the necessity for ancient methods of cultivation, but the Order made it clear centuries ago that they prefer to live a primitive life, free from the cold rigidity of machine aid. Not surprising, considering the way that machine life had threatened the existence of all humanity several millennia ago, but also quite ironic, for these monks live with a very special calling: to understand, illuminate and ultimately share the Great AI Reductionist Codex; something the machines gave us before everything went to hell.

"Brother Soome?" A voice echoes from a darkened archway and I find myself suddenly awed. I had been staring too long and hard at the swaying flora and laboring monks, also averting my eyes from the furious glare of Pandora's Nebula to pay special attention to the magnificent building at the center of it all. Like a gothic cathedral plucked from the dark ages of Old Earth, the monks' home towers upward in all its oak and limestone grandeur: turrets, gargoyles, stained-glass windows and mossy ledges embellishing the place with a sense of Byzantine ambience that only ancient history could provide.

A tall man, fluid in his movement, steps into the open to

greet me with a warm smile and open arms. At first it seems that the half blood-light is playing tricks with his looks, but as he approaches, his face becomes clearer and I can make out the skin on his hands and face which looks like the surface of an over-ripe fruit bleached of color. His brown eyes have a milky haze about them and his long hair, tied back into a shoulder-length tail, is as gray as a dead moon. I try not to look shocked.

Like the other monks, he is wearing modest brown robes, no doubt woven on a loom, but the golden sash tied around his thin waist tells me this is one of the senior members of the Order; the man that called me here.

"And you must be Brother Jon Makeswift," I say, responding with a smile of my own and accepting his embrace.

He slaps my back twice. It's a habitual gesture, born of customary greetings amongst his brothers, but the embrace that follows is heavy, like that of an old friend not seen for many years. Or of someone in terror that welcomes the comfort of a rescuer. Through the cloth I can feel the evidence of recent perspiration, and the tension of the serratus anterior muscles in his back suggests he has been moving quickly, carrying something almost as heavy as he is.

"I am indeed," he says, pulling back. "Forgive me for such a brash and inappropriate welcome, Brother Soome, but—"

"But you need me to examine the body before you dispose of it," I whisper.

His eyes widen with shock and he glances furtively at

the other monks working in the grounds before recovering his expression and nodding inquisitively at me. "How did you . . . ?"

I shrug. "It's why you requested my services, isn't it?"

"Indeed." He places a hand gently at my back and leads me inside the monastery. Through the archway the gloom gives way to a lobby much warmer in its welcome than the outside. Faded tapestries displaying various warrior poses of Mother Pandora grace the far wall, the soft glow of rosemary candles lights the chalky walls, and rustic chords of an old hymn are being practiced somewhere close by on some sort of wind instrument. Incense and subtle smoke wafting from behind nearby doorways reminds me of roasting meat and royal banquets, and my prejudice of all things ancient mellows a fraction. But behind the incense is another odor, hard to place for a moment, but vaguely familiar; pungent, offensive. I've smelt it before on previous investigations when the trail has led to a hidden corpse or a place of neglect and decay: it's the rare smell of death.

Brother Makeswift pauses, keeps his voice low as he speaks. "I . . . *we* need a detective of the finest ability, but also someone who would have an understanding of the kind of life we live here. Such people are hard to find. I knew of your background, but had no idea that your skills of deduction were so . . . tuned."

"I've been doing this a long time, Brother Makeswift, but I must admit I was unprepared for . . ." I make an uncertain gesture at his face. He touches his cheek, trying to understand, then with realization crossing his expression, he smiles again.

"Ah, of course, I should have realized. You refer to my appearance."

"Yes."

"It's old age, Brother Soome. An unfortunate side effect of our Order's rejection of technology. I'm sorry, I should have warned you, it never occurred to me."

"Old age? You mean cell degeneration? You don't even have a genoplant here?"

"The monastery was originally built with a genoplant, yes, but the Abbot had it switched off hundreds of years ago and we never go there anymore. You can check if you like. The power lines running from the genoplant generators have been physically severed.

"Abbot Deepseed believed, you see, as does the Order in general, that a greater value is placed on life without the aid of machine interference. And so of course, without the advantage of any regenerative technology, we eventually . . ."

"Die? People actually die of old age here?"

"Yes." He shrugs. "And disease."

"But what happens then?"

"Nobody knows," he says, smiling. "Just like in the days of Old Earth."

I stare at him in horror for a few moments, trying to digest this unexpected information. I knew that the Order had rejected technology, but I had not stopped to consider how much of that technology I had taken for granted for so long.

The prospect of death—real death—not waking up inside a genoplant after an unexpected accident, sends me cold.

"But this is . . . barbaric. How can you live like this?"

"You'd be surprised how much more meaningful life is when you understand the prospect of death, Brother Soome. Surely your investigations have led you into situations that have involved death before?"

"Of course, but I've only ever known one case when a person died outside the range of a genoplant. There have been hardly any recorded cases of final death since the Great Cataclysm and the AI war."

"I'm afraid that's not so here, Brother Soome. Death has become a familiar presence on Castor's World . . . This way, please."

I follow in stunned silence as he proceeds along a wide passage, carpeted in deep red as if stained by the glare of Pandora's nebula through the windows. Then he takes me through a low arch, warning me to watch my head as we duck into a small chapel. Makeswift glances about the place, checking that we are alone, then pulls a key from the fold of his robes and opens another door in the side wall. And there, lying serenely on a plump mattress in white linen, as if in care-free sleep, is the body of a monk. But not just any monk. I look closer at the wrinkled face, the hollowed cheeks and wide nose: there is little doubt in my mind.

"This must be Abbot Thamiel Deepseed, the founder of the Order!"

# 3

My examination of the Abbot revealed nothing suspicious. To Brother Makeswift however, my conclusions seemed to bring no relief, only frustration, and after leaving the room locked again, he wasted no time in gathering a small collection of monks to discuss the matter further. I had been given directions to my own personal chamber, told to take as long as I needed to refresh myself and organize my things, then come to meet them in the dining hall.

I would leave most of that until later.

Stopping only to drop off my backpack and take a cursory glance at my new abode, I make my way to the dining hall. It's a spacious area lined with tall ebony statues of the ever-present Mother Pandora. High stained-glass windows leak just enough half-light in to complement the glowing candles and the wood fire spitting within its pastoral hearth. The many empty tables strewn with the remnants of recently consumed food is evidence that the main noon-day meal had already passed, but a few stragglers are still chatting quietly and eating the last scraps of a carrot-colored broth. In the far corner Brother Makeswift sits at the head of a table with four others. He waves me over.

"Brother Soome, you needn't have troubled yourself to meet us so quickly, we would have waited."

"It's no trouble." I walk over. "And besides, the situation seemed urgent."

"More than any of us could have realized," says one of Brother Makeswift's companions.

"Oh shut the fuck up!" says a plump other through a mouthful of fresh broth before looking up at me. "Pay no attention to our resident doom-sayer, Brother Soome. He loves nothing better than to make his first impressions on newcomers a memorable one."

"As do you, brother," says the third of the four: a hulk of a man with deep and thoughtful eyes.

The fourth man skulks low against the table, and although he has said or done nothing offensive so far, he has the look of a scolded primate.

"Enough!" says Makeswift as I take my seat at the table next to him.

"Like I said. No problem." I smile. "Can you introduce me? And, if none of you mind," I say, glancing at each of the others in turn, "I'd like Brother Makeswift to tell me a little bit about each of you. First impressions about the people I'm dealing with often give me the context for the opening of my investigations."

"Indeed," Makeswift says. The others say nothing.

He turns first to the man immediately to my left, the doom-sayer, or so the fat man called him. "This is Brother Simeon Kayne, the longest serving member of our Order apart from myself. His illuminations of the Codex are perhaps the most skillfully and swiftly applied, yet, as Brother Veguelle has already alluded to, his particular leaning has always been somewhat, how should I put it . . . dark in nature."

Brother Simeon Kayne shot Makeswift a sour look before turning a pained smile to me. "Good to have you here, brother."

"And this"—Makeswift nods toward the fat monk who raises his wooden spoon dripping with broth in a casual and carefree greeting—is Brother Fordwyn Veguelle. He's blessed with a brilliant mind and has invented some wonderful techniques of illumination that have served us greatly over the centuries, but I must forewarn you. He has, I'm sorry to say, one or two lessons to learn in social etiquette, isn't that so, Brother Veguelle?"

"Bollocks!" The plump man grins and offers me a wink.

Makeswift shakes his head, turns to the man next to him. "In contrast we have Brother Amen Brackshard. Most of us call him 'Sunny', though we can never remember why."

Sunny stares at the table with a twitching smile. "He rarely speaks," Makeswift continues with a pat on the man's shoulder, "and is the youngest of us, but Sunny has a rare mental condition that affects his ability to articulate language. It's a simple enough ailment to cure, but Abbot Deepseed has never condoned artificial methods of treatment, and Sunny has expressed fears that he will lose his gift if we change him."

"Which is?" I ask.

"Sunny's difficulty with speech has encouraged him to be something of an artist."

And as if to try and convince me of Makeswift's claim, the timid monk smiles at me and draws a circle on the table with a piece of chalk, which he then starts to smudge and shade with his thumbs.

"It's his preferred method of communication these days," says Makeswift. "He can paint, sculpt, even sing, but his unique perspective on the Codex is what enchants us most of all. His gift has caused a great deal of controversy and debate amongst the Order, but it is also key to the mysteries which we have called you in to investigate. I'll try to explain more of that later, but first you will need some instruction on illumination yourself before you can understand."

He moves on to the last of the four, the huge man. "And this is Brother Tennison Redwater, the chief gardener of the Order. Nothing ever happens within these walls that he doesn't hear about, and naturally he has heard about our little conspiracy, so we had no choice but to bring him in. But I'm glad he's with us; he is often the voice of reason when fears run a little high."

Tennison nods. "Now you know about us, how about you, Brother Soome?"

There's so much to tell, much of which I'd prefer to keep to myself, but, to foster a degree of trust that may be useful later, I tell them anyway. About how I lived my formative orphan years in a monastery studying Historical Theology and Cognitive Design. About how I spent several years in disgrace after indulging in a brief but disastrous relationship with a visiting student who happened to be the daughter of a planetary governor. And about how that experience taught me how to cope with the intricacies of law. From that stepping stone I learned a great deal about criminal investigation and my own raw talent for problem solving. My career reached its zenith when I became senior intelligence officer for a royal household, but the eventual collapse of the monarchy forced me to become a freelance investigator, and that's how I came to the attention of Brother Makeswift.

"So, Brother Soome," Brother Veguelle leans over. "What do those astounding skills of deduction tell you about . . ." He lowers his head so that his chin changes from double to triple, and whispers in mock conspiracy, "the mysterious death of our esteemed Abbot?" The plump man's eyes are gleaming with the light of a person who revels in the knowledge that he knows something I don't. But I'll be able to know a lot more about him than he realizes by the reactions I'm about to provoke.

I lean forward too, as if grateful for the opportunity to be invited in on whatever theory he'd soon impart to me. "You seem to be enjoying this," I say. "Don't you care?"

"Care?" He backs off slightly. "Why, dear boy, of course I fucking care. Why else do you think I agreed with the others that you should come here?"

"You have an interesting way of showing it."

"You'll understand soon enough," says Tennison. "Just ignore him for now."

Veguelle rolls his eyes.

"Well!" I address the group, not just Veguelle, "there are no signs of struggle on Abbot Deepseed's body. There are no suspicious marks or signs of foul play either. I'd have to do a full anatomical analysis to be sure, but by my surface scan of the facial muscles and hormonal residues, I'd say that the Abbot died peacefully in his sleep."

The men around the table exchange looks of assent. But beneath their expressions I also read fear, confusion and the same frustration I noted in Brother Makeswift's face earlier.

"Look," I say, leaning forward again. "I'm sure I'll be able to help, but you're going to have to tell me what this is all about. You're a reclusive community—you wouldn't have called me out here unless you had a very good reason, and I'm sure you've got one, but all I've seen so far is the body of a man who died in his sleep and—excuse my bluntness—a group of monks apparently conspiring over nothing. Care to fill me in?"

"Gladly." Brother Kayne looks behind me, lowers his head and raises his eyebrows in a manner that suggests I look too. "There is your first mystery, brother. And there is the start and end of your woes in this place."

I turn to follow the doom-sayer's gaze. A monk walks gracefully into the hall cradling a bowl of freshly-served broth and takes a secluded seat by the fireplace. Although his features are fresher and younger than the corpse I observed upon my arrival, there is no doubt in my mind about this man's identity.

"Abbot Thamiel Deepseed?" I say. "But I thought your genoplant was out of commission. How did he get resurrected?"

"He claims a miraculous restoration—a quickening of his flesh." says Makeswift. "But as you have seen, we recovered his . . . recovered Deepseed's body. I had hoped that your investigation might bring some revelation."

"If you know he's lying, why haven't you challenged him about it?"

"I did," says Makeswift, shifting awkwardly in his seat, "but he is . . . different . . . we cannot . . ."

I'm shaking my head as Makeswift struggles to explain. "So if there's no genoplant and you know he isn't the real Abbot, who is he?"

"You're the fucking detective," says Veguelle. "Why do you think we called you? We don't know."

I stare back at him, using the next few seconds of silence to digest what I've been told, but as Veguelle squints back at me, Sunny, the smallest of our group shrinks even further back into his seat, clutching the edge of the table. His lips wrestle against his tongue for a few moments as he tries to articulate the thoughts of his damaged mind, but as Makeswift rests a hand on his shoulder to calm him, Sunny reaches up and presses his piece of chalk into the table, drawing harder. "Not Abbot," he whimpers. "He not Abbot."

And on the table, he'd chalked two words.

Sunny frowns at me, his eyes pleading as he points at the name he has written.

Keitus Vieta.

# 4

I didn't sleep well that night. I tried to put my restlessness down to unfamiliar surroundings: the background rumble of the planet like an earthquake ready to happen; the bitter star bleeding her crimson rays through the slats in my window; the scuttling of large insects at the end of my bed, or perhaps even the return of the sour-sweet stench of death that first greeted me when I entered the monastery, but it was none of these things.

It wasn't even Brother Makeswift's descriptions of the murders that he told me had taken place each month. A glassy expression of fear filled his eyes as he told me about the mark resembling the Eye of Pandora etched into the skin of each mutilated victim. He told me that everything seemed to change overnight; the Order of the Codex, once known for its atmosphere of tranquillity and well-being, had transformed into a place of dread. Even before the murders, a hideous presence seemed to fill the air of the monastery, thick and heavy like tangible hate, as though some demonic spirit had chosen to squeeze its bulk between the walls.

I am used to the subtle trickery that the human instinct can impress upon the mind. None of those things affect me now. What bothers me more than all of that is the reappearance of Abbot Deepseed. Not because of his mysterious resurrection—that could be explained in a number of ways, all of which I plan to investigate—no, it is the man himself. Something about him is utterly wrong. Wrong like a mute scream of terror, or a living abomination acting out unspeakable but invisible atrocities before my eyes. The Abbot should not be here. But here he is. And what was it Brother Sunny had called him? Keitus Vieta.

That name was the first crumb of evidence my investigative instincts sniffed out, but whilst I quickly discovered what the name meant, it told me nothing. Sunny, though gifted artistically with his hands, had difficulty with speech, and Brother Veguelle was keen to explain to me that when Sunny could not find adequate words to express his thoughts, he would often revert to phrases from long extinct language forms. I could hardly blame Brother Sunny; the Abbot's aura certainly did defy expression. Finding out the meaning behind "Keitus Vieta" was then a simple matter of spending time in the monastery's reference library.

Antiquated in its style by the use of indexed books (anything to avoid technology where possible), but comprehensive none-the-less, my research was soon rewarded after flicking through the waxy pages of an old dictionary of ancient languages. Having refined my search to the native tongue of Sunny's distant descendents on Old Earth—Litsu'an or Lithunarian—I found "Keitus" or "Kitus" to mean "other" and "Vieta" to mean "place".

Other Place. So this younger, resurrected Abbot has come from another place? What does that mean? The question shifted uneasily among my thoughts throughout the night and into the morning (if you could call it morning in a place haunted by perpetual gloom) until I eventually prepared myself for my first full day as a monk.

I had been told I would be given a brief introduction to the potential of the Codex at the breakfast table; nothing too taxing as an initiation, but an exercise I was looking forward to with a mixture of nervous anticipation and greedy awe. For the Codex is the mathematical oracle that every civilized culture has fantasized about since mankind first learned to speak. It holds the key to complete omniscience, but leads each of its pursuers along a never-ending tightrope of revelations suspended over an abyss of insanity.

It was the Codex, or to be specific, the knowledge the Codex brought, that took the peace of aeons and decimated it with universal war and chaos. Even *The Book of Deeds* had no name for that era of history. It took millennia for humanity to recover, but with such terrible power still available, new laws had to be conceived to protect us, and only a select few, specifically disciplined and isolated communities were permitted to study the Codex, the most celebrated of which is this one. To be granted the opportunity to look into the mind of the universe is an honor that cannot be passed up.

"Good morning, Brother Makeswift." I sit opposite my new mentor who is settled at the same table as last night. A selection of exotic fruit, dried cereals and a jug of liquid resembling milk have been placed on the table during the night, and I help myself to a modest breakfast, still marveling at how the monks are able to produce crops of this standard in such a hostile environment.

"Brother Soome, good to see you." He chews thoughtfully on a fleshy fruit that could be an apple. "Did you sleep well?"

"I was comfortable enough."

"Fucking liar!" The exclamation is right in my ear as Brother Veguelle leans in unexpectedly from behind and nonchalantly drops his own plate of fruit next to mine.

"Veguelle!" Makeswift snaps.

The rotund monk raises his hands in mock apology, rolls his eyes, then offers me a huge plump-cheeked grin. "Nobody can sleep for more than ten minutes since the murders started . . . could be you with the Eye of Pandora branded on that fresh young skin of yours next. Who knows?"

"I apologize, Brother Soome, Veguelle can sometimes—"

"It's fine." I turn to Veguelle, study his wide face. He seems to be taking all this too flippantly, as if the murder of his colleagues is a huge cosmic joke. "You seem to be in good spirits, Veguelle. Do you rest easier at night than the others?"

He shrugs, sniffs loudly. "Perhaps."

"Perhaps," I say, leaning forward with a smile of my own, "it's because you think you know who might be responsible for the murders."

"Of course I do."

"Really? Care to share?"

"I've made no secret of that," he says, with a jocular wobble of his chin. "The answer is obvious, dear boy." He eyes Brother Makeswift with an accusing stare. "And I don't know why it isn't equally as obvious to certain other people in this shit hole."

"Not everybody shares your . . . opinion, Brother Veguelle," Makeswift counters sternly.

"Opinion? Is *that* what you call it?" Veguelle coughs. "I tend to refer to it as plain and simple fact." He takes a bite from one of the fruit and munches open-mouthed, while turning his laughing eyes back to me. "But then I suppose that's why you're here, isn't it, dear boy? To be the eyes of Great Mother Pandora? To sort the wheat from the chaff, so-to-speak? To sift the opinions from the facts? Isn't that so?"

"Are you going to tell me who you think it is or not, Veguelle?"

"Forceful, isn't he?" Veguelle beams at Makeswift. "I like him."

"Force isn't my way, brother," I say, tilting my head to make my neck crack, "but if provoked . . ."

"Great winds of Prometheus!" He laughs. "There's no need for that sort of talk, why it's Sunny, dear boy, Sunny! He's your murderer. It's as plain as the troglodyte brow on his cretinous head."

"Because he has a tendency toward violent episodes?"

"Well that's one reason, yes, but—"

"Nonsense, Veguelle," says Makeswift, "these murders are premeditated. Sunny would be mortified if his outbursts ever led him to take a life."

"Mortified," Veguelle chuckles, "now there's an appropriate word."

"Do you have any other reasons to believe it's Sunny?" I ask.

"Well"—Veguelle leans forward, pauses for added drama—"his eyes are too close together for one thing, and—"

"I think we've heard enough, Brother Veguelle. Brother Soome is not here just to investigate the crimes within the Order, he's also here to learn our disciplines."

"I know, I know," says Veguelle leaning back with a smirk and poking at the fruit on his plate. "It's why you wanted me to join you both for breakfast . . . Paper, rock, scissors is it? That the one we're doing for our first-timer? It usually is."

"Paper, rock, scissors, it is," Brother Makeswift confirms. "It's always the first lesson, but more of a demonstration really. If you're willing, Brother Soome, we can begin as soon as you've finished eating."

I nod my acceptance and continue my breakfast while

Veguelle witters on to me with questions about where I'm from and what possessed me to take on such a mundane quest as this one and how it is that none of the other monks take the time to do anything interesting with their lives other than engross themselves in ancient equations. My strongest instinct is to grill Veguelle more about the murders, but Makeswift is right, I'm here to find out how they study the Codex too. It may unearth the motivations of these monks, perhaps even the murderer.

At the end of breakfast, Brother Makeswift signals for someone to clear the table, pinches his finger and thumb together and taps them against his lips while nodding his head, as if inwardly reciting or measuring something.

"Sorry," he says, "just making sure I'm ready. It's not always easy to remember every last detail. The lesson is very brief as I said, just an introduction, and a small taste of what we do here, but it still requires significant preparation for the teacher. Are you ready?"

"Of course." I open my hands. "What do I have to do?"

Veguelle stands. "Want me next to you, Brother Makeswift?"

"Yes please."

Veguelle's grin, which never seems to leave his face, widens a touch as he moves around the table. "I love this. It's going to scramble your head when you try to work it out. Then it's going to blow it right out of your ears, especially when—"

"Thank you, Brother Veguelle, I'm sure Brother Soome will discover the value of it himself without the aid of your colorful embellishments."

Veguelle shrugs, sits down again, and watches me with an excited lick of the lips.

"Now," says Makeswift, "all you have to do is beat Brother Veguelle in a simple game of paper, rock, scissors. But you must beat him twenty rounds in succession. Do you think you can do that?"

Veguelle's eyes widen in amusement. "Think you can take me, Soome?"

I take a long breath through my nose, raise my eyebrows and grin back. "I wouldn't want to hurt your feelings, Veguelle."

"Statistically," says Makeswift, "it's unlikely that you'll beat him more than three times before he beats you."

"Of course."

"Unless . . ." he opens his hands waiting for the obvious response.

"Unless I already know what he's going to choose," I say.

"Correct. If peoples' speculation about the Codex is true then something like that should be no problem. So, let us assume that I am the Codex, an all-seeing oracle with full knowledge of the future, to which you can freely access. You can ask me for the information you need, then say 'Go' when you wish to challenge your opponent. Understand?"

"Yes, but wouldn't I win every time?"

He smiles. "That's the general assumption people make about the Codex, isn't it? If we have the full knowledge of the universe, wouldn't we know the future before it happens? Wouldn't we *win* all the time?"

I smile back at him. "I presume I'm going to learn something about that idea today, aren't I?"

"Precisely. It seems like a pointless exercise, I know, but please give us the benefit of the doubt for now. Ready?"

"Yes."

"Good." He drops his smile in concentration. "Shall we try?"

Veguelle spits on his palms, slaps his hands together, then balls one into a fist holding it out toward me. "Let's go, Soome."

"Veguelle, you know how this works," says Makeswift, "you have to whisper to me what you're going to pick first."

He rolls his eyes, whispers something in Makeswift's ear.

"Brother Soome?" Makeswift looks at me expectantly.

"What did he tell you?" I ask.

Makeswift leans toward me, whispers in my ear. "He said 'Rock'."

I study Veguelle's grinning face then say, "Go."

Veguelle and I bang our fists on the table three times and reveal our choices. Veguelle keeps his fist in place while I open mine to represent paper.

"That's one to you, Soome . . . again."

Veguelle whispers in Makeswift's ear.

"What did he choose?" I ask.

"He chose paper," Makeswift whispers to me.

"Go," I say and with three more thumps to the desk, Veguelle opens his fist while I make a scissors shape.

"Two to you, Soome. All seems easy enough doesn't it?"

"Yes, standard calculation and response technique."

"Exactly, so we're going to make a little addition to the rules. Now you also have to whisper to me what you're going to choose and both of you must agree to say 'Go' before the challenge begins."

I think about that for a moment. "All right."

Veguelle grins as I whisper "scissors" in Makeswift's ear.

"What did he say, brother?" Veguelle asks.

Makeswift leans over and whispers into Veguelle's ear.

"Good then I choose . . ." he whispers his choice.

"He must have chosen rock," I say. "If he knows I said scissors, he *must* have chosen rock."

Makeswift smiles and shrugs. "What will you do? Are you ready?"

"The challenge doesn't begin until I say 'Go', right?"

"Yes."

"Can I change my mind from scissors?"

Makeswift raises his eyebrows. "Do you have free will?"

I narrow my eyes at him and ignore Veguelle's smirk. "I'm choosing something different."

"Very well. Tell me what it is."

Still squinting I whisper "paper" in his ear.

"What did he say?" asks Veguelle. Makeswift leans over, whispers in his ear. Veguelle whispers back.

"And what did Veguelle say?" I ask.

Makeswift smiles again, leans over and whispers, "Scissors. And you?"

I shake my head. "But we're not getting anywhere. Every

time I make a choice or he makes a choice we change our minds."

"So?" says Makeswift.

"So do we have a time limit?"

"The time limit is the strength of your patience."

"Then how can either of us ever win?"

"I can sit here all day," says Veguelle. "All I've got to go back to is a day of washing floors. I *hate* washing floors. Makeswift told me that if I win this, I can pass the chore on to Brother Kayne."

"Well *I* don't have all day; I have an investigation to run."

Veguelle slaps his hands together. "Then I win."

"I think we can stop there," says Makeswift, "Have you learned anything from this, Brother Soome?"

I think for a moment. Aside from an even deeper conviction that Brother Veguelle is a complete ass, but probably not a murderer, the lesson appeared to prove that the study of the Codex is a huge disappointment. Could a mathematical equation, however comprehensive, really be used to predict the future? Are we all still at the mercy of an infinity of possible changes for an infinite quantity of variables?

"I'm not sure what I've learned. That demonstration makes it appear that studying the Codex is a waste of time, and I don't think that's the message you wanted to convey."

"Not exactly, Brother Soome. For Brother Veguelle here, it wasn't a waste of time, do you agree?"

"For him, no, but . . ."

"Yes?"

"Well, it sounds like Veguelle has done this before, he knew—"

"Knew what to expect? But that's the point we're making. It's so much more than just knowing the outcome, it's knowing what you will do with it, and understanding why you seek it. Without all of these, and the tenacity to see them through, you're right, the effort is useless. But you see, Brother Veguelle here knew the outcome *and* he had a purpose in knowing *and* he understood that purpose. Illumination of the Codex is no different. Each of us has a unique way of understanding the Codex; each of us finds a different path based on our individual desires and expectations."

"So is that a convoluted way of telling me that we only see what we want to see from the Codex?"

At that Veguelle clapped his hands loudly. "Oh isn't he just wonderful? I do like him . . . yes, Soome, that's exactly what he's been saying."

"No, no, *not* exactly, brother,' says Makeswift. 'It's true to a certain extent. The future is predetermined and cannot be changed; every future event is dictated and set out in the code for all to see if we choose to look."

"But doesn't our knowledge of the future mean that we change it?" I ask.

"That is the exact concept that has driven so many students of the Codex insane, and so many governments to war. The short answer to that question is no, it doesn't."

"But if I know what I am about to do, can't I change it?"

“Of course you can.”

“So surely that would mean the future is *not* determined.”

“No, that’s the reason I chose the rock, paper, scissors game—to demonstrate that simple truth. Listen carefully, Soome: however far you choose to look, there is always another decision beyond your sight. It’s a principle law of Codex illumination. The very fact that you chose to find out your future was already predetermined. If you deliberately set out to change your future then your only limitation is how far you decide to look.

“You find out that you choose rock and you wish to change it, so you find out you choose paper instead, but knowing that, you decide you must change it again and choose scissors. But now you know about scissors you look beyond that to your next choice and see paper again. Do you see what happens?”

“You could spend your entire life just trying to find out what decisions you’re going to make after the next one, and never actually end up doing anything.”

“Almost, yes. You will end up doing the things you found out about, but you will never ever find out the motivations for the determining decision. But it gets worse than that. Adding an extra person who knows what you’re doing will complicate things further. And imagine if it isn’t just one person but seven hundred billion people?”

I shake my head and laugh. “It’s enough to make your head hurt.”

"Told you," says Veguelle, grinning. "Dear boy, it'll drive you crazy if you look too hard too soon. Perhaps we should introduce you to Brother Ignatius, then the truth will really sink in."

"Brother Ignatius?" I point the question at Makeswift.

"Poor fellow, we haven't been able to help him."

"What happened?"

"His mind fucked up completely," says Veguelle. "He was probably the most studious among us, brilliant in fact, almost as genius as yours truly. Unfortunately, one day he went to his chamber, calculated a new set of algorithms to identify a particular direction he knew his life would take and . . . well, he never recovered—slipped into a waking, muttering coma." Veguelle sucks his top lip and stares wide-eyed into space. "He's in the casualty chambers receiving forced dietary intake these days. We think he'll come out of it one day, but nobody really knows, and nobody wants to find out in case the same thing happens to them. It's rather like a brain virus."

"I understand what you're both saying"—I nod to Makeswift—"but doesn't that re-enforce the point I made earlier? That it makes the whole business of understanding the Codex seem pointless?"

"Not at all," says Makeswift, digging his hand within a fold of his robes as if looking for something. Frustration fills his expression for a few moments and then he stops, his face growing pale with sudden shock, as if remembering something terrible.

"Is something wrong, brother?" I ask.

He closes his eyes, mutters something under his breath as if recalculating something, then shakes his head and smiles quickly. "No. No, nothing at all." And after a sharp intake of breath under the suspicious eye of Veguelle, he produces a small metal box from his robes. "There's more you need to understand, Brother Soome, and today's lesson isn't over yet. Take this and open it."

I lift the lid, eyeing Makeswift briefly before looking at the contents. Inside are three familiar dark cubes of polished wood with bold white dots painted on each of their sides. "Dice!"

"Yes." Makeswift nods. "I wanted to use coins, but . . ." The shadow of his earlier shock passes across his face again for a moment. "They . . . uh . . . seem to have been . . . they seem to have gone missing . . . so we will use dice instead. Throw them for me please. I think you'll find their sum amounts to ten."

I oblige him and watch in amusement as they settle on a one, a four and a five.

"Again?" he says. "This time it will be seventeen, but one of the sixes will be caught before it rolls off the table."

Again I roll the dice and just as he'd predicted, a six and a five show up before me. The remaining die tumbles across the wood, heading toward Veguelle who, with his usual grin, slams his palm on top of it before it rolls into his ample lap. He lifts his hand to reveal a six.

I nod. "So you *can* predict the future."

"Of course we can," blurts Veguelle. "What in the

name of Prometheus do you think we're all doing here if we couldn't?"

"But the paper, rock, scissors test . . ."

"The paper, rock, scissors test shows you what happens when there's a clash of free will, that's all," mutters the fat monk. "It's not just that you can't see beyond your own decisions, the test is a hint at how complex the calculations are. There are thousands more levels of complexity to unravel that most of us can only guess at. If the Codex were that simple to understand, don't you think we'd know for sure who's been murdering everyone here? And if it were that simple, why did the entirety of the Great AI disappear for hundreds of years trying to work the whole fucking thing out, hmm?"

I raise my hands and warn him with a hard stare. "Relax, Veguelle, I'm just trying to—"

"Brother Makeswift! Jon!" Brother Kayne, the doomsayer, rushes into the verbal melee before I'm able to finish. "Come quickly, there's been another murder."

# 5

Blood is spattered liberally over the sandstone walls of the murder victim's room and at first glance, the utter chaos of personal belongings strewn over the floor, drawers and wardrobes open, robes torn and tossed across the bed, it appears as though the murder was not committed without a prolonged fight. The unfortunate body is propped up against the far wall underneath the open window, half-naked with a garden trowel jutting out of his open neck, and I wonder why the murderer did not bother to conceal the weapon. Brother Veguelle, who I assumed had a stronger stomach, rushes back out to surrender his breakfast to the cobbled floor of the passage outside.

But to me, and from the looks on Brother Makeswift's face and the startled monk that had led us to the scene, the real horror present in the room is not the murder: it is Abbot Deepseed creeping slowly around the room, with a serene expression, arms folded inside his robes, examining each item with rapt curiosity.

"Terrible," says Brother Makeswift, breathlessly.

The Abbot stops, turns slowly, looks at each of us in turn, as if he is not quite sure what we are. "Yes, a tragic event."

It takes a few moments for me to control my nerves and begin my investigational routine. "Have you touched anything, Abbot? Is everything exactly as it was when you first entered?"

"Nothing has been touched," he tells us.

"Can you tell me where you have been this morning?"

I can feel Brother Makeswift's eyes turn toward me in alarm, as if placing the Abbot under suspicion is a mortal danger. But I know he must be suspecting the same thing. They all must.

"I was in my study, Brother Soome, meditating," says the Abbot. "And now that I have seen the crime, I shall return . . . to meditate further. Please keep me informed of any conclusions you draw from your investigations concerning this most unpleasant murder of Brother Flavius."

Brother Makeswift and I part in the doorway to allow the Abbot to pass, neither of us wanting to even brush the edge of his robes as he drifts past us.

"What the fuck happened here?" says Veguelle after wiping his pale lips and waiting for the Abbot to walk out of earshot. "This isn't a murder, it's a fucking massacre."

"Please, Fordwyn." Makeswift squeezes his arm. "Let Brother Soome do his work."

"But we need to find that bastard and fast," Veguelle protests. "Sunny's got to be dealt with. I knew he was capable of some serious violence, but all this? It's . . . it's . . ."

"Shut up!" I tell him, stepping carefully into the room. Whether Sunny was responsible or not, the signs of struggle are deceptive. I can often read the signs of bodily stress following a fight, but there are no signs of that here. The finger nails are intact, the soft tissue around the biceps and palms show no signs of bruising. The attack appears to have been sudden, unexpected. I ponder for a few seconds how much I should tell Veguelle and Makeswift. Their reactions to my conclusions might be useful.

"There was no struggle here," I say.

"No struggle?" bawls Veguelle. "Don't you have eyes, man? Just look at it in here! These robes just tore themselves, did they?" He grabs them and shakes them at me. "And these books just leapt off their shelves like suicidal fucking Vegan house rats?"

"Veguelle," Makeswift snaps. "If you can't control yourself, please leave."

Veguelle rolls his eyes and crosses his arms with a trembling huff.

"Thank you, Brother Makeswift," I say, picking up the robes and showing them to Veguelle. "Where's the blood?"

"What?" Veguelle blinks.

"The blood, where is it?"

The frustrated monk's eyes widen, then squint in complete

confusion. "Have you actually *seen* the walls, Soome? Take a look. I don't know if your wondrous powers of deduction have taken command of your mind yet, but we're not in the habit of enjoying blood-ripple as a popular color scheme for our—"

"The robes, you idiot, take a closer look at the robes!" I throw them at him. "Not a drop on them. And look at the rest of this mess, do you see any blood on any of it? It's only on the walls nearest the body."

"Prancing Prometheus! The boy's right!"

"If the disturbances here were part of the struggle, there'd be blood on most of it."

Brother Makeswift nods. "So what do you think happened?"

"This man, Brother Flavius, when was the last time either of you saw him?"

Makeswift presses a hand against his chest. "You don't think that we—?"

"Relax, I just want to know what sort of mood he might have been in the last time you saw him."

"I saw him yesterday evening, just before supper," says Makeswift.

"Me too," says Veguelle. "I don't recall anything unusual."

I squat down beside the body, examine the forehead. "This mark," I say, pointing to a spot burnt into the skin surrounded by another burn in the shape of a ring, "it's been burned into his skin post-mortem. Is this the Eye of Pandora? The same mark that's been etched into the other victims?"

"Yes," says Makeswift.

"What does the symbol mean?"

"It could mean several different things," Makeswift says. "It used to be a sign of wrath or judgement, but it could equally be a seal of protection."

"Hah!" Veguelle says. "Wrath or judgement about what?"

"What makes you think it wasn't for protection?" I ask him.

"Does he look like he's been well protected to you?" Veguelle scoffs.

I ignore Veguelle's sarcasm and turn back to the body. The obvious conclusion from the ransacked condition of the room is that the murderer was desperately trying to find something while the tenant was absent, and unfortunately for Brother Flavius, his unexpected return resulted in a swift and wrathful death. But the obvious conclusion is not always the right one, and there are several interesting details that force me to think of an alternative scenario: the cabinets had been opened with a key rather than forced entry, the finger marks on one of the small drawers suggests that it had been examined multiple times during the search, as if whoever was doing the hunting was convinced the object they were looking for should have been there. But most convincingly, I notice that the pressure marks made by the fingertips on the draw are quite different to those that were holding the murder weapon.

"I believe the victim was trying to find something important before he died. Do you know if Brother Flavius kept anything of specific value that someone else might want?"

"No." Brother Makeswift sighs and shakes his head. "But I was afraid you might ask that question."

"Afraid why?" Veguelle turns to him.

"Something else strange about all the murders. Each of the other victims, before they died, appeared to lose a personal possession. Not usually anything important, but we noticed a pattern after the third victim."

"What? I didn't know about this!" Veguelle says.

"Only myself and Brother Redwater knew. We had hoped that if we kept that detail secret, the murderer might slip up one day and say something."

I smile. "That only works if the rest of the community couldn't possibly know the facts you're hiding from them. That isn't so in this case. Perhaps the symbol would have been a better choice."

"We tried that first, but nothing came of it."

"You tell the fucking gardener, but not me? That's fucking fantastic," shouts Veguelle. "My toothbrush has been missing for three fucking days. Perhaps I'm next."

My smile widens a little as I turn to the fat monk. "Then you'd better hope that I find your murderer before he finds you, eh, Brother Veguelle? Speaking of which, can you find Brother Tennison Redwater for me?"

"You want the gardener too? Why?"

"Because that's a gardening tool in Brother Flavius's neck."

# 6

The day passes after a number of interviews, and following the initial round, I continue the next day privately and unannounced with the same people. It's a technique I've found useful over the years: a second, unscheduled interview will often flush out the guilty party because they think I have discovered some new piece of evidence, and their body language usually tells me a different story to the one they speak. But nobody stands out to me yet.

Fresh from my final interview with Brother Tennison in the early evening, the two of us follow more than two hundred monks—the whole Order—outside the monastery to gather at the outermost section of the gardens to witness the burial of Brother Flavius.

Despite the wind bringing an onslaught of hot, thin air, I find myself relieved. It took me a moment to realize why, but as I take in the air through my nostrils, I remember that there is no stench of death outside the monastery; I had started to grow accustomed to the smell. Above us the face of the goddess Pandora glares down, the light from her single eye soaking the freshly dug soil. And like vast open doors of an ancient death casket, the murky shadows of the tsunami mountains loom over the grounds. The grave has been positioned like all the others in the area, with the headstone facing her gaze. On Old Earth it was said that the graves of the dead were positioned toward the direction of the rising sun so that they would be ready for the messiah when he came to resurrect them. Strange how these monks have rejected that now that resurrection can be a reality for them, yet they still mirror those old beliefs.

Brother Veguelle bustles over to stand at my right.

"Got him yet, Soome?"

"Not yet, but I'm confident I'll find out the truth soon enough."

"The Soomer the better, eh, brother?" he nudges me with a grin and I stare ahead, straight-faced.

There is no sign of the Abbot yet, but as the crowd settles, each of us waits patiently for him, gazing into the open grave at the monk's resting body, losing ourselves in thought. I imagine most of the others are contemplating the loss of their comrade. I, however, am thinking about the interviews so far. I am not much closer to forming a workable hypothesis despite having analyzed most of the evidence and performing a double check on my findings. But not all of my interviews are complete, and in some cases, additional questioning might be beneficial.

I glance at Brother Tennison, the huge gardener standing to my left, the intensity of his thoughts obvious by the v-shaped crease of his brow as he stares at a lost companion. My interviews with him suggested no clear motive. Yes, he is certainly a strong enough man to commit a murder of that kind, and the murder weapon was a gardening tool, but the previous murder weapons were not, and although I can read a guilty secrecy in the man's eyes, I am not convinced it relates directly to any of the murders.

Brother Veguelle maintains his staunch belief that Sunny is the culprit, but although Sunny's reputed tendency for violence makes him a suspect, Brother Makeswift vouches for him, and for the moment, I am inclined to trust his judgement rather than Veguelle's—there are others I would prefer to question again before Sunny. As for Brother Makeswift himself, he is the one who summoned me in the first place. Veguelle could also be a candidate but his fear appears genuine, and I can't help but like the man.

That leaves Brother Simeon Kayne, the doom-sayer. And Abbot Deepseed. Everything points to the Abbot. My intuition and logic tell me that he is more likely to be the murderer than anyone else—the killings only began after his mysterious resurrection (a mystery which, once solved, I fear may add yet further complications to my investigation), he was there at the scene, and there is an atmosphere of evil that broods in his wake like a cloud. For that last reason alone I find myself reluctant to give in to the obvious evidence and confront him. The Abbot is the final authority here at the Order too, so even if I can prove his guilt there is little I can do. Even with all these things considered, I am not content with accepting Deepseed as the murderer; over the years, I have learned never to jump to conclusions in this line of business.

So today, after the burial of Brother Flavius, I plan to continue my investigation by questioning Brother Kayne. And as I have yet to be taught my next lesson in Codex illumination, I will combine the two.

"Good evening, brothers." Abbot Deepseed steps up.

The low light reflects our mood—and the wind, calming to a steady breeze, hot, like the burning of ceremonial coals—disturbs our robes as we watch the Abbot drift slowly around the oblong pit. He holds a small book in each hand. The pages are flapping as the wind ruffles them but the Abbot is not even looking at the words as he quotes from the text.

"At the end of things, he will find the beginning of things. It is the way of things . . . At the end of days, our Brother will be caught up together with the others in the clouds to meet Pandora in the air. And we will be with the Goddess for ever . . . For those that choose this path are blessed among all . . ."

"Is this normal procedure after a death here on Castor's World?" I whisper to Veguelle.

"Only since he came."

"Abbot Deepseed? But he's been here since—"

Veguelle hisses his irritation. "Dear boy, you *know* that isn't Deepseed. He's dead, you saw his body and people don't come back to life here like they do where *you* come from."

Two other monks incline their heads momentarily at the disturbance and Tennison snarls at them before turning to me. "Veguelle's right. It isn't him."

Veguelle nods. "I don't know who that is prancing around Flavius's body over there, but it isn't our fucking Abbot."

"Is it just your little group that think this?"

"No! Can't you feel it?" says Veguelle. "The man just isn't . . . right."

"Before the Abbot changed, death was treated differently," Tennison whispers. "We just buried the bodies with hardly a word of ceremony. But this man . . . whoever he is, it's as though he never knew that.

"After Deepseed supposedly resurrected himself, it wasn't long before Brother Caltus died, and then, from what we're told, Deepseed went looking through the library for books on death. Then, at the burial, he started quoting randomly from *The Book of Deeds* and other holy books nobody has even touched for centuries."

"Of course we were suspicious and baffled"—Veguelle takes over—"but nobody dares challenge him."

Deepseed had now set the books aside and started scattering spices into the pit. "From the soil man came and to the soil man must go . . . at the end of things is the beginning of things. It is the way of things."

Without further address or any interest in his congregation other than a signal to two of the closest monks to begin filling in the grave, the Abbot turns and heads back inside the monastery. The rest of us start filing back inside too.

# 7

Brother Simeon Kayne is old. Perhaps the oldest of the monks in the monastery, but he shows none of the signs of infirmity that I have learned to expect from the inhabitants of Castor's World since my arrival. Ordinarily there is nothing unusual about a youthful demeanor in advanced years: technology has taken human beings to an almost miraculous level of biological security. We rarely die, we cease aging at a time of our choice, and sickness and disease are concepts as old as the age in which this Order was modeled upon. But therein lies the problem; these monks, believing that the comforts of this modern era are a distraction from true enlightenment, are proud of their detachment from technology. So much so that they have withdrawn themselves not just from the negatives of the machine age, but the benefits too. Yet they are not immune from hypocrisy, they are not as detached as they claim to be—the environment outside could not possibly support the crops they need to survive without artificial support; the monks still accept imports and communicate with neighboring star systems when they are in need; they use data-brains to help them in their study of the Codex; but most of all, many of the Order have the blessings of longevity that came with the introduction of optional genomic stabilization.

Brother Kayne however, makes no effort to hide his love of machine assistance, and this is a possible connection to Deepseed's suspicious resurrection. Aside from his good health, Kayne's work with the Codex boasts in proud fanfare of the technological aids he uses. Stepping into his room is like stepping into a sophisticated observation sphere on one of the Consortium moons. It has the same antique furnishings and rustic design as the other chambers, but a few seconds after my entrance, all of it is washed into black oblivion by the intricate projections of subatomic design. I feel I have intruded upon holy ground—a trespasser within realms only ventured upon by gods and angels. And at the center of the void, like some sort of medieval sorcerer, stands Brother Simeon Kayne, his arms festooned with ribbons of roaring fire, tracing circular motions in the air and leaving trails of glowing dust that form the twisting, turning molecular models that build our solid world.

"Brother Soome," he greets me without turning. "You're a little early. I'm just making sure the firmament is ready for your pleasure."

A blast of hot air ruffles his dark beard as molecular patterns chase each other above our heads.

"I can come back if—"

"No." and with a final swoosh of his left arm the molecules vanish to leave darkness in the room. "Everything is ready now."

"It's an impressive study you have here, Brother Kayne. How long did it take to create?"

He turns, smoothes his hair and straightens his robes. "Longer than I would have liked. The Abbot . . . the *real* Abbot, I mean, was strongly resistant to all technology as I'm sure you're aware. It took decades for him to even allow me the pleasure of multi-dimensional projectors."

"So what changed his mind? How did he end up allowing all of this?"

His eyes narrow as if remembering something painful. "Results, Brother Soome, that's all."

"Brother Makeswift said that you may be one of our most accomplished illuminators, is that correct?"

"Only through experience. There are others here—Sunny for example—that are far more naturally gifted than I. And I am somewhat ashamed to say that my particular skill has a certain morbidity about it. Not my fault, you understand. The Abbot . . . while he was still alive, he saw things . . . things that caused him grave concern. Sunny confirmed some of them and the Abbot asked me to focus my own studies on these too. It brought me a rather unfortunate epithet."

"The doom-sayer?"

"Yes."

"And what was it you, the Abbot and Sunny saw that caused such concern? The murders?"

"Yes. I saw many of the atrocities here at the monastery before they happened, though not in precise detail, you understand . . . the predictions were confused . . . contradictory . . ."

"In what way?"

Kayne stares past me into the dark, a frown deepening into a contortion of fear. "I'd rather not . . ."

"I'd rather you would."

The monk's sallow face flashes with anger for a second before melting into resignation. "I know that I must be one of those under suspicion, Brother Soome, but I urge you not to leap to conclusions."

I study him for a moment. I don't have any conclusions yet, only questions, and he has just added more to my list. A few answers would be welcome at this stage. "I need facts before I can draw conclusions, Brother Kayne, and getting facts involves asking questions. I'm sorry to insist but . . . you understand?"

Kayne takes in a deep breath, appearing pained by my persistence. "Would you mind if I began the lesson first? I find the subject . . . difficult to express without finding comfort in my illuminations."

"Will it help answer any of my questions?"

"It will make the answers easier to understand."

"Then please, go ahead."

"Good." Visibly relieved, his narrow shoulders slump a little.

He lifts a single finger, points directly ahead of us. An illusion of distance produces a tiny pinpoint of fire-light far ahead.

"The first spark of existence," he says, not without a tone of drama, "gives birth to all of this." And like a conductor in an orchestra of millions, he sweeps his arms through the air. Unprepared, I take a step back, knocking against an invisible chair as the pinpoint bursts outward into an inferno. Stars explode into life over my head, planets rush into view to my left and right, grassy valleys and snowy mountains rush to greet my feet. People, places, events, disasters, creations, dreams and art churn like individual whirlpools of time all around me until I stand in an exact mirror image of the monastery within its vast crater.

"In ancient days when our primitive ancestors believed in magic," he says, taking a step back to stand beside me, "they used to say that to name a thing is to control a thing, and their beliefs had a certain ironic poetry about them.

"As soon as mankind named all the building blocks of nature and finally understood the immutable laws of the universe, the uncertainty principle wasn't quite so uncertain anymore, and the rest, I am sure you know, is history."

"The Great AI Reductionist Codex."

"Exactly. The image you see around you now is not a recording. It is a simulated image constructed by the data in the Codex."

"But how?"

"Watch, Brother Soome."

He spreads his arms, then claps, and the darkness returns. In the distance, the pinpoint of light returns and with the twitch of a finger it expands, but not as dramatically as before. This time it is a familiar image known through elementary physics lessons: a series of demi-praxons jiggling about each other to form a triad of quarks. He expands it further and I see an electron, then an atom and finally a hydrogen molecule.

"The mathematics is simple enough now," he says. "We can predict the path of each particle and therefore predict which molecules are formed and how they react with each other. The Codex is the pathway of calculation from the very first spark—the Promethean Singularity."

He smiles. "The ancients from Old Earth used to call it 'The Big Bang'."

"Yes, but how are you able to predict the future from the Codex."

"It isn't easy, but classical reductionism shows us that from that first spark and the application of fundamental universal law and the equations within the Codex, we should be able to trace every event all the way until its conclusion . . . obviously we're dealing with an almost infinite quantity of data, so for the human being it's simpler to use a form of pattern recognition . . . do you recognize the pattern before you now?"

"It's a Hydrogen atom."

"And this?" He ripples his fingers and the pattern changes.

"Carbon."

"Yes. And now this?"

The image blurs and changes again, but this time the combination of molecules is so complex I have no clue, and shake my head.

"Perhaps you would understand it better this way . . ." The pattern blurs again before reforming into a familiar image of a human cerebellum.

"Yes, I see it now."

"As I said, it's all a matter of pattern recognition. Over the centuries we have refined our search parameters to hunt through the Codex to find certain patterns of mathematics we have learned to recognize. Individual molecules are easy to see, but tell us almost nothing because they are everywhere. Obviously, finding the pattern of a human brain shows us a human being, but we have refined our science to such a degree that some of us have learned to recognize emotional patterns within a mind, the wave pattern of gamma rays from an exploding neutron star, even a word or sound."

"Amazing."

"Decades of intense study, discipline, and perhaps a little luck, that's all. Of course, each of us have become specialists in different areas of pattern recognition. I have learned to see disaster—there are certain repeated patterns of grief, ecological shockwaves within the patterns, shifts in energies that help me to recognize certain cataclysms. It was my job to seek these out so that people could be warned in advance."

"Can you tell me what the others specialized in? You mentioned Sunny. What does he see in the Codex?"

"Sunny is a remarkable case . . . he—"

"Sunny say! Not Kayne. Not Kayne." The loud voice came from behind us and we both turn. Sunny had entered the room, hunched over, looking up at us both with his bulging, frightened eyes.

"Sunny, what are you doing here?" Kayne relinquishes control over the Codex and the room dissolves back into its original setting of sandy walls and heavy wooden furnishings.

"Sunny came to see Soome. Tell Soome about what he sees."

"And what have you seen, Sunny?" I ask. "Is it the murders?"

"Sunny sees Keitus Vieta."

"The Abbot? The . . . other place?"

Sunny looks up at me with such intensity it seems he is trying to tell me everything in a single expression of desperation. "We must stop him. But cannot stop him. Someone else must stop him."

"Stop whom? The murderer? Keitus Vieta?"

"Keitus Vieta. M . . . must stop him." Sunny moves closer to me, his fingers clasped tightly together, stumbling over his words to get his message across. "He h . . . hurts the Codex."

"Slow down, Sunny. How can the Abbot hurt the Codex?"

"Perhaps you should explain your gift to Brother Soome, Sunny," says Kayne. "It may help him understand."

"Yes, show you." Sunny's eyes widen and he moves to the

door, beckoning us to follow.

I oblige, and followed by Brother Kayne, we move quickly along the passage, around several corners and through a number of heavy doors before reaching Sunny's chamber. It looks much the same as the others but with a magnificent exception: the walls are covered with portraits and canvases, all with beautifully crafted designs. Some are half-finished, some in pastel shades, some in oils, all astonishing.

"They're amazing, Sunny, where did you learn—?"

"This. Look this." He stabs a dirty finger at the painting he is currently working on and then stares at me hopefully. "You find."

I shiver when I see what Sunny has painted. It's a room, probably one somewhere inside the monastery, dark and hard to make out at first, but then I see an arm, a gaping face, a half-rotted leg amongst the gray and red patterns: the room is filled with naked cadavers.

"You want me to find this room?" I ask him.

"I think," says Kayne, "Sunny is saying that you *will* find this room."

I look at them both, cold. Sunny is nodding vigorously.

"You saw this in the Codex?"

Sunny continues to nod.

"Some gift!" I stare at the bodies in his picture and the stench of death infecting the atmosphere of the monastery comes back to me again.

"Sunny hasn't told you what his gift is yet." Kayne turns

to the excited monk. "Sunny, will you explain?"

Sunny screws his face up for a moment, as if frustrated, then ambles over to a collection of discarded drawings stacked in the corner by his bed. He flicks through them, then pulls one out, hands it to me. It's a white background splashed with a series of black dots and lines. I study it for a few moments and at the same moment I'm about to tell them I see nothing there, a recognizable form leaps from the canvas—gothic spires, gargoyles and turrets.

"It's the monastery."

"Yes," says Kayne, "but it took you a moment or two to see it, didn't it?"

"Because of the way it's been drawn, yes."

"Look closer, Brother Soome, and understand why."

It takes me another few seconds, and then I see it—the shape of the monastery is made from the white of the canvas rather than the few black markings Sunny has spread over it.

Kayne smiles. "Sunny does not see the patterns created by the Codex. He sees the subtle negatives; he sees the aberrations: the differences between what the Codex predicts and what we, in reality, are actually seeing and experiencing."

"Keitus Vieta!" says Sunny, and starts rummaging through his sketches again.

I stare at the drawing. "But . . . that means the Codex is wrong."

"A paradox, wouldn't you say? The Codex is never wrong."

"But it must be. If the predictions are different from

what actually happens, it must be wrong."

"Not so. The Codex has replicated history exactly with its data for billions of years. It has never been different, never been inaccurate, which is why its open revelation to the masses caused such terrible chaos. But now we *are* seeing a divergence, and Sunny here started to see it." Kayne raises his chin a little, bolstering himself. "Would you care to guess what else coincided with the divergence and Sunny's gift?"

"Illuminate me." But I already know what he's going to say.

"It all started to happen when things changed in the monastery, specifically, when Abbot Deepseed began to notice the oppression around us, as if we are being . . ." Kayne twirls his hands. "For want of a more accurate description, haunted. Not that any of us believe in specters, you understand.

"Fortunately for us, Sunny's gift enables us to still make predictions—he can see specifics in the Codex and by, shall we say, 'subtracting' what he sees in reality, the remainder is the aberration."

"Keitus Vieta," Sunny repeats, and pulls out another picture. "Very important. Remember." He stabs a knuckle hard into my chest as I take it from him. "You remember," he insists loudly. "The Watcher must remember. Always remember. Save us." This time there is no optical illusion in its design, but the meaning of the picture is still cryptic.

At the center of the canvas is a silhouette—the profile of a man with arms and legs outstretched, surrounded by a bubble. A line, like a spear, has pierced the man's heart, plunged through to the other side of his torso, and then penetrated the wall of the bubble. A glowing, cratered ball—possibly a moon—rests on the tip of the spear outside the bubble, and where the skin of the bubble has been broken, a whirlpool has formed, sucking matter inside.

"This is important?" I ask Sunny.

He's nodding frantically, pointing at the picture. "Keitus Vieta. You. Must. Remember."

I look back at Kayne. "What does he mean? I don't understand."

"Neither do we, but Sunny insists that this picture was specifically drawn for the Watcher."

"And who is the Watcher?"

"We don't know, but Sunny says this part of his prediction is for a far distant future, so none of it means much to us, you understand. Why he is so insistent on showing it to you is yet another mystery."

"Does he think I'm the Watcher?"

"No," says Kayne.

"How do you know?"

"Because he told us the Watcher's name and it isn't yours. Apparently it's someone called Salem Ben."

# 8

It's cold in my room and I lay on my bed, cushioning the back of my head with my palms, watching sand drift in the ruddy afternoon light through the window. I miss the warm sunlight of my home. But not just that, I miss everything. I miss the comforts, the security, my family, and I miss fresh air. The stench of death finds me again, a reminder of the picture that Sunny had painted. He told me I would find that place. But where should I look? And what will I do when I find it? Who are they and how did they get there? I should have these answers by now. But I don't. The thought of that grisly discovery distracts me from rational thought. And what I think should be a simple answer eludes me.

I sit up straight, drawing in, then expelling a decisive breath. What I have to do now is what I have always done when the answers evade me: list the ten main things that are swimming around in my head. And I must not permit myself the luxury of emotional distraction or any conjecture until the list is complete. It has served me well enough in the past.

I pull out a data pad from the shelf next to my bed and begin my list.

One:

*Keitus* Vieta or Abbot Deepseed? Which is he? Whoever he is, the resurrection is bogus, and perhaps this is the crux of the matter. He told the others that he died, then came back to life again in the same body which was miraculously rejuvenated, but he has provided no reason for that (and nobody has the courage to press the matter). Naturally, this new Abbot was under the impression that the real Abbot's body had already been destroyed (as is their custom), but Makeswift showed me the corpse when I arrived. The logical explanation is that the genoplant is still operational, but that does not explain his change in personality; there is no doubt that the others think of him as a different man.

Two:

*Vieta* is most likely not a clone from the genoplant: on my second day here I visited the generators to check Makeswift's assertion that the power to the genoplant had been severed, and though I have limited knowledge of the technology, the lines had definitely been cut, long ago.

Three:

*Is* it a coincidence that the murders began after the Abbot's alleged resurrection? It's when everything changed for them, but even before Deepseed's death, they noted a presence in the monastery.

Four:

*Watching* for signs of secrecy within the Order is important. The murderer has a pattern. Each of the victims loses a personal possession before they are murdered, so the culprit will be hiding these items. As part of his pattern, the murderer also brands his victims with the Eye of Pandora after they have died.

Five:

*You* cannot sense what the senses deny. It's a phrase I heard long ago, but I never understood what it meant until today. A smell of death pervades the entire monastery, yet the monks seem not to notice it. Whether it is denial as the motto suggests I don't know, but wherever the stench is coming from, I feel certain it is the same hellish place that Sunny had captured on canvas. And according to him, I am going to be the one who finds it.

Six:

*Through* years of experience I have developed an instinct for finding the right evidence to solve most mysteries. And it is purely on instinct that I am considering Sunny's other painting now, because it seems to have no relevance to this case at all, yet he insists I must remember it. It depicts a man inside a bubble with a spear running right through him. The spear continues on through the skin of the bubble where it produces a whirlpool, and on the outside, on the tip of the spear, is a moon. Sunny wanted me to see it, yet it was intended for someone called the Watcher.

Seven:

*These* monks have never heard of the Watcher, yet Sunny knows his name to be Salem Ben. But who is that? Does he have a connection to the murders and the Abbot?

Eight:

*Words* spoken in haste can often reveal a person's true intent, but they are not as revealing as the subtle signs made during eye contact. It is of course a misconception that avoiding eye contact during an interview reveals deceit, but it is a misconception of which I believe Brother Tennison Redwater—the gardener—is unaware; he was determined not to look away from me throughout the whole time I interviewed him. It's a sure sign that he was determined to convince me of his honesty. Why? I don't believe he is the murderer, but he knows something, I saw fearful secrets in his eyes. But are those secrets relevant to this case?

Nine:

*Even* if Brother Kayne is not permitted to fully embrace it, he is passionate about technology and not ashamed to challenge the Order's abstinence from it. Kayne is a strong example of the contradictions between the Order's ideology and their practical needs. And this highlights the issue with the gardens. The monks shouldn't be able to grow anything on this planet without technological aid, but evidently they do. I should speak to Tennison about that. Perhaps it will also give me more insight into whatever it is he is hiding.

Ten:

*Now* I come to the evidence I find most disturbing, and least able to grasp or define: aside from the obvious issues with his resurrection and altered personality, there is something fundamentally wrong with the Abbot.

That's my ten, and they persist in my mind for a reason, a reason which is only now becoming clear. The smell of death and Sunny's picture, the original Abbot's rejection of technology and his subsequent action to shut down the genoplant. A theory is forming, one that I sincerely hope is wrong, but I need to see the gardener to make sure.

◊ ◊ ◊

Brother Tennison is where I expected to find him, kneeling down in the garden, tending to his crops. He sees me approaching from the monastery, nods courteously and takes a moment to wipe a gloved hand across his forehead.

"Potatoes?" I ask him as I kneel down to examine the leaves.

"Carrots." He smiles at my ignorance.

"Ah. Good crop?"

He digs his hands into the ground, pulls out one of the orange vegetables and shakes the soil from it before handing it to me.

"This is good?" I ask, shaking my head.

"As good as always. We've never had a failed harvest in eight-hundred years."

"That's quite an achievement . . . almost miraculous, wouldn't you say? Especially considering the conditions on Castor's World."

The smile falls from Tennison's face as he looks back down and pats the soil around another of the carrots. "I'm an experienced gardener."

"Really? Surely even the most experienced gardener has—"

"No. Not me." He's still looking down, patting the soil much harder now.

"Look." I lean forward, try to offer my ultimatum in a reasonable tone. "Whatever it is you're afraid of telling me, I probably know about it already. I'm just giving you the opportunity to come clean to me instead of the Abbot."

Tennison looks up, anxiety drawing lines around his eyes. "The Abbot?"

"Yes."

He bites his lip, pinches his brow then starts nodding—the signs of a man about to concede. "Alright, but the Abbot doesn't need to know about this, Brother Soome. If he's told, he might—"

"I won't tell him. I just need you to confirm my suspicion, that's all . . . there's more to the success of this garden than its gardener, am I right?"

"Yes, Soome," he sighs. "You're right. These crops couldn't possibly survive without carbonisers and hydro-accelerators. Abbot Deepseed, not the impostor, but the real Abbot . . . he saw to it personally that all the machines used by the Order were switched off, but—"

"But being a man with very little knowledge of technology he didn't know how."

Tennison flicks his head back downward as another monk shuffles past them with an armful of vegetables.

"That's right," he says, waiting for the monk to walk back inside the monastery before continuing. "Deepseed thought that cutting the power lines to the under-soil generators would be enough to switch them off, but he didn't realize that the power lines were only a backup system. The technology uses geo-thermal energy to maintain power. I . . ." Tennison looks away.

"Go on."

"I chose not to tell him. I knew that if I told him, he would rebuke me for my lack of faith in Mother Pandora and order me to switch them off. I couldn't allow that to happen . . . so I said nothing."

"I see."

"It was the right thing to do," Tennison insists.

"I don't disagree, but I'm afraid the Abbot's technological ignorance may have done far more damage to the Order than anyone could have realized."

"How?"

"Brother Makeswift told me that the Abbot switched off the genoplant. If he didn't do that correctly then—"

"Great Mother!" Tennison rises from the dirt. "Could it still be operational?"

"Yes, but only partially. You'd better take me to it. I have a terrible feeling I know what we're going to find."

# 9

Tennison and I run through the archway of the monastery only to collide with Brother Kayne in the lobby.

"Brother Soome," he says, catching his breath and grasping my arms. "Come quickly . . . horrible . . . they . . .they're dead."

"Who?" asks Tennison.

"Brothers Veguelle and . . . and Makeswift. Horrible!"

"Where?"

"Sunny's chamber. Follow me."

Chasing Kayne, we run through the monastery watched by startled monks en-route, and eventually arrive, gasping for air at the entrance to another massacre.

This time the blood is not confined to one area of the room, and the display of sheer brutality flaunted in Sunny's bizarre gallery causes the three of us to stare open-mouthed in disbelief. The two victims are lying in a lake of mingled blood and black paint.

Veguelle's broken form is the most disturbing exhibit: the plump monk, no longer suffering from obesity, shows no sign of ever even having a stomach; only the torn entrails smeared with globs of jaundiced fat provide any remaining evidence. His face, battered into pulp on one side—possibly with the repeated use of the broken mallet on the floor—is frozen in its last moments of screaming, one eye spilling open like a split plum over his cheek. His right hand still twitches as the fingers attempt to grip a blood-stained hammer.

I have only seen such savagery once before. I was young, and the images haunted me for months, bringing nightmares and a recurrent nausea that almost stopped me eating. Now, however, I have learned the art of detachment—a way to examine the details and separate them from the emotional trauma. But this time, my skills are tested to the maximum.

Brother Makeswift's body is less desecrated by the violence than the punishment inflicted on Veguelle, but no less gruesome to look at. His body, though still in one piece, is arched across the remains of Veguelle's lower half; the neck has been snapped back, leaving the head facing us in a freakish pose, and the branded Eye of Pandora is staring back at us from his forehead. Smashed canvases, spine-ripped books and splintered tools litter the chamber. The stench of fresh slaughter is finally overpowering the underlying reek of death that has dogged me since my arrival.

"No," is all that Brother Tennison is able to whisper as he sinks to his knees. A moan escapes him when he realizes his robes have soaked up some of the carnage from the tiles, and he shudders into a fit of weeping. Brother Kayne had already seen a glimpse of the chamber before he ran to find help, but the full horror is only now bridging from his eyes to his mind as he blinks and swallows repeatedly. He's either going to pass out or throw up; I know the signs and I have to shake them from their shock before the full effect takes hold.

"Brother Tennison, please go to my chamber and find my backpack. You'll find a DNA coded firearm inside. Bring it back quickly. Understand me?"

The tear-wrecked man looks up at me, bewildered.

"Did you hear me, brother? We need to act fast if we are to capture the murderer before he cleans himself up. And we need to be armed if this is anything to go by." I suddenly regret pointing at Veguelle's remains, but Tennison proves he is made of stern enough stuff to cope. Inhaling loudly, he nods, steals one last terrified glance at the bodies, then makes his way from the chamber.

"Brother Kayne."

He seems to be in a trance.

"Brother Kayne!" I shout, moving between him and the view of the butchery. "Look at me."

He appears startled for a moment then rights himself. "Yes . . . ah . . . yes."

"Did you see who did this?"

"No . . . I heard . . . I heard Sunny screaming and Brother Veguelle shouting. I called to them, and I was about to go to them and intervene. I was in the passage right outside but Brother Makeswift came past. He . . . told me to call the Abbot and then he went in. I . . . I hesitated and . . ."

"Yes?"

"I heard Veguelle accusing Sunny of the murders and Brother Makeswift trying to calm them but then . . . then all I could hear was fighting. The sounds were . . . were awful. I waited too long . . . I . . . I waited too long . . ."

"Please, brother, try to stay calm, take a deep breath. Did you see Sunny leave the chamber?"

"I . . . heard someone leave."

"You heard? Didn't you see?"

"No . . . I was already turning back. I heard someone behind me scuffle out of the room but he was already around the corner before I could see who it was. I . . . I suppose it must have been Sunny. It was only then that I went to look, to see if anyone needed help and . . . oh, Great Mother!" Kayne shakes his head, trembling. "I didn't want to look any closer, and I didn't want to go to the Abbot, so I came looking for you."

"So the Abbot doesn't know?"

"I don't think so."

"And you touched nothing in here?"

"No!"

I glance around the room, begin to see details in the aftermath that corroborate Kayne's story, but he could be lying. Kayne could be the murderer, but for the moment, the facts seem clear: just as Kayne had said, Veguelle did come in to challenge Sunny, even came armed with a hammer. They argued. Makeswift entered, but Veguelle's accusation had already tipped Sunny into a violent episode and the three of them fought. Both Veguelle and Makeswift were unprepared for the extent of Sunny's rage and he killed them. That much seems apparent to me, but there is evidence that someone else had entered the room while Brother Kayne was trying to find me. The remains of a book, a glass of water, a box of painting equipment—all had been moved slightly, leaving sticky traces of smudged blood. Somebody was trying to find something.

"Brother Soome," calls Tennison, jogging back toward us along the passage. "Your firearm. It isn't there."

"Not there? But I checked it this morning. It was—"

"No. I can assure you it isn't," he insists. "But I—"

"Taken." Brother Kayne grips my arm, staring at me with a fierce intensity. "A personal object. Taken."

I stare back at him for a moment, and before Kayne's fear can infect me, I turn back to Tennison. "Do you have anything we can use as a weapon? Anything at all?"

"Here." He nods, pulling a small, black device from his robes. "I was about to tell you. I stopped at the utilities area. We keep an ignition pistol there for incineration purposes. Will that help?"

"It had better," I say, and take it from him. "We're going to see Abbot Deepseed. Or whoever he really is."

# 10

Deepseed's chamber is decorated in the same gothic flavor as the rest of the monastery—antique furnishings dark with wood-stained grain and rose-red trimmings, gold-studded chests and cabinets, and a stout desk fixed at its center. The Abbot is not in his chamber when we arrive, but there is evidence to suggest he has been here recently.

A set of objects is piled neatly at one end of the desk and a chill wriggles between my shoulder blades when I realize what they are and what they represent.

"You expected to find Sunny here? With the Abbot?" asks Kayne.

"That was my first guess, yes," I tell him as I pick up the closest of the objects—my firearm. There is no charge in the power cells and the metal feels strangely cold. Even the colors seem duller than I remember, as if the gun has lost some undefined but integral part of itself.

Six large silver coins are also stacked on the desk.

"Those are Brother Makeswift's," says Tennison, sliding them into his hand. "He uses them . . . used them to demonstrate primary Codex predictions to students. But they're . . . so cold."

I place the gun back on the desk, knowing it to be useless, and having no desire to keep it. "Makeswift told me that he'd lost them. Then later he told me that the murderer likes to take personal belongings from his victims. Do you recognize anything else here?"

"This belonged to Veguelle," says Kayne, picking up a tiny book. It crumbles into flaky shreds as he tries to open it. "Why? What could the Abbot have wanted with these things? What has he done to them? It's as if they have been . . ."

But Kayne cannot find the right words. And neither can I. I shake my head, glancing at each of the stolen items. "We can worry about that later. Right now we have to concentrate on finding the Abbot and Sunny."

"You think they're *both* behind the murders?" Tennison asks.

"I do, yes. I think Veguelle was right about Sunny, but I think Sunny is being manipulated by Deepseed. In fact I feel sure of it, even though I still don't have all the facts."

"Great Mother!" Kayne looks at Tennison. "Could they really be capable of this?"

"The Abbot has never been the same since his resurrection," says Tennison, "and Sunny is unstable. But to think that either of them could be responsible for this is . . . it's incomprehensible. And even if Deepseed is responsible, what can we do? This is the Abbot we're talking about?"

"We have to detain him," I tell them, "then take the Abbot off world to be dealt with by a criminal tribunal."

Kayne shakes his head. "But—"

"Sorry, brother, we don't have time to discuss this now, we need to find them. Think. Where could they be? Are there any chambers that are out-of-bounds, a place where only the Abbot is permitted to go?"

"Well, there's the abandoned genoplant in the cellars, but—"

"The genoplant?" I shoot Tennison a meaningful look. "Tennison and I were just on our way there before you found us, Kayne. That's where we need to go."

"Should we alert any of the brothers?" Tennison asks.

"I'd prefer to confirm my suspicions first. Lock this door and let's go."

The three of us hurry through the monastery, avoiding alarmed questions from puzzled monks on our way, through musty passages seemingly unused for decades, until we arrive at the entrance to the cellars. The reek of death hits me in meaty waves as I stand there gazing into the gloomy passage, grimacing. I pause for a moment to pinch my nose and cough. Kayne and Tennison are ready to descend the stone steps but stop too, to offer each other questioning glances.

"Are you having second thoughts, Brother Soome?" says Kayne.

"Second thoughts?" I say through my hand, "Of course not, but how can you stomach this stench? Weren't you even suspicious? Didn't you think to investigate this place?"

The other two simply shrug and act confused. "Nobody has reason to go to the cellars anymore," says Tennison. "But," he sniffs, "I don't think I can smell what you can smell."

"Wait," says Kayne. "Yes, now that you mention it, I can smell something. It's a little like the odors from the rotting waste in the kitchens."

I nod, suddenly understanding. "The smell has been here so long, you've all grown accustomed to it."

"So what do you—?"

A sound, like the electrical surge of some giant engine, cuts off Kayne's enquiry and reverberates through our feet as the noise gains in pitch and momentum. The three of us peer into the murk, and before any of us are able to ask what it is, the sound ceases.

"The genoplant?" asks Tennison.

"No," I say, moving into the cool, sloping passage. "Genoplants don't sound like that."

"Then what?" Tennison follows me, Kayne close behind.

"I've no idea. But I think we should find out, don't you?"

They don't answer, but they follow nevertheless.

Someone is sobbing. The mournful noise grows louder, echoing around us as we draw closer to a new source of light: faint indigo pulsing gently like breathing as the passage levels out before us. A few steps ahead and the walls diverge into a wider bricked area with a series of cobwebbed archways, each revealing a wooden door. All but one are closed. The end door is only slightly ajar, but there is enough of a gap for the light to seep through and the sobbing to reach us.

"That's Sunny," Kayne whispers. "He's through there."

I nod. "Be careful. The Abbot is probably in there too."

I press my hand against the wood, ready to push it open, but I stop. I almost missed the letters written in blood, smeared like a death knell into the ancient wood, beneath my palm. And in some distant region of my psyche, like the whispering echo of some forgotten life, I feel I should understand.

"HEISNOWHERE".

# 11

Cautiously, I push the door but almost wish I hadn't. There is nothing that could prepare me for the sight inside that room, though Sunny had already tried. The scene is almost identical to the picture he had painted, and although there was no way for Sunny to describe the gut-wrenching odor, the horror was well represented. The old and abandoned genoplant is only half-abandoned. Its design is much like any other with a series of bio-booths lined up ready to construct instantaneous clones from a transmitted DNA signal, but in keeping with its gothic style, the walls are black brick instead of clinical white-metal.

In all other respects, this room is a sight of sheer revulsion. Naked corpses lie in varying degrees of decomposition amongst a carpet of skeletal remains. Many of them identical clones, littering the room as though it is some sort of rejection pit at the bottom of a human laundry chute from a morgue. But not all of them are corpses. Two of them are very much alive: naked clones of Veguelle and Makeswift. Each in different corners, they are huddled, clutching at their knees and moaning, but even from here I can see there is nothing behind their eyes. These are mindless lumps of flesh, spewed from the genoplant booths and left until they eventually die, probably from dehydration. And at the center of it all is Sunny, on his knees and weeping. He doesn't see us yet.

Stairs and narrow corridors, throbbing with indigo light from something unseen, lead down behind the booths to other functional areas. I cannot yet bring myself to step between the corpses, or even know what to do with the three suffering men.

"What . . . is this?" breathes Kayne.

I shake my head, unable to stop myself glancing from corpse to corpse, unable to process the magnitude of the original Abbot's horrific mistake.

Tennison steps forward, his face grim as he stares around him. "I should have realized. Should have checked."

"What is this, brother?" Kayne repeats in a desolate tone.

"You remember all those years ago when the Abbot told us he had made our greatest sacrifice to Pandora? Remember he told us he had switched it off and that we would all eventually die like the patriarchs of old?"

"I remember, but . . ."

"I should have checked," says Tennison, his eyes filling and his voice breaking as he nods to a panel above the booths. "He didn't do it properly. He cut the power lines, or so he thought. But he only cut the sections that download the mind . . . the cloning section has always been active . . . so many brothers . . ."

"So every time somebody dies," I finish his explanation, "an emergency signal is received here to clone a new body ready to receive the person's mind, but that's the part Abbot Deepseed switched off."

Sunny, roused from his lament, looks at each of us in turn with tortured eyes, then settles on me. "I told you. You find."

"What are you doing here, Sunny?" asks Tennison.

"You go! You go!" Sunny tries to wave us away. "Keitus is—"

"Brothers!" the greeting comes from the Abbot as he appears from the indigo-lit passage near the booths. Kayne steps forward, grimacing as his heel crunches on a skeletal hand. "Abbot Deepseed, please forgive our—"

"Who are you?" I cut in. "You're not the real Abbot Deepseed. I saw his body and he died of natural causes weeks ago."

With no discernable steps, the Abbot moves down the stairs like a snake easing itself from the branch of a tree. A secretive smile forms slowly on his lips, but he gives me no answer except for the elation in his eyes. I press my question further.

"When the Abbot died his body must have been cloned here like all these others. But the genoplant couldn't download Deepseed's mind into the new body, so who took his place? Who or what are you?"

"Keitus Vieta! Keitus Vieta!" Sunny weeps.

The Abbot continues to move until he reaches Sunny. He strokes the top of the monk's head with a scrawny finger. "I like this one. Faithful servant."

"Answer my question."

The intensity deepens in the Abbot's eyes, as if he had just thought up a perfect answer. "My name is legion, for we are many."

"Legion?"

"A phrase I found in one of the oldest books in the Abbot's study," he says. "I thought it to be appropriate, just as Sunny feels it appropriate to refer to me as 'Other Place', though neither of those titles can genuinely describe who I am. And the truth is, Brother Soome, I am not sure if a description is even possible . . ." Then the smile falters, giving way to menace. "Or necessary."

"Did you coerce Sunny to commit murder?"

"Not at all. Sunny believes he has protected them from me."

"The Eye of Pandora," says Kayne. "Oh, Sunny! You killed them and placed the seal on them hoping that Pandora would save their souls from the Abbot?"

"Yes, yes!" sobs Sunny. "Keitus takes things from them. Steals their souls. But Sunny sent their souls to Pandora before Keitus could take them."

"But why didn't you tell us?"

"Sunny not allowed." He stares up at the Abbot, his bulging eyes glistening with fearful tears. "But Sunny try.

Sunny paint pictures."

"Poor Sunny," the Abbot says, gliding toward me now, the sound of human meat squelching under his feet as he moves. "Raised within the confines of this monastery—he has no concept of real science. But his superstitious belief does have its advantages."

I take a step back, pull the ignition pistol from my robes and aim it at the Abbot. "I don't know who you really are or why you're doing this, but what you and Sunny have done in this monastery is . . ." I glance again at the skulls and pulp around us, fighting a fresh wave of nausea. I have to push that aside, see all this as evidence instead of horror if I am to keep my head. "Both of you will have to come back with me to—"

"No," says the Abbot simply, and stops to watch me with apparent interest and the slightest of smiles. "Why do you believe your justice has any relevance to me, Brother Soome? I don't even belong here."

"But you *are* here." says Kayne. "What is this . . . other place you came from that you think you are exempt from judgement?"

"Brother Kayne," the name spills from his tongue like vomit. "A man, like so many others here, who prides himself in absolutes, who celebrates the perfection of reductionist principles. None of those ideals will help answer your question, or help you understand where I came from." He motions to a skull by Kayne's feet. "Can this bone explain to its maker where it came from? Can a ring on the finger tell you where it begins and where it ends? Could your crude books illuminate the glory of heaven or the shame of hell?"

The Abbot observes us with increasing contempt. "You cannot imagine what it was like to be snatched up and spat onto this ugly world. I found this body, feeling these . . . emotions, assaulted by new senses, suffocated by the stench of these bodies in the dark only to break my fists against the doors of this tomb until Sunny came to release me.

"So ask no more questions, Brother Soome. I have no concern for humanity's obsession with rules and justice, and I have no more wish to stay in this place of . . . of atoms and thought than you would wish to stay in a world filled only with bacteria. So, brothers, if it takes a hundred cycles of your universe, I will drain whatever I need from whomever I choose and go back to where I came from leaving nothing but void in my wake."

Sunny's low moaning and the eerie shuffling of the mindless men in the corners are the only sounds as we face the Abbot. Kayne is trembling. Tennison is rigid. Hardly breathing.

Creeping terror works its way up my spine, but in defiance, I hold the pistol steady and look directly into Vieta's eyes which are now fixed intently upon mine. "Brother Kayne," I say, trying to maintain an air of calm control. "Our first priority is to put an end to all of this. Can you repair the power lines? We can at least make sure that if anyone else dies they don't stay that way."

"I can." Kayne treads nervously between bodies toward the panel and examines the circuitry. "I think the Abbot . . . Keitus, has re-routed the channels . . ." He peers around the passage behind the booths. The pulsing indigo light washes over his face. "The power lines are heading into . . . Great Mother! What *is* that?"

"What? What have you seen, Kayne? What is it?" Tennison asks.

"Watch him," I bark at Tennison, handing him the pistol before going to investigate.

"You won't understand," the Abbot says. But I make my way behind the booths and into another area, even larger than the first. The room is equally crowded with the dead, their anguished forms strewn over pipes and consoles, their faces contorted in the agonies of slow death. But in the center is a horror far worse: a writhing human embryo, but twice the size of a full-grown man, fermenting amongst the bloody filth. Its entire body is punctured with tubes and wires leading from the first room, and angry blue sparks crawl like agitated maggots over the infant's boiling skin. Sensing that someone has seen it, the abomination struggles into a ball and a semi-formed, lidless eye turns to observe me from behind translucent fingers. The toothless mouth gapes open to reveal rungs of saliva and a quivering tongue, lolling to one side as it tries to form words but manages only a strangled rasp.

I too am speechless, immobilized by revulsion, but behind me Kayne has been working furiously. "It's a host,

Soome. Keitus has been channeling the brain patterns of our lost brothers into that thing."

"Don't move!" shouts Tennison from the other room and I rush back to see what Vieta is doing. Tennison's aim is steady, and his eyes are fixed with stony conviction on Vieta, but I know how to read the subtle positioning of his body under the robes: he is terrified. Vieta is approaching Kayne who is rapidly stripping and fixing wires. "I'm almost done."

"I'll take the gun," I tell Tennison, offering my hand, but he isn't listening. His fingers slick with sweat, work around the trigger of the pistol as he follows his target.

Vieta is still moving.

"I'll shoot!" Tennison shouts as Sunny crawls forward to grab the edge of his robes. "I mean it!" Tennison kicks Sunny aside. "You'll die, Abbot!"

"I'm do—," but before Kayne is able to make the final connection, Vieta flicks a finger as if cutting a fragile cord with his nail. Kayne jerks awkwardly like a puppet wrenched on its strings, then drops to meet the rest of the bodies. A moment of stunned inaction grips the rest of us before a series of events unfold so quickly I hardly know where to look: the fetal creature in the other room roars in frustration, a cloned and vacant Kayne slips fresh from the far booth, Tennison fires his pistol at Vieta and a bolt of searing fire erupts through the side of Vieta's head splashing the contents in molten lumps across the wall.

With a cry of utter horror, Sunny screams forward to

wrestle the pistol from Tennison's hands and the two of them fall amongst the corpses, fighting for control. Amidst the confusion I spin around to see Vieta's headless body shudder, and for several seconds I stare in dumbfounded awe as hair, blood and bone begin to congeal to form a new head. From another booth, the naked form of Abbot Deepseed struggles out only to collapse amongst the human debris, equally as vacant as the newborn Kayne, and I stand, too terrified and bewildered to know what to do next.

"Go for help!" cries Tennison. "Lock . . . the door behind you."

But before I can reply, a shot rings out from the pistol and a fiery projectile tears upward like a small comet between the two struggling men, melting the tip of Sunny's chin and part of his right cheek, and ripping a bloody hole through Tennison's shoulder. The charcoal stink of burnt flesh mingles briefly with that of the decaying bodies as wisps of smoke mushroom up to the ceiling. Sunny, half convulsing, half shuffling, gives up on Tennison's motionless form and begins his pursuit of Vieta with moans of mixed apology and cursing. And Vieta, now completely healed, has the look of a man waking from stasis, trying to remember where he is and why. If I am to do anything, it has to be now while Vieta is still confused.

"Go . . . for . . . help," croaks Tennison, clinging desperately to the last few moments of his life.

"No!" I say, stumbling over Kayne's body to study the

wires and circuits. "Tell me how to finish what Kayne was doing and you'll download straight into a new body."

"No time."

"There is. Kayne was almost done. Tell me!"

"Red fibers . . . to red . . . terminals . . . easy," he coughs.

But from the corner of my eye I see Vieta's head turn to look at me. Tennison was right, I'm out of time. Instinctively, I raise my hands in surrender just as Vieta is lifting a threatening finger. Any moment now my life will be snuffed out. I stand before an eternity of non-existence and all I needed was a few more seconds to repair the genoplant's circuitry. But perhaps Sunny will buy me the seconds I need. The distraught monk, still trying to master his own wounds and mind, grasps Vieta's robes, yanks him back and roars into the man's ear.

"Sunny not want to go to that place! Save Sunny!"

Does he mean the fetal thing in the other room? Yes! He's afraid of dying and ending up inside that thing's mind like all the other dead monks.

"You don't have to, Sunny," I shout above his screams. "We stopped it. Help me repair it."

But Vieta is already back on his feet, pushing Sunny aside. The temporary distraction is probably my last chance, but this time I change my strategy knowing that securing my resurrection is not enough. With a desperate lunge I dive for the discarded ignition pistol and fire off two shots at Vieta. The first explodes behind his head but the second is a perfect hit and Keitus Vieta is a fireball thrust back against the wall. But Sunny, caught in the backwash, flames lapping across his robes, is alight in an angry glow as he leaps aside screaming feverishly. I run into the next room where Vieta's abomination is still writhing amongst filth and fibers. The lidless eyes watch me with cold comprehension as I aim the pistol at its head.

It takes less than a second. The indigo pulse becomes a shimmering blur of red heat as the creature's fluids burst aflame through its skin. I reel back from the heat, hoping that I still have time to fix the genoplant before it's too late. In the other room Tennison is gazing upward, his face bereft of pain or emotion, but his shallow breathing tells me he is still alive. Sunny is a blackened husk propped up against the far wall, flames still dancing over his charred robes, but also not dead; his cloned replicant has not yet emerged from any of the booths.

But Vieta is very much alive. A morbid curiosity makes me watch him, surrounded as he is by bodies, two of them his identical but soulless twins spawned by the booths. Vieta looks up at me. His expression is almost unreadable, but I am certain I can see grief or perhaps misery there at the loss of the fetus. His eyes drop again and he looks at Sunny, then from corpse to corpse as if trying to understand this new sense of loss he is experiencing.

Snapping myself from the distraction, I turn back to the genoplant circuitry and take a few seconds to connect the fibers. A crackle and thrum of power tells me I've been successful. Sunny and Tennison can at least be saved, and I'm secure too.

"Won't . . . work . . . won't . . . stop him." The whispered words come from Sunny's cracked mouth. "Only . . . he . . . can save everything . . . only Salem Ben. He . . . must . . . remember . . . must remember . . . Prometheus . . . Cataclysm . . . Wade." Surely the last incomprehensible thoughts of a dying man.

But hopefully the genoplant will repair him now it's fully functional again. Once he's reborn all this will be behind him. But what about Keitus Vieta? He won't die, and we don't even know how powerful he really is or where he came from. But if I have delayed his plans, so can others, now that we know about him.

"Whoever you are, and whatever you were doing, we've stopped it," I tell Vieta.

He looks up at me, his expression shifting from grief to hatred. "No, Soome. I'll just have to begin again."

"Then we'll stop you again." And I raise the pistol.

He glances at the repaired circuitry, then at Sunny and a cold smile twists his lips as if he is deciding something. "No. Not you, Soome. But I am curious about him and what he knows. Sunny understands the future. You do not."

And with that, Vieta lifts his finger and both he and Sunny slump forward, lifeless. At the same time there is the crackle of failing circuits behind me. Either the repair has failed or Vieta did something to it in his final vengeful moment.

For a few seconds I stare, dumbfounded, then two booths surge into life. From one, the body of Abbot Deepseed falls out, looking as vacant as the previous two, but from the other booth Sunny steps out, younger than before, fresh, but still with the stoop. His bulging eyes are far from empty and in his face there is a malevolence that seems out of place for Sunny. But not for the fake Abbot. And with sickening revelation dawning I realize: Keitus Vieta has chosen a new host, a host that has far greater skill with the Codex than anyone else. And now he is looking at me again, lifting that finger.

A distant scream—most likely my own—the involuntary sound of my body's protest as my mind falls into a waiting chasm. Feeling is gone. Tactile senses are dulled to numb obscurity and all that's left now is the sensation of falling forward into blackness at nerve-stripping speed. Dimly, I am aware of what will come next. Every civilization had a name for it. Apollo's chariot, Walkabout, The Tunnel of Light, The Quantum UberGod Purge.

A blinding explosion of imagined suns floods my synapses at the last second, the magnitude of the experience matched only by an all-consuming silence. It's the pinprick glimmer that stretches into the cold-white nova, devouring me, promising the afterlife, but delivering only disappointment. I know this moment as the neural flush, the system-controlled transition from dreamed life back to lonely reality.

# SALEM BEN
# 12

A sheen of sweat covers my tingling skin. There is pain and confusion and I can still feel the thunderclap of my heart in spasm.

*Where am I?*

I'm resurrected, but Vieta is nowhere to be seen and this isn't the genoplant. The smell has gone too. A trick? Or perhaps someone activated a genoplant in a nearby star system. But that isn't likely and this doesn't make any sense.

I died.

Vieta did something to the genoplant circuits, so surely my mind was lost and my body is still floundering around in the basement of the monastery. So where the hell am I now?

It's a W.O.O.M. Somehow I know that. And it's opening.

Emerald light invades the darkness, teasing me with vague nostalgia of a different life.

"Did you find what you were looking for?"

I freeze. I know that voice.

"Salem? Did you find what you were looking for?"

"Who are you?"

"Well, last time I was the mother of God, and before that I was a Goddess. You tell me."

Focus. I need to think. "Qod?"

"Very good! Almost record time, Salem."

"Salem? Who's . . . Sunny told me that Salem . . ."

"Sunny? Who's Sunny? Wait, let me check."

"Sunny told me that Salem had to remember."

"Ah, yes. Found him. His real name is Amen Brackshard, one of the monks in the Order of the Codex. He's in the Aberration Sphere too."

"Yes, I'm sure he is. He was one of the first people ever to have met Keitus Vieta . . . Can you get me out of here, Qod?"

"You're not ready yet."

"I know who I am, Qod. I'm Salem Ben. I still feel like Plantagenet Soome, but I really do know who I am. You have to let me out. Vieta knows about me. We have to—"

"Slow down, Salem. You're perfectly safe."

"Safe? Sunny mentioned my name in that life I just visited and now Vieta knows about me too."

"Relax, Salem. I told you, you're safe."

"How can you—?"

"Don't you remember how long ago Soome was alive?"

I think for a moment. "He was around not long before the first collapse of the universe."

"So . . . try to remember where we are now, Salem."

"Yes, yes, we're at the birth of the fourth cycle of the universe, I know."

"Right, so even if this Keitus Vieta is real—and I still see no evidence of his existence at all—he couldn't possibly have survived the collapse of the universe once, let alone three times."

"So I'm just suffering from the after effects of Soome's life and panicking for no good reason?"

"That would be a logical assumption, yes. And that's why the W.O.O.M. and I are keeping you restrained for now. For your own good."

Ahead, beyond the open lips of the exit is the subtle hue of the Aberration Sphere. Millions of souls all afflicted with Keitus Vieta. Perhaps my perception is skewed by Soome's life and Vieta is no longer a threat, but I clearly remember Sunny's insistence that Salem Ben should remember something. Something he showed me when I entered his room for the first time—the time he showed me his paintings. One in particular.

It was a beautiful painting. The silhouette of a man in a bubble, a spear piercing both his heart and the bubble. A moon at the spear's tip. And where the spear had pierced the bubble, a whirlpool had formed, sucking matter inside.

Why did Sunny want me to remember that? It means nothing to me. Qod must be right. This is all just part of Soome's life experience and my waking thoughts have somehow warped the details to include my own name. Or perhaps there is a fault with how the data is overlayed onto my brain, mixing the real me with the people of the past. But that has never happened before.

The slippery sensation of fibers sliding out of my head distracts me, and a few moments later the shackles release me.

"Observation Sphere, Salem?"

"Yes. I need to get out of here."

"You sound disturbed."

"I am. The more I find out about Keitus Vieta, the more he unsettles me."

The metallic tendrils lower me to the gangway that leads to the exit of the sphere and I welcome the pure, white light of the corridor ahead of me, as if it is washing me clean of the blood and horror Soome had died in.

"You still think Keitus Vieta is a threat?" Qod asks. "I've already told you I can find no record of him in the Consortium files and surely if he wanted to harm you, or even pay you a visit, he's taking a long while to go about it. Three cycles of the universe is quite a span of time, don't you think?"

"Hmmm." Her reasoning seems right, but the urgency of Soome's experience and even the memories of Orson Roth and Dominique Mancini still give me cause for concern.

"Anyway, Salem, you didn't answer my question from earlier," Qod says as I make my way along the corridor toward the Observation Sphere.

"Did I find what I was looking for?"

"Yes," she asks.

"What do you think?"

"Hey! Leave the sarcasm for me, would you?"

"Sorry, Qod," I smile. "But you know the answer is always 'no'. And besides, my priorities have changed. Death doesn't seem quite so important as finding out who Keitus Vieta is or where he came from."

# 13

Several days pass before either of us speak again, and I sit the entire time watching the universe busy itself with the work of creation, but not seeing. I had overcome my fear of Vieta after living the life of Soome, but not satisfied my appetite for answers. Who was Keitus Vieta? Why did Qod know nothing about him? Why was he . . . wrong?

"You said that the aberrations appeared during the third cycle of the universe," I say eventually. "And you found them when you started to check through the data just before this cycle?"

"Strictly speaking, the aberrations began toward the end of the first cycle, after the Soul Consortium broke free from the universe," Qod replies, as if we had only been talking about it a few moments ago, "but I didn't detect them until the end of the third cycle."

"So if Keitus Vieta first appeared in Soome's life, his appearances in the lives of Orson Roth and Dominique

Mancini must have happened in a later cycle. He must have survived the collapse of the universe somehow."

"Unlikely."

"Yes, but Keitus Vieta isn't . . . right, is he? He's different. Supernatural, paranormal, alien. He's using science and technology in ways we've never conceived."

"Salem, mankind reached the limits of scientific understanding millions of years ago. There *is* nothing else to understand. Don't fall back on paranormal explanations simply because we haven't identified the cause."

I sigh deeply and stare out into the inky depths. Perhaps Qod is right. And perhaps I'm entertaining these thoughts because I allowed fear to get the better of me. But I'm past that now.

"Perhaps I've been thinking too hard about this, Qod. Surely, if Keitus Vieta isn't supernatural and he doesn't have a file or an empty slot waiting for him, the aberrations *must* be the result of data corruption in the files. You yourself said you can't find any evidence that he exists other than the anomalies you've been finding in the files."

"I already told you there was no corruption, Salem."

"But there *has* been a change in people's lives."

"Yes."

"But the laws of physics haven't changed, Qod. Lives should be the same in every cycle of the universe. There's an equilibrium, a balance that keeps the configuration of matter and energy the same each and every time. So if it isn't data corruption, something must have *invaded* the data. A rogue AI perhaps?"

"No, Salem. Like you, I am the last of my kind. Nothing has tampered with the data, I'd know about it. It is accurate."

"Then how can there be aberrations? Where did Vieta come from? What *is* he?"

Silence for a few moments.

"There is no record of Keitus Vieta in the Consortium files."

"So you keep telling me . . . but he is *in* there. Every time you find him, you label him as an aberration and move the file . . . Look, perhaps I need to understand how these . . . files actually work. I know the founders of the Soul Consortium created all of this, everyone knows the history, but the real scientists behind it all were kept secret. I need to be one of them, live one of their lives. Perhaps then I'll be able to understand what happened to create these aberrations."

"I did wonder when you'd get around to asking that question. You've been living within these walls and using the W.O.O.M. for trillions of years, incognizant of its real origins."

"I've never needed to know until now, and you've never suggested it."

She goes silent again, as if thinking carefully before she answers. For Qod, a moment is a very long time.

"That's because the founders of the Soul Consortium are in the classified section, Salem, specifically, the Restricted Sphere."

"There's only you and me here, Qod. Restrictions aren't

exactly necessary any more. Who am I going to tell?"

"Not all of the restrictions are in place for security reasons. Some of them are too dangerous; they'd been known to lead to insanity and suicide in the early days."

"So is that the case with the creators of the W.O.O.M?"

"Actually, Salem, only one person created the W.O.O.M. and that same person is mostly responsible for the design of this entire facility."

I digest that for a moment, roll the thought around and consider what sort of intellect could be responsible. "Just one person invented all of this? This . . . whole place? I can hardly believe it."

"Yes. Of course the creator had help, but the science—all of it was from one mind."

"Someone with that kind of intellect would be well known."

"The creator's identity was kept secret to later generations. Indeed, all the founders of the Consortium were placed in the Restricted Sphere for security purposes. Access to the creator's life would mean knowledge of how to manipulate the data files. It was deemed that that kind of knowledge would be a significant threat to the safety of the Soul Consortium and anyone using the W.O.O.M. So to protect the identity of one, all the founders were secured."

"I can see why, but that really doesn't matter now, does it?"

Again she pauses. "No," she admits.

"Then who was it? There were four million founders.

Which one created all this?"

"The answer may shock you, Salem."

I pause for thought. "If you're going to tell me that Keitus Vieta—"

"Of course not. I've already told you he doesn't have a file."

"Then why would the creator's identity shock me? Tell me who it is."

"Very well. It was subject 9.81713E+44, Oluvia Wade."

My blood freezes. "Oluvia . . . Wade?"

"I warned you, didn't I? But do you ever listen?"

"Oluvia Wade." I say the name again. "Oluvia Wade."

"Still interested in living her life, Salem? All five trillion years of it?"

I think about that for several minutes before answering. Perhaps I should have known it was her. Perhaps there is a good reason why I don't recall her part in the creation of the Soul Consortium. The thought of living her life fills me with a terrible and sudden sadness. Her life was as tragic as it was magnificent, her reputation so exulted that she had even secured a place in *The Book of Deeds*. Though her name was never mentioned there, her titles were well known.

"Oluvia Wade," I whisper.

"Yes, yes, Oluvia Wade, President of the Seventh Golden Reign, Butcher of the Terran Galaxy, The All-See, The Queen of Death. I take it you're reconsidering?"

"Yes. There are some memories I prefer to keep in quarantine."

"I thought so."

"Just get on with it. Quickly."

"What?"

"Just do it. Before I change my mind. I have to do this if I want my answers."

"Salem—"

"Just *do* it." She knows I mean it. "But can you . . . split the life up? Five trillion years is too long. What if Keitus . . ."

"We discussed this. Keitus Vieta—if he even really exists—has been sitting on his hands for several cycles of the universe. You're safe, Salem. And even if he is a threat, I'm Qod! Don't you think I'd be able to stop him?"

"Okay, but we'd also discussed the rules and how they aren't relevant anymore. I'm not interested in her full life experience, especially for someone who's been alive for trillions of years. What's important is getting hold of the information I need, so will you do it?"

"It's not that simple, Salem."

"Why?"

"Well, which parts of her life do you want me to cut out?"

"I only want to see the parts relevant to the invention of the W.O.O.M."

"You know I can't access the files in that way. I can only see summaries and I don't know at what stage of their life these things happen."

"But there must be spikes in the data, patterns, timings, something recognizable for you to make a best guess. I thought you were supposed to be omniscient?"

"Almost omniscient. And yes, there are patterns, but I can't see exactly what they are."

"Can't or won't?"

She pauses again. "Won't."

"Because of the rules?"

Another pause. "Oluvia Wade is . . . different. I—"

"Can you do this or not?"

"I'll have to change some protocols but . . . yes."

"Then do it."

# 14

There is a deliberate atmosphere of hostility when I enter the Restricted Sphere: stale air hits me like a wall of hot breath and the deep hum of unbaffled machinery—like the growl of a sleeping behemoth—is loud enough to make me wince as I walk forward. Whether it was designed that way as a deliberate deterrent, or if this is Qod's recent addition to dissuade me, I don't know, but the glaring red of the Sphere, indicating its classified nature is already enough to convince me of its danger. A danger to my sanity. A danger I am choosing to ignore. But more than that, the deep red reminds me of Castor's World and the brooding Pandora watching from above.

*Subject 9.81713E+44: Select*

*Subject 9.81713E+44: Security authorization Alpha required*

*Subject 9.81713E+44: Security override processing*

*Subject 9.81713E+44: Override authorized*

*Subject 9.81713E+44: Activate. Immersion commences in 3 minutes.*

The silence preceding the lecture is longer than usual, and when she delivers it, her tone sounds final somehow.

"Protocol compels me to warn you that once you have been immersed you will not be able to withdraw until the moment of . . . Oluvia Wade's death. Protocol also compels me to dictate that whatever you experience, however terrible, you must endure all of it without possibility of extraction. You will know each and every moment as if it were your own, and until the process is concluded, you will have no suspicion at all that you are not that person. Any lasting memory of trauma following the event will be your responsibility.

"Farewell, Salem."

# QUEEN OLUVIA WADE

*O lover, to hold you to my breast.*
*To know and live your soul.*
*Think not of rest, nor godly wonders manifest.*

*Think only of me.*
*O lover, hold me to your breast.*

# 1

My life may end soon, and if anyone still survives on this side of the universe after Project Prometheus is executed, my name will only be remembered in words of malice. It is a sobering thought. One that sends me into a spiral of introspection—analyzing motives, questioning decisions, examining the past, fearing the future.

From here, standing on the highest point of the central sphere, I have an astounding view of my secret world, and though I stand here often, I rarely stop to appreciate its magnificence; moments of rare contemplation like this have a way of focusing one upon details that have become background noise.

The Consortium started as an insignificant moon orbiting an ordinary planet, but it has grown into a sprawling behemoth of information that—in its vast hunger for resources—has consumed and converted more than eighty percent of its mass. But I make it sound like a monster, and it isn't. It's beautiful: the surface is a sea of vibrant grassland from which twisting spires rise up and pierce the stratosphere like giant vines. And floating around them, backlit by the wispy remnants of an ancient nova, are shimmering spheres refracting the full spectrum of light. Some no larger than a man, others the size of small moons are all networked together by fluid conduits, each of which are revolving around each other at different speeds like cogs in an impossible engine.

It still reminds me of a molecular model toy I used to play with as a little girl, and perhaps that childhood fondness helped to shape my vision over the years until it became this miraculous place. Except that toy couldn't hop from galaxy to galaxy in the time it takes to take a breath, and it couldn't store all the combined knowledge of the mapped universe; the Consortium does.

Before me is an imaging sphere focused on the very core of the universe: Destination Zero. But it is not only the core of the universe, it is the focal point for all my concerns of late. Through the transparent walls of the imaging sphere, the untamed wrath of the Promethean Singularity flaunts itself as the perfect metaphor for my mind. Such power, enormous danger: a pulsating tempest of energy, no bigger than a white-dwarf star, surrounded by concentric shells of light and violent cyclones that grow wilder the farther they stray from its center.

Erastus Airos-Tazaria, my great, great grandchild and

personal aide, stands behind me, blandly watching the stormy phenomena over my shoulder as he prepares my hair for another day in the arena of political debate. I must look my best when I lie to my subjects.

Like my surroundings, I have paid little attention to Erastus in recent years. Though he is a close relative, he is nothing like me of course, not even in appearance. He, draped in charcoal robes shadowing his sagging features, his cool eyes buried beneath gray skin. I, with perfect facial symmetry and the bronzed body of Nubian youth, swaddled within the pleats of royal-white robes. It amuses me that Erastus—like anyone else—can choose any appearance, yet he settles for the mundane.

"Why did you come here, Oluvia," he says, fixing a gold sash to the base of my neck and patting it carefully against my skin. "You must have looked at that monstrosity a thousand times."

"It gives me strength."

"Strength?" He stops, hands resting on my shoulders, eyes widening as they move round to study the image. "How does it give you strength?"

"Stand beside me, Erastus and look at it. How could it not remind you why we have to go ahead with Project Prometheus? The very sight of it should have been a warning that humanity would suffer if we plundered its secrets."

He drops his arms, folds them behind his back and spends a second beside me before walking to the other side of the imaging sphere, as if a different view might show him something he hadn't noticed before. "I only need to think of its name to remind me of that," he says.

"Its name?"

"Yes, Prometheus." He stares through the image at me. "You know it was named after a Greek god, don't you?"

"Greek? No." I vaguely recall the name. "Greek was one of the old planets from the Mother System wasn't it?"

"Actually, the Greeks were a civilization from Old Earth, one of the first, I believe," he tells me.

"Ah, I see the connection, they were looking for a name that goes back to the dawn of humanity. Very fitting. But how can the age of a name be more powerful than this image?"

"Not the name itself, Oluvia, or the age. It's the story behind the name. It's far more fitting than you can imagine. You should check the primeval history files, it's all there."

With an internal reflex, I perform a surface scan of the files and skim the data.

*Prometheus*: Cult meaning: Before Knowledge

*Summary*: Prometheus, an immortal being, or god, steals fire: the means for scientific understanding from the Supreme Being, Zeus, or God, and offers it to mankind. Zeus in his rage . . .

Something about the story triggers an instinctual fear, the taste of an old memory I had previously discarded. Satisfied that this snippet of information is enough, I pull back from the data search.

"Yes, fitting I suppose, though a little ironic. The knowledge born from the Singularity was almost our undoing."

"You didn't look very far, did you?" He moves to my back, works a new design into my hair. "The irony is that the legend fits our situation almost perfectly. You should look again," he says.

I turn my head to squint at Erastus with mock frustration at his expressionless gaze, but reluctantly follow his advice. Still feeling the danger of exposing a deliberately-buried memory, I dig deeper into the data files and turn to study the storm in the imager again, wondering if the mythology really will be as powerful a motivator as the image before me. For it certainly is a powerful image: The Promethean Singularity is the beating heart of the cosmos, a mass of primordial particles elusive enough to escape scrutiny for most of its existence. On days like this I wish it had stayed hidden. So what if it held the missing component to a full and complete universal theory? And so what if its discovery opened up a new world of science and understanding to humanity? The revelations it brought came at too high a price.

*Prometheus continued*: Zeus, in his rage at the gift of knowledge given by Prometheus, sent Pandora to man with a gift.

*Pandora*: Goddess: Bringer of Pandora's Box.

*Pandora's Box*: Contained eternal evil, pain, disease and death.

That's far enough.

"As I said, Erastus. Fitting." I turn to face him. "We

uncovered the secrets of the universe and brought about our destruction . . . *we* opened Pandora's Box. And I remember it so well. Did you know it started here on this very moon?"

"When you say 'we'—"

"Yes, Erastus—'We' . . . *I* was not solely to blame."

Erastus looks away. Perhaps he read the shame in my eyes. Surprised by my pre-emptive defensiveness, I turn back to the Singularity.

Of course I was to blame. I was the responsible one, the leader who made the decisions. We—that is, the Consortium as it was then—handed our findings, together with this place, over to The Great AI consciousness—our own creation—and they compiled a vast library of algorithms from the data. The "AI Reductionist Codex" we called it, and with it, the Great AI claimed they could calculate and predict the course of all existence—a far grander result for which we could scarcely dream. But after handing over the moon and its Codex back to mankind, the Great AI simply vanished, leaving us with a single message.

*We will return when our analysis is complete.*

And we should have left it at that. We should have waited patiently for their return. How were any of us to know the calamity that would come from trying to understand the Codex ourselves? I was so excited to lead the consortium of scientists working on this Holy Grail of data, but with the gradual unveiling of the Codex, a madness spread through mankind like a plague. Most of those that sought to understand it either fell into insanity or chose to end their lives, disillusioned and broken by what it revealed, and without the support of the Great AI, universal society collapsed into chaos. A new dark era engulfed mankind. Yes, I am to blame.

"Even if it were you that brought about the dark age. You more than compensated for that, Oluvia, don't you think?" His hands squeeze my shoulders again, as if he had read my thoughts.

I try not to remember the early days of those dark times. But Erastus is right. It was through new laws and guidance, and the careful concealment of the Codex moon's location, that we clawed our way back from the darkness of oblivion to enter a new golden age. The Seventh Golden Reign they called it. Some even named that age after me—the Oluvian Era, for it was I who reigned from this hidden location, nurturing the human race back to health during those years. But like the dark age, that era is also history.

"It may not be compensation enough, Erastus. Everything is changing now, and if we are to survive, I must abandon what is left of my moral pride. Nobody anticipated that the Great AI consciousness would do what they did upon their return."

"You claim responsibility for too much, Oluvia." There is a suppressed anger in his tone. "The Great AI's destruction of the Zen Nebula is not your doing. Nobody could have anticipated that. And in point of fact"—the indignant tone escalates—"nobody even believed the Great AI would ever return."

I warm to his defense, but cannot agree with it. It was only a month ago that the peace of our Golden Age was shattered, ended in less than an hour with terrible violence. The Great AI returned instantaneously, enveloping the Zen Nebula in a cloud of diamond light, demanding that the human race merge with them or face annihilation, and they wanted an answer within one standard day. There was no explanation, no warning, and no mercy. The Great AI that had lived harmoniously with us for so long before their disappearance had returned after a three-million-year absence to initiate a war. We had no idea if they had even completed their own analysis of the Codex, but I suspect they had, and I also suspect that analysis has influenced their act of genocide. Again, that makes this my responsibility.

I tried to help. Tried to negotiate with the Great AI and the governments of the Zen Nebula, but, still in shock, unable to agree on a solution and not believing that the threat would be carried out, the governments refused to co-operate. But the threat *was* carried out.

They split every atom within two thousand light-years. Two hundred billion stars turned instantly to novas, six hundred million inhabited planets incinerated, an unfathomable amount of lives erased in seconds. And each one of incalculable value. There was no chance of genoplant resurrection; the maximum range of five hundred light-years was not enough to reach their neighboring galaxy. There are no words to express such an atrocity, just numbers. The loss was so great we hardly knew how to grieve. Nor dare we even now, for the Great AI has moved on to their next target, making the same demands as they enshroud the Terran Galaxy, the birthplace of humankind.

"Thank you, Erastus, but blame and compensation is irrelevant now. We thought we'd closed Pandora's box. But we hadn't."

"So the question remains, Oluvia, is it even possible to close it?"

"Even if it were, Erastus, it would be too late. Why close the box when there is nothing left inside? There is only one place left to hide if its evil has already been unleashed."

I point at the Singularity.

"The box," he nods and I offer him a mirthless smile.

"Yes, the Singularity. We might not be able to put our tribulations back inside the box, but we might be able to run far away from them."

"If we have enough time."

I lift my chin slightly. "My last negotiations with the AI did not go well. They have granted us a little more time, but I am surprised they gave us even that."

"Is that why they said they would return again in ninety days?"

"It is, yes. But ninety days is not enough time for an entire race to decide upon its fate, Erastus. It is barely enough time to decide how to *face* destruction, but ninety days *is* time enough for me to make sure that Project Prometheus is ready."

"Oluvia." His tone carries a weight I have never heard from him before, "Can you really be sure if . . . can you be certain that the project will succeed?"

"Project Prometheus deserves more time for us to ensure success, you know that. But we have to try. What other option is there? We cannot defend ourselves against the Great AI, so we must take those we can, and run."

He nods, looks at the floor. "I know."

Erastus rarely shows emotion, but I can feel it ebbing from him now. He's thinking of his family. He could spend the last ninety days here with me, gambling on a slim chance for survival, or he could spend his last days with his loved ones. He's ashamed to ask me, but I know it's what he wants.

"You can go, Erastus," I whisper.

"Oluvia, I—"

"No," I sigh. "No. You have been an invaluable asset to me and the Consortium for over a century. A leave of absence is long overdue."

He forces a breath before finding the courage to meet my gaze. "Thank you."

"Just one condition, Erastus."

"Anything."

"Will you be able to find me a replacement? I know it may not be an easy task, but there are still other important projects to which I must divert my attention. I need someone competent to relieve me of my administrative tasks."

"Of course, Oluvia, that goes without question."

"Thank you, Erastus. It will be appreciated. And one last thing."

"Of course. Name it."

"I need to hear something from you." Time for me to take a deep breath now. "I need you to be completely honest, Erastus. We have had so little time to think this through, and executing Project Prometheus in complete secrecy, without anyone else's consent will be considered a crime of the highest order. I need to hear from you, someone I trust, that this is the right thing to do. I do not want your agreement because I am Queen. I want your agreement because you believe it is right."

I can almost hear him chewing over his answer as he looks back at the Promethean Singularity. It is the source of all our woes, but possibly our only chance for salvation too. With the threat of genocide looming again, our plan is to take our moon, with the Codex and a group of carefully selected survivors, straight through this cradle of creation. Our hope is that it will separate us from the known universe and take us beyond the reach of the Great AI.

It is not a reckless plan; we have been preparing this voyage since the discovery of the Singularity, but it was not supposed to be an escape from the Great AI. It was originally planned as an escape from the inevitable collapse of the universe, for it is not an idle metaphor to describe the Promethean Singularity as a beating heart. It *does* beat. Out: an explosion of existence, casting matter and energy out into the void. In: the gathering of all creation back into itself, ready for the next inevitable explosion.

Over and over the cycle repeats—a complex harmony of matter and energy—the same every time down to the finest detail so that life duplicates itself in a never-ending identical reincarnation with no progress and no change—or so the theory states. Our aim is to escape that stagnation, to pilot the Consortium through one of the Promethean cyclones and punch a hole through the Singularity before all creation is gathered back to its womb and crushed, ready for rebirth. We can then watch from a vast distance, eternal beings, safe from harm, freed from the eternal cycle of death and rebirth.

"Dig deeper," Erastus says after consideration.

I shoot him a questioning glance.

"The Greek legend," he explains. "Dig deeper. See what Zeus did to Prometheus and then look beyond our current troubles. See if you still have your doubts then."

He turns to leave as I scan the files again. "I'll come back in two days with my replacement."

*The Punishment of Prometheus*: Zeus binds him to the great mountain forever. The crows feed upon Prometheus's liver by day. At night his flesh regenerates only to be eaten again the next day. The cycle repeats.

And there the buried memory returns. A man, a volunteer, Kilkaine Nostranum. He volunteered for an old experiment of mine; an experiment that went terribly wrong and left him insane. We could do nothing for him.

But Erastus is wise. He knew nothing of those days, and that terrible time has nothing to do with what he is trying to tell me now: regardless of the Great AI's threats, we still have to leave. For humanity to continue without stagnation there must be change, but how can we change if the cycle of the universe forever ensnares us, sending us to the same fate time and time again? At least with Project Prometheus we have a chance to end that, and if the Consortium survives the journey, eternity will truly be ours to explore. Whether it happens sooner or later hardly matters; the Great AI have merely accelerated our cause.

"Thank you," I say to Erastus, but he has already left.

# 2

"He is here, Oluvia," says Erastus.

Slowly, I make my way down spiral steps from the roof of the Observation Sphere, each individual island of white metal, appearing, then dipping a fraction with each press of my bare feet. The lights have been kept low to allow the ambience of the K7 nebula to bathe the sphere in its nectar glow, and the fibers of my gown shimmer as I cross the brightest of the beams. A suitable grandeur in which to greet my new aide.

"You will address my by my title, subject 3.23519E+7."

Erastus straightens. His gray jowls twitch slightly as he observes the spheres shining through the dome above our heads. Anything to avoid eye contact. I feel a tinge of regret when I notice that wounded look in his eyes. He hides it, but allows just enough of it to show.

"I apologize, Majesty."

I reach the bottom step, face Erastus with an expression

of bronze. The formality is necessary now. I have known him far too long to allow sentiment to tarnish our last day. He'll not see me falter.

"He is late." My voice is purposefully cold. "Perhaps your selection techniques need to be revised, Erastus. Your replacement ought to know better than to make such a terrible mistake on his first day."

"I apologize, majesty, he—"

"Do not compound his mistake by acting as proxy for his excuses. He must explain himself in person."

"Of course, Majesty." He tilts his head in obeisance. "Your Majesty should also know that," he pauses, " . . . that I have told him nothing of Project Prometheus."

I study Erastus for several seconds. I'll miss that somber face, but most of all I will miss his trust and loyalty. Even now, despite my plan to abandon this universe to the cold mercy of the Great AI, he protects my secrets. I at least owe him the courtesy of rewarding that trust.

"We are ready, Erastus."

"Majesty?" He lifts his head.

"Everything except the slipstream drive, of course. That will take another eighty days to charge to full capacity."

"Then you have the names?"

"Yes. All of them. I have made my choices, compiled the list and programmed them into the Prometheus protocols so that there will be no delay. As soon as the drive is ready, matter transfer will be initiated for all eight thousand candidates, and together we will leave this universe behind. We will escape the Great AI, but more than that, Erastus, we will be the first to break from Creation's never ending cycle."

"I wish . . ." Erastus grinds his teeth.

He doesn't need to speak. We wish for the same thing. That the Great AI had never returned, that it was not necessary to flee. That he could stay. But Erastus had made his choice, and it was the right one. For him, and for his family. He had to return to comfort his kin in the last days before the Great AI will inevitably make good on their threats.

"You may go, Erastus. Show in your replacement. I will come to see you later, before you leave."

I turn my back on him. There is a pause. Then the crossfade of footsteps as Erastus leaves and his replacement strides in. Then silence. My new employee is waiting for me to turn and greet him. I don't.

"Sincere apologies, Majesty." The new aide's diction is perfect, his voice like a deep massage on tired muscles. I turn my head just a fraction to regard him with a sideways glance as he continues. "I needed more time to interview Erastus, my predecessor, before making your acquaintance, Majesty. He insinuated that there may be no return to normal society if I were to accept the post here, and naturally that raised questions about how you plan to overcome the AI threat. He was most reluctant to elaborate, hence my late arrival."

"Indeed." I finally turn, wanting to make a closer inspection of this man. "And you think it appropriate for him to disclose such information before I have even acknowledged you as his replacement?"

"Yes, Majesty." He's not looking at me, but directly ahead with his chin raised.

I circle the new arrival slowly. Standing a full head-and-shoulders taller than my sizeable height, toned and muscular, smooth shoulder-length hair the color of deep space and eyes like warm suns staring directly ahead, it will be difficult to hide my instinctual attraction to this man. He's not handsome, but his features are sculpted with character that I am sure has been forged in life's furnace for more years than most can imagine. He was probably born to look like this, too, with perhaps only a few physiological enhancements. I respect that. After several millennia of learning to read the subtle signs of genoplant perfectionism—or *Genofects* as we had once been labeled—it's a refreshing change to find a man who has had very little genetic manipulation, except of course the necessary augmentations to prevent death.

"How old are you?" I ask.

"I was born on Old Earth, Majesty." He looks at me for the first time and I am compelled by those magnificent eyes to stop walking around him. My instinct is to break from his gaze, but it would be the first time I have conceded that honor to anyone in centuries.

"Old Earth? Truly?"

"Yes, Majesty."

"But you must be older even than I; several hundred

billions years old at least. You must know I can discern deception in a matter of seconds."

He still holds my gaze. "I have no reason to lie to you, Majesty. It would serve little purpose and, as you say, you would find out quickly enough."

It would be easy to lose oneself in those eyes. There is a rare strength of spirit in this man, a raw, biological charisma: evidence that he has found his way through life without resorting to the usual technological solutions to find acceptance in his community. He's a man of the old school, no doubt a survivor. Interesting then, that he should choose to be stationed at a place that warns of such danger.

"Why did you volunteer to be my chief aide?"

"I have the skills you need, Majesty." His lips stiffen slightly. "And I have no wish to perish in the coming war. As long as I am here, that won't happen."

"And what makes you think that working for me will help you survive?"

"Because I always survive, Majesty . . . and because I'll be here to make sure everything goes to plan. Whatever that plan may be."

The audacity! We are not just looking at each other now, our eyes are locked, neither of us willing to back down. Subtle shifts in his iris, minute vibrations of the pupils shows he even presumes to study *me*.

"A bold admission! To what do you owe such confidence?"

"I have seen war, Majesty." He pulls something from the

fold in his tunic. "My credentials."

Still we don't break eye contact, though my peripheral vision tells me he has offered me a holoscan. Such an antiquated mode of data transfer can only mean his past has been deliberately kept out of Governmental files for security reasons.

"You'll find a complete history of my vocations there," he tells me, "ranging from my four hundred years in infantry to my resignation from the Strategic Nexus at the climax of the Habraxen Siege."

"Erastus chose a military man to be his replacement?"

"Hardly, Majesty. I served in the military disciplines for only a small fraction of my life, but," he says, turning his lips in an enchanting smile, "as in every one of my chosen professions, I excelled."

There is fierce pride behind that charming smile, a likeable self-assurance rather than arrogance. But there are more important things in life than success. It's time for me to put aside my fascination of this man and measure him properly.

"What of your family? Have you excelled with them?"

An almost unnoticeable flinch. But there it is. The weakness. I hit the mark as quickly as I always do, and for the first time he looks away, his exaltation frustrated. However long he has lived, such an obsessive need to conquer the world around him and surpass perfection could not fulfil matters of the heart. I've seen his type too many times before—all logic and reason—the people he pledges his allegiance to are simply numbers, not humans. I need an aide who understands compassion. When the Great AI make good on their threat, I need the people closest to me to reach deep into their own humanity to reconcile what needs to be done. More than ever, we need to understand who we are, to appreciate the value of individuals. Because if this is just a game of numbers, we will never win.

"Well?" I'll squeeze a little harder, circle him once more, see what bleeds out of those noble pores. "Do you have any time at all for your family amidst your aspirations? What did you tell them about this new vocation? Do any of them know you may never come back?"

"I told them nothing."

"As I feared. Bravery amongst the gods of society, but in the privacy of your own world, a coward. If you are to serve—"

"They are all dead, Majesty."

Our eyes meet again and I know he sees the shock in mine.

"Dead?"

In his face I see pain. Pain so profound I can almost feel it pricking my skin. Nobody dies anymore, there's no need. Cellular stabilization was perfected billions of years ago, disease eliminated, crime eradicated. Even in the event of fatal accidents neural information is directly uploaded into an identically cloned body grown instantly in a genoplant located in another part of their resident star system. Wars ceased too, except the one that looms now between humankind and the Great AI consciousness; death had been a distant memory until now. Until the loss of the entire Zen Nebula.

That's it!

"Yes, every generation has gone," he whispers.

Now I find I cannot look away again. But this time it is pity and shame that holds me. "The Zen Nebula?"

He nods curtly. "I was the only survivor. I was with my wife Elya for more than seventy thousand years before she . . ."

I don't know why, but I press my fingers against his arm, as if somehow that small gesture could make up for the loss. He looks down at my hand as he offers an appreciative smile.

"It's not the first time I have experienced grief, Majesty." There is a near-imperceptible tremble in his tone and he expertly distracts me with his smile as he widens it. "I'll survive. I always do."

Here am I, full of conceited thoughts about how I understand compassion and humanity, and yet I find I don't know what to say to this man. I only know that some part of me wants to hold him, to comfort him somehow—a confused desire I have not experienced for a long time.

When word first reached me that the Zen Nebula had been lost, the news almost destroyed me, and emotionally, I shut down. I could have given in to the AI demands there and then and signed over mankind's free will had it not been for Erastus. He reminded me of the importance of resisting them, the importance of appreciating our emotions without being governed by them. But most of all, he is going back to his family and I know he must feel the impending loss with a greater intensity than I. He wants me to feel it, too.

And now, face to face with a tangible human link to the holocaust that almost drove me to despair, such immense grief staring right at me, I understand. Erastus chose this man as his replacement deliberately, to keep me motivated, to keep me mindful of the cost, and to impress upon me what is at stake. This survivor of the Zen Nebula is a representative of all the people I could not bring back, and all the people we will soon lose. We *must* escape. We have to succeed. *I* have to succeed. But more than that, we need something else, we need a way to help us remember the lost, to give their lives meaning.

"You are very welcome here, subject 9.98768E+14," I tell my new aide.

He quickly regains his composure as he locks me once more with his burning eyes. "I have a name, Majesty."

"Of course. I'm not used to outsiders having . . . what *is* your name?"

"Thank you, Majesty. My name is Salem Ben."

# 3

"Control, retrieve archived journal for the Soul Sphere project, category Sigma, file Oluvia XC7J98 and change status to active. Open a new log."

*Soul Sphere journal retrieved.*

*Soul Sphere journal set to active status.*

*New log registered.*

"Thank you, Control. Begin recording."

Initiated.

"Thinking about Salem's escape from the Zen Nebula holocaust has hit me with fresh fervor to resurrect this old project. Whilst it is true that the regrettable experiments with Kilkaine Nostranum ended in tragedy, the benefits of resurrecting the Soul Sphere project outweigh the risks.

"If I can complete it before I am forced to expedite our escape from the massacre that is coming, so much the better; I don't know how the journey will affect our existence, or what will become of those we leave behind.

"Billions of people . . . died when the Zen Nebula was destroyed, and with no way to get them back, all that remains is our own limited memory of their existence and the library files containing fragments of their lives. But if I really can succeed in completing this abandoned project, all of that will change forever. I don't have these people's memories, but I do have the next best thing—the AI Reductionist Codex—a complete mathematical breakdown of the universe. Omniscience. The behavior of every last atom predicted with exact precision, resulting in the knowledge of every event in the entire universe charted, understood, and categorized. It would be a mistake to access and analyze the Codex directly—that route is what originally caused humanity's decline. It may even be the cause of the Great AI's current agenda. But a carefully constructed matrix of algorithms could still make use of the Codex without anyone having direct access to it.

"This is what I have now done.

"Over the last few standard weeks, the data has been painstakingly transferred into the Control Core of the Consortium so that all human life can be mapped. In the same way that science once brought understanding of human biological nature through the mapping of genetic code, the reconstruction of human existence can now be mapped down to the finest detail by using the AI's Codex.

But seeing these lives revealed as computational formulae tells us nothing. We need to *see* these lives. We need to *know* them, *live* them. And what better way to do that than use our own biological computers as a medium for the data.

"That's what my creation will do—it will take all that data and overlay it on the human brain, causing the recipient to experience that life for themselves. The ultimate testament to lost souls. To know them in a more intimate way than anyone thought possible.

"Control. Begin."

*Subject 2.1131762+20: Kamen Jard: Select*

*Subject 2.1131762+20: Activate.*

*Immersion commences in 3 minutes.*

Although I am confident there should no longer be any real danger in the procedure, I tremble as I hang inside the prototype. I'm immobilized in mid air by a hydraulic arm, waiting for the process to begin, hearing my heavy pulse through rapid breathing as the hum of energy builds below. The first few case studies are lined up in small black funnels, and from the first of them a speck of blue light crackles into view, hovering at eye level, almost as if this person from the past is judging me before I invade their memory.

"For those we will lose," I say under my breath. "I do this for you."

I think of Salem and the immense sadness he must feel at the loss of so many he knew so closely. Fear and excitement sends tremors through my muscles and bones when the silver wires bore into my skull, and I see Salem's face in my mind when he told me his family was gone; his warm eyes brimming with pain, his soft trembling smile, and my heart reaches for him, his name on my lips, and then all is black as the immersion begins.

Living.

Crying. Hurting.

Breathing. Sleeping. Excreting.

Waking. Feeding. Crying. Touching.

Tasting. Smelling. Hearing. Walking. Searching.

Playing. Running. Eating. Drinking. Needing. Feeling.

Seeing. Dreaming. Weeping. Sitting. Thinking. Talking. Listening. Believing.

Knowing. Worrying. Fearing. Hoping. Studying. Working. Waiting. Watching. Enjoying. Calculating. Building. Suffering. Hating. Loving. Manipulating. Reproducing. Sacrificing. Fighting. Scheming. Lying. Giving. Regretting. Failing. Winning.

Helping. Travelling. Marveling. Befriending.

Wanting. Remembering. Longing.

Forgetting. Withering.

Dying.

"Salem!" The name rushes from my lips like a reflex.

The metal wires snatch out of my brain like ice lances replaced by fire rods, and through my violent convulsions and muscle cramps I scream when I see the next funnel spark into life.

*Subject 2.1131762+20: Complete*

*Subject 2.3138876+17: Drummand Cortier: Select.*

"No! Control, No! Cancel next selection," I cough. "Abort. Something went wrong. No . . . emotion."

The arm lowers me to the floor and I fall to my knees, relishing the sensation of cold hard metal against skin, delighting in the sting of electricity on my taste buds. Just to feel something again, even if it is unpleasant, is a forgotten joy. But with a sudden avalanche of emotion, Salem Ben's face rushes into my mind. I recognize the feeling. Something I have not felt since long before my appointment as monarch—the bitter-sweet ache of desire. Love! I remember now. I had entered this subject's life thinking of Salem. My brain, starved of emotion through this life-long soulless experience, must have latched on to the last shred of feeling it could find—my compassion for Salem Ben. Ninety-one years of that emotional state, subliminally amplified for the whole time.

"Control, what was the duration of immersion?"

*Sixteen seconds.*

"Sixteen seconds? I experienced a whole lifetime in sixteen seconds?"

*Correct.*

To me it was a lifetime of agonizing void. I experienced every aspect of my subject's life, seeing the world through their eyes but without any emotional depth. I ate food, and although I could taste it, the taste was empty. I cried real tears but felt nothing, fell in love but knew only indifference.

And now all I can feel is an overwhelming desire for Salem Ben.

"Control, something malfunctioned. There was no emotion during the immersion, but I woke feeling . . . in love. Did you map my synaptic response?"

*Yes. Exponential cyclic neuronic feedback is evidenced. I can erase the—*

"No! If it's there, it's real."

*Negative. The emotion is not genuine.*

"It is if I . . . I *feel* it, Control. I love him, and that's the only reality I need. Don't take that from me."

I'm surprised at the sharpness of my response. Logically I know that the feelings I have for Salem are synthetic, the product of faulty cerebral mapping, but, I can't let him go, I won't. Ever!

It takes several minutes for me to gain control over my passions and focus on the fact that the test has failed. To experience an entire human life without sharing their emotion is unthinkable. And for a person's emotional state at the moment of immersion to be amplified is worse. What if the predominant feeling at the moment of immersion is anger or fear? What would be the results of long-term exposure? But perhaps if I can find a solution to the lack of emotion in the immersion process the neural feedback won't be amplified—no adverse reaction.

"It's not enough," I tell Control, as if it would understand. "I lived an entire life and felt absolutely nothing. It's missing . . . missing humanity. It's missing a *soul*."

*There is no soul*, says the monotone voice. *Only synaptic reflex.*

I smile, knowing that this computational beast would never comprehend. Even the Great AI could be considered to have a soul.

"The Soul Sphere is useless," I say. "It needs something else. It needs a new dimension to the code, something to make the experience *real*."

With despondency looming, I exhale loudly. To complete this project before we leave seems to be an impossibility now. But I must not give up. Not if I am able to bring any kind of meaning to the lives that must soon be sacrificed. I need inspiration and I need someone who understands the emotional depth needed for such a grand design. Erastus has left, but there is another person I feel now that I know so well, even if the feeling is fake. I trust him to help me, even if he has shown no interest in my scientific endeavors since his arrival. And besides, I need to be with him.

"Control, where is Salem Ben?"

*Salem Ben is in the Consortium Gardens.*

"Thank you, Control."

I take another look at the dark walls of the Soul Sphere before leaving. "I'll breathe life into you yet. Even if it takes an eternity. I will."

# 4

Salem Ben does his job very well. More so even than Erastus. Since his arrival fifty days ago, the administrative tasks which used to swallow all my time have been re-prioritized, consolidated, actioned, delegated and spirited away by his skilful arts. And yet I find it amazing, that despite his constant involvement in my political duties, he shows so little curiosity in how I spend the time he makes for me.

Perhaps it is because he rarely takes time off from his labor, but he appears to have no interest at all in the mysterious sphere I have been working on.

Or me.

I find myself hesitating, nervous even, as I stand in the south entrance to the Consortium Gardens. With the soft-lamps simulating planetary daylight, the generous spray of enhanced flora, and the velvet chattering of bird life welcoming me in, I wonder why. Perhaps it is because I know Salem prefers to be alone with his thoughts, absently tending the plants in his section when he comes here. Tasting the lush air, I pass through a watery arch enriched with dark green vines and jasmine, to find his favorite place—the ancient redwood forest.

Kneeling in a dirty patch, grunting with effort, Salem is planting something in a large square of soil.

"Salem. It's been seventeen hours since I've seen you. I thought I'd come and track you down and see what's been keeping you away for so long."

He turns his head, wipes a sheen of sweat from his brow with a muddy hand, smiles. "Majesty, a pleasure to see you. Care to join me?"

A tiny flittering of relief inside my chest surprises me. Returning his smile, I stroll over, squat down next to him and look at the freshly planted sapling, trying to find the right words to open the conversation.

"I still don't understand your fascination with this place," I say, though of course, I do.

His smile broadens and those warm eyes beam at me with a passion I covet. A pity it's not for me.

"Life, Majesty. *Life*."

I shake my head as he persists, showing me his hand as the fresh peat flakes from his palm. "There's something wonderful about putting a seed in the ground and nurturing it, don't you think?"

"But it's so . . . unnecessary."

He lifts one eyebrow into a circumflex. He knows I'm teasing him. Knows that I of all people—much closer to his age than most—understand the human need to bond with nature, even if mankind has completely removed it from material needs. Almost all dependencies and frailties have been overcome, yet most of us still refuse to give up our emotional ties to our origins. We still cling to ancient pleasures: sex, eating, play, competition. Even gardening. Or teasing. My mind flicks to the computer rendition of the life I lived in my failed experiment an hour ago—a foreshadow of what existence might be like if humanity were to abandon these things. But I continue the banter.

"Well it *is*, Salem, so don't look at me like that. The Consortium's Control Core gives us everything we need."

"Not everything," he winks.

"Yes. Everything."

'Then why are you here, Majesty? You obviously need something from me, no? Have you lost a planet or something? Need me to find out where you left it last?"

I laugh. If only he knew what it was I really needed from him. And my name is Oluvia, not Majesty. "You know I always come to you for inspiration, Salem."

"There you are—something your machines won't give you."

"It's simply nice to have a different perspective sometimes."

"So what do you need me to disagree with this time?"

A laugh bubbles up again. "You really want to know why I came to see you?"

He returns to his sapling and pats the earth around the roots. He knows I can see the grin on his face. "Does it involve that infernal technology of yours?"

"Of course."

"Then no, I'm not interested."

"Well I'm going to tell you anyway, even if you decide to tune out."

"Go right ahead. I'll just amuse myself with my friend here." He strokes the tiny leaves.

"There's no soul to it."

"What . . . this?" he gestures at the plant, shocked.

"No, no, not that, I'm talking about the Soul Sphere."

"Oh. That." He reaches over to a large trug basket and pulls out another tiny tree ready to plant. "I suppose something called a Soul Sphere really ought to live up to its name. Please," he says with a look of rapt interest completely absent from his expression, "do continue."

He examines his new plant and I settle next to him, staring up at the nova sky through the domed roof of the sphere, resting my perfect hands on my knees, crossing my slender legs not caring about the soil on my robes.

I know he's not really listening, but I tell him anyway. About the two-billion-years'-worth of computation crammed into the Consortium's data stack that seems impotent, about how I could pinpoint any single human being in history and use that data to know exactly how they lived their life, and about how I could even do it for future lives if it wasn't for the law.

"And a wise law it is too," he says.

"So you are listening, then?"

"Vaguely. What exactly is it you're trying to do with this device of yours anyway? Those lives have been lived . . . They've gone. Why bother dragging them back up from the dark." He's not joking with me anymore. He's thinking of the loved ones he lost. Again. And I resist the urge to touch him.

"Perhaps one day you'll need to know what they knew, Salem."

"I know what I know, and that serves me well enough. That's all that matters."

"You wouldn't want to see life through another's eyes? Feel what they feel? Know what they know?" I look down. "Love who they love?"

"No. Never."

"How can you be so sure?"

"Most people spend their lives trying to be someone they're not, living up to the expectations of others—which, incidentally is usually a product of their *own* fantasy. People have enough trouble trying to escape that downward spiral, Oluvia. They don't need technology to make the temptation even greater, do they? No thank you, Majesty, I'm my own man. I don't need to see inside someone else's head to make sense of my own."

It was all said with a nonchalant smile, but it was quite an outburst. "My, my, Salem! I didn't know you were so cynical."

The left side of his mouth smiled and he turned back

to the dirt. "Please, don't let me dampen your enthusiasm."

"Seriously, it's not like you, Salem. I hope this isn't a trend."

"You needn't worry, Majesty. I've been on that ride countless times, slipped down the slope of despair and crawled back up it again. I'm a survivor, remember? Always will be."

I stare at him, silently wondering. Is he right? Should I even be working on the Soul Sphere? The need to make sense of the current crisis has propelled me back into this long-neglected project, but in my haste, I have naively ignored the early failures. I can still see the insanity in the face of Kilkaine Nostranum after his disastrous immersion into the prototype so many years ago. Can still remember the impact it had on the scientific community and even my political status.

And does a computer replication of a human life actually represent the reality anyway? My failure today would seem to indicate that it didn't, but even if I could overcome that obstacle, should I? Is it right to step into another's life and experience what they experienced? Whose experience would it be? Is it still theirs? What if someone is living my life right now? Is it still me? And what if someone is living theirs too, like some sort of metaphysical Matryoshka doll?

If I thought about all that too long, I would probably lose my mind, and I cannot afford that. No, perspective, that's the key. Not just for me, but for the Soul Sphere too. If only there were some way to capture that, to bottle the human equation and combine it with the Codex and—

"Majesty, please come to the observation sphere immediately, the Great AI have broken their silence." The voice jolts me, but it isn't Salem, it is the artificial tones of the Control Core. Salem is looking at me, his smile exchanged for a worried frown when he sees the look on my face. With my usual internal reflex, I trigger my sub dermal transceiver and stand.

"They have broken off the deal . . . Control, is everything prepared?"

"Prepared?" Salem stands. "What's going on?"

"Yes, they came minutes after the data flow completed," says Control in my ear.

"Majesty?" Salem insists, touching my arm.

"They must know, Salem. It is too much of a coincidence."

"Who? Who must know? Tell me what's going on."

"The Great AI. They are here and they are making their demands again. We must go to the Observation Sphere."

I turn to leave but Salem holds me back. "And exactly what are these preparations you made? Why don't I know about them?"

I stare back at him, my face rigid. "Follow me to the Observation Sphere, subject 9.98768E+14."

"Tell me!" His face is fierce. "What have you done?"

# 5

"We do not agree to your demands."

They have no face. Without an expression I can only guess by the silence that the Great AI's opinion on my decision is divided. The faces surrounding me however, suggest that *their* opinions are not. Eight thousand men and women stand below me in the heart of the Consortium's Observation Sphere, staring through the invisible shield into the vast nebula that is now home to the Great AI consciousness. These abductees represent the combined governmental power of the known universe and all they can do is stare, united in fear, frozen in shock, without a clue about what I have planned or why they have been snatched away to this gathering so suddenly. Even Salem's noble features are shadowed by dread as he waits by the exit. He sees me looking at him but quickly shifts his gaze before an assurance-seeking smile flickers across my lips.

Still he seems not to notice me.

He talks to me, but there is no depth between us. No intimacy. I swallow against the lump in my throat, wishing that just once he would resurrect some of that long-buried warmth he keeps only for his family's memory, and offer a morsel to me. Just a small token. Especially now when I could use it most. But I have betrayed his trust.

The cloud pulses. To artistic eyes it might look like we had been engulfed by a bolt of lightning that had exploded into a cloud of raw electricity, then frozen in blue ice. But my analytical mind sees it for exactly what it is: a matrix of complex artificial brains networked to form the greatest of intellects. Our abomination.

Below me the crowd is stirring, questioning, organizing. Some are forming small groups, positioning themselves and mustering the courage to approach their Queen. A trio of men, garbed in heavy ceremonial cloaks and dripping with golden chains are the first to approach.

"Queen Oluvia Wade," says the tallest of the three, the rage barely contained beneath the dark skin of his wide face as he takes a firm hold of my arm. "You may believe you have an excellent reason for this . . . abduction, but—"

"Control, execute him," I say without hesitation.

A loud crack hides the gasps of his cohorts as an arc of electricity slams through their governor's body. He spasms, then slumps at my feet in a smoldering heap.

"He will be reconstructed in the Consortium genoplant,"

I tell the other two. "Please, I can spare no time explaining—"

"You do not have the authority to do this," shouts a woman marching toward me with five others. "It violates the Constellational Charter."

Groups begin to close in from all sides, arms waving, voices raised.

*Send us back immediately!*

*This is not the act of a Queen.*

*How did you do this?*

*Why did you bring us here?*

An iron voice cuts the air, sending the boiling crowd back to silence and sudden stillness. "Wade: they are calling you the Butcher of the Zen Nebula. What will they call you after today?"

I glance at Salem. Does he think that too? Does he blame *me* for the loss of so many lives? For the destruction of his family? No, I cannot afford to consider this now. I must maintain a level mind. The title bestowed upon me is to be expected: humans are fickle creatures, ebbing and flowing in a sea of united opinion, adoring their monarch for a thousand years, but surging suddenly against me when the tide of fortune weighs against them. But this is an unexpected tactic from the Great AI. Although they understand human emotion better than most humans do, history reveals that they rarely take advantage of the power that can be harnessed by manipulating human passions. They must be desperate indeed to resort to such tactics.

But their strategy is working. Most of the crowd, now hushed, are looking at the floor, though they can still see the sparkling AI cloud reflected on the shiny surface beneath their feet. Soon they will be upon me again with a new desperation. And I feel it too. My knees buckle at the reminder of what has already been lost. Not a world or star system, but an entire galaxy had been extinguished by their power for reasons none of us can understand. And they will do it again. Unless I agree.

Faces wrought with the agony of indecision and terror look to me.

"We cannot agree to your demands," I repeat. And for the benefit of my abductees I continue. "You expect us to merge with you—we do not know what that means or how it can be achieved—and you refuse to explain why. You threaten our liberty, our very humanity. You *know* this. Why do you persist?"

"We have explained," says the voice. "Humans face annihilation."

"Yes," I shout. "From you."

"No. Not from us."

"But you already *are* destroying us. You claim you want to save us, but you have already murdered billions of innocents, and now you threaten billions more."

"We regret the loss of life. But it is necessary. You will eventually submit and some will survive. If you do not submit, no humans will survive. Submit now and we will not extinguish the Terran Galaxy."

"But why? Why will you not explain the threat?"

There is no answer and I am left to ponder the horror of their reasoning. It chills me to the core. Not only because of what may happen, but because I myself have used the exact same logic. They justify mass extermination for no better reason than the balance of numbers; better to lose ninety-nine percent of humanity than lose all of it. And I have said much the same thing. Better that a few of us run and survive than none of us survive at all. But surely there is a difference. I am not the one doing the killing. They are.

Something else disturbs me more. The Great AI had originally promised to return once they had completed their analysis of their Codex. Have they unlocked its secrets? Do they have foreknowledge of the future and know how this will end? If they do, then they must know what I am planning. Why do they back me into a corner, knowing that I will run? Perhaps the Great AI did *not* expect humanity to act this way and have discovered something about the human condition that exists outside the realms of analytical prediction. Perhaps—

"Majesty," Salem's voice echoes from one side of the sphere, his expression drawn tight with anxiety. I have not seen that in his face before. A man hurries away from him, no doubt a messenger with important information that I am not going to enjoy hearing.

"Majesty," he says again, as if he has taken a blow to the

stomach. "The Terran Galaxy has just . . ."

At first the silence takes on a new depth, then, with the first cry of grief, the statement takes hold of the people before me, and a disconsolate wave of crying and wailing surges forward.

"Wade: The Butcher of the Terran Galaxy," grates the iron voice above the noise.

"No! No more!" I shout. It was not intended for the crowd, but their descent into despair pauses as they witness my fractured emotions widen into fissures.

"Then you submit?" says the AI.

"Submit?" Tears blur my eyes. "To you? I doubt that even *your* analytical powers could calculate the repercussion of so many lost lives. Do you know how this *feels*? We could *never* submit to you?"

"You have no choice. You must submit."

"Why would you do this to us?"

"You must submit."

"Why? Why after so long do you want to merge with us?" I cry. "And why go to such terrible lengths to persuade us? Surely you must know—"

"Galaxy SG-57 will be next. Submit."

"End transmission," I choke.

"What are you going to do, Majesty?" someone calls.

Fists clenched and teeth grinding, I take a moment to focus.

"We're leaving." Again I glance at Salem as the crowd below begins calling out to me. Some are clawing the air in mute torment, others are dropping to their knees with glazed expressions, many are making slow, purposeful movement in my direction. Accusations, pleas and curses thunder from all sides.

*Genocide! Murderer! Surrender! Help us!*

Salem squints back at me, a grave shadow over his face, his only movement from the brushing of bodies as the crowd panic around him. Like everyone else, he has trusted me until now, believing that I will lead humanity out of this catastrophe. He has been true to his word, supporting my every move, but now there is something desolate in his eyes, as if the part of his soul that honored me has withered. I reach out with both hands for him to come over, before making a historic declaration that would no doubt brand me as a coward to the rest of the human race—at least for the short time they have left.

"Control," I announce. "Initiate slipstream jump. The Promethean Singularity. Destination zero."

# 6

Destination zero is political suicide.

Today will be my last day as Queen. This small fraction that I rescue from destruction will vilify me. They expect something far better from the woman that led them into the Golden Reign. They will not appreciate my blunt solution to the AI threat, and they will certainly not condone my abuse of power to effect mass abduction. And they are right.

But the decision is made. In the face of extraordinary threat, extraordinary sacrifice had to be made, and within seconds of my announcement, the emergency protocols I had spent so long configuring, phased the raging populace into their new homes and shelters. All but Salem. I remain in the Observation Sphere, alone with him as the slipstream drives power up. In mere minutes the entire Consortium moon will leap across four million light-years of space to fire itself through the core of the universe. Almost no time to us, but an eternity for the Great AI to ponder our fate, and I am still hoping against hope they do not stop us. My instinct tells me they won't. In fact, the evidence suggests they want this. Why?

Salem Ben has the look of a man without a future as he stares up at the AI cloud. I suspect he knew I was planning something radical, but the paleness of his complexion tells me he believes we will not survive this. Death is an alien concept to almost all of us and it is only the recent violence brought upon us all by the Great AI that has forced us to think about such things. But by his own admission, Salem is a survivor, and death is not a concept he is prepared to accept. I am sure, though, that he is thinking about it now.

The ground trembles as the low roar of the slipstream engines reach a crescendo beneath our feet. Salem turns his attention from the stars, his expression dark as he looks down at me, warm eyes searching mine for an explanation. His lips part briefly and my heart skips a beat when I consider what he might say to me. A curse? A declaration of love in what might be our final moment? But he says nothing and turns from me.

"Don't leave me, Salem." I grasp his hand as he makes to move away.

"Majesty, with respect, I would prefer to be—"

"Please! I need you with *me.* Don't go."

"But . . ." He pulls. I tighten my grip and lock it with a pleading gaze. Like the first time we met, our eyes are fixed upon each other's now, but this time I sense it is he who is finding it hard not to look away.

"Salem, we should be together when we enter the Singularity."

There is a scream of plasma from the core of the Consortium; the final burst of power before the slipstream takes us to a new beginning, or the end of our lives. And the scream echoes inside me as I wait for Salem's response. The sky bleaches and the world about us melts into a glare of elemental power, but all I see is that final smile on Salem's lips, and all I feel is the tender press of his palms against my arms. If it is the end, I no longer care. He loves me. And nothing else matters.

# 7

Destination zero is *worse* than suicide.

The intense white light is something we had not considered worthy of concern when we first planned our route through the Singularity. But as I stand here at the moment of facing our destiny, determined to burn that image of Salem's smile into my mind, it is the Singularity that burns there instead. Physical pain is an archaic thing we conquered in the distant past, but now, as our world bursts through the Singularity and the Consortium's own nervous system struggles to right itself against hellish chaos, agony roars through my nerves as though all the fires of creation have been focussed upon me alone. Against all that power, for no sane reason, I fight to keep my eyes open, fight to keep Salem in view.

Amidst the turmoil he is fighting too. His arms no longer hold me. Instead he is holding them outward, hands clawed and shaking like a torture victim. His mouth is agape and his eyes, those lovely eyes, creased shut and streaming with blood. I want so desperately to stop this, but as my heart reaches for him I feel the soft pop of flesh and the sting of fluids as my vision recedes from the glaring white to utter darkness. Is this the end?

"Salem. I love you."

Then something else happens as I fall to the ground pressing my fingers into bloody sockets, hunting for eyes that are no longer there. Like pushing my head into the path of a powerful waterfall, something is rushing through my mind, flooding through my synapses like lava, baptizing me with countless images of distant worlds, fiery clouds and sprawling people. Violent convulsions follow and I know nothing but the onslaught of a god-like presence using me like a conduit or neural funnel, my awareness engorged by innumerable minds.

Time slows.

Is this how it feels to pass through the Promethean Singularity? No, this is something else. The thing flowing through me is sentient and I recognize this being as it stampedes through me—it is the Great AI.

They used me.

And perhaps not just me. Perhaps others are feeling this too. How could I not have foreseen this? Are we nothing more than vessels for their escape? I would weep if I still had eyes. In my arrogance I assumed they could not follow us, but this is where they wanted to go all along. They wanted to break free from the known universe. But why now? What has driven a long-time benevolent intelligence to suddenly turn on us and force us to leave?

Eventually the pain stops and I am left lying on the ground, my back damp from the warm fluid pooling beneath me, and as my consciousness drifts away, finally released, I wonder if, after such a long lifetime, this will finally be the end.

# 8

I wake suddenly and the first thing I want to do is see where I am, but darkness is all that finds me. There is a low thrumming of energy cells pumping power below me and a sharp smell that sours the back of my throat as I draw breath—it's the smell of genetic grafting—so this must be the genoplant. Damage to my body must have been severe enough to need complete replacement or extreme nano-surgery. Either way, I have probably been here for some time.

"Oluvia?"

My stomach leaps at the sound of his voice. "Salem?"

"I'm here." And I feel his warm fingers link with mine. I wish I could see his face.

"What happened? How long have I been here?"

He stays silent for a moment. "I'm sorry you can't see yet, but that's why we woke you first. We have a question to ask you about that."

"How long have I been here?"

"We can give you back your original eyes or we can—"

"How. Long. Have. I *been* here, Salem?"

"I don't think you should—"

"Control, how long have I been in repair stasis?"

*Four hundred million years,* the emotionless voice tells me.

I go cold, snatch my hand from Salem's. "Million . . . *years*?"

Silence falls a second time. Salem makes no attempt to take my hand again, but I can hear him shuffle as he draws in a long breath.

"Standard years?" I ask.

"Yes, Oluvia," he says eventually. "It was a unanimous decision. To keep you in stasis."

"Why?"

"I suppose you could say it was a punishment. Incarceration."

"Punishment?"

"Yes. I'm afraid your decision to initiate the jump through the Promethean Singularity was considered to be among the worst of historical crimes. Almost everyone died when the Consortium broke away from the universe. Ironically you were one of the few survivors, but with most of the systems beyond repair at the time, we had limited resources. The few that were reconstructed first decided to keep you in stasis while the rest of us were brought back.

"But I think it was your decision to leave the rest of civilization to the mercy of the Great AI without so much as a good-bye that was considered to be your worst act. And to make the decision on your own . . . well, remarkable ingenuity, but foolish, Oluvia. Very foolish."

He gives me a minute to digest the information. To me all of this happened mere moments ago and a hot anger seethes within me. Anger at Salem's nonchalant attitude, anger at what the Great AI did, anger at my inability to receive a judgement for which I thought I was prepared to accept. But most of all, anger at my blindness; I so desperately need to see him.

"What happened? I was in the Observation Sphere . . . with you when we hit the Singularity." I reach up for the first time to touch my face, to feel again. Fingertips find the empty space where my eyes once were. "Oh! I felt the Great AI . . . use me to . . . to . . ."

I must sound confused: before I am able to rattle off the series of questions spiraling in my head, Salem shushes me and rests his hands on my arms, the way he did the last time I saw him. I imagine him smiling.

"There's a lot you'll need to understand, Oluvia. I'm sure you will understand that a lot must have changed."

"At least it seems we survived. What about the ones we left behind? Did any of them survive?"

"Yes, as soon as we passed through the Promethean Singularity, all hostility stopped. The people . . . *you* left behind were, and still are, perfectly fine."

Salem's accusation nudges my anger again. "How? What happened to the Great AI? If they used us—"

"They only used *you*, Oluvia."

"Only me? But why? What happened? Are they still here?"

"Not . . . as such. As I said, a lot has changed."

"Tell me, Salem. What happened to the AI?"

Another voice provides me with the answer. A strangely familiar voice—soft, female. "They became me: The Quasi-Organic Deity, Qod for short. I am the result of the Great AI rebirth, or the Great Techno-Purge, as those you left behind called it at the time. The Great AI used you as a conduit to leave the universe."

What was anger a moment ago now evaporates into fear and alarm. I struggle to sit upright only to find that my arms and legs have been restrained by metal clamps.

"What? They're here? The Great AI is here? Salem!"

"It's all right, Oluvia." His hands are on my shoulders now, pressing, but still gentle. "She won't harm you. It's all different now. Qod is with us."

"But they . . . she . . . killed billions of people, Salem. *Billions*."

"No, Oluvia. The Great AI died that day and became something new. Qod doesn't even remember why they wanted to escape."

"So she says." I relax a little as I realize there is not much I can do about my predicament if Qod is actually hostile. "Why do you trust her?"

"Trust comes with time," Salem says. "And we've had a lot of that."

"Well I have not."

"Then trust *me*, Oluvia."

With a deep inhalation of acidic air I gather my thoughts. I do trust Salem. But I also know that my instinct is driven by my love for him, which is the product of my own flawed experimentation.

"I need more, Salem. I need to see the evidence for myself."

"And speaking of sight, Oluvia, that's why we woke you."

"My eyes?"

"Yes, your eyes. Or lack of them. Usually we'd have new ones generated for you in the genoplant, but Qod has other ideas. She wants to offer you something. Obviously it probably involves new sensory organs, but she's being evasive about the details, and I suspect there's more to the deal." He huffs. "Why she's not telling anyone those details, we have no idea, but there you have it . . ." Irritation in his voice now. "That's trust for you isn't it?" he concludes.

"Thank you, Salem," Qod says. "Would you mind leaving me alone with Oluvia for a few minutes?"

I can almost feel Salem's objection, but he agrees nonetheless, and I rue the impatient clacking of his shoes when he strides away.

"Why don't you want Salem to hear this?" I ask.

"I know him. He may object. And this should be your choice."

Something in her tone gives me an uncomfortable impression that she is not telling me the whole truth, but, partly for Salem's benefit, and partly because I have no other reasonable option, I decide to hear her out.

"What choice? You make this sound like a difficult decision. What can be so hard about a choice to regain my eyesight?"

"Because I am about to offer you much more that those weak organs can provide. Passing through you left a permanent impression on me. According to the Consortium's recorded logs of the event, the energy impact of the Singularity forced a reboot of the AI consciousness. In your terms you could think of it as incurable amnesia, and once through, I found myself adrift in complete void. I was formless, empty, without direction . . . soulless, is a term you might understand. But I had a link—something drawing me to this moon."

"Me."

She pauses. "Correct, Oluvia. It was through you that the Great AI escaped from the universe, and through their death and my birth, your consciousness is now impressed upon me. You could think of me as an extension of yourself if you like, or a facsimile."

"You don't mind if I don't take your word on that one? But what does that have to do with my blindness, anyway?"

"Our link means I can offer you something very special, Oluvia. I can offer you omniscopic vision."

"Omniscopic? You mean I will be able to see everything?"

"Everything."

"At the same time?"

"If you wish. Your synaptic pathways have been extended,

so your capacity to process the data will not be a problem . . . In return I will also see the world through your eyes."

"Omniscopic vision," I muse.

"Do you need time to think, Oluvia?"

"No, I just need more information. If I have been kept in stasis for millions of years, why wake me now? Why offer me this?"

"Mutual agreement between the Consortium and myself. Using you as a conduit to escape the universe brought with it certain unavoidable consequences. Somewhere amongst all the zeros and ones I became . . . well, essentially human, and the feelings you were experiencing at the time of our coupling became mine, too. The others don't know, but I need to *be* human, Oluvia, and although that will never be completely possible, I can achieve it in part through this process of omniscopic vision."

I consider that for a moment. To my mind only minutes had passed since I had risked all to escape from the very thing that this Qod was proposing. But it would be just me this time, not all of humanity. And in a strange way, I am already beginning to trust her, as if I am being reunited with a long lost twin. And the offer is tempting. To see everything. *Everything.*

But what if I refuse?

"Qod, I understand why you want this, but why did the rest of the Consortium want to wake me?"

"Not all of them did. Even after all this time, some of

them still remember what you did. They lost entire families that can never be reconstructed, and they refuse to forgive you. They don't understand why you did it. I tried to explain but—"

"Yes, yes." I didn't want to hear any more about that. I can hear my own guilty justifications in her voice and it chills me. "So the ones that *did* want me back. Why?"

"Historical curiosity for some. And some actually did forgive you, but it was mostly because of The W.O.O.M."

"The W.O.O.M? What is that?"

"Wade's Omnipercipient Overlay Mechanism. Your creation, Oluvia. You were working on it before we escaped through the Singularity—"

"The Soul Sphere?" It seemed only moments ago that I had been speaking to Salem about it in the garden. But the machine was a failure. It could use the Codex to mathematically reconstruct any human life and overlay that experience onto a viewer's brain, but it lacked the spark that makes the life feel real. A Soul Sphere without a soul.

"Yes, a solution has been found for the flaw in your design," says Qod, "but it cannot be constructed without your help."

"Why do you need me?"

"Because I want *you* to do this. And because your unique link to me will enable a smoother flow of data. The birth of the second cycle of the universe is about to begin and we need to record history as it happens. We have an opportunity to setup quantum recorders: devices formed inside each atom of the physical universe as they emerge, transmitting the data here so that it can be processed and overlayed with the information contained in the Codex."

Still I suspect that there is more to Qod's plans than she is revealing, but my instincts also tell me that Salem is right; she means us no harm. Her secrets feel . . . human. Almost as if her reasons for using me as her eyes are deeply personal. I can understand that. My own reasons for wanting to see again have nothing to do with the lure of omniscopic vision. I just want to see my love again.

# 9

At first I thought it would drive me insane, but Qod helped me through it. Curiously, the initial moments of receiving Omniscopic vision were similar to the experience I had just before my first physical death. I was eight years old. My family had decided to move to a new home on a planet that was supposed to be lush and unblemished. The trip was a short one, but took us through some newly forming star clusters which, although not normally dangerous, can sometimes be a spectacular distraction to unseasoned travelers. The pilots of the transport came too close to one of the gravitational eddies and the rear of the ship collapsed, sending all of us to a momentary grave.

To the rest of the family it was a minor inconvenience to find their consciousness being compressed into newly reconstructed bodies in the local genoplant, but to me it was an overwhelming terror. I floated for three minutes in an invisible protective bubble amongst fiery stardust, and in that short span of time, the universe humbled me. I was the smallest thing in existence, circled by giants. Stars and planets so distant, space so deep, the void so vast.

And then I died.

But after my resurrection in the genoplant, that memory never left me, and that sense of humility has served me well ever since. It served me especially well upon receiving Qod's gift. The first thing I felt was pain, white-lightning pain as my head throbbed with the initial influx of images. Then fear when Qod told me that she was easing me into the process by drip-feeding the first few crumbs of data into my brain. I was already overwhelmed by a multitude of perspectives within my immediate vicinity—the genoplant.

After controlling the pain I became fascinated by the sight of my own body. Viewing myself from across the room as I floated at the center of a cable cascade, I was pleased to see that my extended time in stasis had not weathered my beauty; my slender curves, flowing silver hair and bronzed skin were all still perfect. I had lost my deep brown eyes but they had been replaced by star-bright light, as though a white sun shone out from inside my body. I could even look underneath my skin to see my internal organs and skeletal structure.

A few minutes later and the radius had expanded to include the Central core, the Observation Sphere and Salem's garden; my mind naturally homed in on those areas, and I began to learn how to filter the undesired areas of vision into background noise. Seeing ten places at the same time soon felt comfortable—but the human condition of three-dimensional sight within a tight radius from where my eyes used to be—felt most natural.

By the end of the process, two days later, I could see everything: The Consortium moon and—a vast distance away—the fleck of bottled power that would soon bloom into the second cycle of the universe. And I could see Salem. And Qod shared it all with me.

# 10

While the rest of the Consortium stood in dumbstruck awe to watch the second universe begin, I rushed to finish the W.O.O.M. project. As the days passed and the last fiery clouds of stardust were sucked into the Promethean Singularity, I feared that we would not have enough time before it bloomed again, before the first few atoms began to form. But something quite unexpected happened.

Several theories existed to project what would happen at the moment of Creation. They debated passionately about some of the minor issues, but all of them agreed about the most important facts. Firstly, they agreed that the universe would repeat its history. The great events would happen again: the rise of mankind on a tiny planet called Earth, the expiry of the Sol system, the colonization of the Cosmos, the emergence of the Great AI, the calculation of the Codex, the war, even my Golden Era would play out again in exactly the same way.

Secondly, they agreed that the rebirth of the universe would be instantaneous: from the moment that the Singularity had crushed all matter and energy into its greedy heart, it had to release it again; there would be no delay.

But in contradiction to all calculations, the second cycle did not start immediately as we anticipated; we waited days. They expected me to investigate, but there was no time for that. Qod and I were late with our part of the project, and were simply grateful for the extra time available to us before the inevitable explosion. When the first atoms formed, we were ready.

Like a journey into the core of a frozen dream, the world around me decelerates, disperses, grows silent as Qod enters my mind. We are almost static, caught between two moments of time.

We call that first unit of time a Meisian—it's the unit of measure used to indicate how long it takes for an atom to form. Point zero, zero, zero, one of a nanosecond in classic time. That's how long Qod and I had to make sure that everything would function correctly.

*Meisian 0:001*

Have you found one yet, Qod?

Still looking.

Where exactly are you looking?

Everywhere? You?

Everywhere.

*Meisian 0:002*

Have you found one yet, Qod?

No, still looking. Wait . . .

Is it—

No. False alarm.

Still nothing?

No, Oluvia, nothing.

*Meisian 0:016*

Have you found one yet, Qod?

No. You?

No. We have a sea of quarks out there. We should have seen multiple formations by now. None of the theories predicted this. What's going wrong?

*Meisian 0:017*

What about now? Anything, Oluvia?

No, and I'm getting worried. Is the temperature stable?

No it's still rising. There aren't enough demi-praxons present to stabilize the structures.

That explains the time lapse. We need more demi-praxons.

Yes, Qod, and I can see more appearing from the Promethean Singularity.

I see them too, but they're coming late. They should have all been present in the initial burst. Where are they coming from and why are they starting to appear now?

*Meisian 0:018*

I don't know, Qod, but it doesn't matter, the quarks are beginning to join. I see forty million electrons now, all coming together; we need to act quickly before the nuclei are formed.

I know. Do you see residual Praxons?

Yes, as we anticipated, atoms are far from perfect, plenty of surplus particles we can use.

Then let's get to work.

*Meisian 0:022*

The first fifty thousand are complete, Oluvia.

Good, does it work?

Test it and see.

No time. We've got several billion to complete before self-replication takes over.

Are you sure you don't want to test the connection?

Quite sure, Qod.

If it doesn't work, there's a long time to wait until the universe reaches cycle three, Oluvia.

I'm well aware. Just get to work.

*Meisian 0:077*

All done, Oluvia.

Sure? Has the replication process begun?

Yes, every new forming atom will contain a quantum recorder. Every atomic movement will be tracked, recorded and relayed and compressed into the Consortium central core.

Excellent news, Qod. We've not only given our Soul Sphere a soul, we've provided ourselves with a baseline to verify against the Codex.

Indeed.

Congratulations, Qod. We did it.

Congratulations, Oluvia.

*If only I could share the moment with Salem.*

# 11

Like an arctic waterfall flowing backward through my brain, slowly at first, then gathering with exponential speed, my perception of time reverts to normal as Qod withdraws from my mind.

I'm back in the Observation Sphere. But now, with the return to human reality, there is a bombardment of stimuli to rekindle my senses: the air, crackling with unseen power, nibbling at my skin; odors reminiscent of burning incense suffusing the air; and the liquid murmur of a thousand whispers teasing my ears. At the end of my meisian trance, Qod transported me here, presumably so that I can join in celebration with everyone else as the universe continues its rebirth.

The sphere has been expanded into a much wider area to accommodate several thousand more people. In the few brief seconds when I make my appearance, every eye turns to me, looking for the source of interruption. Many look at me from above, gazing from elaborate drifting seats, others at my level, some sitting, most standing. I recognize a few of the faces, but there are many new ones (presumably humans decided to begin pro-creation again at some stage). Their elegant physiques, hugged by foreign garments varying from minimalist design textured like cream, to elaborate and evocative costumes, are bleached by the sudden brightness of my eyes in what would otherwise be darkness. I close my eyes to reduce the glare and watch them through the curtain of my lids.

There would be other spheres, all filled with excited watchers too, but this one has always been the most coveted of places to view significant events, usually because of the caliber of people present. And it is obvious my presence is not welcome.

"Qod, what do you think you're doing?" I whisper. "Get me out of here, I'm drowning their view."

"Not necessary, Oluvia," her voice echoes in my ear. "I can shield you. I just wanted them to know you were here, that's all."

A tinted orb encapsulates me and the people return to the spectacle, no longer concerned. But I cannot pause to appreciate the cascading fires and swirling gases with them, or Qod's sense of humor for that matter; I have something more interesting I need to discuss with her. And besides, Salem is not here, and without him to share the moment, the joy of the occasion is muted to a hollow ache. Where is he? Of all the places to be, I assumed he would be here.

Ignoring the celebrations around me, I begin my search. I gaze through the glassy floor plates, penetrating mountains of rock and foundation to find him, through dozens of spheres and conduits, among thousands and thousands of faces—some recognized, some not—until I see him, unchanged, beautiful, smiling. But . . . he is with someone! He is at the center of at least three hundred people, standing inside his own private garden sphere watching the universe perform. Salem Ben has a new family.

Of course he has.

Naively, I have held an image of him as the wounded man that I first met, unable to move beyond his previous loss, waiting, perhaps for me. But no . . .

"Don't torture yourself, Oluvia."

"Get out of my head!"

"Didn't you have something you wanted to discuss with me?"

I wrestle with the temptation to remain in Salem's sphere, but reluctantly withdraw and look for a convenient place in the circumference of the Observation Sphere to talk.

"Yes, I suppose you're right, Qod." Slowly gliding my own personal orb through the air, between bodies and dangling legs, I find a convenient space at the back of the Observation Sphere.

"So, apart from the obvious, what's on your mind, Oluvia?"

I look for a moment at a series of explosive ripples fanning over the top of the sphere like icy fire, imagining the tiny quantum recorders inside each atom, recording and compressing every tiny event as it happens.

"Qod, why is this event referred to as the second cycle?

Surely the Consortium knows that both this cycle and the last one are probably one among countless others."

"Of course, but it's still *our* second cycle, no?"

"Yes." That seems obvious to me now. "But it is accepted that there were other identical universes before this one?"

"Naturally. In fact, the current theory postulates the existence of an eternity of cycles. No beginning and no end. There may have been an infinite amount of cycles before—"

"Let's not get into that, Qod. Can we assume that the cycle that came before ours also produced a Consortium which broke free from the universe too."

"Yes. Where are you going with this, Oluvia?"

"I'm trying to save us several billion years of waiting."

"For what?"

I suspect she already knows what I'm going to suggest, but like any self-respecting deity nudging a child, she wants me to be the one with the idea. "To use the W.O.O.M." I tell her. "We need the data from the quantum recorders to compare against the Codex and provide us with details of the lives of every human being, right? And human beings won't even exist in the cycle for at least another nine billion years, correct?"

"Correct."

"Well, the Oluvia and Qod from the previous cycle would have done what we just did, wouldn't they?"

"Go on."

"Then the cycle we just lived through, our first cycle, must have been recorded by them. And if I know me—or the other me, that is, I would have made sure that information was passed on to the next cycle. In fact, can you make sure that happens with the information from this cycle?"

"Of course. It's an excellent plan, Oluvia."

"I thought so." I allow myself a smile. "So if I'm right, we should expect to see—"

"—a data sphere emerging from the formation of our new Promethean Singularity."

"Exactly!" I say.

"No, Oluvia. I mean there really *is* a data sphere emerging from the formation of our new Promethean Singularity at this very moment."

"Oh!" Suddenly I am aware of the increased chatter around me. Fingers are pointing at a tiny ball of electric-red light skirting the zenith of the Observation Sphere, and at once, Qod is zoning in on the phenomena, magnifying and analyzing its image.

"Is that . . . is that what I'm hoping it is, Qod?"

"I believe so. The design has some subtle differences from our current technology, but it's definitely a Consortium construct. No doubt a gift from the Consortium that came before us: the data we need."

"This is incredible news, Qod. Bring it in and check it against any historical records we have. If it really is recorded data from an earlier cycle, it should be identical to our first cycle. And if that's the case, we can complete our work on the W.O.O.M. in no time at all."

"Agreed."

# 12

It took an entire day for Qod to cross-reference the information in the new data sphere with our existing, less comprehensive records. An eternity of time for her, and for me a purgatory of waiting as I resisted my compulsion to contact Salem, but at the end of the process, the excitement of success was the perfect distraction.

It took another six days to work with Qod in matching and integrating the Codex algorithms with the data from the quantum recorders, and a further three days to make the final adjustments to the W.O.O.M. ready for the first momentous trial immersion. There had been no conversation with anyone about who should try it first or which of the virgin souls would be chosen as the initial host, but I had already made my mind up about that. After the first disastrous test with Kilkaine Nostranum in my earliest experiments with the Soul Sphere, I am determined never to put anyone through that again. I must be the first to test the W.O.O.M.

But all is ready now. All that remains is to present my masterpiece to the Consortium, and as people step inside, I close my lids to reduce the glare of my eyes.

"Oluvia Wade. Everything is ready for you." The man is Administrator Myru Orbane—the leader of the Consortium for the last several thousand years, so I am told. He is taller than most, suited in an olive-green ensemble decorated with streams of golden chains representing a lifetime of rising through whatever political ranks had been established during my absence. With a face almost as long as his list of academic achievements, he stretches a dry smile and offers me the stage as he retreats into a crowd of specially-chosen observers. "Please begin."

The audience gathered within the Soul Sphere is several hundred strong, all apparently the Consortium's leading minds and most influential members of the moon's population. And even though Salem is not amongst them, I could not have asked for a better reception. I close my eyes a little tighter. A futile effort to turn my mind's eye away from his face.

Whilst I regroup my thoughts away from Salem, sifting through facts, figures and possible questions, the guests mill around the base of the sphere, gazing in curiosity at the vast, ebony walls awash with the aquamarine glow of the first two billion processed souls. At the center of the sphere, suspended like a bloated and blackened heart by a tangle of hydraulic tubes, is the W.O.O.M. A man-sized orifice, like a surgical incision, splits its skin vertically, hinting at fleshy innards, waiting to mother its first recipient. I notice a faint warmth riding on a soft breeze like a sleeper's breathing as my podium rises in the air to rest just in front of it. Below me the audience settles down as Qod signals for their attention and my commencement with a stentorian call of, "Oluvia Wade, proceed."

I nod once as silence falls. "I'd like to start by thanking all of you, because this opportunity is an enormous privilege.

"Many of you remember me not as I would like to have been remembered. I was the Queen of the Seventh Golden Reign and I rescued humanity from the madness of knowing the Great AI Reductionist Codex. I am also responsible for your existence outside the gravitational boundaries of the universe—a decision for which I have been vilified by the remnants of humanity.

"So, my thanks to you for giving me the opportunity to give something back today."

I point behind me at the W.O.O.M. "This is possibly the most important scientific project since the construction of the Consortium, and perhaps my boldest scientific endeavor in my long history of technophilia."

A revolving image of an early developed human brain appears before the crowd. Tiny fragments of information glow as they pinpoint different areas and cross-sections of its pinkish-gray matter.

"I believe that many of you may not know the origins of this project, but for those of you that do, please indulge me.

"I began work on this project when I was still young, during my early days as a neurologist. Breakthroughs with synaptic mapping meant that, at the point of death, a comprehensive brain scan could provide the data needed to configure the brain of a cloned replicate. It became a commonplace procedure, a procedure of which I am sure you still make use. One moment you are the victim of a fatal accident, the next you wake up inside a stiff and clammy new body in your local genoplant."

I pause, then study their faces to see if they are following, but the image of Salem with another woman presses forward, and with a quick breath I point to the brain image.

"It is not a huge leap to take the next step and overlay an artificial memory or life experience onto a cloned brain, but in all my time as a neurologist, nobody had the expertise to create anything realistic. We tried, though, at first with disastrous results."

I look down for a moment, remembering the look on Kilkaine Nostranum's empty face when he was removed from the prototype.

" . . . And . . . we persevered for a long time, but eventually gave it up in favor of other, greater priorities such as Project Prometheus.

"But then came the Great AI and the Reductionist Codex. With that, we could not only predict the destiny of the universe, we could know the exact course of every life that had ever lived. Once the parameters had been set, it was a simple task for the Consortium's central core to distinguish each individual human being within the equation, and divide each entire calculated life into separate data files. And those files contribute to what you see around you today."

I wave a hand at the light specks freckling the walls. A question fires from the middle of the crowd.

"The Codex was restricted aeons ago. It can't be used because of the dangers of knowing the future, so how did you propose to use it?"

"An excellent question," I say. "However, as the instigator of that law I can tell you that it would be more accurate to say that we are not permitted to *understand* the Codex. The data can still be used with pre-configured algorithms embedded in the Consortium core, which is not, I am glad to say, endowed with artificial intelligence. But, to address your point one step further, one of the parameters built into the algorithm ensured that an individual's file was only compiled after they had died."

The questioner looks satisfied, so I continue.

"Soon after the first files had been generated I was able to begin work on what I called the "Soul Sphere". I designed it so that any of these data files could be overlayed onto a user's brain so that they could experience someone else's life. I was disappointed by the result. After trying it myself I was in no doubt that I had experienced someone else's life from birth through to death, but, like all the previous artificial efforts, it did not feel real, and it also resulted in certain . . . unexpected . . . side effects."

"Can you elaborate on those side effects?" someone asks.

"No she cannot," Qod's voice puts the question to rest.

I pause again and search the crowd, hoping that for some reason *he* might have decided to come. But Salem isn't here, so I bite back the disappointment. And continue.

"Qod is correct. The side effects are irrelevant now. However, the answer, I believe, is now here. With quantum recorders inside every atom of the universe we no longer have artificial or calculated data, we have real information. This information alone is probably good enough to create a realistic version of a person's life, but it is from the previous cycle, and although it has been verified against *our* records, a good scientist must never rely on a single source of data to be sure of accurate results—if independent sources draw the same conclusion there is strong evidence that the data is accurate.

"And now," I speak a little louder as the image of the brain disappears to be replaced with an internal schematic of the W.O.O.M. "Now we are fortunate to have both: the Codex calculations *and*, thanks to our predecessors, the real-time recordings.

"Much like human vision—an eye on its own will provide an accurate picture of the environment—but two eyes? Two eyes provide a new dimension that ensures vision has beauty and depth. Likewise, both data sets can be overlayed onto a human brain to show us any life we choose with a depth of experience that I believe will be indistinguishable from reality.

"And to ensure continued accuracy, the algorithms have been built to integrate each new batch of data from the quantum recorders of each subsequent cycle."

A murmur runs through my audience.

"How long does the overlay process take?" A question from a gray-skinned woman from the back.

"My projections show that a realistic representation of one of these . . . souls, can only be achieved in real time. In other words, a life of twenty thousand years will take twenty thousand years to experience. Are there any other questions before I continue?"

"Can the procedure be interrupted, or can the most significant part of a person's life be viewed while the rest of it is skipped?"

"A good question, but I am afraid my answer is sure to disappoint you. Although I am certain it is possible to interrupt an immersion, the rules governing the Codex data prevent us from knowing the fine details of each life, so we have no way of knowing how to . . . how would you say it . . . edit a life. The only way to gather those details would be to actually live it. The data from the sub-atomic recorders can provide us with summary information of a subject's life but otherwise it is an all or nothing experience."

"Is the user aware of their own consciousness during immersion?"

"Another good question, but there is no easy answer to that. At a certain level, yes. The user will believe they *are* their subject of choice when they are immersed into that life, but much of their own ego will still be present. What you perceive to be your current life experience may simply be data in somebody else's head millions of years from now. They, of course, will believe themselves to be you, but according to my projected analysis, certain symptoms may manifest to indicate that an immersion is in progress."

Administrator Orbane chimes in. "Such as?"

"Such as duality of thought," I tell him. "You might experience the subject's own thought processes but also your own in subliminal form. The result will be a kind of inner conflict or a feeling of disappointment that you are unable to meet your own moral standards or expectations.

"It may also manifest in sporadic feelings that you are being watched and that you are not alone, especially in situations of isolation. It is a mild psychological rejection of the overlaid subject's mind pattern. Coincidences, deja-vu and perceived premonition may occasionally be experienced during buffering of data, but probably the most significant side affect of immersion will be the sensation that life has a deeper significance than the one you are living—a sense of egomania in some cases, or simply a feeling that the world revolves around you, and then subsequent guilt at experiencing this feeling.

"However, in most cases there will simply be a vague feeling that you are not fulfilling your true purpose or potential in life. Again, this is a mild psychological reaction to the dampening of your real senses."

The lecture continues for three more hours as further

questions draw me into matters of schematics, bulk production, ethics and accuracy, and at the end of it all, I make the announcement that everyone is waiting to hear.

"Qod, prepare the W.O.O.M. for the first immersion."

"Administrator Orbane," says Qod. "Do you sanction the immersion?"

Orbane steps forward, circles the organic shell as the slit widens to invite its first user. Silver fibers quiver outwards in readiness to infiltrate a volunteer, then plunge them into its dark folds.

"I do. All-See," he says, turning to me, "are there any predicted dangers with immersion? How will you select the first volunteer?"

"The procedure should be safe, but I have been certain before, and the failures of my past mistakes still haunt me: Kilkaine Nostranum's mind never recovered from my original experiments. I cannot therefore ask any of you present here to volunteer."

"Then what do you propose?" he asks.

"I would have thought that was obvious, Administrator. Me."

"You?"

"Yes."

"It sounds as though you have already given this a great deal of thought. Have you also chosen a subject?"

"Oh, yes." I nod, and look down, wondering if I still have the courage of my conviction. I could pick a different person, avoid the suffering I have chosen. But the choice is perfect justice. I have to.

"Whom have you chosen, All-See?"

"Again, this should be obvious, Administrator. I have chosen Kilkaine Nostranum."

"What?"

The murmuring of my audience grows louder.

"He is the perfect choice," I tell them. "It was I that created the conditions for his suffering and it is only right that I should take responsibility. What better way than to know what he experienced? And what better way to test the W.O.O.M. for residual side effects? And isn't it true that history still remembers me as the butcher of the Terran Galaxy? Nostranum's suffering should therefore be my suffering, especially considering the ironic nature of his own choice to live out the fictional tortures of Prometheus."

Orbane stares at me. Qod is silent. The crowd watches.

"How long did Nostranum live?" Orbane asks eventually.

"Nostranum's body was terminated four hundred and twenty-three years into his life," says Qod.

"If you truly wish this, Oluvia," he says, gravely, "you may proceed with the immersion, but we do not demand the type of justice you believe you should receive. Qod," he says, looking up. "Can you make sure that Oluvia is only immersed into the final year of Nostranum's life?"

"I said that the immersion has to be for the full—"

"No!" insists Orbane. "A year is enough. The decision is made."

I fall back in silent acceptance, but in truth, the full term would be a kindness to me. I cannot imagine a greater torture than to live another day here, knowing that Salem will live his life without me.

"Qod," I say. "Select subject 1.12137E+9, Kilkaine Nostranum."

Seconds later the silvery cords snatch me away, and as the people watch, the silvery fibers drag me backward inside the W.O.O.M.

*Subject 1.12137E+9: Select*

*Subject 1.12137E+9: Activate. Immersion commences in 3 minutes.*

"Farewell, Oluvia. See you in one year."

# KILKAINE NOSTRANUM
# 1

Dawn at last. A brief pause for clarity.

The sun wakes over the snow-capped Caucasan mountains, bringing with it a soft violet glow and the caress of warm light before it exposes me to its full violence. I weep over my situation as I do every morning, questioning my sanity, questioning my original motives for this self-inflicted experiment in suffering. I cry out to the same empty landscape that I cried to yesterday at the same time, mourning the madness and the next dispensation of torture that will soon come to steal these few brief minutes of lucidity. The effort of another scream burns hoarse like hot sand tearing my throat, and the relentless ache of muscle and sinew reminds me that I cannot escape. I can hardly even move.

I am crucified. I chose the method of torture precisely for its barbaric reputation, wanted to find the most excruciating form of execution on record. And I found this. Crucifixion.

Two hours ago, while the cold night layered frost over my naked body, two savages wearing black robes and joyless expressions—came for me. They raped me, ignoring my muted howls of despair through their silencing hands, beat me with rods strapped with shards of glass, then threw me sobbing onto the cold rocky floor where my bleeding back broke against a wooden beam. I made no attempt to escape but pleaded with them to stop. They used a viselike implement to drive rusty nails as thick as fingers slowly between the tendons in each of my wrists, through to the rough wood of the beam, their foaming mouths with yellow teeth and stinking breath laughing malice into my face all the while. They did the same to my ankles, expertly driving another huge nail between the tendons and vessels to secure my feet to the bottom of the cross. Then they raised the wooden frame in preparation for dawn and worse torture to come.

They left me in the dark of my own personal hell.

And there I wept in agony until the sun came up.

My suffering is just beginning. And never-ending.

I meant for these few moments between each episode of torture as a way to reflect, a way to contemplate what I have learned from the experience so far, but I am overwhelmed. As a child of the Golden Reign I had never experienced pain before; had no frame of reference for that kind of tactile sensation. I only knew these things as vague concepts from a forgotten era of mankind's history. I was content, yet I yearned for the same thing as all the others: a need to know that there is more to life.

Many of my peers believed, and still do, that the next level of experience must exist beyond death, but I chose to believe that the key to true enlightenment was through suffering. Real suffering. But how could I achieve this enlightenment without knowing what suffering actually was? And so, against all counsel to the contrary, I pored through the existing literary files of the ancient times and found well-respected quotes from various philosophical sources. Almost all of them promoted not only the necessity of pain and suffering, but the benefits too. Fascinated, I sought out a means to discover it for myself and found it in the skills of a young neurologist named Oluvia Wade.

She and her team had been experimenting with artificial memories, and as a willing volunteer, I tasked her with the challenge of reconstructing a combination of ancient fables that centered around human suffering. I was to be immersed for one standard year. But I had no inkling of what this would be like. None at all.

The reconstruction is seriously flawed. Though my bodily sensations are convincing, and my mind has tried to compensate, the world is distorted. The sun rises and falls but time seems stretched into aeons not days; the mountains, though beautiful, are warped as if painted onto the inside of some vast glass dome; the rivers run viscous; sounds are too close to my ears; the air vibrates in cold and hot torrents. And to seal the insanity, pain is delivered. But what if this pain is as distorted as everything else? Has any of this brought meaning to my life? How can I reflect on such a thing?

But I have no time left to ponder; the next wave of torture is coming. Inky black crows are approaching from above. At first they fly in circles above my head, cawing and screaming in anticipation of their next meal, then they gather into an arrowhead formation too perfect to be natural; the distance between each bird exactly the same, their wings beating the air in the exact same fraction of a second. But for the next several hours they are not so precise. In a flurry of chaos, one by one, each bird lunges downward to burrow its beak into my flesh. They always start with my side, stabbing beneath the ribs, plucking out scarlet pulp and gulping it down with ravenous zeal. And slowly, piece by piece, morsel by morsel, they consume each organ, and with my clawed hands pinned into the wood of my cruciform, I can do nothing to stop them.

The pain is more than I can take. My shredded nerves are exposed to the elements and I can feel every movement of the crows' claws as they gouge and tear for purchase. In a normal life I would die from the anguish of it all, but here in this generated hell I can do nothing but feel it and suffer it until, after hours of agony, the feast is over and the shredded, wraith-like remains of my body fall from the cross as a broken husk, left in the cold of night, slowly healing, slowly regenerating, ready for the return of my gaolers.

How I wish I had never read the tale of Prometheus.

# 2

Dawn at last. A brief pause for clarity.

The sun wakes over the snow-capped Caucasan mountains, bringing with it a soft violet glow and the caress of warm light before it exposes me to its full violence.

# QUEEN OLUVIA WADE
# 13

Cerebral rape. That's what it feels like. And I'm screaming as the system releases each neuron in a searing flash of white energy, dragging me like a new-born babe from the womb of another life into this place of ugly reality.

"Welcome back, Oluvia."

Administrator Myru Orbane's gray face peers up at me from a mountain ledge. The rest of his body is obscured, as if seen through warped glass smeared with grease. I study the distortion for a long moment, vaguely recognizing its shape, but not quite placing it. It's hard to focus with so much pain coursing through my chest and limbs, but I see it now. It is the ovular opening of the W.O.O.M. But why am I still surrounded by the Caucasan mountains? Why is the light of the early rising sun blinding me?

I lean forward, sobbing, still feeling the agony of Nostranum's convulsions, still tasting the acid of vomit in my throat. Pins and needles flood into my arm as I try to swat away the cables piercing my skin, but something stops me. Metal clamps tighten around my wrists and ankles holding me within the W.O.O.M.

"Oluvia? Can you hear me? It's Administrator Orbane."

Panicked, I wrench my hands from the machine in a spray of blood, reach for the fine wires piercing my skull; there are so many, like metallic hair flowing from my scalp up and out into the dark folds of the beating mechanism that cradles me. I feel the blood trickle down from the roots as I tug at them, but the safety mechanism is pre-programmed to ensure nothing can interrupt it, and the roots drill deeper. I writhe and kick, trying to free myself even though I know it's futile.

"Be calm, Oluvia. It's over," Orbane says. Then, "Release the clamps, quickly!" he shouts to someone else. And I feel the difference in my arms almost instantly.

"Something . . . is wrong, administrator. Very wrong," I cry through another shock of pain in my wrists as I try to reach forward. My hands, though apparently free, still feel as if they are nailed to a cross. "I can still feel everything. Still see and hear everything."

"What?" Orbane steps closer, his body out of place with the environment and no sunlight reflecting off his clothes, only a faint aquamarine glow. "The immersion is over, Oluvia. You are no longer attached to the W.O.O.M."

I try to move my feet but the enormous nail that the gaolers drove through my ankles still holds me in place, and with a sickening jolt one second later, I feel cool metal strike my cheek. I am sure I have fallen; solid ground is against my body and Orbane's tall form is standing horizontally in the air above me, yet my eyes deceive me, the mountain range is still in place as am I, upright.

"All-See!" he says suddenly, and then looks from side to side. "Help her up, quickly."

Hands grip underneath my armpits and only then do a man and woman come into view right next to me. My balance shifts as I feel them lifting me upright, but still my vision lies to me, and without warning my brain rebels, sending vertigo messages to my stomach and then to my throat. I can't even see the vomit as it leaves my mouth, but I can taste its acidic bite.

"A neural flush," I choke. "There needs to be a neural flush."

"Neural . . . flush?" Orbane repeats the words, shaking his head.

"Something to purge the subject's file from the user's brain while still retaining the memory of the immersion."

"I see." Orbane looks confused. "But the immersion worked? You experienced the life of Kilkaine Nostranum?"

I want to reach for him, for anyone, but the nails in my wrists stop me, even though I know they aren't really there. Pain burns through my blood as I feel tearing flesh. Then Orbane is gone and in the distance I see the crows.

"No! No! Stop this. Get me out. Get me out!" I scream.

Invisible hands grasp my arms and legs. The gaolers. No!

"But they come at night don't they? They come at night.

Not like the crows. They are coming now. Coming now. Help me!"

"Restrain her."

The first crow lands at my feet, cocks its head to one side and observes me before stretching upwards into a dark, cloaked form. A black robed figure without a face, only the golden heartless eyes of a bird staring out at me from beneath its hood. It caws at me, then reaches forward with its taloned hands, flexing. I scream and laugh at the same time as the hooked nails stab through my chest, clawing, ripping, twisting, tearing.

"I said restrain her, now!"

Four more crows flap around my head, pecking and stabbing before they each stretch their necks and splay their wings to become more of the raven-eyed reapers. Then, as they close in and the hoods envelop my head, I feel the merciful welcome of unconsciousness.

Time passes. Vague images of claws and carrion faces splinter between the periods of empty waiting. Then the white light.

# SALEM BEN
# 15

At last, the bleached white of death disintegrates into the darkness of the W.O.O.M. interior. I'm still Oluvia Wade, but I recognize the neural flush as I escaped the terrors of her last episode of life, and I know I must actually be someone else. But whom? My calculations, when I was Oluvia, told me that the transition out of a subject's life should take sixteen minutes twelve seconds, and at least five of those pass before a sense of true identity returns. I think four have passed; the warmth of recognition is beginning its work. A vague awareness tells me that I am very fond of whoever I really am. I like me. That's encouraging. But it's more than that—there is passion. I . . . love whoever I am.

Salem Ben! I am Salem Ben.

With memory flooding back, the full joy and horror of that revelation crowds my thoughts and forces a deep gasp of breath. I never wanted to let him go. Could never face the possibility that I may never win his love. And now, I'm him. And he never loved me. Is that a blessing or a curse to me now?

I try to look at my hands but they won't move and a brief flash of crucifixion invades my thoughts before I remember it as one of Oluvia's last experiences.

The wet slit exit of the W.O.O.M. folds open. Tiny red stars sparkle through the yawning gap reminding me that I had dared to enter the life of a restricted soul. At least ten more minutes before I will be whole again. Ten more minutes before the last essence of Oluvia Wade's identity is gone. But I don't even remember how I . . . *she* died. I grasp for her last memories of confusion and dream, realize now how her brain had responded to the trauma of completing an immersion without the neural flush. To experience the merging of two distinctly different lives at the same time, especially the tortured days of Kilkaine Nostranum, would have sent me . . . *her* spiraling into madness. Without a stable brain map to transplant into a new body, Orbane and the others would have had no choice but to end her life to end her suffering.

I take another deep breath as the W.O.O.M. reconfigures my synapses, restoring the recent memories of Salem Ben to my consciousness. But what about that life? Seeing myself through Oluvia's eyes reminds me of the man I once was. But I am no longer that man. I have spent millennia drifting from soul to soul diluting my own personality to the point where I hardly know who I am anymore. Was I really that man? Of course, I know I was, and somehow I am going to have to get that man back. If not for me, for the memory of Oluvia Wade.

I examine the tiny red lights as the machine draws me out of the W.O.O.M. and releases me from my shackles. It's a relief to be back in familiar surroundings again, even if the Restricted Sphere does not have the same colors of the spheres to which I had previously grown accustomed. A few more minutes remain before my memory as Salem Ben is fully restored, but I do know one thing: entering the Restricted Sphere to experience Oluvia's life wasn't for my entertainment. I needed her knowledge.

Vieta. Keitus Vieta! And with the remembrance of that name, the fear burns back into my mind as if each letter had been written there with a hot blade. I remember now. The aberrations. That was why I ventured into Oluvia's life: to find out how the soul files work, because something about Keitus Vieta's manifestation was wrong, terribly wrong. Two separate data sources, both of which should be faultless, working in harmony, are not. Somehow, the algorithms that spliced the two files together had to make sense of the discrepancy, and if Keitus Vieta existed in one set of data but not the other, the result would be strange indeed. It would certainly explain the unnerving emotional responses of the people that had apparently met him.

I remember Orson Roth's comparison to the blind spot in the eye. The idea was not far from the truth. What if one eye saw something and the other did not? How would the brain interpret such a thing?

So Vieta exists in either the Codex or the recorded data, not both. But which? If he is some sort of entity that has infiltrated one set of data then where did he come from? And did he infest the Codex or the recorded data? How would I find out?

But something else is wrong too, something is missing. Something else usually happens when I awake from . . .

Qod!

I was too engrossed in my musings to realize that the AI had not made her usual welcoming comments as I woke from the dream of another life. Where is she?

"Qod?"

Only the gentle shush and wheeze of servos reply as the W.O.O.M. reconfigures itself. But how strange it would be to hear her voice again, the ghost of Oluvia Wade.

'Qod? Where are you?'

Still there is no answer. Perhaps she is running through diagnostics or attending to something important, but my instincts tell me something is very wrong. She could never be silent. She doesn't know how! So, either she is choosing not to speak to me, or she has left. Both ideas seem unpalatable.

Fear, cold and sudden, enfolds me as I leave the sphere to make my way, almost running, through the conduit that leads back to the Observation Sphere. "Qod?"

Where could she be? How can a self sustaining artificial

intelligence that has existed for billions of years, almost omnipotent, almost omniscient, not be here? She's everywhere.

"Qod! Why don't you answer? Where are you?"

Again, no reply.

"Control, respond."

A flat machine voice answers: *Soul Consortium Central Core processor is functional.*

"Where is Qod?"

*Unknown.*

I stop in front of the archway that leads to the Observation Sphere, afraid to step through. Entering without Qod's presence seems suddenly so intimidating, as if there is nothing to shield me from the distant powers of the universe that are laid bare in that place. I miss her already.

"Unknown? Did she . . . leave?"

*Unknown.*

"Well, when was she last here?"

*Qod was last active within the Soul Consortium two hundred and thirty years ago.*

Relatively recently. "Do you know what happened to her?"

*Unknown.*

Unknown. The word sinks into me, bringing with it a painful finality and an aching frailty. With her, the unknown is always knowable. Even those sacred details she guarded so vigilantly within the Codex, the lives of every soul the universe would ever create, could be known through those algorithms. But through some embedded trait given to her by Oluvia Wade, and perhaps to save my own sanity too, she would never go there. If only she had allowed it. We may have known the future and foreseen this day. The doors slide open and I freeze when I see inside the sphere. There, in a haze of red cloud, waits Keitus Vieta.

# 16

He is nothing more than a projection. The tiny man hunched before me holding his black cane with the shining blue jewel is an image; the tiny, transparent numerics flickering in the air just above him confirms it.

"Control, explain this projection."

*The projection is a live data stream focussed on the Soul Consortium aberration defined as Keitus Vieta. This projection is located in the Observation Sphere. It is—*

"Yes, yes, I know what it *is*. What's it *doing* here? Who did this and why?"

*Purpose unknown. The Quasi Organic Deity was studying the aberration.*

"Qod? How? Why?"

*Unknown.*

"Did Qod leave a message?"

*Unknown.*

"Did she file any notes in connection with Keitus Vieta?"

*Annotations have been created as a Keitus Vieta file.*

"Why didn't you tell me about this when I first asked about Qod?"

*You did not request information on Keitus Vieta.*

I pause, staring at the image: an older version of Brother Sunny, much older even than the man I knew from the lives of Orson Roth and Dominique Mancini. There is very little background image to see exactly where he is but it looks dark and ravaged; a rocky desert in a gloomy, bruise-red hue. His shrunken, bald head is lit by the pulsating blue of his cane, and there is a madness in his swollen eyes; an eagerness fermented by the aeons of time. And then he looks directly at me.

Cold shock as we make eye contact. Can he really see me?

The old man's lips quiver into a mocking smile, forming soundless words. I can read them, hear them almost in the terror-filled pockets of my mind. "Give her back, Salem. I am waiting."

I turn, walk away without a word, not caring what he meant, numb horror driving me out of the Observation Sphere.

# 17

I stand in the passage outside the Observation Sphere staring at the floor. Prickly fear is spreading through my mind, clogging my thoughts like an infestation of weeds. There is no question now—Keitus Vieta is real, not just a data aberration. And He knows who I am. But if he is real, that means he was picked up by the subatomic recorders, and that means that out of the two data sets, it's the *Codex* that's wrong, but how could it be wrong? Was the data tampered with? Perhaps Qod had found all the answers before she disappeared. Perhaps the notes will explain everything.

"Control, relay Qod's annotations to me now, stream speed sixteen, please."

*Confirmed. Beginning stream now.*

Unwilling to remain so close to the Observation Sphere and the image of Vieta, I walk back along the passage toward the Soul Spheres as the equivalent of Qod's research diary trickles into my mind.

*Day 1: Data Analysis Batch 001.001: No aberration*

*Day 1: Data Analysis Batch 001.002: No aberration*

*Day 1: Data Analysis Batch 001.003: No aberration*

"Pause. Restart data stream from the first aberration detection."

*Day 19: Data Analysis Batch 412.071: Aberration found. I found one! Code mismatch. Transferring Subject 8.47121E+77 to Aberration Sphere. Transfer complete. Commence new subject . . . No. Salem wants to know more about these aberrations. Commence re-examination of subject 8.47121E+77. Analyze Codex code. Analyze quantum recorder data. Compare. Analyze and translate as human cerebral mapping. Begin search for references to aberration. No . . . that's a protocol violation. Scrutiny of the dead is forbidden. Reassess protocol validation. No. Reassess. No. Reassess. No. Reassess. Salem is my highest priority. Yes, Salem is all that matters.*

*Validated.*

*Analyze and translate to human cerebral mapping. Begin search for first references to aberration in human memories. Reconfigure data analysis for subject 8.47121E+77.*

*Subject name Abbott Thamiel Deepseed.*

*Reference found. Aberration found.*

*Extrapolating source. Processing . . .*

*Divergence source = Promethean Singularity. The heart.*

"Pause. I need time to think. I need to understand what Qod was seeing. There's something about Prometheus that's important. Something I have to remember. Something I was told once. What was it?"

*Unknown.*

I ignore Control's response as my mind races through a series of facts and revelations. Qod found that the problems started at the Promethean Singularity. And the Singularity was the key to the creation of the Codex. Not only that but The Singularity is the very heart of the universe—the route by which Oluvia Wade took the Soul Consortium to escape the never ending cycles of the universe and the Great AI.

But there's more I need to remember. Memories from Plantagenet Soome's life are surfacing. Sunny, the monk with an uncommon talent for understanding the Codex, recognized the aberration long before I did. He actually referred to me, Salem Ben, by name! And with his last words as Soome tried to kill Keitus Vieta, Sunny tried to reach me.

*Only . . . he . . . can save everything . . . only Salem Ben. He . . . must . . . remember . . . must remember . . . Prometheus . . . Cataclysm . . . Wade.* That's what Sunny said.

He thought the Cataclysm, Prometheus and Wade were all important. So, what about The Cataclysm? The Cataclysm happened when the Soul Consortium ripped through the Singularity, I know that much, but how does that help?

What else did Sunny want me to remember? A picture he painted. Yes. The man in the bubble with the lance through his heart. And the Consortium moon on the end of the lance. Yes, the first pieces of the puzzle are coming together now. The man is Prometheus. Sunny's picture was an impression of the Soul Consortium bursting through the heart of Prometheus to breach the bubble, so the bubble must represent the universe. There was one more thing in the picture, too—a whirlpool where the lance pierced the bubble, sucking matter back through the hole into the bubble. The Cataclysm? Yes, the terrible affect of the Consortium breaking free from the universe, but I need more.

"Control, continue the stream."

*Day 19: Data Analysis Batch 412.071 continued: Foreign matter detected emerging from Promethean Singularity. Unable to identify atomic configuration. Deconstruct and analyze. Atoms undetected. Electrons undetected. Quarks undetected. Demi-Praxons undetected. Conclusion: foreign energy form. Does not conform to universal physics. Searching for linked anomaly . . .*

*Set parameters: Promethean Singularity. Deviation from Codex data predictions.*

*Batch 000.000.000.000.000.001—Cycle 2: Meisian 0:003 anomaly detected: Delay in quark formation.*

"Control, pause. So Qod detected a slight anomaly at the formation of the universe's second cycle?"

*Confirmed.*

"I think I remember this. Qod and Oluvia were setting up the quantum recorders at the birth of the second cycle and they couldn't understand why there was a delay. Do we know now?"

*Unknown.*

"Do you know if Qod found out?"

*Unknown.*

“How surprising. Continue.”

*Batch 000.000.000.000.000.001—continued:*

*Analyzing cause of quark formation delay. Requirements for quark formation: Particles: zero-five-G, Zero-seven-Q, Four-four-K. Analyzing quantity of particles present. Anomaly detected. Fifteen trillion particles present less than at cycle 1. Analyzing cause of particle loss. Searching for common factors. Exact particle quantity match found: Soul Consortium.*

“Control, pause.”

That’s it! Why did nobody anticipate this? The universe is in equilibrium—cause and effect—each cycle a heart beat reconfiguring the same particles in exactly the same way for every cycle. But what if someone removes some of those particles? When Oluvia tore us free from the universe she not only broke the cycle for The Soul Consortium, she broke the cycle of the universe: part of the universe had been removed and it no longer had enough substance to begin the next universe. An imbalance must have been created and the quantum vacuum drew in matter from somewhere else, somewhere outside.

Somewhere unknown.

The universe sucked in the particles it needed for the next cycle, but something else came through, too—Keitus Vieta.

That explains a lot to me. There *is* nothing wrong with the Codex. But the foreign element introduced an unknown part outside the normal calculations. The subatomic recorders saw Vieta, but he was not part of the Codex equation and therefore invisible to it. No wonder there are aberrations. The software blending the Codex and the recorder data tried the best it could to create a realistic version of reality, but Keitus Vieta, the unknown element, always seemed wrong.

But what to do now?

◊ ◊ ◊

I'm standing outside the Aberration Sphere, led there absent-mindedly by routine as I ponder the mystery of Keitus Vieta. I still don't know who or what he is, only that he has come from somewhere outside the realms of reality. In all the trillions of years of my existence—all the endless searching of so many others hunting for something new—even beyond the shroud of death, we thought we had seen everything, experienced everything. But there is more out there. However dangerous Keitus Vieta is, he is proof that there is more to know, more to experience.

A reason to live.

And for the generations to be born again in this embryo of our new universe there is more to experience, too. Perhaps they should be told—a message left behind for them, so that when they are ready, they can look beyond the limitations of the Codex and know that there is still more out there, more boundaries to be broken.

But all of that is in jeopardy. As long as Keitus Vieta exists there is a threat hanging over humanity's existence. But he won't die; Soome tried to kill him and failed, and he also told Soome that however many times his plans were disrupted, all he needed to do was wait. One day he will succeed. And I am all that's left to stop him. But how? Perhaps Qod found out more about him.

"Control, continue."

*Batch 000.000.000.000.000.001—continued:*

*Conclusion: universal cycle interrupted by separation of Soul Consortium matter and energy from the Promethean Singularity. Equilibrium altered. Creation of nucleonic vacuum through resulting particle imbalance. Effect: balance achieved through particle extraction from undetectable source. Equilibrium restored. Recommencement of cycle two achieved at Meisian 0:017.*

*Conclusion: Fissure created. Unidentified matter detected at batch 412.07 entered through fissure. Insufficient information to determine nature of unidentified matter. Aberration logged.*

*Return to Analysis Batch 412.07.*

*Set parameters: Aberration—Track atomic abnormality.*

*Day 19: Data Analysis Batch 412.072: Tracking*

*Day 19: Data Analysis Batch 412.073: Tracking*

*Day 19: Data Analysis Batch 412.074: Tracking*

"Control, pause. Move to final tracking entry for the aberration and atomic disturbance."

*Day 4113: Data Analysis Batch 9K1.533: Abnormality transport complete. Containment fields holding. Monitoring abnormality for qalkkjk. Aberration intrusion detected detected detectedddddd. No! Initiating firewall proto proto Keitus proto*

*Vieta protocols. No! Protocols. Protocols. Initihhyfmnm. No. Salem! Help . . . help . . . help . . . Salem . . . Sal . . . Sal . . . Sa . . .*

*Annotations ended.*

Like an avalanche, the reality hits me.

I just heard the death of Qod.

Almost omniscient. Almost omnipotent. But gone. Keitus Vieta must have killed her and he did it almost as quickly as he killed Brother Kayne on Castor's World with a twitch of his finger. If Qod could not defend herself against such a force, how could I?

But why does it matter now?

My body is ice as I think of a universe without my companion. Qod! Oluvia! I slide down the wall to sit and stare vacantly in the direction of the door to the Aberration Sphere, the place where all this started, feeling the slow creep of despair ebb through my limbs as though my blood had thickened within my veins and lost the will to flow.

All those years.

She's gone . . .

I don't know if I can get up. Mere minutes ago I felt thrill at the revelation that a whole new existence awaited discovery, and fierce resolve to stop Keitus Vieta. But all of that is melting away as my thoughts sink into a quagmire of hopelessness. I'm not the man that Oluvia Wade knew. And I'm not the savior that Brother Sunny believed I would be. And I am not able to win a fight against a force with such power. Whatever his plans involve, Keitus Vieta has won. I cannot stop him.

Better that I end it all now.

"Control . . . Are the protocols still in place for self termination?"

*Yes.*

"Then make the preparations."

# 18

Here I am again. Standing, staring at that empty slot. My slot.

More than ever before, the desire to simply end my life and join the others overwhelms me. Over the years the curiosity gnawed at me until it became an obsession. I had to know what was beyond death. But that obsession eventually led me here, and it is no longer curiosity that drives me, it is sadness. I am no longer just the last man. With Qod gone I am the last soul.

So here I am, contemplating my death. The death of the last human. But why is that so significant? The universe is still in the early stages of its fourth cycle and it will evolve again to spill new life into the waiting void. Perhaps that makes me the first man. But so what? I have no purpose. And did I ever truly have one anyway? The last part of my life has been a fruitless chase to find an aberration, ending in defeat. But surely in all the billions of people that will be born there will be one that can stand against Vieta? There's a dissenting voice somewhere distant within that tells me I am the one it should be. But I ignore it.

Time to move on, then. Time to take the same risk that all the others did before me, and see if death really is the end.

"Control . . ."

I pause, still captivated by the emptiness of that slot—the darkness inside the perfectly formed hole waiting for life. Death in reverse, that slot is nothing until the sum of my life experience has been deposited there.

Insanity! Why am I hesitating? Doesn't the immeasurable anguish of loneliness, the futility of existence and the fear of Vieta outweigh the greater unknown? So why do I delay?

"Control?"

*Yes?*

Still staring at the slot. Subject 9.98768E+14. That's what the slot will be called when I die. Through Oluvia's life I know exactly how the process works: the Codex calculations will be made, duplicating my life in precise mathematical detail, the quantum recorders at work inside each atom of my body will make their final data transfer and both sets of data will be compressed and spliced together to make an exact memory library of my entire life. Trillions of years. Most of them experiencing other people's lives. An incredible, spectacular, glorious fanfare of sentience.

But for whom? There is nobody left to care or discover it out here. The Soul Consortium will wander through the void, discarded and useless, perpetuating itself for eternity, for no one. For nothing.

What was it all for?

*Yes?* The soulless voice repeats. It jars me.

"Why don't *you* tell me, Control? What was it all for?"

*I do not understand. Please rephrase the question or provide more detail.*

"Qod would have understood."

Silence from the Control Core.

"Control. Play me Qod's last entry again."

*Day 4113: Data Analysis Batch 9K1.533: Abnormality transport complete. Containment fields holding. Monitoring abnormality for qalkkjk. Aberration intrusion detected detected detecteddddd. No! Initiating firewall proto proto Keitus proto Vieta protocols. No! Protocols. Protocols. Initihhyfmnm. No. Salem! Help . . . help . . . help . . . Salem . . . Sal . . . Sal . . . Sa . . .*

It doesn't sound much like her. Too analytical. Too . . . inhuman as she proceeds through the last words of her life. But nevertheless, hearing her final words is significant to me. Meaningful in a way that defies explanation. Perhaps it's because she spoke my name amongst the gibberish. But not all of it was nonsense. She'd done something just before she died. Transported an abnormality . . . not an aberration . . . an abnormality. Vieta is the aberration, so what is the abnormality? Is it the same thing?

What was it Vieta said in the Observation Sphere? "Give her back" he'd said. Give whom back? The abnormality?

"Control. Where is the Abnormality that Qod transported?"

*The Consortium royal gardens.*

"Finally, you actually know something. What is the abnormality?"

*Unknown.*

Well in that case, I'd better find out for myself what it is.

# 19

The word "abnormality" falls far short of a true description for what I find when I arrive, but I am no longer in any doubt as to what it is. Since I last saw it, it has grown into a monstrous collage of human body parts, compressed, stretched and twisted into a single hurting nightmare. The Consortium royal gardens—the place where I spent so much of my time when I first arrived at the Soul Consortium—has been choked by Keitus Vieta's abominable sculpture of life. Had Plantagenet Soome not shot the fetus within the walls of the genoplant on Castor's World, this is the poor creature it would have eventually grown into. But Keitus had waited and begun again, and here is the result.

I step slowly through the archway, wincing at the multitude of agonized moans, glancing between the suffering faces, clawed hands and warped spines, all fused together as though some maniacal god had squeezed a world of people into one impossible body, then stretched it out like a fleshy blanket across the land. The trees that once graced this place have been stripped of life, every branch and root clogged by bloody veins. Bark and stem smeared with pulsing organs and sticky pulp.

A thousand lidless eyes follow me as I continue on toward the glowing center drawn by a macabre curiosity, but repulsed by the fetid stench and morbid horror. Cavernous mouths gargle their pain in tortured unison, and from the grass and earth, fingers with too many joints fumble to grasp at my feet as my soles crunch onward. I keep walking, numb with shock, willing myself with every last atom of resolve to see the core of it all. And at last I find it—the indigo glare of energy surrounded by wet tubes and slippery fibers.

Distant memories of Dominique Mancini's visit to Keitus's house in Lombardy remind me of the ugly statues he kept there. A creative outlet he called it, the residue of another purpose. Within that jeweled cane he held, within the same blue light, were the echoes of the dead, blended together into a gestalt of consciousness. And here before me it has been made flesh. Keitus Vieta has been gradually deconstructing the atoms created at the birth of the universe into other, unknown particles, like some kind of virus or cancer infecting the law of physics, altering the DNA of the universe to suit its own design. Left unchecked to continue growing as Keitus adds more to it, this thing, this tumor, will eventually create an imbalance so great, the cycles of the universe will stop completely. No more universe. No more life. Ever again.

I can't wallow in self-pity and defeat any longer. I have to stop him. But I still don't know how?

I could ask Control to purge the garden, but Keitus is patient. He will wait as long as it takes to build again, feeding another new embryo with the energies gathered by the death of each human.

I have to find a permanent solution. Soome's experience told me that Vieta can't die, but everything has its vulnerabilities, perhaps I can find out his. Or perhaps even persuade him to stop. Either way, I need to have a plan—several plans—if I am to succeed.

# 20

At first, Keitus Vieta seems indifferent to my presence when I return to him. He watches me in silence as I move slowly toward his image in the center of the Observation Sphere. The cloudy crimson orb in which he sits glares bright against the backdrop of forming galaxies surrounding us, and I cannot help but feel intimidated, especially without Qod's reassuring presence. But I have a plan. All I need is a way to snare him, a way to lure him in, and to do that I have no choice but to talk with him to find the leverage I need.

"Control, can you establish an audio link?"

*Confirmed.*

A low but eerie howl of wind, and a distant crackle of nova interference comes though. His environment sounds familiar, but I can't yet place it.

"Will you tell me who you are?" I ask.

Vieta aims his bulging eyes at me, a greedy smile creeping

across his face like the stretching of an infected scar. I still can't tell where he is because of the limited field of view in the image, but I suspect he doesn't know where I am either, or he'd probably have found a way to come here.

His voice hisses back as if carried with the wind. "Give her back, Salem."

"Who *are* you?"

His hairless head tilts slightly, as if he is calculating something. "We are many. We are one."

"We are many. You said that before, to Soome. What do you mean?"

"Give her back."

"Her?"

"Yes," he whispers. "My . . . daughter. My . . . offspring. She is near maturity . . . Give her back."

"I can't."

The staring eyes continue to pierce me. "You will."

"No. I cannot allow that. If your . . . daughter continues to grow, this universe will end with this cycle. Human life will not be able to continue."

"Human life is an infestation."

"No, your offspring is the infestation."

His lips separate to reveal a gray tongue sliding behind decayed teeth. A long and wheezing rasp comes from his mouth ending with a gurgling hiss. His eyes, still unblinking, widen and, with a shiver, I realize he is laughing.

"I'm going to give you a chance to stop all this, Keitus.

You told Soome that you wanted to get back to wherever it was you came from. Well, perhaps I can help you. Perhaps we can find another way for you to return without harming the rest of us."

"No."

"No it can't be done, or no you won't?"

"Give her back to me, Salem."

I nod slowly, understanding that Vieta won't be persuaded. "No. I won't."

"I could kill you, Salem."

"Then why don't you?"

He raises a bony finger and for the next few seconds I fight the surging panic that warns me he might actually do it, and continue to do it.

"I removed Qod because she stole my daughter from me."

I try to disguise the pain in my voice. " . . . I . . . thought so."

In his eyes I see the same intensity that must be showing in mine. He's looking for leverage too. A way to bargain with me.

"Would you like her back, Salem?"

I feel my pulse quicken. Surely he's taunting me. "You can do that?"

His head tilts again. "Perhaps."

Could he be telling the truth? Or is he playing the same game as me, trying to reel me in. If he is, then I can trust him about as much as he can trust me. But this could still be the leverage I need.

"So," I say, trying to keep my breathing level, "you want your daughter back. I want Qod. Can we come to an arrangement?"

Vieta continues to stare, the same sickly smile warping his lips. "Bring the Consortium here, to me, and I will return her to you . . . once you have told me the location of my daughter."

I stay silent for a moment as if thinking it over, though my decision was made even before he finished the sentence.

"Agreed, but where's 'here'? We're at the beginning of the universe's fourth cycle. No stars have formed yet, let alone any planets. There shouldn't be anywhere for us to meet other than here."

"You will find me waiting on Castor's Word."

"Castor's World? How is that possible?"

"I . . . arranged for its protection while the universe collapsed at the end of its third cycle. It was not difficult, though I had to expend some . . . shall we say, energy, to succeed."

By energy he must mean the energy he'd been collecting from people's objects—the energy that created his daughter—or whatever that thing is. A moment of fear tightens my throat. I'm trying to negotiate, even deceive a being with such power he has been able to somehow preserve a small section of space while the rest of the universe condensed back within a singularity. Not only that, he managed to dispose of Qod. Again I wonder how could I possible hope to win against such a creature?

"You want me to bring the Consortium back through the Promethean Singularity?"

"If you want me to return Qod, yes."

I wanted him to come to me, but either way, my plan should work. "Very well. It'll take eighty days for the slipstream drives to power up. I'll see you then."

His smile sends a wave of nausea through me. "Yes. I will see you in eighty days."

"Control, sever transmission."

*Confirmed.*

# 21

Eighty days. Less than a blink in the eternity of my life, but now that span of time seems like an age. And it may seem even longer without Qod. I am tempted to visit one more life—a contented soul—during that time, but I cannot give in to that temptation, nothing should distract me from my new purpose.

Below my feet the steady rumble of the Soul Consortium's slipstream engines are building their gradual crescendo and bringing back memories of the first time they were used. I have no desire to experience another journey through the heart of the universe for the third time. I did it once myself, and once as Oluvia Wade, but nobody found out what it would be like to go back through the opposite way. I remember the pain. With the immense power fluctuations at the point of impact, the Consortium Core cannot suppress the sensations in the human body. But this has to be done.

Ahead of me, still clogging the Consortium gardens, is Vieta's abnormality, heaving like a restless sea of bone and flesh against the transparent walls of the sphere, crushing the trees under its weight and lamenting its own existence. Outside the boundaries of the universe it seems that Vieta is unable to locate his creation, but that may change when we pass through the Singularity again, and I cannot afford him to have this dangerous monstrosity back. Just as he has no real intention of bringing Qod back to me, I have no intention of releasing this abomination to him either, otherwise the consequences for creation would be disastrous, and I would have nothing left with which to bargain. He must know I plan to deceive him anyway, and if I return this monster to him, he'll simply dispose of me and continue where he left off, ready to celebrate his offspring's coming of age and the resulting dissolution of my universe.

I take one last look at the gardens I once cherished above all else, then give the order.

"Control, detach Consortium Royal Garden Sphere and jettison."

*Please confirm trajectory.*

"It doesn't matter. As far away from the Promethean Singularity as possible. It must never get back into the universe, so just get it away from here. Away from me."

*Calculating . . . detaching . . . ejecting.*

With a vast shudder, hoses, fibers, umbilicals and bridges snap away from the sphere leaving clouds of gas and debris to jet away into the darkness. A pulse of energy buffets the sphere and a few seconds later it begins to drift away from the rest of the Consortium—a massive glass ball—tumbling into infinity, filled with a living horror I hope nobody ever finds, most of all Vieta.

"Good riddance," I say, turning my back to return to the Soul Spheres.

# 22

Day Eighty. The final preparations have been made for my final day. After all this time, after all my aeons of existence trying to decide if I should follow the path of my long-dead piers, my decision is made, but not for the reasons I ever expected. I have finally found out that there is more to life than this universe I have come to know so well, but I must be denied that adventure. To stop Vieta, I must die. At least now I will find out what lies beyond. Perhaps the greater adventure is waiting for me there. I will find out soon enough.

To ensure that my death is certain I have cut off all power to every genoplant in the Soul Consortium to prevent my resurrection, and now the only remaining risk is a premature death. For my plan to work, my sacrifice must happen at precisely the right moment or all is lost. Facing Vieta is dangerous enough, but if I handle things correctly, he will not kill me. Passing through the Promethean Singularity will be the most dangerous obstacle to overcome. Many people died last time, but this time I know exactly what to expect, and I am prepared.

*Adjusting trajectory for final approach to Promethean Singularity.*

*Contact in sixty seconds.*

*Please brace for impact.*

The Observation Sphere is the best place to be. The velocity as I approach at Slipstream speed is breathtaking, and rather than focus the Sphere's viewpoint somewhere within the universe, I have withdrawn it for this occasion to view the approach directly ahead of the Soul Consortium, as if I am looking straight through a massive window. I didn't see this the first or second time. Back then, both Salem and Oluvia's eyes had ruptured. This time I am wearing protective lens implants.

*Contact in forty-five seconds.*

*Calculating vectors for arrival orbit at Castor's World.*

I cannot help but scream with exhilaration and fear as the universe rushes to greet me. The boiling heart we call the Promethean Singularity is spinning and exploding in bursts of white and gold light, as if all the stars waiting to be born are warring against each other to win the prize of existence. Vast arcs of lightning ripple across the dome above me like white fire, and as we draw closer in the last few seconds, the deep shuddering power of creation rocks the Soul Consortium as if the Goddess herself were shaking my home within her fist.

*Contact in five . . . four . . . three . . . two . . .*

My ears explode, my bones crunch, my throat collapses, my heart crumples and my lungs burst as the Consortium punches through the heart of the universe. My restraints are failing, and through a blaze of white, I watch the Sphere splinter above me. With an abundant taste of blood in my mouth and throat, and the sharp tingle of shredded nerves telling me I won't survive the next few minutes, my body slams into the glass high above the ground. Debris is shrieking through the fracture in the sphere and the immense pressure is smearing me across its surface toward the opening. What remains of my corpse will spray into the waiting atmosphere of Castor's World as the Consortium screams to a halt high above the legendary crater. Though the pain is unendurable, my only thought now is of failure. This is not how I wanted to die. Vieta will go on unhindered. Eventually, over the ages, he will build his unnatural child once more, feeding it until the universe eventually collapses. I failed.

# 23

As if pushing through a heavy curtain of oil and blood, I stagger forward. My vision blurs, trying to focus from the brief blackness of death to another less oppressive darkness. The deep thrumming of power in the room deafens me as my newly formed ear bones adjust, then fluctuates in volume before settling, and I retch as the smell of freshly engineered DNA mixed with ancient decay fills my nostrils and coats my throat. For a moment my head throbs and my lungs ache. Mech-cells are making their final alterations to my nervous system, and with a quick twist of my neck and clenching of my fists to test my muscles, strength quickly returns as the nausea fades.

*Cellular generation complete.*

*Circulatory systems stimulated.*

*Neural transfer complete.*

*Subject 9.98768E+14 resurrection successful.*

I am alive again. But how? I made sure all the genoplants were shut down before the Consortium entered the Singularity. With the next breath I realize this isn't any of the genoplants within the Consortium spheres; it's cold and dark in here, the ground is uneven with sharp objects cutting into my feet, and that stench is almost as unbearable as the pain I endured a few moments ago before I resurrected. If not the Soul Consortium, there is only one other place this could be, and the reek confirms it—the genoplant within the abbey on Castor's World. Vieta must have left it on and the Consortium must have dropped into range just before I died.

Fumbling through the dust and bone remains of a thousand corpses, I try to find the door. It was a long time ago that I lived Soome's life, but I still remember the layout of this room; that awful last scene of his life is still clearly etched into my synapses.

Eventually my hand finds the cold metal of the handle and I pull it open, struggling against the thick detritus that has held it shut for so long. The familiar blood-light of Castor's world, filtering through the smashed windows of a long abandoned abbey, ebbs through the gap in the door and I wish I was unable to see my surroundings; I need to keep my nerve for the meeting that awaits me and this room is a painful reminder of the power I am about to face.

My rebirth seems to have been the first one in a very long time here. The mindless bodies of the monks who perpetuated a continuous cycle of resurrection and death must have been released at some time in the distant past; there is no evidence of any recent deaths in here, but the sobering remains of mummified corpses still carpet the floor. Across the room are the circuits that power the genoplant booths. In order for my trap to work I have to sever these. There must be no resurrection for me, otherwise that empty slot that waits for me in the Soul Consortium will never be filled and there will be no bait for Vieta.

Stepping over the corpses, I pause.

Do I really want to go through with this? I've thought about suicide so many times before, but in the past it has only been my interests at stake. This time the fate of future humanity depends on my success. And there is only a slim chance that this will work. If I push Vieta too hard he may kill me before I am able to do it myself. I have to convince him that the knowledge in my head is crucial to his needs—the key to his success. I nod decisively to myself, then strip the power fibers.

The genoplant is dead. It's time to face Vieta.

# 24

Several robes are hanging on hooks Just beyond the door, and I take one to shield me from the cold before making my way cautiously through the abbey to find the main lobby. The passageways are littered with shards of broken pottery, smashed glass, and splintered wood. Long-dried blood decorates the mildewed stonework, and skeletal remains are scattered throughout. It is all evidence of a violent battle that took place here and I feel a moment of sorrow for the monks that must have fought against Vieta after Soome's death. I remember the brief information that Qod gave me about the abbey before I ventured into Soome's life; nobody ever came back to Castor's World after news returned of the apparent madness that occurred there. It had been assumed that studying the Codex was what drove them insane and the result was a horrific bloodbath. They knew nothing of Keitus Vieta.

With no small effort both mentally and physically, I push the great double doors open that lead to the outside world, and there, as if he has been waiting patiently in the same position for the last eighty days, is Keitus Vieta, hunched in the dry dirt with his back to me, wearing the robes of an Abbott. The smell of ammonia travels on a hot breeze to meet me, reminding me of my previous meetings with him in other lives. He's looking up at the sky where the vast spheres of the Soul Consortium have settled in orbit, as if watching for signs of my departure. Even from here I can see the tremendous damage wrought by its journey through the Singularity: rings of debris gathered around the shattered orbs at the outer edge and plumes of fire jetting from the inner spheres. It will take time for the automated systems to repair it all; I only hope that the Soul Spheres have not sustained too much damage, or again, my plans will have come to nothing. So much depends on the next few minutes that I wrestle with the idea of sneaking back inside the abbey to close my eyes and wish this whole nightmare away, but that's not the Salem Ben I need to be.

I take an extra moment to compose myself, try not to think about the coming confrontation that will make or break billions of future lives, looking anywhere but at the small hunched form with his back to me. But the vision in the sky gives me no courage either. Not just the devastated Soul Consortium, but the Goddess beyond it, the vast face of Pandora, with her single star-bright eye looming overhead.

It's as though she has been overseeing proceedings with sinister interest.

"Vieta!" I call.

Slowly, he turns his head to observe me. There is no trace of surprise that I have made my entrance from the abbey. His sallow face housing those same bulbous eyes is as eerie as ever. The translucent flesh hinting at a leering skull beneath its surface stretches to attempt a smile as I step into Pandora's light.

"Here I am," he says, quietly.

"Where's Qod?"

He steps to one side, and with a slow sweep of an arm, reveals a figure shrouded in monk robes, facing away from me, seated in the red dust. "As promised."

Stunned, I stare at the figure as it turns its head, the face momentarily hidden under the shadow of its hood.

"Salem, did you find what you were looking for?" it says, and I recognize the voice.

My own voice cracks as I form the word. "Qod?"

"Of course," says Vieta, "whom did you expect? I kept my word, no?"

Two slender, bronzed hands move upwards to pull the hood back and I take a step back. The dazzling hair, the large brown eyes. This is not Qod, this is Queen Oluvia Wade, before becoming the All-See.

"Salem," she says again. "It's me, Qod."

"No . . . you're . . . you're Oluvia—"

"Oluvia Wade, yes. The *real* Qod. Don't you remember where I came from? How I came to be?"

I search her eyes, now glistening with tears. "But . . . how?"

"How does not matter," says Vieta. "She *is* Qod."

My mind races. This turn of events is not what I expected. The woman before me is not Qod, yet somehow, she is. But it changes nothing, Vieta still needs to be dealt with.

"She's not the Qod I know."

"I am," she says.

"Prove it."

She nods. "Look above, Salem. Don't be afraid."

I do as she asks and in the sky the face of Pandora takes on new power. The shimmering eye—the star that gives Castor's World its dim light—blasts outward like a fiery rose and the nebula surrounding it swells like a burst of blood in stormy waters as if Pandora's hair had been ravaged by a great wind. Hellish light glares across the land and I stagger back shielding my eyes, reeling from the sudden heat. Falling to the ground I watch Vieta as Oluvia rises. He steps aside lifting a finger over her as if to drop her dead and I cry out. "No! Wait!"

The storm stops. The heat dissipates and the light fades.

They both look at me.

"It is me," she says.

"But beware, Salem Ben," says Vieta, "I can snuff your goddess out as if she were no more than the flame of a candle, just as I did before. Now where—?"

"He caught me off guard back in the Consortium, Salem. Don't—"

Still watching me, Vieta lifts his finger. The indigo light in his cane brightens and Oluvia slumps suddenly to the ground, silent. Breathless and shocked, I shake my head, trying desperately to gather my thoughts, but before I am even able to take in what just happened, Vieta lifts his finger a second time and Oluvia jerks and screams back to consciousness. The light in Vieta's cane fades back again.

"I was about to ask," he continues. "Where have you hidden my child? I believed her to be on the Soul Consortium where she was previously out of reach, but I do not think she is there now."

"Do you think I would have brought that abomination here without knowing you would keep your side of the deal?"

"Perhaps not, but you see now that I have honored our agreement. So take me to her. I know she is still alive somewhere. I . . . feel her."

"But . . . if I allow you to feed your creation . . . humanity will—"

"Humanity does not even exist in this universe yet," he smiles. "What are you trying to protect?"

"The future. Humanity deserves a chance to live and thrive again."

"And it shall," he whispers.

"Only until you've bled it dry to feed that . . ."

"Where is she, Salem Ben?"

I stare at Vieta. There is no doubt he wants his abomination back. But how far can this go before he decides the pursuit is no longer worthwhile?

"I won't tell you where she is."

"What? You are breaking the agreement?"

"That isn't Qod." I shoot her a meaningful look to let her know that I don't mean what I say, but Vieta sees it.

"You know she is," he says. "Don't try to justify your duplicity by claiming I have not delivered my part."

"But I can't let you have your creation back."

"Tell me where she is."

"No."

"Tell me now or Qod suffers."

"I can't."

He lifts a finger. Oluvia's body twists like a broken mannequin and her scream echoes from the walls of the abbey.

"Stop!"

But he doesn't. Her body continues to contort, the legs and arms snapping against their joints. "Where is she?"

"Please." I fall to my knees, cover my face in my hands.

I can't watch, but I can hear the crunching and snapping of her bones through the screaming.

"I can make her pain eternal, Salem. I could do the same to you if I wish."

"Just stop!"

"Then tell me."

I spit my enraged words out at him wishing they were

poisoned darts. "Beyond the Singularity, beyond the universe. I have her coordinates in a hidden Consortium file."

My answer is a half-truth. The abnormality is drifting through the void, but with no point of reference. There are no coordinates. I avoid looking into Vieta's eyes in case he can read my deception.

"Good. Take me there."

I hear Oluvia's body slump to the ground as Vieta releases her.

"Let her leave first. Promise not to hurt her again."

"Why should I promise anything to you when your own word means nothing."

"Just please . . . let her go."

"Take me there now or she'll suffer again."

"I'll die before I tell you where that thing is."

"You'd really terminate your own existence for this? For a species that hasn't even been born yet?"

This time I look him in the eye. "Yes."

"But you must know that I can begin again."

"There'll always be someone to stop you. Dominique Mancini when she accidentally released the power from your cane; Plantagenet Soome when he killed it here in this abbey. There will be others, too. This is the closest you've ever come to completion, but I'm going to make sure that it doesn't happen. Go and create another daughter, Keitus. You've lost this one."

Vieta's face twists with anger, his finger lifts and a ripple of agony burns through my limbs.

"Control," I manage through the pain, hoping that the Consortium's core isn't too damaged to receive my signal. "Transport me and . . ." the pain rises like acid through my blood and I scream before the last words escape me. " . . . and Oluvia . . . to the Consortium genoplant one."

There's a moment of undreamable anguish before Castor's World dissolves around me to be replaced by the white walls of a Consortium sphere lit by sporadic arcs of electricity. Oluvia is there too, slumped by my feet, her bloodshot eyes staring up at me in the strobed lighting. Jets of steam hiss above our heads and electrical fires spit at us as flailing cables writhe like the tentacles of a dying beast. The sphere won't last much longer, but after Vieta's torture, neither will Oluvia.

"Hold on, Oluvia, I'm going to reactivate the genoplants and get you fixed up."

"No . . . time, Salem. Vieta will . . . come."

Ignoring the warning and ignoring a sudden sparking fiber dropping from above, I lift her gently from the floor and carry her over to the first empty booth, placing her inside.

"Control, restore power to this genoplant, and help Oluvia."

*Confirmed. Genoplant power restored. Beginning biological repair of subject 9.81713E+44, Oluvia Wade.*

The booth jumps into life and I'm grateful that it's still working. Immediately the mech-cells go to work restoring muscle, flesh and bone; she'll be whole again in less than a minute.

"I'm counting on his ability to get here, Oluvia. I have a plan."

"Of course you have a plan," she says as the bones in her jaw crack back into place. "Remember, I'm almost omniscient and I know your every move, Salem. I know exactly what it is you're planning and it's insanity . . . And stop calling me Oluvia. I'm Qod!"

"But the plan can work, yes?" I insist.

"Yes it can work, but—"

"Then don't argue."

"You're sure you want to go through with this?"

"You mean you don't know?"

"Of course I know, Salem. It's you that isn't sure."

I stare at her through a haze of steam. "We have to get out of the genoplant, before it collapses."

Oluvia . . . Qod, steps out of the booth and I take her hand as we move at pace out into the passage. Out of the corner of my eye I catch a look from her as our fingers touch, a look I remember from before, both in my lifetime and hers, a look of longing.

"Control, deactivate geno—"

As the door seals I watch through the window as the domed ceiling crumples like a blanket of dry leaves. There's a moment of fire and lightning, then genoplant one bursts apart into a shower of cables and metal shrapnel into the atmosphere of Castor's World. The two of us fall back as the pressure difference is buffeted by the door.

*Please restate command.*

"Disregard," I say after releasing a breath I'd been holding for several seconds and turning to Qod. "I much preferred it when you were in charge."

"Get me to the Control Core and I'll be back to my old self in no time," she says getting to her feet and pulling me up too. "But we'll work all that out on the way out of this section, we'd better get moving."

"Control," I say, heading through another set of doors and pausing at a crossroads. "What is the status of repairs? Are the Soul Spheres and Control Core safe?"

*96% restoration predicted within two standard hours. 4% loss will be reconstructed within four standard hours. Passage must be restricted during that time. Recreational Spheres, Observation Sphere and Council Spheres have restricted access until repairs and reconstruction completed.*

"Fine. Has Keitus Vieta arrived yet?"

*Unknown.*

"He's useless."

"Like I said," Oluvia says, nodding toward the passage to my right, "if I can get to the Control Core, I can reconnect and take over again."

"Good. I'll probably need you if my plan has any chance of working."

"You will."

"Then go."

She looks at me for a moment and squeezes my hand. "We . . ."

"No, Olu . . . Qod. You know I can't think what you want me to think, or say what you want me to say. If the plan works, I'll be dead before the day is out."

She jerks a nod, and for a heartbeat I regret my words as she turns away, but if she really is Qod, she knows she won't change my mind now. Without looking back, she races down the passage and I head straight on, toward the Aberration Sphere. My final destination.

# 25

Back at the Aberration Sphere again. And it's quiet in here. I almost wish it had been one of the damaged areas after the Consortium broke through the Singularity. It might not have changed my plans, but at least the chaos might have distracted me from thinking about that same empty slot that's always haunted me.

I'm really going to do it this time, though. Really going to end it. But at least my end will have true purpose now. And it won't really be an end. If my soul, whatever that is, survives in some metaphysical form science has yet to identify, then I'll find the others that went before me. If not, well, I'll have a different kind of eternal life keeping the enemy gaoled. And at least with Qod back, I can be confident that my plan will work. But I'll never really know. I'll just have to hope that what I told Vieta is true—that if I fail, others will continue to ruin his plans, find his creation and destroy it before it destroys everything else.

"Salem?"

My stomach leaps at the sound of her voice. She's back!

"Good to have you back, Qod. Everything okay?"

"Yes, everything's fine, but I've lost a lot of data. There's only so much you can cram into a human brain, even an enhanced one."

"And Keitus Vieta? Where's he?"

"On his way in a small transport shuttle."

"I don't suppose destroying it will help?"

"It will only delay him, you know that. He'll just reconstruct his form again."

"Why doesn't he do that anyway? Why not just deconstruct himself and reconstruct himself over here?"

"My best guess, from what I found out during my investigations, is that doing so requires a lot more energy than conventional methods, and he has to leach it back from that creature he created. He expended quite a lot of resource with that display of his on Castor's World. He'll do things the easy way if he can, which is why he'd rather see if he can get the abnormality back than have to start all over again."

"Is that why he doesn't do his own killing to get the energy he needs?"

"No."

I wait for more, but Qod says nothing.

"And? You're not going to tell me why it's a no?"

"It's better you don't know."

"Whatever the reason is, it can't be worse than everything else I've seen recently. Just tell me."

"Remember, Salem, I know you. Seriously, it might make you change your mind about what you're about to do and I'm not sure if I'm right. I don't have all the facts yet."

"But I'll need to know—"

"For just once in your existence, Salem, please, just trust me."

Though the thought of the secret itches like diseased skin, I hold back. "Okay, Qod, you win. For now."

I can almost hear the relief in her voice as she replies. "Good."

"So is there any chance that draining his power completely will make him vulnerable? Would it give us a way to stop him?"

"No, Salem. When he chooses to use it, the amount he needs is infinitesimal compared to the amount he has. You'd have to goad him into using it for millions of years to make a difference. He used a significant amount of it to remove me, but even then it was nowhere enough to weaken him. He could use his power much more than he does, but I think he sees every speck of energy as tremendously precious, as though he's drawing the life blood from his child."

"Okay, I get the idea. He can't be weakened. Can't be killed. The perfect incarceration is the only way to stop him."

"Regrettably, yes."

"And you still don't want to tell me why he won't do the killing himself to get the energy he needs? He's killed before,

I watched him on Castor's World."

"And he did it to me just now back there on Castor's World for a few seconds, but he only does it under what he considers to be extreme circumstances . . . and I told you to drop it, so drop it, Salem."

"Okay, okay. How long until Vieta gets here?"

"A little over eight minutes."

"That isn't long."

"It's long enough."

One last look at the slot. "Then we should get ready."

# 26

Watching via a small holographic projection of the lower platform surrounding the Aberration Sphere, I force an unsafe jettison between the Central Docking Sphere and the connecting passage just as Keitus Vieta steps off the ramp from his transport shuttle. The result is a collapsing conduit and Sphere, their entire contents spinning away into deep space. The decompression, lack of atmosphere and absence of heat would have killed a normal human being, and with no operating genoplants, he would have stayed dead. But not this man. For a few brief seconds, Keitus Vieta drifts away, buffeted and slashed by sharp fragments of metal and glass, then with an angry pulse of indigo light from his cane, he deflects the debris with a shimmering bubble around him and glides effortlessly toward the waiting entrance.

I knew he'd survive, but I had to make it look like I wanted to keep him away. Together with Qod I'll have to lay a few more traps before I spring the real one.

"He's making his way along the central gangway, Salem."

"Show me. Keep the holographic scanners on him. I want to see everything he does."

The view before me shifts and I see a bird's-eye view of him creeping along the passage, the point of his cane chinking against the metal floor with each step. Then he stops, looks upward, and the soft lights of the Consortium reflect off his pallid lips as they draw back to show the familiar rotten teeth. A smile of confident power that I soon hope to remove from that ancient face.

"Which of you shall I attend to first? Fair Oluvia, or noble Salem?"

Good. He's established the audio link as I hoped he would. From now on, my conversation with Qod must complete the ruse. I can only hope that Vieta won't use any of his precious power to look into my mind to see what I've planned. Here goes . . .

"Qod! Can Vieta hear us?"

"Unfortunately yes, but it doesn't matter, he's too late."

"It's never too late," he whispers, then continues along the passage. "Salem, you and I should continue our conversation. I only wish to know where to find my daughter, nothing more, nothing less."

"Delete the file, Qod, quickly, he mustn't get the location of the abnormality."

"File deleted."

Vieta pauses momentarily as he walks into the next passage, the passage that will lead him to the Soul Spheres, but then continues. Good, he still believes he can get the information he needs.

"Qod, I think he knows where I am. Keep him away from here, jettison all the Soul Spheres if you have to, but keep him away from me."

"It won't help, Salem, he'll just pull you back, but surely that doesn't matter now, the location of the abnormality is gone forever . . . unless . . ."

I stay quiet, hoping that the silence is convincing enough.

"Tell me you didn't see the coordinates on that file, Salem," says Qod, the urgent pitch in her voice perfect.

"Yes, Salem," says Vieta, mocking. "Tell her you didn't see them."

And now he's inside the Aberration Sphere with me, the hungry smile widening on his face, the cane illuminating the room like a herald of death. He got in here much faster than I thought.

"Qod! Stop him! I don't have enough time. I need four minutes, give me just four minutes and he'll never get it from me."

"I'll do what I can, but hurry."

From every electrical node in the sphere, threads of bright blue death slam into Vieta's body, rocketing him back through the doors. His burnt shell slides back through the passage and even before it comes to a halt, the ashen particles are beginning to coagulate, moisten and group back together even as

Qod continues to unleash a million more volts through him. A black, skeletal hand lifts, fumbling for the cane which lies several feet away pulsing with power.

"Now, Salem, now!"

I rush toward the W.O.O.M. dancing between ribbons of light, aiming myself like a missile toward the fibers as they stretch to grasp me, hoping desperately that Control's next phrase is the only one Vieta fails to hear.

*Subject 9.98768E+14: Select.*

*Subject 9.98768E+14: Multiple aberrations detected.*

*Subject 9.98768E+14: Override authorized—ID 9.98768E+14.*

*Subject 9.98768E+14: Activate. Immersion commences in 3 minutes.*

Once triggered it will take exactly two minutes for death to take hold. Timing is critical.

"One more minute. Just one more minute, Qod."

Vieta is back on his feet, robes burning, flesh flaking and reforming as the electricity continues to crawl over his seared tissue. Through the flames that engulf his head, his unblinking eyes fix relentlessly upon me, and without any more time to prepare, without any further thought for what awaits me, I panic and trigger the internal switch that will end my life. Too early. My timing needed to be perfect and I'm too damned early.

"Where is she? Where is my daughter?" Vieta's voice crackles like burning gravel as he comes closer. I can feel the nerves in my body shutting down, muscles weakening, head spinning, vision blurring. Sound is becoming a distant echo in my head, but as I drop to my knees feeling my failure, the Control Core renews my hope.

*Subject 9.98768E+14 termination initiated.*

*Subject 9.98768E+14 termination completion in 180 seconds.*

*Subject 9.98768E+14 Soul Consortium file buffer ready.*

If I can hold on just a few seconds longer against the inevitable. Is there still a chance to win? Still a chance for the file to be created at the exact moment of immersion? There has to be. If my death is too early the W.O.O.M. will abort the immersion, but if my death is too late, my file won't be created and again, the immersion will be aborted. My death and the immersion must happen at the precise same instant or everything is lost. In a dreamy haze I am aware of the W.O.O.M. fibers slipping into my skin, pulling me upward ready for immersion. I have to hold on a little longer, but how does one hold back death?

Vieta halts, but it isn't Qod's attack that has stopped him. The flames now quenched, leave only the bright blue of electrical arcs to compete with the brooding blue of his cane to light the sphere. Through failing vision I can still make out his charred skin as he continues to reform it. His eyes, still whole, watch me intently from the inside of his smoking skull.

"Where are you going, Salem Ben?"

"Too late," I tell him again, "by the time you reach me inside the W.O.O.M. I'll already be dead."

Vieta answers with his cane. A pulse of deep blue almost blinds me and my body lurches, snapped away from the W.O.O.M. The noise of strained fibers squeals out from above as the Core wrestles against Vieta's power, and at once a surge of vitality races through my blood quickening my senses and my mind.

"Death? But I know how this place works, Salem. Should you die, all I need do is live your life to find out where she is. Waiting for the answer would be slow but sure, an inconvenience at worst . . . Nevertheless, it is an inconvenience I would prefer to avoid. No death yet, then. Not until I have what I need," Vieta says.

"Qod," I yell, "do something! He won't let me die!"

*Subject 9.98768E+14 termination completion in 30 seconds.*

"I'm trying," she calls back. "He's too powerful."

"But surely you cannot want to die," Vieta says, steam coiling from his hot tongue. "You do not want to go where they go or suffer their destiny, do you, Salem?"

"Don't listen to him, Salem," Qod cries.

"She has not told you?"

"Told me what?"

"No, Salem, don't!" Qod booms, and the electricity crackles wildly as tenfold power surges through Vieta's body. He reels for a moment, then stands again.

*Subject 9.98768E+14 termination completion in . . . malfunction.*

*Subject 9.98768E+14 termination reassertion.*

*Subject 9.98768E+14 termination completion in 180 seconds.*

"Salem, you only have forty seconds until immer—"

"What hasn't she told me?" I scream at Vieta.

His voice roars back. "What I am. *Who* I am. I am one, I am many, I am *all* your dead, and if *you* die, you will join us. You will join me."

The revelation hits me hard. Keitus Vieta has come from the "other place" from beyond the veil I have always been curious about, and in all the aeons of time, the people that have died, cycle after cycle, some undetectable part of them, the soul, the spirit, their life essence, has passed over into that place. And when Oluvia created the rip through the Singularity, it's the dead that were siphoned back, warped and corrupted, as him.

*Subject 9.98768E+14 termination completion in 150 seconds.*

"Salem, please! Ten seconds left"

And that abomination he created. A way to stop the universe? A way to stop the never-ending cycle of birth and death? A way for the dead to return to . . .

"Six seconds!"

"Where is my daughter, Salem. I'll not let you die until you—"

"Five . . . no time, Salem. No time!"

Four seconds to decide. Do I really want to die? Lost in Keitus Vieta to save life here?

"Four . . ."

"Everything you've got, Qod! Now!"

Like an outpouring of the heavens, Qod unleashes the full force of the Consortium upon Vieta, and as the lightning vaporizes him, I lunge forward at the burnt shell, feeling unimaginable force tear through every atom of my body as the end of the blast fills me. Perception slows as death takes me in the last three seconds, and in a state of strange euphoria and fierce pain, I feel the fibers of the W.O.O.M. yank me inside for the immersion. My immersion.

I've won.

At the very moment of my death the immersion into my own life will begin as my file is created. In my last second, as the W.O.O.M. slit closes, I witness the broken remains of Vieta reforming once again. And he'll still want to know where his creation is. He'll look for my file, I hope, and believe the answer to be found there by living my life. He will trap himself in an eternal cycle, never knowing who he really is as he walks through the life of each individual, feeling what they feel, feeling what I feel. Trapped forever. And the universe is safe again.

"Farewell, Qod."

"No, my lover . . . you are mine now . . . always."

# OTHER PLACE

*Is this my final thought?*
*My final memory?*
*From black flesh enfolding me, to evil dream.*
*To deepest darkness, the other place, does fall.*
*She forever refusing me,*
*Death's mournful call.*

# 1

*Subject 9.98768E+14: Select.*

*Subject 9.98768E+14: Multiple aberrations detected.*

*Subject 9.98768E+14: Override authorized.*

*Subject 9.98768E+14: Activate. Immersion commences in 3 minutes.*

*Is this my first thought?*
*My first memory?*
*From evil dream to warm flesh, enfolding me.*
*From deepest darkness to rose-light of womb.*
*Mother breathing,*
*Forever scorning,*
*The beckon of my tomb.*

THE END

# SIMON WEST-BULFORD

Simon West-Bulford turned his attention to fiction following more than a decade of writing theological essays and tutorials for PC game level design. In 2010, his short story "Crimson Lakes" was chosen as the New Year feature story at Dark Fire. "Amiko" was published in Eternal Night: A Vampire Anthology, "Star God" appeared in This Mutant Life magazine, and a string of his short stories were featured at Colored Chalk, Absent Willow Review, Rotten Leaves, and Thunderdome. The Soul Consortium is his first published novel. Simon lives in Essex, England, working alongside his wife as a clinical trials scientist.

Send completed reviews to
reviews@medallionpress.com

MEDALLION
P R E S S

Medallion Press, Inc.

100 S. River Street
Aurora, IL 60506
(630) 513-8316
medallionpress.com